# GOD COMPLEX
## OF A
## SUICIDAL FREAK

# GOD COMPLEX OF A SUICIDAL FREAK

## ZERO

VOL. I

J. Hunter

Summary: At an elite boarding school, a "cursed" and depressed student becomes responsible for the life of a classmate after his own suicide is interrupted when he finds her about to jump from the same bridge he is.



Cover art *versions 1-3* by Damian Cole

Title Font by Leon Ning

Cover art *version 4* by Leon Ning

ISBNs: 979-8-9914688-0-0 (pbk), 979-8-9914688-3-1 (hardcover), 979-8-9914688-1-7 (e-book), 979-8-9914688-2-4 (audio)

Sakayume LLC 2024

zerohale.com

*A foreword from Zero:* **The first thing you should know is that I am cursed.**

Zero * 7

# TABLE OF CONTENTS

Zero * 10

# Zero's Character Inventory:

| Description | Name |
| --- | --- |
| "Protagonist" | Zero Hale |
| Troublesome Girl | Briar Thornswood |
| Student Council President | Jordan Adrian |
| Captain of the Soccer Team | Myles Adrian |
| Popular Girl With No Real Significance | Marina Almandez |
| Teacher (English) | Kyouka Kurima |
| Teacher (N/A) | Natalia Sharp |
| Teacher (Media & Tech) | Jackson Henderson |
| Senior Student Representatives | Analisa Weston, James Hudson, & Thomas Kang |
| Junior Student Representatives | Daniel Blackwell, Nina Taylor, Maggie Arrowood, & Alek Slate |
| Sophomore Student Representatives | March Haskins & Sam Dixon |
| Student Council Members | Avni Anand, Charlotte Atwell, & Annie Obraztsova |
| "Ice Princess" & The Most Popular Boy at Kane Academy | Alina Carter & Jake Parker |
| Chairman | Callan Adrian |

# Chapter 1:

## My Suicide is Interrupted

I'd prefer for there to be no funeral.

I understand that if I'm dead, I won't get much say in the matter, but if this is only wishful thinking, then there's no harm in allowing some self-indulgence. You see, I simply can't imagine a single thing to be said at a funeral in my name that wouldn't cause me to wake myself in my coffin just to kill myself again.

Of course, there's always a possibility I wouldn't actually get a coffin, or any sort of reception, anyway. If Lila's desires were seen to, as they usually are, she'd probably ensure some method of stealing my body for herself and preserving it—the little creep. Not that it would matter to me. At least I'd be spared the humiliation of a reception of strangers.

If there *were* a funeral, and Lila *was* forced to behave, that might just be the worst-case scenario. I can imagine the ordeal now: "He was such a bright boy, with such a bright future," or "You would never have expected this from him." Perhaps I'd be able to let those comments slide, but if there was a single "Oh, I am going to miss him dearly," then all hope would indefinitely be lost. For the very people who ignored or feared your existence in life to proclaim the opposite after your death, that is a true curse, I think. (Though not the worst curse.)

Really, in my own case, if people wanted to pay their respects properly, they'd come up to my coffin one by one and pronounce their congratulations to me for finally doing it. Then they'd burn my body to ash so the least amount of me could be left in this world as possible. I—

Oh.

I'm sorry, is that too much to say to you right off the bat? I get that I may have come off a little strong. You can handle it, though.

Otherwise, you never would have picked up this book, RIGHT?

The corner of my mouth tugs upward for the first time in weeks. Hollow laughter follows, bubbling up from my chest. It's abruptly cut off, however, as I erupt into a fit of coughs. Lungs burning, I have to sit up and lean over, pressing my hands into the snow that's been steadily burying me for the past few hours.

When the unexpected fit finally subsides, I grip handfuls of my hair and let out an animalistic noise caught somewhere between a groan and a growl. *Seriously?* Am I really serious right now? Has my health actually come to this? It's almost funny in a horrific kind of way that nearly gets me to laugh again. But as pathetic as it is, in all practicality, it's good I cut myself off.

Self-indulgence has its limits, after all.

With a deep breath, I straighten up and look from the snow on the ground around me to the large river flowing fifty feet below me.

I promise it's not natural for me to be in such an embarrassingly manic state. By way of explanation, I'll point to the sun rising idly on the horizon. Considering the time the sun rises in Darkwell in early February, this means I've been up for a total of ninety-three hours. Last I checked, the dark circles under my eyes have gone from noticeable to straight-up bruised-looking, as if someone had punched me in the nose and then punched me again with double the force for good measure.

"Ah, but that's just how it goes, isn't it?" I murmur.

I dig my fingers into the snow for no particular reason and lift a handful, watching the flakes melt slowly on the flesh of my palm—a sparkling color that is even whiter than the winter hat on my head.

(I'm speaking of the snow here, not my complexion; I may be pale, but I'm not *that* pale.) Anyway, allow me to pose a question to you: If something as pure as snow has such a fleeting existence, where its demise is brought about by any contact with another thing, living or otherwise, what does that say about my own existence? About your existence?

Answer: Nothing. I am once again talking about snow here.

But that sounds exactly like the sort of pretentious, overripe prompt several of my teachers might throw around at my impressionable classmates. An academy for the elite doesn't mean an academy for the invulnerable, needless to say. (I can feel myself getting a headache now just thinking about it.)

An adult asking such terrible, vacuous things of young people trying to learn seems almost a crime to me. And yet, such teaching methods are all but a staple of upper-class education. This is why, no matter how fine an institution I get sent to, I've never been able to comprehend the concept of school. Or, no … that's not quite right. A better way to explain it would be to say that I've just never been able to comprehend people.

That is the truth at the heart of my existence. Longer lasting than snowflakes melting in my palm, but just as lacking in substance. A human who cannot understand other humans is a sad, pathetic thing. One barely qualifying as a person in their own right.

*Well,* the ghost of another smile traces my lips, *I suppose that's why I'm here.*

...

Right then. I've certainly given this enough thought. No point in delaying it any longer.

I get to my feet and hold onto one of the bridge's support beams as I look out over the frozen wasteland below. The urge to take another step is almost unbearable; here, at the very edge, staring down at the frosted-over river, I'm certain there's nothing I've ever wanted more.

*The setting is perfect.*

If I land right, I should be able to snap my neck in a way that even I can't survive. And since you don't know me, it won't cause you much distress for things to end like this.

"Besides," I release the support beam, "I'll be sure to give you to someone else when I go."

The beating of my heart is as steady as it's ever been.

There's no feeling left where the soft flecks of ice melt on my skin as the warmth of my final exhale meets the frigid air.

I close my eyes—

---

*"I know who you are, Zero. I know the real you, and I still want you."*

A certain girl's face is the first to flash through my mind. Tangled black hair, pleading gray eyes, standing atop the roof with a blinding sunset behind her.

*"Don't you understand?"*

Another flash; instantly, the girl is replaced by a woman—no— by *that* woman, sitting on the stained and tattered mattress of the old apartment, reaching for me.

*"Zero, you can never leave me."*

Blonde hair spills over her shoulder as that woman leans closer, and closer.

*"There's no one else in this world who loves me the way you do."*

That woman, who could never, since the day I was born, leave me alone.

*"Isn't that right, darling?"*

And lastly …

"*Tch. Zero.*"

Still clutching to me, she dissolves in my grasp as a tall man wearing a dark suit fills my vision, suddenly standing in the grand hallway of our family home.

He turns away from me, lip curled in disdain and eyes shrouded in shadows.

"*You are no son of mine.*"

---

My eyes fly open as I stumble back a step.

"Really? Now? Of all times?" I seethe through my teeth. "Why? Why, why, why, *why?*

Can't my mind just be quiet in the end?

Just a second of peace … just *one*.

But a second is too much to ask for. (It's always been too much to ask for.)

I purposefully picture the girl's face. If my father is right, and I end up in Hell, then perhaps I'll be seeing her again soon and she can finally get what she "wants," after all. Or perhaps she'll simply exact revenge on me instead. After all I've taken from her, I'll have no right to protest either way.

"Hahaha!"

The sound of giggling, not in my head, but from down below, slaps me across the face.

I search out the source and see [Two Oblivious Girls With Poor Survival Instincts] standing out on the river. They're fellow Kane Academy students, going by the black skirt and tie uniforms and matching stockings. But while I have a clear view of them, neither one notices me from my perch on the bridge. Instead, they're talking and peering down at the ice, as if in search of something.

I sneer on instinct. It's barely dawn, what could they possibly be doing here? Anyone out in this cold, at this hour, has something seriously wrong with them. Unless … oh god. I squint and peer closer. That would be worse. So much worse. They can't seriously believe that stupid legend, can they?

*"Did you know, if you stand on the Black River before daybreak, you might see the face of your soulmate in the ice?"* I once overheard a girl ask her friend (or something along those lines). *"If you do, it means they'll love you back!"*

These *idiots*. It's barely below forty degrees right now—that might be cold to human flesh, but it doesn't exactly do it for solid ice. Besides, day has already broke, so they're late. If they really want to see their soulmate's face, they ought to get their asses out of bed an hour earlier.

I rub at my temples, fighting off my growing headache.

*What a pain.* Now is no longer an optimal time to take my last step. As unpleasant as I'd likely find the two girls, I don't need my last act on Earth to be traumatizing them for the rest of their lives. However, I can't simply walk away now, either.

"They could have come here on any other morning," I mutter.

If this were a normal situation, I'd say I know the ice has around a fifty-fifty chance of breaking under their weight—they're on the thickest part, where the water is deepest, but if they'd bother to look down the rest of the river, they'd see such solidity isn't the case anywhere else. And, knowing the lack of practical skills possessed by people at this academy, I'd give them each a fifty-fifty chance of being able to swim.

However, since I am here, **this is not a normal situation.**

I stare at them a bit longer, considering my options. Leaving them and heading back to the dorms is tempting, I'll admit. So is yelling at them to get off the damned ice if they know what's good for them.

Then I wonder, would the world really be worse off if it were poorer of two giggling high school students with an enthusiasm for debunked romantic folklore? It's a cruel thought, not that I've ever pretended to be anything else.

*But it's also a foolish thought.*

I know how this is going to end. It's happened too many times before. Given the situation at hand, my very being here has all but sealed both my fate and theirs.

So that's it.

With a last heavy sigh, I climb down from the bridge and begin my descent to the river.

I'm still holding out hope I'll be wrong, while already taking off my coat and hat in preparation, when it happens. A terrible cracking sound rips through the quiet morning air, followed by high-pitched shrieks and the swishing noise of a body slipping into the water.

One of the girls has fallen in.

She struggles violently at the mouth of the hole she's created, fingernails clawing and legs thrashing while her friend looks on in horror, utterly fixed in place.

But the girl in the hole isn't fixed in place. She's losing grip by the millisecond, her body being pulled deeper and deeper as she screams her head off. The kind of screams a dying animal makes— terror-stricken, wailing howls that pierce me like bullets as I run straight for her, unthinkable thoughts bounding through my head with each step.

*If I let her drown, would I feel something? Would I actually feel something? Or am I going to save her so I never have to find out?*

The girl goes under.

And I already know my answer.

My coat and hat land on [Unfortunate and Predictably Useless Friend] as she stands there, stunned.

"Get off the ice!" I yell. "Now!" Then I sprint along the bank of the river, kicking myself for not having moved this way when I first came down.

[Girl I Am Now Intent on Saving] is nowhere to be seen. *Dammit.* I continue downstream as fast as I can until I'm certain I am farther than where she'd be, quickly scouting out a place in which the ice is thinnest.

*There.*

Kicking off my heavy boots, I shatter the light coating of surface frost and immediately curse to death every single person who has ever perpetuated a lousy local legend intended to excite teenagers. It's hardly what I would even consider chilly today, and yet never, in my life, have I felt something so absolutely encompassing of the word "cold."

*Fuck. Me.*

Has the Black River always been this large? Staring out at the dark, rushing current, it suddenly feels like the vastest stretch of water I've ever seen. *And it's moving so fast.* If I fail to calculate this precisely, I'll be carried downstream in an instant, sans the girl. I'll only have one shot.

(But, shit, if *I'm* this cold, she must be *frozen.*)

What if she's already—no. No, whatever the case is, whatever shape she's in, I'll deal with it.

And here the girl comes now—I can see her dark shape sweeping toward me from under the "ice" barely fifteen feet away. I have no choice.

I dive.

But—*oh god.*

Everything seems to happen at once.

One. The shock reflex to inhale hits me the second I'm submerged.

Two. My body explosively collides with the girl's.

Three. My arms wrap around her entire torso, leaving no chance for the current to separate us as I resist the reflex and steel myself.

*Ok.*

Our heads break the surface together.

*I've got her.*

But how much time does a person have in freezing water before their ability to move is stolen? Five minutes? Ten? I'm sure the addition of another person to the equation changes things. There's no time for relief.

Grunting with the effort, my burning muscles already going numb from the biting temperature, I continue lifting [Girl I Am Now Intent On Saving], determined to keep her head as far above the surface as I can manage. For just an instant, I fumble and her face tips forward, but before I can correct this idiotic mistake, her head flings back and she gasps, taking me by surprise as she immediately flails about in my grasp. *This is bad.*

"Calm down," I command, my voice rough and strained—perhaps a little harsher than is ideal. (Or not harsh enough.) "You *have* to calm down."

"*Help,*" she heaves. "Help me!"

"And what do you think I'm doing right now?" My grip on her tightens, desperate to put an end to her squirming. "Taking an early morning swim?" I need to flip her and lean back so I can carry her to shore on my chest.

"Help!" she says again, though slightly weaker this time.

"Stop—ugh—" I dodge her flailing hand by a few centimeters. "Stop moving!" How does she even have the energy for this right now?!

My head submerges again briefly as I fight to hold her up, glacial torrents flooding down my throat. A single ill-timed breath. I spit out the water and grip her struggling body tighter.

"*Fuck.* Are you trying to make this harder?" I grit.

"Oh, please, help me!"

"I can't if—"

"Please!"

"I'm tryi—"

"*Plea*—"

**"You're going to drown us both if you don't listen to me right now!"** I shout, firm and loud enough to overwhelm her other cries.

Finally, she shuts up and looks at me, something settling in her large brown eyes as she gives me her focus.

"Good," I say, ensuring to keep my tone calm, "very good. Now, I'm going to get us out of this river, but I need you to hang onto me and stop squirming around until I do it. Got it?"

I glance over my shoulder at where we're headed. The current is still carrying us downstream, of course, but as strong as it is, there at least doesn't appear to be any more chunks of ice ahead.

The temperature of the water is my main concern. We don't have much time before my muscles stop working at full capacity, and if we're not out of this river by then, we're both dead. While part of me might be ok with that, another part of me is certain this is *not* the way I want to go.

I turn back to face her and she blinks at me, nodding once.

"I'm going to turn you," I say, already flipping her around and leaning her back against my chest as I continue to kick, angling at a diagonal to the shoreline. "Just relax and keep hold of my arm."

Magically, [Girl Who is Finally Letting Me Save Her] listens.

Ok. I can do this.

*Breathe, stroke, kick. Breathe, stroke, kick.*

Everything inside me burns as I repeat these movements, and I can feel my limbs slowing as my clock for muscle mobility runs out.

*Breathe, stroke, kick.*

My lungs are weighing me down.

*Breathe, stroke, kick.*

But there's no air left in them.

*Breathe, stroke, kick—*

CRACK!

I hear it before I see it. A giant, leaning pine tree splitting in two.

Over our *exact* position.

"Oh, come on—" are the last words to slip from my mouth before the thing crashes on top of us.

With less than a hair's breadth of leeway, I shift my grip and duck, diving straight for the bottom. But sword-like branches follow, skewering through the surface as the tree continues its downward trajectory with seemingly murderous intent.

There's no time to prepare or suck in a deep breath or consider the dangers of the cold shock reflex—there's only time to give 120% of my focus to each and every tree limb that slices toward us.

Of course, one is coming right for the girl's head. I flip us, wincing as the blow scrapes directly down the center of my spine. *There goes another uniform shirt.* More branches come for her neck and chest. I twist to avoid them, but with the force of the tree's fall, its size, this current, the air pockets in the wood, there's no doubt—the tree is rolling with us.

As a limb presses into my back, I do the only thing that's left to me; I clutch the girl to my chest and wrap my entire body around her—a less-than human shield—and let us tumble.

Needle and dagger-sharp branches prick my skin all over. The sensation isn't pleasant, but ... *It could be worse, too,* I think just as an especially large limb whacks the back of my head.

*The entire world is dark.*

My eyes snap open. I blacked out for a—

Wait.

Where is the girl?

She was in my arms less than a second ago.

I twist my head around wildly.

*Where is she?!*

I'm still sweeping forward, so is the tree, but I'm in front of it now. Which means—so is she.

*There she is.* Up ahead.

But she isn't floating to the top; she must have screamed all the air out of her lungs. I can tell from the way her mouth is opened wide and grimacing, the only thing wider than her saucer-like eyes.

Her arms are also open and outstretched toward me, those eyes saying everything her underwater voice cannot: SAVE ME.

It's all so familiar.

I've seen this expression before, on another face.

Suddenly it's like I'm looking at someone else entirely. [~~Girl I've Killed~~] [Girl I'll Save] is sweeping farther away, her dark eyes turned light and her hair turned black.

In a moment, she'll be too far for me to catch up.

But that grimace ... it's turning into a smile.

*No, there's no smile.* There is no [Girl I've Killed] here. It's just me and the innocent girl I'm letting slip from my grasp.

I hesitate.

Then, **I push forward.**


The second I get her onto the dry river bank, I collapse.

Panting breaths wrack my body as I lie beside [Girl I Somehow Actually Saved], my chest surging up and down while I slowly will back control over my cut-up arms and legs.

*God, this should have been an easy save.*

Sure, the tree complicated things, but I should have gotten her out long *before* we ever reached it.

Have I truly gotten so weak?

Hah. My old man would be looking at me with such disgust if he could see me right now.

But he can't.

And neither can the girl from the rooftop ... or that woman ... *They're not here. They're* not *here.*

The only ones who can see me are this girl and her sobbing friend. A friend who rushes over to us, practically sliding through the snow in her haste to throw her arms around my fellow river-surviving companion as she proceeds to force both my coat and hat on her, crying all the while about how she was certain we were dead the second the pine crashed down.

Somewhere in the blubbering, I catch the girl's name: Marina. It's familiar, as is her face.

I turn my head toward her and get a better look. Olive skin, dark curls, large hazel-brown eyes. *Ah, so that's her.* Unclouded by adrenaline and hallucinations, her identity is obvious. We have a class or two together—she's actually a very popular student, not just within the junior grade, but across virtually all class levels, making it even stranger that she'd be the one I'd run into all the way out here …

Then, at seemingly the same time, both girls sense my gaze and slowly look over at me.

Staring, Marina stutters out her first words since coming out of the river: "Z-Zero Hale?"

***

The walk back is painful enough that I consider heading back to the river and letting it finish what it started. But it was partly of my own volition that I conceded to the girls' pleas of escorting them to the dorms. (You have to know when to fight, when to run, and when to just give in—this situation constituting that last option.)

It's clear Marina is in a state of shock, and getting her someplace warm and familiar is crucial for both her mental and physical well-being. And I am more than a little dubious of this friend's capability in getting her there alone; after all, why didn't she go call for help the moment this all happened? Not to mention, Marina is still wearing both my hat and coat, so I didn't have much of a choice.

It was out of my hands.

The only real question was *how* to get them back.

I briefly thought of carrying the girl, but, while that's surely not impossible, my muscles have yet to recover and the prospect of holding another person so close to me for such an extended period of time makes my stomach roll. It was better that I simply give her my boots (ie. place them, along with my socks, on her soaked and freezing feet as she stared blankly ahead) and walk the half mile back beside the two girls barefoot.

A light trail of blood follows my every step.

From a purely physical standpoint, this is a contender for the most uncomfortable and downright miserable I have ever been.

Well …

No, that's a gross exaggeration, but I really am displeased right now. My entire body aches, frozen feet crunching through the melting snow as my head pounds incessantly; aside from the many cuts and the drenched uniform clinging to my skin with malice, it's impossible to tell what pain is caused by my spontaneous dip in the water and what is thanks to my lack of sleep.

But anything physical is mere child's play in the face of my mental frustration. My half-hearted attempt at persuading the friend to allow me to escort her and Marina directly to the school nurse was unsuccessful, which means I will now have to deal with quite possibly my least favorite person on this entire 1,800-acre campus … the exact person that Marina is apparently set upon seeing.

The decision is not a particularly logical one. The main school building is only about five minutes farther off and the nurse would be more readily accessible. But further opposition is futile.

All I can do now is hope that, having gone through this most recent, and notably dramatic, incident, I won't be forced to go through any others before I get another chance. Believe me when I say it'll be better for everyone when this chance presents itself and I am finally able to take my unlucky curse with me. It'll be better for you, too.

Yet any momentary feeling of calm this knowledge provides me for the rest of the journey back is destroyed the instant I see him.

***

### Zero Hale

- **Year/age/student ranking:** Junior, 17, 149 of 150
- **Hair:** dark brown
- **Eyes:** dark, off-putting shade of auburn that makes them appear almost red
- **Height/Weight:** 5'11, 161 lbs.
- **Notable features:** red eyes, pale complexion, dark hair in need of a cut, large tattoo on his back, silver ring he never removes from his right index finger, (he also has multiple piercings in both ears, but don't ask him about them)
- **Favorite item:** white winter hat
- **Likes:** manga, video games, horror & thriller fiction, piano, MyTube
- **Dislikes:** soda, poetry, whipped cream as a substitute for frosting, Type-A personalities, uncomfortable clothes, modern art, horoscopes, reality tv, experimental film, oatmeal raisin cookies, group activities, dilettantes, self-righteous fanatics, the *Fantasy Five* series, waking up in the morning, most everything else

- **Personal comment:** "Is this seriously a required part of the profile?"
- **Fact:** Zero believes he is cursed to always have bad things happen around him.

# Bonus: Zero's Student ID Portrait

Hey, wait a second, I don't recall giving you my student ID picture. No—don't just go to the next chapter, I want to talk about this—

***

# CHAPTER 2:
# THE STUDENT COUNCIL PRESIDENT MIGHT BE MORE OF A FREAK THAN I AM

"I knew it," [My Personal Devil Incarnate] says with a disturbing combination of superiority and weariness as we approach the senselessly large, castle-like structure of the Eastern dorm building. "I knew you were still out." He's resting back against the front entrance, eyes closed and long legs crossed, as if he's been waiting for us for some time. "You've been out all night, *Zero*."

"Congratulations," I grumble, "you got me. But if you can find it in yourself to get past that and shut up for two minutes, these girls could really use some assistance."

"I'm aware." His eyes shoot open and Student Council President Jordan Adrian, also conveniently the dorm president since one position of leadership just isn't enough for him, takes his first good look at me. "You three weren't exactly inconspicuous making your way down here."

"Oh, well, how kind of you to rush forth and assist us so benevolently, then."

He ignores my remark, instead focusing on assessing my state and the state of the girl leaning against me. I catch the briefest flicker in his sharp eyes—as if things might be worse than he originally thought—before his expression settles into one of understanding. (Seriously, it's unnerving how quickly he can adjust to a situation.)

"I see," he says just as two more boys appear from the double doors directly behind him, almost like they'd been waiting in the shadows for their command. "You two," he directs at them, no longer interested in me, "get these girls inside and by the fire. I want heated blankets and dry clothes on them immediately. One of you will fetch the school nurse once they're settled."

"Understood, President," one says. He looks tired, like he's not used to being awake at this time. (Is there a particular reason the president had them on standby?)

Both boys nod before their eyes catch on me, halting them mid-step. Recovering with hard swallows and twitching hands, they reluctantly come forward as if they wish to be doing anything else. The taller of the two veers to my right, still keeping his eyes on me, and quickly leads the friend indoors while continuously looking over his shoulder. [Little Henchman Left On His Own] glares helplessly at his supposed partner before continuing over to me, shaking like he's the one who jumped into a freezing river.

"Sometime today, Samuel," the president snaps, fed up with his underling's hesitation. (Is this man a student council president or a twentieth-century dictator—wait, at academies like this, those can pretty much be synonymous, can't they?)

I say nothing, knowing any words from me will just frighten the boy more as he pulls Marina off of me and directs her toward the entrance.

She willingly releases her death grip on my arm but pauses before she can be led all the way inside. "P-President Jordan?" she says, looking up at him pleadingly.

"Yes, Ms. Almandez?"

"Aren't you ... coming with us?"

"I will check in with you when you're ready to see the nurse. Until then, there is another matter I must see to."

He's giving her his full, overwhelmingly undivided attention, but it's obvious he's not about to change his mind or succumb to her request. Marina knows this. Rather than argue, she hangs her head and allows Samuel to move her forward—my coat (student ID and phone in its pockets), hat, and boots going with her.

Right before she steps inside, she pauses a final time and glances over her shoulder. I expect her to be glancing at the president, but instead she's looking at *me*.

And she's glaring.

Hard.

Before I can decipher what such an inexplicable expression means, she turns and disappears behind the ten-foot tall, black iron doors.

That look wasn't comforting, and I'll have to get my things back from her later, but a sigh of relief emits from between my lips at the thought that responsibility for her no longer rests with me.

As always, however, the relief is short lived. Because, finally …

We're alone.

The president turns back to me, no longer burdened by witnesses as he looks me up and down with what I can easily distinguish as disgust. I look him over with a mutual sentiment.

Despite the early hour and the dark circles under his eyes that suggest he's slept about as much as I have in recent days, he still looks perfectly put together. Not a single wrinkle defaces his pristine uniform, his light brown hair is brushed and styled without a strand out of place, and the bright amber of his eyes gives him such a fierce intensity that he would make any normal student cower in the face of his undisguised displeasure. My eyes may be a strange color as well, one that I've heard gives them the exact shade of bloodlust incarnate, but I firmly believe they have nothing on the president's.

(How anyone can think *I'm* the scary one at this academy when this monster exists is beyond my comprehension.)

"Getting other students mixed up in your acts of delinquency, Zero?" he asks, cocking his head. "I guess I shouldn't think of you as capable of anything less. You certainly do love meeting my expectations, don't you?"

"Don't insult me while phrasing your insults as praise. It's creepy."

"Creepy? That's quite the choice of words coming from you."

I stumble a step toward the doors. "As much as I'd love to verbally spar with you right now, President, I don't think this is the time. Unless you wish to be going at it with an iced-over corpse."

Honestly, if I stay in these clothes for another minute, I'm fairly sure *I'm* going to go into a state of shock, and possibly lose a limb or two to frostbite—a fate I do *not* want for myself. I wish to die, not be permanently disabled.

My fears are further realized once I reach the doors and am unable to get my fingers to cooperate in holding the handles to open them. Sighing like I've burdened him with a major inconvenience, the president opens them for me, pushing me inside from behind—his fingers pressing directly into the fresh cut marking my spine. From what I've seen, I'm the only student he gets rough with like this, a side of himself he'll only show when we're alone. I guess some habits really do die hard. (Perhaps I should be flattered.)

"You need to get out of these clothes," he states, already typing away at something on his phone. "You won't last much longer in them."

"Oh? Are you going to change my clothes for me? If I had known how much you cared, maybe I wouldn't have broken curfew to begin with."

(If I thought he looked disgusted before …)

"You're not in a position to be making jokes right now, Zero. However, since you are incapable of doing it yourself, I have contacted someone to escort you to your room and assist you."

His eyes might as well be pinning me to the wall like a bug in a child's insect collection.

"Someone to assist me?" I repeat. "And who, at this school, could you have possibly convinced to do such a thing?"

"One of the select few who do not entirely fear you."

I quickly run through a list of possible people in my head. He may simply mean a person who happens to fear *him* more than myself.

"I trust there won't be a problem with that. After you've finished, you will meet with me back down here."

"Whatever you say, Prez." Usually, I'd put up more of a fight. But I'm finding it difficult to care much about anything right now.

What a strange state I'm experiencing … If he were to order me to strip down and change right here in the dorm entranceway, I might actually do it.

I laugh aloud at the thought, though the sound comes out much weaker than I expected and promptly turns into a rather pitiful coughing, much like up on the bridge. The president's expression doesn't change. He turns to face the back wall just as my coughing subsides and I hear footsteps coming down the stairs.

"Be nice to her, Zero."

These are the last words I hear before a small hand encloses around my shoulder. Words that I can all but hear the cruel satisfaction in as he says them. All feelings of "not caring" drop away as a sense of dread takes their place.

The girl the president chose isn't one I recognize (someone on the council, no doubt). She's cute, I'd say, in an underclassman-younger-girl sort of way, but not at all someone I'm happy to have undressing me. Is this another divine punishment? Was the walk back from the river not enough? Does God actually hate me?

It wouldn't be so bad if I were oblivious to the way she's looking at me. But I am not.

She's one of *those* girls.

The kind who might still be scared of me but get off on that fact. The kind who say things like, "Zero, I don't care if you don't like anyone else. You can just like me!" because they can never get it through their heads that I am simply not capable of liking anyone *at all.*

[Girl Who Will Soon Try To Undress Me] pulls me into my room after getting me up the stairs—a process which I undignifiedly had to accept her help with.

The moment the door shuts behind us, enclosing us in the privacy of my personal suite, I am hit violently by two sensations. The first being that my room is much colder than the entire rest of the dorm building (seeing as I carelessly left my window open and it has not been shut since I was last here). And the second being that, despite appearances, we are not alone. *There is a third presence watching us.*

It's such a strange, unexplainable feeling that I don't know what to do with myself. Whatever it is, it's all-consuming, seeming almost … vengeful, and I suddenly wonder if I should worry for the safety of the girl at my side.

"Is something the matter, Zero?" she asks, completely unaffected by the presence. "Wh-what's wrong?"

From the large, four-poster bed to the stone walls to the massive fireplace, everything feels wrong.

But the sensation of the dark presence is gone sooner than I can place its cause, and so, shaking my head, I say, "It's nothing. I'm fine."

In the corner of the room, however, from between my dresser and bookshelf, a pair of unblinking yellow eyes stares at us.

"Marius, look away," I say to him. "There's no need for you to see me in such a state." He must have gotten in through my window. It's not the first time he's miraculously done so, despite my room being on the second floor.

"Marius? Who are you talking to, Zero?" asks the girl, confused.

"A friend who doesn't know the meaning of boundaries."

"A friend, who—ah!"

Marius jumps from his hiding spot without warning and lands on my bed. [Girl Who Dislikes Cats] makes another unnecessary shriek and starts shooing him toward the window.

"You shouldn't be here! No animals allowed in the dorms! Shoo, shoo!"

Marius evades her swats with ease, an air of boredom following him as he pounces from furniture piece to furniture piece, the girl pointlessly chasing after him. Eventually, he seems to tire of the situation and jumps out of the window of his own accord. I bid him farewell, vaguely wondering if I'll see him again.

The girl presses a hand up to her forehead and takes in a deep breath as if having completed a formidable trial. "Gosh, Zero," (gosh?), "I can't believe you left your window open like that. But what are the chances of a cat getting inside? A black cat, no less. That's a sign of bad luck."

Bad luck? My, what an amusing comment for her to make.

Mistaking my silence for gratitude, she turns to me and smiles. "Well, now that that's out of the way ..."

Thus begins the process of undressing me. I notice the girl, whom I suppose believes she's being discreet, eyeing all the places my still-wet uniform clings to me. Girls usually think it's the guys who stare at their bodies, and that's true, but some don't seem to realize how it's just as obvious when they do the same. Such lack of self-awareness has always made my head spin.

For now, though, I'll let it slide. I won't be here for much longer, so it doesn't matter if this one develops a slight crush—as unfounded and superficial as it may be. I only stop her when her hands start to tug at my pants. My shirt is one thing, and I may not be self-conscious when it comes to my body, but I draw the line here. She frowns just a little but opens the door to my bathroom where I find that she's already drawn a warm tub for me.

Good.

I might pass away from embarrassment right in front of her if I had to struggle with the faucets while she watched. I tell her "thank you" and that I can handle the rest on my own. Then I stumble into the tub without waiting for a response.

The warm water burns at first, but the pain soon melts into pleasure, washing out my cuts and thawing my frozen muscles as I allow my head to fall against the back of the tub, eyes closed. (What a morning.)

I hear a throat clear and realize the girl has yet to leave. I crack my eyes open and slide them over to her. She's staring, of course, and twisting her hands like she doesn't know what to do with herself.

When she informs me that she was told by the president to see my bath through to its completion, I am neither upset nor surprised. I am once again resigned. In the end, the feeling of her small hands running through my hair as she rubs the shampoo into it is almost nice. And though I'd rip my own fingernails off before telling anyone this, I've always liked to have my hair played with. It's just not something that's happened since ... Well, it's not something that's happened in a long time.

[Girl I Might Fall In Love With If She Keeps This Up] continues running her fingers through my hair after she's finished washing it.

"I'm sorry about all this," she whispers, likely thinking I'm no longer awake enough to hear her. In a way, it's almost true. "I'm not sure exactly why President Jordan—wait ..."

I fail to do a single thing even as she runs a finger over my bare collarbone. But what is she—oh, that's right, I nearly forgot. (Though I really thought they would have faded by now.)

"I-I thought it was just cuts from the accident, but these aren't ... W-what—what is this?" Her fingers run down my chest before coming up to my neck, very tentatively turning my head to the side. "Bruises and b-bite marks? Zero, how did you get these?"

For the first time in what officially amounts to ninety-four hours, I fall asleep.

It's an incredibly brief rest, however, as [Girl Who Decides To Interrupt My First Chance At Peace] eventually rouses me and tells me I must get dressed to meet with the president again. A clean pair of boxers and what appears to be an ironed and pressed uniform are laid out for me on my bed. I change into them myself, now that my mobility is mostly, if not miraculously, back (reminiscent of all the times my bones were broken in multiple places only for them to heal fully in a few days).

For the sake of the show I'm putting on, I once again thank the girl. She responds by blushing and stammering out something I don't quite catch. It seems when we're making eye contact, she's much shyer than when she has me stripped and half-conscious in a bathtub. Or maybe seeing those marks on my body have simply brought out her bashful side.

Quietly, she reminds me to go straight down to meet with the president. Then I see her out of my room and lock the door behind her.

I waste no time in proceeding to fall backward onto my bed where I fully intend to stay for the rest of the day.

There's no point in me going down to see the president. Even when we were kids, I never minded if he got angry with me, and now any repercussions won't matter. Besides, it's not as if my exhaustion has been fully cured or anything. Really, I deserve to take off what may very well be my last day.

No sooner have I thought this than the door to my room swings wide open and *he* walks in.

"Tell me, Zero, did you enjoy the special treatment Annie gave you?"

Annie. So that's the girl's name.

"President." My head lifts off the mattress just high enough to glance at him standing over me at the foot of my bed. "Just because you have the ability to break into people's rooms doesn't mean you should use it. Without probable cause, this is a violation of my privacy. Feel free to see yourself out the same way you came in."

"I knew you wouldn't listen," he says, ignoring me.

My eyes roll back in their sockets. "Yes, well, you seem to know everything."

"Sit up."

The command is sharp and, sighing, I decide there's little harm in following it. Though if my obedience pleases him, he doesn't let it show. Instead, he glances down at my ID, running over the statistics shown there.

"Your student ranking is pathetically low. Do you ever intend to take school seriously, or is this truly the best you're capable of?"

"Snooping through my private information only to disparage me with what you find, huh? Well, sorry to disappoint, but it looks like I'm just not as smart as you think I am." Images of my father appear in my mind as I say these words. I shove them all aside.

The president appraises me for a long moment, but I keep my face composed, revealing nothing. "The day an honest word escapes your mouth is the day you'll finally take me by surprise, Zero."

"I really have no idea what you're talking about."

"Indeed, I don't intend to hold my breath."

Beginning to tire of this game, I say, "You can do whatever you like, it makes no difference to me. Just tell me why you're here."

In place of an answer, he crosses the room and sits in the chair at my desk, fixing me with those amber eyes from hell. Then he promptly tosses my student ID and phone beside me.

"Apologies for not taking you inside immediately when you arrived. It was a choice made to satisfy my own curiosity." He says this out of nowhere, and it catches me off guard. It's not like him to apologize for *anything*. And I know that's not what he's really here for.

"Curiosity?" I question, pocketing my ID and phone. "About what? Seeing how long I could last while my clothes froze to my body?"

He doesn't so much as nod or incline his head. Not even a shrug. He just looks at me, his chin placed on top of his delicately folded hands, elbows propped up on the back of the chair.

"It's just that ..." Uncharacteristically, he trails off, waiting several seconds before finishing his thought. "It doesn't make sense."

I'm generally good at reading people and picking up on what they're thinking before they say it, but so is not the case with the president. It never has been. There's a certain predatory cunning behind his way of thought that strikes me as coming from a cold, hidden, true personality covered up with an impressive veneer that cannot be made complete sense of no matter how long I've known him.

"You're going to have to give me more than that," I say.

Annoyance flashes across his expression, but he continues. "You walked all the way here completely drenched, bleeding, without a coat, and without shoes. And now, aside from a few superficial scratches, you're perfectly fine, almost as if none of it ever happened. Are you even *human?*"

"I ask myself that question every single day." So far, the answer is undecided. At times I feel so unlike everyone around me as to be an alien lacking all human qualities. And at others, I feel I am the *only* human I've ever encountered.

"You would answer with that. Completely unhelpful, as usual." He stands and walks toward me, lip curled. "To have all that happen and still walk out of it looking like a fairytale prince straight from a storybook, complete with a maiden dangling from your arm and everything; you sicken me." Never have "kind" words sounded so vitriolic. "But no matter my personal opinion of you, this is not why I'm here. I'm here to speak of your attendance, a topic I'm sure you remember us discussing in the past. And," he checks the fittingly uneconomical watch on his wrist, "if you don't leave within the next five minutes, you'll likely be late to your first class."

Wait, what?

I stare at him openly. "You … want me to go to class? That's what this is about?"

"Must I repeat myself?"

I stare for another moment before breaking into a laugh. "That's quite adorable of you. But I—"

He abruptly leans down and slams the headboard just inches from my face, successfully shutting me up.

"Listen to me, Zero, and listen closely. You are going to class. And you are going to behave yourself."

"……"

"Is that clear, or do I need to speak more slowly for you to understand?"

"… You should know, President, it really does things to me when you take control like this. Are you sure you meant for it to be Annie who gave me my bath? Want a chance to make it right?"

For once, my teasing seems to bounce off of him. "Your mere existence causes trouble for this academy; a fact I think even you are aware of. But believe me when I say we have enough to deal with at the moment. I won't tolerate any other disruptions from *you*."

His words—truer than he even knows—hit me, but they lack any sting. I am incapable of feeling that kind of pain right now. *Still …*

"Do you honestly think that old family ties hold any meaning to the rest of our student body?" I ask, meeting his potent gaze head-on. "That it will somehow cause people here to associate my issues with you? You've already won Student Council President three years in a row; that ought to be enough proof to the contrary. Or are you too paranoid to realize that?"

He looks away, breaking our stare-off in a manner that somehow manages to make me feel like the inferior one, and drops his hand from beside my head. Standing upright, he walks back toward my door. "Consider it preparation for future possibilities. I'll see you in class."

I blink disbelievingly at him just as he pauses in the doorway.

"Oh, and, Zero? Don't think I've forgotten how you broke curfew yet again last night. That makes it, what, the seventh time in the past month? Test me again and I might just make good on my promise to give you a roommate."

With that, he's gone.

"Did all of that actually happen?" I murmur to myself.

That was one of the strangest interactions, if not *the* strangest interaction, I've had since transferring here. The president has always disliked me, sure, and he's often seen fit to lecture me or demand that I do something for him, but never has he been so forceful on the matter. And considering he is aware that my "mere existence" causes disruption at his beloved academy, why would he not want me to disappear as quickly and quietly as possible? Why force me back to class?

Since he despises me on a personal level, there is really only one possible explanation: he intends to make use of me for something. Yet even that explanation still comes with numerous unanswerable questions and holes.

Also, some of his wording sticks out to me … *"Believe me when I say we have enough to deal with at the moment."* Here, "we" undoubtedly refers to the student council, and the mention of "at the moment" implies that there is something going on specific to a current issue, one that is important enough to be on his mind amidst all that's happened this morning. When I made my retort, I didn't for a moment think that the president's true reason for saying what he did was that he's worried about my connection to his reputation. But the fact that he didn't correct me is interesting. Is the student council dealing with an issue right now that is difficult enough to give even Jordan Adrian a hard time?

Then again, perhaps none of what seems to have transpired has actually happened and I am still sitting up on that bridge. I've always considered that I might one day become so against accepting reality that I myself would end up being rejected by it completely.

Ah, but no. That is impossible, too, given the president's final threat. Not even in a hell of my own making would I ever pose such an awful fate as having a roommate.

So, what do I do now? Attempt to sneak out the window and get back to the bridge, or follow the president's orders?

Eh, I'll just wait until tonight to end things.

It'll be simpler that way.

And who knows? In the dead of night, with no one else around, maybe, just maybe, I can experience that second of peace.

*Wouldn't that be something?*

Pleased with my astounding optimism, I take my book bag (still unpacked from where I left it two nights ago), pull on my spare pair of boots, and take off for class.

***

# Jordan Adrian

- **Year/age/student ranking**: Junior, 17, 1 of 150
- **Hair**: light brown, cut sensibly short and typically worn brushed back
- **Eyes**: bright amber
- **Height/Weight**: 5'10, 159 lbs.
- **Noticeable features**: intense eyes (as Zero has pointed out)
- **Favorite item**: Jordan does not care for sentimental things (that being said, it would be his watch)
- **Likes**: ???
- **Dislikes**: Zero, incompetence, people who refuse to listen to him, Zero
- **Personal comment**: "As if I'd ever give you more information than necessary."

- **Fact**: Jordan is the first student to have been elected Student Council President his freshman year in over 30 years. Also, he never takes any meaningless actions.
- *Note from Zero*: "I don't know why anyone would want to know more about what this man looks like, but here he is, I suppose."

*Zero's room*

***

# CHAPTER 3:

## LOST ONE'S WEEPING

Ughh, *why did you allow me to do this?!*

I regret my decision the moment I step foot into my first-period classroom.

Predictably, a sea of heads belonging to the twenty-three other students present turn to watch me as I enter.

"Ah, so you've decided to grace us with your presence, Mr. Hale," is the first thing my statistics teacher sees fit to say. "And on time, too? This must be a truly special day."

Special indeed.

Since stupid comments don't deserve even mediocre responses, I continue straight past him and toward my desk in the back right-hand corner.

"If only Ms. Thornswood would follow your example of punctuality."

It's true that she's missing today. As the one who sits directly to my right and the only person who speaks even less than I do, she's easy for me to remember. I silently salute her decision to cut class and slip into my desk seat beside her empty one.

It is, without a doubt, the optimal seating position of any classroom, mostly out of the teacher's line of sight and directly next to the large, floor-to-high-ceiling windows facing the academy grounds. I can fantasize about jumping from them while avoiding being called upon for answers all in one.

Not that this precaution has been particularly necessary considering most teachers in my first week here had already become disinclined to force me to participate. It seemed that, much like their students, they could sense the sinister unpleasantness of my presence. My lingering reputation as a gang leader and potential murderer at my previous high school didn't help, either. This has resulted in most teachers either avoiding me as much as possible or treating me with outright contempt. So is the nature of humans when they come across something they don't understand, something they fear: either run from it or kill it.

I suppose that is reason enough to acknowledge my statistics teacher, Mr. Davis—the only teacher aside from Ms. Kurima who is willing to actively give me a hard time while not completely despising my existence.

I continue to receive more stares from my classmates than usual throughout the rest of the period. Some at least attempt to be discrete, whether out of a desire for self-preservation or a base level of conscientiousness, while others stare blatantly in a way that verges on insult.

Now, what could be the cause of this? Perhaps my punctuality is just that shocking.

Mmh, don't buy that? Then I guess it could be *your* presence that's to blame. This is your first time accompanying me to class, after all. Maybe they can sense—ah. Do other characters tend not to notice you stalking the main character everywhere they go?

Fine, fine, that's not it, either. Well, that only leaves one explanation: news of my river rescue has already begun traveling around (or river disaster, depending on who started the spread.) I didn't expect word to circulate so fast, but it would've happened eventually.

It always does.

I'm just glad no other disasters occurred on my way here.

Unless, of course, the act of me showing up counts as a disaster in itself ... (Surely that can be blamed on the president, not me.)

Finally deciding I've had enough of being the day's zoo exhibit, I muster up the energy to pointedly glare in the direction of anyone who looks my way. An effective tactic. Rumors have a tendency to get out of hand, but it's times such as this, when a single look sends all of my classmates eagerly back to minding their own business, that I'm fine with the way I am perceived.

No one looks at me for the rest of the class. That is, until on my way out of statistics, I have my first (albeit small) incident of the school day. I'm quietly packing up the notebook I did not use when I catch wind of what's about to happen.

A boy is performing a magic trick using a penny in an attempt to entertain a group of girls.

I can already tell from his exaggerated motions that it's the one where the performer reaches behind their back and places the coin into their elbow crease, letting it fly out as they pretend to choke it out from their mouth. Judging from the girls' playfully enraptured expressions, it's going better than one might expect (although his technique is all wrong and the trick will surely be fumbled at this rate).

But what [Boy With A Lot Of Confidence And Little Talent For Magic] does not see is the ballpoint pen lying on the ground that he is about to step on as he dramatically stumbles backward, immersed in pretending to shove the penny through the back of his neck. I am prepared for the misstep and also considering allowing his fall to happen when I notice the two girls only a few feet behind him.

When he does fall, as he most assuredly will, he will take those girls down with him. Likely not the end of the world, but my limbs have already begun carrying me toward them.

Right as [Magic Boy] steps on the pen a second later and begins pinwheeling backward, shouting out a warning of surprise as the girls let out their own shrieks of fright, I wedge my way between him and them, causing his weight to fall against me instead. It's not my cleanest interference, and his head knocks roughly into the side of my jaw, but, taking care not to make a big deal out of it, I promptly straighten up and move the boy off of me. The less thought people give to these occurrences, the better.

"Take your performance elsewhere next time," I say in a low tone just as one of the girls cries out, "Oh, god—a-are you ok, Myles?!" (Myles? Wait …)

Slowly, the boy turns over his shoulder and I hold back a string of curses at the reveal.

The worried girl steps forward as if to rush to him, but then takes one look at me and pauses. When I look at the two girls Myles had been about to fall on, they, too, are staring at me with wide eyes. But his eyes are by far the widest.

He's looking at me with such a shine in his dazed expression that, if I didn't know better, I'd think he'd fallen in love with me. A complete impossibility, of course. There's only one person at this school by the name of Myles. I hadn't recognized him at first, be it because of my state of general disorientation or a plain lack of observation, but now that I'm looking at his face, at his light brown hair and golden-amber eyes, there's no mistaking who I just allowed to fall into me.

Myles Adrian.

*Of course.* My hand comes up to push back my hair, a heavy sigh emitting from between my lips.

It turns out the president's brother has an affinity for bad magic tricks.

He remains tongue-tied a bit longer as I make my way out of the class. I've nearly forgotten the entire incident when I feel a hand on my shoulder, an act that just about shocks me out of my skin. I haven't been purposely touched by another student—not counting the strange events of this morning—in over a year. That this boy, the president's twin brother no less, would touch me so casually is unthinkable. The halls naturally part where I walk, and yet …

"Wow, I can't even believe that actually just happened! You really saved my ass, man," he says cheerily, letting go of my shoulder and coming around to walk beside me. "I mean, the trick was going pretty well up until then, but who could have known a *pen* would be right there on the floor!? Your reflexes were inhuman! But I guess it's not too weird for you—this is just how you've always been, huh?"

I say nothing and Myles takes this as a prompt to continue.

"It's too bad the girls got scared off, though. I mean, to be fair, you were kinda scary." He pitches his voice low for an imitation. "*Take your performance elsewhere … Or I'll take it there for you.* So cool, but kind of over the top, don't you think? Oh, I'm Myles, by the way."

"I'm aware. We've been in several of the same classes."

This statement is a bit unfair, seeing as I don't remember many fellow students' names aside from the previously mentioned Briar Thornswood. But it's difficult to forget anyone in the Adrian family, even if this clumsy, wanna-be ladies' man *is* a far cry from the devil the president is. (What I really ought to have brought up is the fact that my father used to bring me to his family manor on numerous occasions growing up. But surely this boy can't be so dense as to have completely forgotten that.)

Myles laughs and scratches the back of his head, somehow making the gesture an annoyingly charming one. "I guess you're right. Can you believe we haven't spoken until now, though? In the same class and everything. Not to mention, you used to come over for family dinners all the time back when we were younger. But we never really spoke then, either. Ah, well, look at us now—talk about crazy, huh?"

"Yeah. Shocking." So his memory is intact. Good for him. If I continue walking without looking his way, maybe he'll take the hint and leave.

"So, are you eating lunch with anyone today?"

Or maybe not. "No."

"Then I guess you'd like to eat with me?"

"No."

"Haha! You're a funny guy, Zero, you know that? It's all right if today doesn't work, I guess. I figure you wouldn't want to eat with a large group, anyway, am I right? And the guys would definitely wonder what was going on if I all of a sudden ditched them for us to eat alone."

"Hmmm."

Several people in the hall, both girls and boys, greet Myles cheerfully before seeing me beside him, at which point they uncomfortably shift their gazes away. To his credit, Myles continues as if all is normal, smiling broadly and welcomingly, saying "hello" to no small number of students as we continue walking. He might not have the same incomparable distinction as his brother, but I'd almost forgotten just how popular he is. (I guess a lack of skill in the art of magic doesn't mean a lack of skill across the board.)

"So, Zero," he begins, switching his focus back to me after exchanging a passing inside joke with one of the other boys from his soccer team, "what are you doing later today?"

"You really want to know?"

"Well," he chuckles, "that's why I asked, of course."

"Fine, I'll tell you then. I'm dying."

"Dying?" He looks at me for another moment before letting out a laugh. "Hah! And you said it with such a straight face. Like I said, funny guy. I don't remember this side of you when we were kids. I used to think you were so scary every time you'd come to visit—and Jordan always took up all your time, anyway, so … Actually, now that I think about it, I still kind of find you scary, but I see now that's just part of what makes you cool, right?"

Myles gives me a toothy grin before clapping me on the back, thoroughly taking me by surprise once again.

(What fresh hell is this?)

Each sentence he says is worse than the last. And this whole thing is … weird, to say the least. He's unquestionably what one would call a friendly guy, the kind of who can get along with just about anyone—in fact, I can't think of a single person at this school who has a known dislike of him, aside from, perhaps, his brother—but there's no way my saving him from a little fall has suddenly opened his eyes to me for a new bond of friendship like this.

*Myles Adrian, why are you just now making your move?* I think to myself. Then again, there's always the possibility that I'm being overly suspicious and he's just *that* friendly of a guy. It makes no difference to me either way.

"Hey," I say, turning over my shoulder as if I'm trying to double-check something, "is it really ok for you to just ignore her like that? Seems a little cruel."

"Huh? Ignore who?"

"That girl who was trying to get your attention back there."

"What girl?" Myles asks, stopping abruptly and looking over his shoulder, too.

"Oh, you really didn't see her? Well …" I proceed to describe an imaginary girl whose imaginary description does *not* match that of any other girls currently in the hallway.

"For real? Uh, I don't think I know who that is, but I better make sure she doesn't need anything."

"Yes, I think you'd better."

I watch with little satisfaction as he bounds off in search of someone he won't find, shouting over his shoulder for me to go on ahead.

Doing just that, I find myself alone once again.

All around me, students clamor on with each other. One boy questions why a friend of his doesn't return his romantic feelings, another complains about a missing assignment, and—

That's when a particular conversation catches my ear.

Girl 1: "Really, you saw it happen?"

I instantly know what they're speaking of.

Girl 2: "No one saw it happen, you dummy. It was at the Black River, like, way early this morning. Honestly, I don't know what Marina was thinking."

Girl 1: "How unfair—someday, *I* want to be the one getting saved. I hear stuff like that happens all the time, so why has it never happened to me?"

(Does it count as saving when you're also the cause of the issue to begin with? I'm inclined to say no.)

Girl 2: "Hah, you're joking! He's probably the one who pushed Marina in the first place."

Girl 3: "Well, I did hear he tried to drown her before she eventually made it out ..."

(Is that what people are saying? I wonder, did I magically jump out of the water to cut down that pine tree before or after the drowning attempt?)

Girl 2: "Exactly. Either way, if it were me, I wouldn't want him anywhere *near* me."

Girl 3: "Yeah, I don't think it'd be the way you're imagining, Lacey. But, well, whenever there's trouble, he always seems to be at the heart of it, so you might just get your wish."

Girl 2: "Are you two serious? Zero Hale is bad news no matter how you look at him. You'd have to be blind to think otherwise. Haven't you noticed the color of his eyes? Or how pale his skin is? Either he's a vampire or Freddy's theory is right."

Girl 1: Freddy's theory?

Girl 2: You know, about him being the long-lost Prince of Hell, or whatever? All I'm saying is maybe it's all true, and that girl at his old school *didn't* kill herself after all ..."

(Prince of Hell? That's a new one. Deduction of points for farcicality, addition of points for creativity. Who knows? It's possible I'd be more at home burning along with the flames of the damned.)

Girl 3: "You're being ridiculous right now, and so is Freddy, but, you may have a point ..."

Girl 1: "What do you mean, Kate?"

Girl 3: "It's just ... is it not weird how often he's 'saving' someone? I mean, we can joke about it all we want and all, but ..."

Girl 2: "It goes way beyond weird. There's something seriously off about him. Sure, he might be beautiful—in an inhuman kind of way— but you'll stay away from him, Lacey, if you know what's good for you."

Well, this just got boring.

I decide to continue ahead of [Girls With Poor Awareness Of Their Surroundings] so I don't have to hear any more. All three cease speaking the moment I draw near. In fact, I wouldn't be surprised if they ceased breathing. It seems they cannot even get themselves to move over as most everyone else does, perhaps petrified at the idea that I overheard them.

Eyes glued to me in some horrible fusion of fear and morbid fascination, they watch intently as I pass by, their stares following me all the way down the hallway as an unpleasant pricking sensation crawls along the back of my neck and spine.

Turning the corner, I take a glance at the windows to the Kane Academy grounds. It's begun snowing again and everything, from the large rose bushes to the many water fountains, is covered in a dusting of frost. It's … pretty.

… Ah, god, I'm so *tired* …

Well, I gave it all a shot. You can attest to that. And the atmosphere outside is so nice, it's not a bad time to meet my end. Really, it would be a shame to waste it, don't you think? These windows are more than high enough—

I see *him* coming toward me from the other end of the hall. Two council members are on either side of him and though he's deep in the middle of what sounds like an urgent conversation, those freakishly intense eyes manage to pin me to the wall for a second time today, holding me there until he passes.

The president really is a piece of work. If ever I were to count myself lucky for something, it would be that I have had only a single class with him this year.

Honestly, it would actually be more work to attempt to get out now. For the least amount of effort and probability of being disturbed, I'll wait until the end of the school day. Yes. That's the smart move to make.

(Hey, stop looking at me like that.)

***

My other classes pass much in the same fashion as the first. When not talking about her beloved dog she named after her favorite character from that godforsaken *Fantasy Five* series she refuses to shut up about, the art teacher is as unnecessarily serious about her craft as usual. Today, she goes on and on about the dreaded paired projects that will count as our course final. Despite the semester having only started a few weeks ago, she will already be revealing our partners tomorrow, *giving me just one more reason.*

I get several apprehensive glances over shoulders at the mention of this news, no doubt emulating the inner dialogue they're all experiencing of "Please don't let me be partnered with him." I can't say I feel any different.

My aversion to working with others is demonstrated perfectly when, in chemistry, the unfortunate boy who is paired with me for an assignment on calculating molar mass ends up dispensing a sizable amount of his own mass into the lab's trash can. After retching up his breakfast, [Boy I Have Apparently Scarred For Life] runs from the room without a word, face white as a sheet, lacking even the tinge of redness in the cheeks that generally comes from your entire class seeing you vomit.

The teacher, rather than going after him, turns his attention to me, eyes narrowed in suspicion as if I somehow managed to poison my lab partner before we even paired up. He then tells me it's my job to dispose of the soiled trash bag. On my way to retrieve it, he mutters, quite loud enough for me to hear, how difficult I make it each time an experiment calls for a pair.

I elect not to return to chemistry after throwing the trash bag into the hall closet, instead going to sit at one of the windowsills to look out at the snow.

What I need to do now is get back my belongings from Marina Almandez. Since it would not make sense for the academy nurse to remain in the dorms, it is almost certain that Marina was moved to the nurse's office on the second floor of this building. That is where I'll find her.

I wait until lunch to head over, since going early wouldn't be worth the questions about why I'm not in class. On the way there, I face my second incident of the school day.

This time, it's a girl.

She's walking with a friend, headed down the third-floor staircase and turning around to make a response, when it happens.

She missteps on the turn as her right foot places itself down on air rather than solid ground—I manage to reach her faster than I expect, but I don't properly take into account the weight of her body, so I compensate by tugging her to me forcefully. *Too forcefully.*

I can feel her shaking pressed up against my chest. And I'm not sure if I am the cause or if it's the near fall that likely would have resulted in a broken bone. Out of consideration, and in an attempt to get to where I'm going, I release her slowly while keeping her steady on her feet.

"It was just a little fall," I say, my voice coming out in the gentler tone I sometimes use in events like this. "You're ok."

Her hand shoots up and fists around the material of my shirt before I can pull away entirely. She doesn't make eye contact, and she's still shaking, but she doesn't let go.

"Is … everything all right? Did I hurt you?" I'm almost certain this isn't the case.

She shakes her head. Then, so quietly I have difficulty making it out, she says, "Thank you."

Wait, *what?*

Did I hear that right? I couldn't have.

No, I did. She really said that. And her voice was soft and sweet and perfectly matching the innocent appearance of her large brown eyes and the two buns on either side of her head. (Is this love?)

Unsure of what to do, I reach a hand out and pat her head—girls tend to find the gesture comforting, I think. "You're welcome."

"Dude, did you see that?" a boy says to a friend in a whisper loud enough to be a mockery of the concept of quietness. "I thought for sure she was a goner."

"I thought for sure he was gonna toss her over the railing," is his friend's response.

After that strange encounter, I finally make it to the nurse's office.

Part of me has a feeling I will regret entering it, but I must do what I must do. I've put up with enough bullshit to get me here; there's no way I'm exiting this world without my hat. Same goes for my coat and boots. Besides, I want nothing tying me here when I'm gone—that includes the responsibility for a potentially injured classmate.

It's best I see what state she's in so I don't have to think about it anymore.

So, before I can be talked out of it, I raise my hand and knock.

3 ½

Nothing. I knock again. Still nothing. On my third attempt, when I still fail to get a response, I let myself in.

There, sitting up in bed and rocking back and forth with her eyes closed and earbuds in, singing some pop tune to herself while wearing *my* hat, is Marina Almandez.

She doesn't hear me when I clear my throat, nor when I say her name. She just keeps singing, bobbing along to the music, a content smile on her little face.

Well, this is just wonderful.

I walk over with my patience bar in the red zone and take out one of her earbuds.

"Hey!" she cries indignantly. "What are you …" Then she sees who it is that's interrupted her—well, whatever the hell she was doing—and her cheeks bloom a dark pink. "Zero. So, you finally decided to come visit me, have you?" Still looking flushed, she sticks a finger up, pouting as she does so. "Next time, you should try knocking first before just walking in like you own the place."

"I'm here for my things," I say, getting straight to the point. "Where are my boots and coat?"

"That's all you have to say to me? *Give me my stuff back*," she imitates, pitching her voice offensively low. "Come on. That is so *not* what you should be saying right now."

Judging from her words, and the way she's glaring at me, I'd say she really isn't happy with me. But I can't even guess as to the reasons. So I simply watch and wait as she crosses her arms and stares up at me.

"*Ugh*, like, seriously? The least you could do is sit down so I don't have to hurt my neck trying to look at you! Haven't I suffered enough today? Jeez, it's like you don't know the first thing about being a gentleman."

This is … not the response I was expecting.

I sit in the chair pulled out by the bed, crossing my arms as well. "I see you've taken a liking to my hat."

She lets out a huff, chin tipping up in defiance. "Yeah right. It's just warm, that's all."

"Then you won't mind if I take it back."

"Huh?" Her hands come up defensively to the hat, holding it to her head. It looks ridiculous on her, far too big in a way that makes it fall nearly down to her brows. "That's not—I mean, why *should* you get it back? I can't believe it took you so long to check up on me—you don't deserve any of your stuff back!"

"What are you talking about?"

She gives me a long-suffering sigh and flops back against her pillows, arms stretched out to the side. "I've been all alone here and you didn't even think to come see me when you got to school."

"And why would I have done that? I don't even know you. You're not making any sense."

"What, you think just because you got me out of that river you deserve some kind of reward now? I guess that's what you're really here for, then."

"I wouldn't consider getting my own clothing back a reward."

She rolls from her back to her side, facing me fully. "You want me to kiss you or something, don't you? Well, I'm sorry to say but I'm not interested in you like that, Zero. I'm not saying you're not attractive or anything, so don't take offense, but there's someone else I want, and there's simply no way you could ever take his place."

"You are getting way off track—"

"So whatever dirty motives you might have, you can keep them to yourself."

This is no longer worth it. Forget my effects. "I'm leaving." I stand up, but Marina catches my wrist.

"No, you're not going anywhere, Zero! Look, we can't just forget about the matter of the 'rescue' itself."

"Oh, I suppose you have an issue with that, too?"

"Yes, as a matter of fact, I do. Do you have any idea how long you let me float down that river?"

I look down at her with something akin to amazement. Is she actually mad about the length of time it took me to get to her? Looking back, sure, there were things I could have done differently, but I did it as swiftly as I could in the moment.

"Plus, when you finally *did* get me, you were so mean about it!"

"Mean about it?"

"Yelling at me and trying to scare me into obedience, you should be ashamed. Everyone knows you're scary, there's no reason to rub it in my face while I'm *dying*."

"I wasn't trying to scare—"

"But worst of all," she raises her voice and draws out the words, "at the end you ... **hesitated**!" This time, she doesn't even give me a chance to interrupt. "How could you do that?! I really thought you were gonna leave me!"

Hesitate? "I didn't *hesitate*." *See page 25 (Zero's precise words: "I hesitate.")*

"Yes, you did! I saw the way you paused before reaching me. Not to mention, you—" Marina gasps as if just remembering something important. "*Oh*. The entire time, you had me pressed up right against you, didn't you?" she exclaims, pointing an accusatory finger at me while clutching her shirt to her chest. "While you were swimming and when we tumbled underwater! Were you taking advantage of me?"

"What?" I respond, unable to process such absurdity. "Is this a joke—I *saved* you, or would you have preferred if I left you in that river?"

"Well now I'm not so sure."

"Think carefully, is the idea of me touching you so appalling, you'd actually give your life over it?" I look down at where her fingers still remain clasped around my wrist. "Considering how you're holding onto me, and how you clung to me all the way back to the dorms, I'd say that's an impossibility." Leaning down beside her, I say in a low voice, "But you should know, it certainly would have been much easier for me to let you drown."

Marina drops my wrist like I've burned her, a fresh flush washing over her face. She then makes an indignant huffing noise and turns her nose up, determined to appear unfazed. "That sure makes you sound like quite the good guy."

"I never said I was a good guy. Next time I'll be sure to let you freeze and die. Or get crushed by a giant tree, if you prefer."

She gasps again. "How could you say such a thing?! I've had enough of this—get out of my room!"

"To think I came to check on you. Just forget I was ever here." It may have been only a short while ago that I mentally corrected someone when they said I "saved" Marina, but *she* doesn't know the truth. And no matter the circumstances, I'm *still* the one who got her out of that river.

Tired of this back-and-forth, I try to leave once again, as she told me to, but she's faster than one would think, catching me this time by the hand.

A feeling of perplexion envelops me when looking down at our joined hands.

"Wait. You were actually going to leave?" she asks, more quietly now, her eyes trained on her bed sheets. "You didn't even get your stuff back."

I don't know what's happening anymore, but I'm certain I'm going to suffer from whiplash if her mood changes any quicker than it has been. At least any concerns I had about her being injured or sick have officially been proven unnecessary. My conscience is clear.

"I thought I didn't deserve any of my stuff back," I say, pulling my hand back and begrudgingly taking the seat again.

"I didn't mean …" Marina trails off. "The very least you could do is stay with me over lunch."

Yes, I truly have no idea what's going on.

"You want me to stay with you the whole time?" I ask incredulously. "Isn't there someone else you'd rather me get for you?" She's a popular girl, surely she has friends that would come to her side the minute she sought them out.

Marina just shakes her head, dark curls bouncing from underneath my hat. "Some of them already came to see me, and I told the others to … wait until after classes are done so I could rest."

"Yes, rest is important. I should let you get back to that."

"Hauhmmmhh." She doesn't say anything, rather, she just makes some indiscernible noises that might be best categorized as whining groans. (^ This is the best I can do to get the noises down in literary form for you.)

Though I'm loath to admit it, there's something a bit endearing about the silly, irrational girl sitting in the bed across from me. And when she looks up at me with round, hazel eyes, I am fearful of my own willingness to leave her right here and now. If I can't be affected by her objective cuteness, a fact which I have pointed out myself …

What is wrong with me? I must be losing emotion by the minute.

Still, to walk out the door right now as easily as I could would be to drag her into a mess of my own making. So, regardless of what I want, I know I won't be leaving this room until lunch ends.

"Now that you have me, whatever will you do with me?"

"Please, Zero," Marina wrinkles her nose, "that sounds so dirty."

"Marina, I will walk out."

"No, wait! Actually … I do know what I want to do with you."

I let out a low hum. "You're right. That does sound dirty."

This elicits a frown. But I can feel a chill crawl across my skin when her downturned mouth slowly becomes a sly grin. Oh god … *Is it possible this is how I'll meet my end?*

"I want you to tell me a story, Zero." The grin grows wider. "A scary story. And make it a good one—one I've never heard before. One no one's ever heard before! Just like … you know … how you used to do back when you were still …"

I feel my jaw slacken and a few seconds go by before my expression recomposes. *I see.* It suddenly makes sense why Marina was so insistent on keeping me by her side.

So then, this makes her the first to discover this part of me—or, of my past, I should say. I can't say I saw that one coming. Not even the president knows of this particular secret, and I really could have sworn I deleted all the videos, but …

For the next ninety minutes (I somehow stay through my free period as well), Marina Almandez proceeds to have me tell her scary story after scary story. Just like I used to when I still had my [REDACTED]. At one point, she hides under the covers, coming out only when she realizes I'm taking the opportunity to escape, and at another point, she uses my hat to bury her face into while kicking her feet under the sheets until I have to forcibly hold her legs down to get her to stop. For someone so obviously obsessed with horror, she certainly doesn't have a good stomach for it.

When the period finally comes to a blessed end, I take my hat back, ignoring her protests, and ask where the rest of my belongings are. This causes her eyes to tear up as she reverts to accusing me of being coldhearted and only coming to see her to "get my stuff." I don't mind, however, since asking her was only a measure of politeness. The truth is, I've known from the very beginning where my coat and boots are; there are only three places they could be out of sight in this room (the coat closet, chest, or under the bed) and Marina's glanced at the closet each time my belongings are brought up.

"It's not fair," she whines as I step into my boots, "you give your things to me, and then you just take them all back? What kind of a gift is that?"

"A life-saving one," I retort. "If it makes you feel better, I can leave my other pair of shoes with you." It's not as if I'll be needing them.

"Are you messing with me? You are messing with me. That's not nice, Zero."

I flip my coat over my arm and shake my head at her, beginning to walk away. Then I stop by the door. "Marina, about what you know, I don't think I have to say this but please don't go spilling it to the first person you see." Even in death, I'd rather not give people anything else to talk about concerning my life.

"Of course I won't! Why would I do that when I can keep you all to myself this way?"

"Of course."

She winks and smiles widely.

Deciding it's of no consequence to me, I slip off my uniform jacket, leaving me in only the black button-down.

"What are you doing?" she asks, watching me closely.

I throw the jacket so that it lands perfectly on Marina's head. She squeals at the abruptness and then takes it in her hands, looking it over.

Her eyes grow larger and a hand comes up to her chest. "I see," she breathes. "You're giving me your jacket knowing it will smell like you, hoping it'll make me fall for you because I won't be able to stop thinking about you when I wear it. It's not a bad plan, but I'm afraid it just won't work, Zero. Like I said, I already have someone in mind."

I roll my eyes. "Why would I ever want someone like you to fall for me? I gave that to you to stop your whining."

Marina's entire face goes red for a third time. Scowling, she abruptly gets up and walks over to me, opening the door while simultaneously attempting to shove me out of it.

"I'm already going," I say. Then, knowing it will get to her, "Is this just an excuse to touch me again, Marina? You've been doing this all day. My my, what about your special mystery man I can't take the place of—"

"Your voice and looks are wasted on you, Zero Hale!" she shouts over me. "And you better come back tomorrow, or I won't forgive you!" With that, she slams the door in my face.

*Come back tomorrow?*

What a dramatic child. Even if you were blind you'd have to see that she's fine—physically speaking, at least; there's no way she needs to stay the night here. So even if I were still around tomorrow, coming again wouldn't make sense. (Well, she's fine unless you take into consideration the possibility of a mix between bipolar disorder and borderline personality disorder. Maybe a touch of narcissism?)

Turning to go, I place my hat on my head, wondering why today has been so goddamn weird. I've talked to more people, and been touched by more people, than I have all year long. The other question that remains in my mind is who was it she was trying to see in the ice this morning? There's no doubt that's what she was doing, looking to find the reflection of this boy she "has in mind." I guess I'll never know the answer.

Regardless, one thing's for sure: a girl's mind is a seriously scary place. Especially if that girl is Marina Almandez.

But the sheer boredom and desire to be just about anywhere else I experience upon the start of my US History class is enough to make me wonder if I wouldn't have been better off remaining trapped in Marina's room. Attempting to listen, even half-heartedly, to the lesson being lectured at us by the old, frail teacher up front has me feeling such a dark depression that I consider leaving mid-class. It's no stunt I haven't pulled before.

On top of this, I have to fight off the urge to pass out over my desk barely a quarter of the way through the period when a vicious wave of exhaustion sweeps over me. (Though I may prefer passing out to enduring much more of this.)

It is all so unbearably unchanging.

The same people sit toward the back so that they can slack off with their friends, passing notes back and forth and chatting, only to realize they know nothing come test day at which point they freak out, struggle through it, and come out the other side with a below average grade, a dropped student rank, and a feeling of self-pity, asking "Why me?" while being consoled by their equally academically ungifted friends. And the same people sit toward the front who raise their hands for every little thing, even when no question is expressly asked, in the desire to gain the teacher's favor and end up being seen as one of the coveted "Kane Academy elites" by the rest of us, undoubtedly hoping to raise their student rank and get the prestigious invitation into the student council in the process.

That is the way they are.

The only differences today are the empty seat in the left-hand corner of the room generally taken up by the Thornswood girl (just as in statistics and art), what I can assume to be Marina's vacant seat in the middle, and the upper right-hand seat that should be occupied by the president. His not being here likely means he's in a meeting for the student council, a meeting that might just offer a good opportunity for me to sneak away from this place undetected ...

I can't blame my classmates for being the way they are—surely they are all just doing what they can to exist, too—but I also can't help the heaviness in my chest from just being in the same room as it all. So when the teacher begins having students take turns reading aloud from the textbook, I take myself up on my own offer and walk out.

"Mr. Hale!" he calls, sounding genuinely surprised.

I turn to look at him, an icy glare naturally twisting my face. Unfortunately for him, I'm too tired to put on a mask.

"Wh-where ... are you going?"

I look at him a moment longer before I answer, noticing the way his eyes flicker down to the floor and back up to meet my gaze several times. "I no longer have any desire to be here."

With no more to say, I turn and leave.

Mr. Rubin is far too nervous a man to contact the office about my little stunt just now, so I should be in the ... I should be ... the clear. In the ...

*In the ...*

The fatigue hits me again out of nowhere; I stumble directly into a wall the second I reach the hallway and begin using it to drag myself along.

Reaching the first windowsill I see, I clumsily climb onto it and look out at the increasing snowfall. (It's really coming down now. I guess today's below forty degrees after all.) I undo the latch and push both panes open, letting the cold air and incoming snowflakes whip me across the face. The moment I do, I see a familiar black shape staring up at me from below, standing out against the stark whiteness surrounding him. I'm too far to make out the yellow of his eyes, but I can sense his gaze with certainty.

It's as if Marius has been waiting for me in this exact spot.

There's nothing I can do when he's staring at me like this. Nothing except stare back. Approximately thirty seconds go by before he gets up and walks away like he was never there to begin with.

I blink and lift my right foot from the floor, releasing the sides of the windowsill.

"It's a bit strange to be wearing a winter hat indoors, don't you think?" The voice freezes me. "Then again, I suppose you've always been pretty weird."

My hand slowly comes up to my head, feeling the soft fur there. I … hadn't realized I'd put it on again.

Right as I turn to look at her over my shoulder, slender fingers enclose around my wrist, holding onto me firmly as the scent of lilac perfume fills my senses.

"I wondered if I would be seeing you soon, kiddo—I'm glad I ran into you," she says, a smile in her voice as she tugs me to her. "Come with me, Zero."

***

Marina Almandez

- **Year/age/student ranking**: Junior, 16, 119 of 150
- **Hair**: loose brown curls often worn in some fashionable hairstyle with accessories
- **Eyes**: hazel-brown
- **Height/Weight**: 5'2, 120 lbs.
- **Noticeable features**: button nose, curls
- **Favorite item**: butterfly hair clip
- **Likes**: scary stories, "cute things," shopping, fashion, sweets, pop idols, the *Fantasy Five* series, Stargram, certain video games & RPG events, action/spy movies, a particular boy who shall remain nameless

- **Dislikes**: people who won't give her attention
- **Personal comment**: "Do we really only get one of these?"
- **Fact**: Marina was too indecisive to pick out a good fact ("I just have too many to choose from—wait, why are you walking away?!")

**Kane Academy Fact**: Students are ranked twice a semester, after midterms and after finals. This rank is separated by grade level and is used to determine many factors in a student's life. There is also an unofficial ranking revealed at the end of every week to give students an idea of where they stand and what they will have to score on the midterm and final to maintain or improve their standing. While rank is primarily determined through tests and assignments, factors such as individual class placement, attendance, club activities, and outstanding achievements also contribute to a student's overall placement, along with numerous unknown factors determined by a select few higher-ups.

### Bonus: Read Between the Lines of Zero & Marina's Interaction

M: If only you didn't have such a horrible personality … It's really a shame.

Z: Stop insulting my personality. That's the same as just outright insulting me.

M: But it's just too bad. If you weren't so awful on the inside, just think about how popular you could be, you know?

Z: Excuse me?

M: Hey, what were you even doing all morning that made you so late to see me? You know, I heard they gave you a bath and everything. You must have enjoyed that, huh? Having that girl rub her hands all over you like that.

Z: How do you even know about this?

M: *completely ignoring Zero's question* I bet you really had fun. You probably wish you were still there. You do, don't you?

Z: What exactly are you imagining right now …?

M:

Z: ... This is so disturbingly incorrect that I'm going to end this bonus installment here. Where are the roses coming from? Why am I making that expression?

M: Huh? Isn't that just how you normally look?

***

# CHAPTER 4:

## SAKAYUME

After a cup of what must be magical tea that Ms. Kurima all but forces down my throat, I actually feel much more myself again. (As for whether or not this return to self is a good thing, that is not up to me to decide, I think.)

It occurs to me, now that my head is back on straight, that I haven't had my book bag with me since I left chemistry. Luckily, I don't have any embarrassing paraphernalia in there, so even if it's currently sitting like a museum artifact in the lost and found, its contents shouldn't mortify my memory too much.

Finally finished walking around her classroom and sipping at her tea in near silence, Kyouka Kurima takes a seat behind her desk across from the chair she pulled up for me.

"So, you're here," she says, folding her hands over one another and resting her chin on them.

"Looks like it."

"And early at that." She tilts her head to the side, causing me to take note of her hair, jet-black and fashioned in a shoulder-length cut that frames her small face well. I'm not usually partial to short hair, but it looks good on her, making her appear younger than her already youthful thirty-two years. "Good," she continues, smiling in a way that lets me know none of this is in fact *good*. "I was ready to file a missing person's report if you didn't show up today."

"Please, it was a single school day, Ms. Kurima. If missing persons reports were filed over such trivial occurrences, think of how overwhelmed our police departments would be." My fingers tap along the desk to a piano piece I've been replaying in my head. "Rather than only thinking of what you want in the moment, you need to start thinking of the greater good."

Ms. Kurima frowns. "You know, you're not as cute as you think you are. Anyone ever tell you that?"

"On the contrary, I've been told I don't value my looks enough. Perhaps we both need to see an optometrist. I'm free this weekend if you are."

"You little punk." Her brow ticks, her smile frighteningly back in place. "You're talking big for someone who's clearly skipping out on his other class period right now. What if I were to turn you in? That would be considered part of my job, you know. I *am* your teacher after all …"

The rest of what she says goes right through me as I realize the mistake I've made in my careless speech. There is no "this weekend."

Of all the people at this academy, why did she have to be the one to find me up on that windowsill?

I was in a bit of a daze at the time, but if I'd gone through with it, this would all be over. However, Ms. Kurima might just be the one person I can't walk out on. She's certainly the only person I feel any semblance of genuine human emotion toward, so it's natural for me to want to keep her out of my "antics" as much as I can. I might not understand why, but she's also one of the few people who, no matter how often I'm around her, never seems to fall victim to the unexplainable bad things that happen around me.

With the necessity of always being on guard diminished, I could almost mistake myself for a normal person. And who knows? If this was as life was, just living alone with Ms. Kurima—

*Do you think that would make you safe?* a dark voice says in the back of my mind. *Is anywhere truly safe when you're there, Zero?*

The image of a girl kneeling over me—long hair flowing to the ground around her, the rest of her features completely hidden in shadows—flashes in my head, startling me. As quickly as it appears, it's gone half a second later.

Did I ... even actually see it? I couldn't make out her face, but her shape didn't look familiar either. She was a stranger, I'm sure, so then why ... Why did she seem so sad?

As sad as anyone could be.

*I must be hallucinating again.*

"Hey, Zero!" Ms. Kurima calls out obnoxiously loud, tapping my hand with her own. "Anybody there? Come on, have you even heard a word I've said?"

"Ms. Kurima, I believe I said I might have a problem with my eyes, not my ears."

She sits back and folds her arms, appraising me. "Jeez, kid. Where did you go just now? It's like you were in a different world."

"Well, that's not far off. I was just fantasizing about a world with only the two of us in it—for the sake of my mental peace, a life like that might be necessary."

"... If this is your way of confessing to me, then I'll have to let you know that I am both in shock and in need of enough time for you to graduate before giving you my answer."

I shake my head at her silly response. "Never mind all that. What was it you were trying to say to me?"

"Oh, so you're just going to make a comment like that and then brush it off?" She eyes me with no lack of suspicion as she plucks my hat from my head to ruffle my hair. "As if anyone would ever be interested in a cheeky delinquent like you, anyway."

"Ahh, what're you—"

"Hey, isn't wearing a hat inside the equivalent of wearing sunglasses inside?" She laughs at her own observation, hand still mussing up my hair. "You really are a weird one. "

I grit my teeth, accepting the hair ruffle. "So you keep saying."

But then she doesn't stop; her fingers just rub into my scalp harder.

"Hey," I protest, swatting her away, "that's enough." As I've said, having a woman run her hands through my hair isn't exactly something I hate, but when that woman is my teacher who finds joy in teasing me and treating me like a child … it kind of takes all the allure out of the activity.

"So temperamental," she says, giving me a you're-actually-kinda-cute-when-you're-mad smile that has my temper flaming hotter. "But your bad attitude wasn't what I was trying to talk to you about earlier."

"Then please, put me out of my misery. I'm drowning in suspense."

"Interesting choice of words. Because as it turns out, you *did* in fact rescue a girl from drowning in the Black River this morning. And then you walked her back in nothing but your shirt and pants, barefoot. That trek is over three hundred acres." She cocks her head, refolding her hands. "How impressive."

Gossip travels through the faculty as fast as it does through the students. "Just say a half mile like a normal person. And if that's all you have to say to me, I'm going to skip your class early as well."

"I'm not bringing this up to tease you, Zero. I want you … to really think about what you did, about the actions you've taken today."

"You make it sound like I committed a crime. Are you suggesting I need to be punished?" I tilt my head to the side, widening my eyes. "Do you have something specific in mind?"

Ms. Kurima levels me with an unamused glare. "Stop joking around, you brat. The only reason I'm talking to you about this is because it's relevant to your progression as my student."

"Oh?" How will she spin this one?

"In your last book analysis, you essentially made the entire thing into an essay on nihilism, saying how *everything comes from a meaningless beginning only to come to a meaningless end* and whatnot."

"What is it with everyone and imitating my voice so deeply?"

Ms. Kurima slaps her hand down on the desk, hard. "Are you listening? Your paper didn't even have anything to do with the book by the end! Honestly, it's really a wonder you've managed to keep your ranking as high as you have with work like that. How can there possibly be five students worse off than you? It was like you were just writing your own Manifesto of Pessimism or something, going into detail about the pointlessness of life and humanity and all that. It was seriously depressing."

Ah. "I think I know where you're taking this," I say, finally figuring out Ms. Kurima's roundabout lesson and not bothering to inform her that my rank has recently sunk from fifth-to-last to the penultimate slot. "You want to point out to me that the simple fact that I got Marina Almandez out of the river means I actually *do* have some respect for life and therefore have the potential to extend beyond my studies in 'nihilism' to—"

"Dammit, Zero, that's enough!" My eyes go wide as hers close, her chest rising slowly in a deep, calming breath. "Why can't you ever just *listen?*"

When her eyes finally open, Ms. Kurima has a seriousness in her expression that I don't recall ever seeing before. It's no look of amusement, and it's not like the expression she wears when lecturing me to hell and back for any number of things she constantly sees fit to get on me about.

There's something … different about it. A solemn heaviness along with an unfamiliar emotion that I'm wary to place.

Just when I think I can't bear her stare a moment longer, she speaks. "You can make light of it all you want, but the fact is that a girl owes you her life, Zero." Despite knowing they're coming, I cringe at those words. "She's alive because of you. And that *does* mean something, no matter what anyone else thinks, or what *you* yourself think. In a way, you're a hero—" She puts a thumb under her chin thoughtfully, muttering to herself, "Though I'll admit you fit the physical description of a villain much more accurately."

"It's not heroic if it's just setting things to how they should be. Really, a more accurate way to think of it is me making up for my existence in the only way I can." I place my chin in the palm of my hand, a strong feeling of dejectedness hitting me suddenly. "The same goes for all the other incidents you're probably thinking of bringing up right now."

"You always say the strangest things. Would it kill you to make sense every now and then?"

"If making sense were enough to kill me, I would be the most eloquently spoken student this academy has ever seen."

"What?"

"What?"

"What did you just say?"

"Nothing." I break eye contact. "A bad joke."

"… Is this the sort of thing you were thinking about when I found you standing on that windowsill just now? For a second there, Zero … I almost believed you were going to jump. I mean, the look on your face …"

I smirk, pushing the dejectedness aside. "All I was thinking then was that I needed some fresh air and how everything in my life would be so much better if only all my other teachers could be as intelligent and charming as my English teacher—"

"All right, *smart guy*, I can tell you're in an especially difficult mood today." She sticks her nose up in a childish way reminiscent of Marina in her nurse's bed. "It almost makes me not want to give you your present now."

Present? "You mean like a reward for '*being a hero?*' Careful, Ms. Kurima, if you go around giving gifts like this, people might start to think you're prone to favoritism."

She surprises me by smirking back. "And what's so wrong with that?"

Then she reaches into her desk drawer and hands me a manga volume—the newest volume in a horror-suspense series I had mentioned I was reading a while back. She has always had a good memory ... Of course, there's no way she went out and got this for me as a reward for earlier today; no, she's likely been waiting for the opportune moment to use it. On the surface, it seems like a thoughtful gift, but there's a catch. *As there always is.*

"This is one of your favorites, is it not?" she asks.

This time, the catch is obvious the moment I glance down at the title. I shake my head and flip through it, holding in an amused snort. We've exchanged manga before, but this is the first time she's given me one in Japanese.

Ms. Kurima sighs dramatically and spins around in her chair as I look it over. "Such a shame it's not the English-translated version. But since it's such a new release for such a rarely printed series, that I only got through my special contacts, it's going to be a while before the translation is available. I guess," she stops spinning, turning her head to look at me over her shoulder, "you'll just have to let me read it to you. Unless you can wait, that is."

A *three-in-one*: she'd get to tease me, show off, and keep an eye on me. That is, it would be a three-in-one if her plan panned out the way she wants it to. Which it won't. Even if I was staying around …

"I assure you, Ms. Kurima, there's no need for you to trouble yourself." I stand with the volume in hand, lifting it up. "Luckily, I can read Japanese, so it's not a problem."

"… What?" She must think she misheard me.

"I said I can read it, so it's fine."

Her mouth falls open for just a moment before she recovers. "No—no you can't. You said as much yourself just before summer."

"Yes, that's correct. And then I amended the issue by learning Japanese several months ago." I taught myself out of sheer boredom, partially just to see if I could and partially because I knew it would be useful in regards to reading manga (I did the same thing with Spanish when I was a child and interested in telenovelas). Though judging from the look on her face, Ms. Kurima thinks I've picked up Japanese just to spite her.

"That's not possible … no one could learn an entire language in such a short … Zero you …"

If she thinks this is strange, what would she think about the games Lila and I used to play on a regular—wait. No. I'm not going to think about *that* right now, or ever again as a matter of fact.

"You're right, I'm just messing around," I say. "But I'll keep this volume, anyway. Got to start somewhere, right?"

Slowly, Ms. Kurima's expression melts into a semi-bitter "you're unbelievable, you bastard" smile and I let out a small sigh of relief. "You really are something, kiddo."

"Yurushitekudasai, sensei," I say with a small bow before turning to head to my seat at the back of the class, lips twisted in a once-again-intact half smile. My speech is far from perfect—always too formal—as are my writing skills, but I really only used it for reading and understanding, anyway.

"Sou ka?" Ms. Kurima murmurs to herself, hardly phrasing it as a question.

The smile lingering on my face fades as I realize this is the last I'll ever see of her. So …

"Kyouka."

She startles at my use of her first name. "Hm?"

"Thank you." This only seems to confuse her more, but I continue. "I know I haven't been the easiest student, but you really are a wonderful teacher."

She stands perfectly still behind her desk, staring at me. A few seconds go by in silence. Then, she opens her mouth to speak, but—

"Dude, did you hear what happened in Mr. Henderson's class?"

"Of course he has—Alina Carter's in it, he basically stalks her every move."

"Shut up, dumbass. You say that like you haven't been losing your shit over Marina all day."

"Oh, so that's how it is, huh?"

The ~~NPCs~~ other students have begun arriving for class. And, just like that, my final moment alone with Kyouka is over.

Myles Adrian and his friends from the soccer team make it in the last four seconds before the bell rings, uttering a dramatic "Safe!" while skirting through the door together. He spots me right away, grinning and waving energetically like we've been great friends for years.

He clearly wishes to come and say hi, but he's forced to take a seat by Ms. Kurima who glares white-hot daggers at him while asking why he didn't get to class early to discuss his previous paper as she'd asked.

Given what I know about him, Myles strikes me as the kind of student who gets by on his family name and the sort of boyish charms that would have women across the country labeling him something as harmless as "mischievous" for any number of crimes ranging from homicide to cutting up cats in his basement. Not that Myles would ever have the stomach to do such a thing. (His brother on the other hand …)

However, speaking of the type of boy who could be cutting things up in his basement, Alek Slate, who sits directly to my right, has left his desk vacant. The embodiment of unpredictable, dangerous mischief, and someone who is generally unafraid to speak to me, Alek makes the short list of people I remember well.

"Isn't that interesting?" I mutter to myself once the rest of the class has filed in.

Apparently today is the day of playing hooky as I notice, for the fourth time, that Briar Thornswood is also still missing. It would seem rather than ditching only some of her classes, she decided to skip the entire day. I silently salute her once again. Attendance is such a valued thing here at Kane Academy, it takes real courage to break it. Courage, or, in my case, an apathetic yet all-consuming desire for a way to escape the reality of academic life.

Of all my classes, it goes without saying that Ms. Kurima's is indeed the one I find most tolerable. Her teaching methods are occasionally unorthodox and she can become too invested in my personal affairs for my liking, but as I said before, she is still the only person here I feel anything toward.

Despite this, mid-class I revert back to a state of being half-awake, half-driven mad by fatigue (I suppose the tea was only a temporary solution ... maybe I should have eaten something this morning). At this point, if someone asked me what color my boots are, I'm not sure I'd be able to answer.

What I can do is picture that girl standing up on the school rooftop, angry tears dripping down her face: *"Why, Zero, why can't you accept me? I—I don't understand!"*

I wasn't there to witness what happened next, and yet I can see it clearly, unable to get it out of my head.

I nearly begin a bout of hysterical laughter in my seat, having to cover my mouth and bend my head down to suppress it. My outgrown bangs fall in my eyes, partially blocking my vision, but I can tell the girl a few seats to my right is staring at me—no, several people from class are looking. *Oh well!* I sit up straight and my hands fall to my sides. *Who cares?*

"Is he ... smiling?" another girl whispers to her friend.

"What the hell? Is something wrong with him?" someone else says quietly.

Though I am not meant to hear any of this, my hearing has always been excellent—something else I've found to be more curse than blessing.

When class ends, Ms. Kurima looks like she wants to come over to me. As does Myles. But they both get in each other's way when Ms. Kurima is forced to be a responsible teacher and bring up Myles' falling grade and how to fix it. It offers the perfect opportunity for a clean escape; there's just one last thing I need to do here before that.

I discreetly slip a note under Ms. Kurima's flower vase on my way out while she's preoccupied with yelling at a now sheepish Myles. If I had time, I'd go and replace the flowers with fresh ones—though I'm sure one of her many other adoring students will do so sooner or later.

I don't precisely recall what is written on the note to her since I wrote it down several months ago, but it's something about how I appreciate all she's done for me and an apology for making her give up her time to such a hopeless student. (Basically, a more thought-out version of what I'd attempted to tell her at the end of our conversation.) It ends with me wishing her well and has been stuffed in the side of my book bag all this time, there in case I needed it, or, more likely, *knowing* I'd one day need it.

Without speaking, I send up (down?) a prayer of thanks that I had the mind to slip the note from my book bag into the pocket of my uniform before the end of my first period. Tracking it down now would have been a pain.

It's all I can do to hope that Ms. Kurima takes my note for what it is and does not blame herself in any way. She's a smart woman; I'm sure she'll be over it and have moved on to more productive projects soon enough.

4 ½

Before leaving the academy's main building, I stop by the practice rooms on the fifth floor to indulge a final time in my one true talent. I haven't played a piano in over six months, meaning I'll be a bit rusty. It's no matter, though, for as I said, piano is the one worthwhile thing I'm truly good at.

I wait for some kind of rush to hit me as I sit down in front of the keys. Instead, emptiness awaits me. Emptiness, and calls from that woman:

*"Won't you play your mother's favorite song, Zero? Please, darling?"*

It's not even technically a piano piece so much as a piece I translated onto the piano for her back when I would still do that sort of thing. But it seems, regardless of the years that have gone by since then, the memory of my fingers is still intact as I begin Mozart's "Lacrimosa." What a terrible, haunting melody. The majority of his pieces were written in major keys, as per the trends of his time, yet "Lacrimosa" is both in minor key and widely considered among his best compositions.

Also the song he wrote on his deathbed, it's somewhat of a grand goodbye letter to the world. (Personally, I've always favored songs written in minor—and even those that aren't originally written as such tend to sound even more entrancing when modulated.)

Continuing on, I make a transition into an arrangement of "The Moon Over the Ruined Castle." It's a lesser-known piece here in the US, and one I have always felt a connection to. Its emotion is deceptively tricky to convey; when done right, I've witnessed it bring tears to the eyes of its listeners on more than one occasion.

Quiet loneliness and longing bleed from the keys with an elusive feeling that I've chased after ever since the first time I heard it. When even this piece fails to move me, I decide to go back to the dorms.

But the second I stop playing, I hear something—the sound of scuffling outside the practice room door. It's not entirely unusual for another student to be on the fifth floor since there are other practice rooms, art studios, and dance studios—some clubs even have their meetings up here. What is unusual is that rather than choosing a dance studio with a piano, I specifically chose the smallest practice room on the farthest side from the stairs so as to nullify the possibility of being interrupted, and yet still I was not alone when I thought I was.

Someone … has been listening to me.

But when I walk over to the doors and look down both ends of the hallway, no one is in sight.

*******

I attempt to read the manga given to me by Ms. Kurima once I'm back in my room and make it forty percent of the way through before setting it aside.

I don't want her to believe it was the last thing I read and get the wrong idea, so I place the volume on my shelf and grab something from a different series to place on my bed. Then, once it's past curfew, I throw my coat and hat back on and climb out my window and into the snowy night.

After seventeen years of this, it all seems rather anticlimactic.

I left no official suicide note because I have no one I'd wish to send it to and nothing of importance to say. I haven't spoken to Lila in months, and my father may be dismayed for a time, upset that all the training he put me through was for naught, but I have no doubt he'll recover quickly. (Perhaps he'll even be glad.) And Marius will be taken care of by another, more attentive student at the dorms.

There is ... one person who may truly be pained by my passing, but he'd have to find out that I've died, first.

As for everyone else, I can say with certainty that once I go, one of two things will happen: either the universe's natural balance will be restored as I suspect and everything will go back to normal, or *a lot* of people will start dying.

If not dying, then getting moderately to severely injured. Of course, I do not believe this will be the case. Getting rid of something that fundamentally does not belong can only be beneficial to everything else going on around that something. I've known this since I was a young child, back when I'd wake with a feeling of wrongness so strong, I wouldn't be able to get out of bed until someone came and pried me from it. Getting dragged to school kicking and screaming, saying I wouldn't stay unless they chained me in place ... huh. I guess it's kind of funny looking back on it now. Even then, each day was a painful chore to get through. A chore of expectedly unexpected events, frightening accidents, and near-tragedies. Some things never change, do they?

Whatever the exact reason for these events and their connection to me—whether it be that I was never meant to be born, God's personal dislike of me, or something more sinister—I do not care.

There is only one thing I desire now.

I suppose this means this really is about to be the end of us.

Sorry to be cutting our time together short, and for misleading you the last time it was nearly cut short. I'm sure this isn't what you'd anticipated. Or maybe it is, seeing as where we started. Maybe you've even grown attached to me since then, if only just a little. But I doubt it. You're a pretty cold and pragmatic person yourself. If someone doesn't have anything else to offer you in a story, you're ready to move on to the next. Am I wrong?

Heh. That's what I thought.

Don't worry, though, like I've made clear before, I'll be sure to pass you along to another before making my exit. Of course, if you stop reading the moment I'm no longer the focus, I won't blame you, either—

*Ah.*

Jesus Christ. The snow and wind seem to have suddenly picked up, hitting my face from all directions with a constant, cold spray. I squint and tilt my head down, but that offers little protection.

As I continue to stumble on my way to the bridge over the Black River, I fall face-first into the snow several times. My sense of balance is so off now that it was a given this would happen. So, each time, I pull myself back up to my feet and trudge forward.

If I have to crawl there, I will.

It's fine if it's not the peaceful end I once imagined as long as it's the end. (But since this is so humiliating, I'd prefer it if you don't watch too closely.)

Predictably, after one of my many stumbles, my stomach-twisting memory flashes begin again. At the start of the first, I fall for a fifth time. Only now, I can't get back up.

As I said I would, I begin crawling.

"Even now, you can't give me a moment of peace, Selene," I grit out to the hallucination of the familiar girl as she kneels down beside me, still wearing her high school uniform.

"Oh, Zero, you have no idea how much joy I get from seeing you this way. You really are *pathetic*. If this is how you were going to end up only a few, short years later, you should have just jumped with me that day, don't you think?" Selene croons into my ear, her sweet voice like poison pouring down my throat. "Or better yet, you could've just given in and accepted my love as you should have from the beginning! Yes, that would have been the smart thing to do, hmm?"

But Selene isn't alone; close behind, that woman appears.

"Don't touch him, you vile slut," she spits. "Step away from my *son*. There is one person and one person only that he belongs to."

Just like that, Selene is gone and *that* woman has taken her place, kneeling down beside me, reaching for me. I swear I feel the warmth of her hand on my frozen cheek.

"Mom?" I don't sound like myself as I say the word. It's as if I have reverted back to the age I last saw her.

"Yes, darling. I'm here. But you must get out of the snow before you catch a cold." Her fingers move from my cheek to thread through the ends of my hair. "You know how you are when you get sick. You should really let your mother take care of you more. It would be so cruel of you to leave me all alone."

"Stop," I mumble, snow getting into my mouth as my head hangs down. "Please, just … stop. I have to do this. I have to."

"No, you don't, my angel. You can come back to me, stay with me—"

**Zero.**

My head snaps up as my mother is interrupted by someone else calling out my name.

**Zero.**

This voice … is different. It is not from a memory, or belonging to a person I know. Nor does she seem to be yelling, yet the sound of her saying my name feels as if it's all I can hear; coming from everywhere or nowhere. And most importantly, this is—*this is the most pleasant voice I have ever heard.* So beautiful and comforting, yet powerful.

(Who is she?)

**Zero, it's time to wake up.**

Before I can attempt a response, the voice is gone. And Mom is gone with her.

"What ... the hell ... is happening to me ...?"

I fight my way to my feet and begin forward.

In these final moments of reaching the bridge, I am left completely alone. Not even my hallucinations appear beside me, nor do their malignant words resound in my head. The wind itself has died down to nothing more than a breeze, leaving the night perfectly quiet aside from the slowly lessening flurry of snowfall and the sound of my panting breaths.

*Wake up.* What a funny final thing to hear after a lifetime of dreaming.

At last, I stand upon the bridge over the Black River: my favorite spot on the academy grounds and the place I should never have left this morning.

The moonlight shines especially vivid tonight, casting a shimmering blanket of illumination over everything in sight, from the white mountain tops in the distance to the moving currents below. I look out at it all, vacantly, for an indeterminate amount of time. Then I step between the railing and a pillar.

At least I got to see something beautiful in my last—

My breath catches in my throat all at once.

*No.*

*No. No. No.*

The beating of my heart swells from a near-nonexistent pulse to a deafening, blood-rushing pounding as, slowly, I turn my head to my left.

*This isn't possible. This isn't—*

My eyes must be taking up half the space on my head.

*I don't understand. Is this really happening right now? Can this truly be real life?*

I say nothing, my mind wiped blank in shock as I stare.

Wide, unblinking golden-brown eyes stare back at me from a heart-shaped face framed by long, dark hair.

It can't be, but she's … right there.

Standing exactly as I am on the other side of the pillar—so close to the edge, her feet are in danger of slipping off—is my classmate, **Briar Thornswood**.

And just like that, my hell (and yours) is indefinitely extended.

Only …

Hang on. Why is she turning toward me …?

"No!" I breathe instantly. "Don't!" The edge is too close! A centimeter more and she'll—

Fall.

The girl is falling.

Right off the bridge.

***

Sakayume: a dream opposing reality.

**Zero Fact**: When considerably sleep deprived, in dangerous situations, or emotionally distressed, Zero often suffers vivid hallucinations, or "memory flashes," that can appear so real, they look as if they're actually happening. When he was taken to the doctor about it as a child, no explanation for the phenomena was found.

***

# Chapter 5:

# God's Least Favorite

*Briar.*

Her name sounds in my head as I reach for her.

If there's any time between when I see her about to slip and when I catch her, I don't notice.

It's like, suddenly, I'm just *there*. And her body feels so delicate in my arms. If I hold her any harder, she might shatter. But I can't let go yet. *I can't.*

All this rushes through my mind in the second it takes for me to crash backward into the snow and for the girl to crash with me.

...

(What just happened?)

...

I got her.

That's what happened.

She didn't fall.

*I got her in time.*

And now, she's on top of me.

I can feel her breath on my lips.

Her weight on my body.

Her hands on my chest.

And I ...

I ...

"I found you." The words slip softly out of my mouth in a single breath, but what it really sounds like I'm saying is, *I've got you.*

She's so close, I can't even see her face—I'm practically whispering into her ear, my arms still holding her.

(Wow.)

I release her all at once. *"Hah."*

The first sound I make as my brain catches up to my body is a quiet laugh.

"Hah ha ha—" *This is insane.* "Hahahahaha—" *This luck of mine.* "HHaHaHaHaHHHaHaHaH!"

In *Tokyo Ghoul*, Ken Kaneki once said if his life was a story, it would most certainly be a tragedy. I've always been inclined to agree concerning my own life. But sometimes, I think it's all a joke. (Is there anything more tragic than a comedy that forces laughter out of you when all you want to do is cry?)

This girl ...

This girl was missing all day, which means she had *all day* to do this. And yet she waited until right now? What are the goddamn chances?

*Oh,* but I guess you're right—they're 100%, aren't they?

My neck arches back, hysterics attacking me all the while. *How utterly comical!* I must truly be God's least favorite child, for he has never once wanted me to be happy in life and yet he really, *really* does not want me to come back to him.

Another few seconds go by before my laughter slowly dies to an on-and-off trickle. The Thornswood girl is silent, and still on top of me. Distantly, I'm aware I need to get my act together, but all thoughts melt from my head as a hand touches my cheek.

My body stills.

Then, of its own accord, my head lifts to look her in the eyes. They're so ... large. So bright. I wonder if my eyes are as wide as hers look to mine. *But no, I don't think that's possible.* She's sitting back now and peering deep inside me with those eyes, hand still on my cheek, an expression of utter astonishment twisting her features.

It's like she doesn't believe I'm real.

*She's so close.*

Though it's hard to tell in this lighting, it looks as if there's some coloration on the left side of her face. A bruise forming? I can't really think enough to make sense of—

That's when the overwhelming presence from this morning hits me for the second time in my life.

We're … **being watched.**

There's no doubt. Someone, some*thing*, is here with us.

It's malevolently vindictive again, whatever it is, but my focus is still mostly on the girl in front of me. The one who continues to stare at me. It's hard to say for exactly how long; in this moment I feel aware of everything and nothing. My body no longer exists except for the exact part of my face her fingers hold, I can see the individual flakes of snow falling around me, and I can hear what I believe to be the beating of her heart but not that of my own.

The instant her hand falls away, the presence of evil dissolves as if it were never there.

Briar Thornwood's look of disbelief also dissolves, leaving behind what looks like an expression of annoyance.

That's right. She was up here for the same reason I am, which means I've spoiled her plans the same way she has mine. That slip just now may have been accidental, but there wouldn't have been anything accidental about it if I'd shown up even a few minutes later.

I know it.

*She really would have jumped.*

And that means …

I get to my feet first and offer her a hand. She looks at it for a moment too long before taking it, allowing me to pull her up beside me. Taking in her appearance, I notice she's still in her uniform and has no jacket on—interesting attire considering she wasn't in school today. Looks like I will be walking back to the dorms improperly clothed for a second time. (I'll just count my good luck that she happens to be wearing shoes.)

I don't ask for permission as I place my coat around her shoulders and my hat on her head. Half expecting her to push me away, I'm relieved to only have to deal with a disgruntled look of surprise. Her slim form is swallowed by the coat she now wears like a cloak, and while the hat isn't ridiculous looking like it was on Marina, it's clear it was not made for her small face.

"I found you," I say once more, my voice low and deep, covering for the hoarseness from the laughter. "Now, let's go back."

She doesn't nod or say anything in return, but the full, undivided attention she stares at me with lets me know she's listening. And when I descend from the bridge, I can hear the distinct sound of her footsteps following me just a few paces behind.

...

(Fuck.)

What have I gotten myself into?

And what am I supposed to do now? What's the right way to deal with something like this? What even *is* this?

There's been no acknowledgement from her of the fact that she almost just *died*, but it doesn't feel like something I should bring up. Definitely not right now—maybe not ever.

*Briar Thornswood, what do I do with you?*

I glance over my shoulder to see her eyes suddenly trained at the ground, expression displeased but otherwise unreadable. Whatever openness I'd seen in her just moments ago is now hidden. Is she ... genuinely upset? Sulking? Disappointed? What? What is it?

I slow my pace to force her to walk by my side.

Then, I ask, "Did I hurt you when I caught you?"

There. That should be a safe question. It doesn't imply anything but still addresses what happened.

"I had to grab you pretty roughly. I'm sorry about that."

"No," she answers quickly, just above a whisper, "you didn't hurt me." But her quiet voice somehow reaches me with ease; this is the first time in a long time that I've heard it, and the very first time it's ever been directed at me. It's a soft voice, but far from weak—in fact, I'd say there's an edge to it.

"That's a relief."

"....."

"You live in the East Dorms as well, correct?" I ask this next question out of politeness. Truth is, I've seen her exit the East Dorms on several occasions and I also know she has no friends to speak of, crossing the possibility of visiting someone else there off the list.

"Yes," she answers.

"Right. We're almost back, then."

"How will we get in?"

Oh? She's actually asking me something? It's a fair question considering the strict curfew rules, but ... it's also not something she needs to concern herself with. "Just leave it to me."

Along the way, I pick up a sizable rock and place it in my pocket. I'll only need one more. She doesn't ask me anything this time, though whether that's because she's figured out what I'm doing or because she just doesn't want to bother, I'm not sure.

The rest of the walk is quiet, with me stopping only once more to pick up a second rock. I don't feel the need to talk again until we reach the dorm building.

"Thornswood, come here," I say, walking around toward the back of the building rather than up to the front.

I don't need to see her face to know that she's making one, but she does what I ask, anyway.

Directing her to the large, stone statue of a lion, I press lightly on her back until she bends down behind it. This is as close as I can get her to the back doors without her being obviously visible. "Wait here until you get the opening. Then move as quickly as you can to catch one of the doors before it closes. I'll follow close behind you, so hold it for me."

With this, I walk over to the right side of the building and take out one of the rocks, aiming for the large tree branch hanging over the right-side roof. Then I throw it.

Since it's been snowing so heavily the past several hours, the sound of the snow falling onto the roof is just as loud as I expected it would be.

I wait a few seconds behind a tree several paces away from the one I just threw at for [Security Guard Who Was Likely Reading Dirty Magazines And Is Understandably Upset For Being Interrupted] to come rushing outside.

He's even more fired up than I expected him to be, shouting heated curses into the night as he run-hobbles in the direction of a noise he won't be able to locate.

(Just one more.)

I don't have a direct line of fire from my current position, so I aim the second rock to ricochet off the trunk of a tree further up and hit the roof again.

"What now, you spoiled, godforsaken sons-a-bitches?!" the guard yells, taking off toward it the same time I take off for the back doors. "You think this is funny? Well, you won't be laughing when I find you, you little devils!"

The Thornswood girl followed my instructions and is inside holding one of the doors for me. I slip in behind her and we both head for the stairs.

As I pass by the security desk, however, I discreetly pocket a small plastic card that I believe could be useful in the future.

"That was … an interesting plan," she whispers to me as we make it to the stairwell.

I shrug and open the door for her. "It was a pretty simple one, actually."

If we had used our IDs to tap in and unlock the doors, it would immediately show up on our records as breaking curfew, sending a notification to the president. If we'd knocked to get in, feigning as though we forgot our IDs, the security guard would have to let us in and would likely report us to the president regardless. Either that or go straight to administration about it. The best solution was one that worked around both those options. This happened to be what I thought of in the moment.

I'm just glad the tree hanging over the first-floor awning on the security desk side was as I remembered it in my head. (Then there's the fact that if I were a regular student, my plan wouldn't have just been simple, it would have been downright stupid with no guarantee that my aim or the force of my throw would be true.)

"Simple, you say, and yet somehow it worked."

"I said I would get us inside, so I did."

"What would you have done if I didn't catch the door?"

"I'm sure we'd work out some other way." I'd probably have kicked them in. After all, they still have yet to put up the dorm security cameras they've been mentioning for the past *two years*. Or I'd have climbed back up the side of the building so that I could open the doors from the inside. So many options.

"Right … well, you're certain he didn't see you?"

I give her a look and she huffs, wordlessly taking off my hat and coat and shoving them into my chest before turning and walking through the door.

She's acting tough and unbothered right now, but I can see the slight tremor in her body. She's probably still cold. (Or maybe a near-death experience is having more of an effect on her than she's letting on.)

Once safely on the second floor, we use the internal connecting staircases to get to the third floor (her floor). I then walk her directly up to her room, ensuring she gets inside.

"You'll be ok now," I say quietly, trying not to disturb the room's other occupants. "I'll let you get some rest."

"Wait, I—" the girl starts as she whips around, staring at me again with a look similar to the one she gave me on the bridge. "I-I …"

"Yes?"

A thousand unspoken questions and emotions flick through her expression. But all of them remain unspoken as she lowers her eyes and turns her head to the side, shutting me out.

"Thornswood, whatever it is, you can tell me."

A small shake of her head. "It's nothing … Zero."

She says my name so gently, so carefully—making it sound almost intimate. (Or am I just making a bigger deal out of this because I rarely hear my name coming from the lips of another student?)

I take a step back from the doorway to get a better look at her.

She still refuses to make eye contact again, her bottom lip trembling ever-so-slightly in a way that she seems to be working hard to prevent the rest of her body from following suit.

"You should take a warm bath before getting into bed," I advise. "You were out in the cold for too long, and your muscles need to relax."

No response.

Hm …

There's always the possible concern that she might try to sneak out again to finish what she started, but I find that to be a very low possibility. It'll be difficult to make it out a second time without waking her roommates, she's likely exhausted, and the security guard is going to be in an extra vigilant mood. I think it's safe to call it here for tonight.

For good measure, I add as I leave, "I'll see you tomorrow, Thornswood. Sleep well."

She says nothing, as I expect her to.

What I don't expect is how the minute I hear the door to her room close, I feel dizzy to the point that I might fall over. Whatever strength I'd been holding onto in order to get us back safely has been completely used up.

"You've got to be kidding me," I slur, leaning into the wall to get myself to the stairs.

It takes far longer descending one level than it should, but I make it to my floor and into my suite. Now, believe it or not, the hard part begins. Because how the hell am I going to do this?

*Do what?* you're probably wondering.

But I bet a part of you has already figured it out.

I could tell myself that I don't know Briar Thornswood's true feelings, that I don't know she wants to *die.* Maybe there's even some truth to that. Maybe she just wanted some fresh air and a quiet place to—ugh. No, even thinking it feels stupid.

I *know* that look I saw in her eyes. I know because it might as well have been a mirror reflecting my own.

So how … how could I see a girl with that expression and be allowed to go off and end it all for myself?

There's no way.

Because now, no matter how I look at it, I am officially responsible for a life other than my own. Again.

That is until … I can figure out a way to resolve this problem—**the problem of Briar Thornswood**—therefore taking responsibility off of myself. That's the only option ahead of me.

But that's fine, right? It can't be as complicated as I'm making it out to be. She's just one girl. Just one problem.

I fall onto my bed, heavy eyelids flickering closed.

If I figure out this one thing, I'll finally, really be done.

*And what about that voice you heard? You don't think that's important? Not something worth your time, Zero?*

That's right. The voice I heard—does it … belong to that vision? The stranger kneeling over me? Was it really just a hallucination? Or is it connected to the presence I felt watching us?

No.

That's not what matters right now. What matters—the only thing that matters—is solving what's before me. She's my one obstacle to overcome.

Briar Thornswood.

The girl standing atop the bridge at midnight.

Heaviness leaches from my eyelids to the muscles of my limbs, weighing me down to the bed.

Now, to brainstorm some … brainstorm … some ideas …

The last image I see before falling unconscious is a pair of large golden-brown eyes.

I come-to early in the morning and quickly get ready for the day.

Surely the increasingly weird and vivid visions of yesterday can be blamed on my disgustingly extreme sleep deprivation, but, thanks to my first time sleeping through the night in months (possibly all year), crippling fatigue and spontaneous hallucinations aren't something I'll have to worry about anymore. It almost makes me believe the good rest I've just had was worth the struggle leading up to it.

(It's like finally being able to think straight.)

However, despite what my past-self said last night, I currently have *three* objectives to take care of: the most important, of course, remains finding a solution to helping Briar Thornswood—my depressed classmate with a wholly ridiculous name.

Next in line of importance and first in line regarding urgency is getting back the note I wrote to Ms. Kurima before she finds it. Not the end of the world if she does, but sure to be a hassle I'd rather not deal with.

And lastly, I need to get back my book bag from the chemistry room (assuming it's still there). I could always get another bag— they're more expensive than one would guess but that's no issue for me—however, now that I am going to be sticking around a while longer, I realize there's something inside it that would be best if not discovered.

This "something" is my detailings of the game I occasionally play when feeling exceptionally bored in which I score at the precise class placement or percentile of my choosing.

At times, I'd aim for the exact score needed to tip the class average in a particular direction, and other times I'd choose to go from the first slot in the class down to the second, third, fourth, and fifth before reversing in the same fashion over a certain period of tests, etc. The boldest I ever got with this game was in my freshman year at my first high school when I continued to score exactly 65% on all of my tests (the score directly above failing) until the teacher of the class asked if I was making fun of her.

Really, it depended on my mood.

And while it's not something I've played in a while, I'm sure that excuse wouldn't matter in the slightest if another person at this academy were to find out about it.

There's no time to waste in getting to work on these objectives so, after a quick shower, I head out the door. Classes start at eight-thirty a.m. and it's barely past seven a.m., but that's the only way to—

I stop and look down at the two items at my feet directly outside my room.

It's my book bag. And my note to Ms. Kurima.

Both are sitting in front of me as if they'd nicely delivered themselves to my doorstep upon hearing that I was going to search for them. Placed atop them is a second note; one I didn't write. I pick all three items up and bring them inside my room, looking over the mystery note as I do so. It reads in a red-penned, aggressive cursive, **Be Careful Where You Leave Your Things!**

Well, isn't that pleasant?

"You missed my boots," I say to no one, thinking of the pair I'd left in the nurse's office. If they were going to creepily return all my misplaced things, they could have at least been thorough.

I check the back of the note, discovering nothing. Just the one message, then.

It's not handwriting I recognize, but it's also obvious that whoever it was has purposefully disguised their real handwriting. That alone tells me they're likely someone I have regular contact with in a setting where I'd have seen their handwriting. Since I'm not in any clubs, that would mean one of my five classes (not including free period).

I suppose the fact that the note I placed under Ms. Kurima's flowers is here means that they're likely in my English class. But then there's the matter of my book bag which I most definitely left in chemistry. Cross-examining the students I share those two courses with should give me a very narrow pool of suspects. But would they really be so obvious?

I stare at the note for another five seconds and proceed to toss it onto my bed and walk out the door. I'll deal with whatever the hell this is later. There's something I've got to do now.

My original plan was to break into the school early to retrieve both the missing items that have now been so conveniently returned to me. But the other half of my plan—the half that concerns my first objective—still requires that I go in early.

As I carry out this part of my mission, let's review all the information I have on Briar Thornswood to prepare for the next step: getting close to her and becoming someone she trusts to help her as efficiently and effectively as possible.

If I were to make her a profile using this information, it would look something like this:

Briar Rose Thornswood

- Year/age: Junior, 17
- Physical appearance: waist-length brown hair, fair skin, very large golden-brown eyes, relatively small mouth—when I put it like this, I feel as if I'm describing a manga character ... I'll stop here
- Height/Weight: 5'5, 110 lbs. (approximation)
- Personality characteristics: A/B-average student—impressive for the difficulty level of this school, quiet/introverted, can be cold when approached, used to be in a fairly popular friend group freshman year but a falling out happened before the summer, used to be asked out regularly until all the boys gave up on the endeavor, doesn't seem to get along well with girls either, relatively untrusting, no clear interests—need a lot more info here
- Student Ranking: fairly high?
- Clubs: none
- Friends: none
- Conclusion: my profile is pathetically lacking

It's possible that an upfront approach to getting closer to her could work. But it's risky, especially considering how displeased she appeared with me last night, so I'll settle for the approach I'm taking now.

I make my way around to the back of the main building and find the steel, moss-covered entranceway I discovered when walking around the grounds in the middle of the night my sophomore year. It's somewhat of a "secret passage," and while I've never had cause to use it before, my research of old Kane Academy floor plans shows that it's an out-of-use entrance for cleaning staff leading directly to a first-floor closet.

A quick glance over my surroundings assures me I'm alone, so I lift my leg and kick with all my force.

I'm hit with a slight surprise when the door immediately flies off its hinges—I knew I'd be able to kick it in, but I didn't expect it to give so easily. My strength is undoubtedly back to 100%. If only I'd been in this condition yesterday, getting Marina out of the river would have been like lifting a flower from a pond. (It's true I could have tried using the card I picked up from the security desk last night to get in just now, but I'd rather save it for an emergency in case I'm wrong about the longevity of its usefulness.)

Once inside the building, I head to the art classroom and sit down behind the computer at the desk up front. It's easy enough to figure out Mrs. Michaels' login info given her obsession with her dog and that popular *Fantasy Five* series. Knowing both letters and numbers are required in a Kane Academy password, a combination of the dog's name and the birthday of the character for which he's named does the trick.

I pull up the document I'm looking for: the partner assignments for this semester's final. I change Briar Thornswood's partner to be myself and, to avoid the modification being traced back to me, proceed to change two other pairs as well just on the off-chance Mrs. Michaels notices the list has been tampered with. That would ruin everything, but I'll worry about crossing that bridge should it come to that.

If this works out the way I believe it will, I'll have successfully made an opening to come into regular close contact with the Thornswood girl. It'll give me an "in" with her as well as time to figure out a permanent solution that doesn't require me being around anymore.

Hearing this, you might be tempted to point out the matter of my curse with the question "But, Zero, won't closer contact with you mean closer contact with near-constant danger?" And I'd have to tell you that you have a good point there. But it is also true that if I am closely watching her at all times, I should be able to prevent anything from happening to her before it happens. And she can't ever be safe if she kills herself, so … the added risk is worth it.

There's still roughly an hour until classes begin, so I carefully head down to the first floor to wait out the clock in the backroom of the faculty lounge—a space I have access to thanks to a certain someone. On my way, I pause briefly in front of the display boards for student rankings.

"Hmm."

I take note of something **interesting** and continue on, quietly ducking in through the back entrance to the lounge.

"Is this going to affect my plans, or can I ignore it for now?" I wonder to myself, facing the ceiling as I lie on a long, well-cushioned couch. I'd prefer if someone else took care of it altogether, but it would be foolish to bet on a losing horse … Well, if the situation really starts to look dire, I'll act.

Later on in statistics, I see Briar Thornswood for the first time since the disaster of last night (really, I've been on a roll, haven't I?). We make eye contact but she hastily looks away while I continue to watch her. During the break between statistics and art, she almost looks like she'll come up to me but the ever-persistent Myles Adrian beats her to it.

"Hey, man! How's it going? I didn't see you at lunch yesterday. What have you been up to?"

"Well, I did tell you I wasn't going to eat with you." It seems I should have let him slip on that pen when I had the chance.

"I guess you'll just have to eat with me today, then. I already let my friends know ahead of time, so there won't be any issues."

"That's not how this works."

Myles grins, tilting his head to the side. "Actually, there's something I wanted to ask you about."

I continue packing up my things, uttering a flat, "That so?"

"Yeah. I … I want to ask for your help with something."

"Not interested." I already have someone who needs my help, there's no way I'm adding another. If I do too many "nice" things, I might start to mistake myself for a good person.

"I don't mean to—"

"Yo, Myles! Come on, dude, we're gonna be laaaaateee!" [Impatient Friend Who Is Strangely Worried About Tardiness] shouts from across the room. "What's taking you?!"

"Just a second, Logan! Hot damn, give a guy a minute. Anyway, what I—"

"You should go ahead with your friend. Like I said, I'm not interested. There's no point in making him wait."

Myles laughs a bit but he sounds unsure. "Right, well, you see … this thing I need help with, it's sort of something only you can do."

This catches my attention. "Oh?"

"Yep, so if you could meet me for lunch today, that would be great. If not, I'll just find you later on. Is there another time that works for you?"

Being considerate of my schedule? He must be serious—there's something he needs that only I can help him with. But what the hell could that be? He could ask anyone at this academy to do anything and they'd do it with a smile on their face, yet he wants *me*?

"I'll get back to you sometime tonight. But don't bother looking for me at lunch; I'll be busy."

"Busy? Oh, sure. No worries, I just want to make sure—"

"Mylllleeessss!" [Friend Who Is Surprisingly Still Waiting Around] wails from the doorway.

"Calming breaths, my guy—I'll catch up with you! So, Zero—"

We both freeze at the same time, our eyes traveling to look down at the hand placed on my shoulder. Wait, is that …

Briar Thornswood steps up beside me, her hold on my shoulder remaining.

"Oh, hey, Briar. What's up? Did you need something?" Even Myles, who has no issue talking with anyone in any of our classes, can't hide the fact that he's been caught off guard.

"Yes," she says, her posture perfectly straight. "Zero and I are going to be late to our next class. I think it would be best if we got going now. Umm …" She looks to me as if to get confirmation, but I'm too focused on the fact that this girl is touching me. (Is that a burn mark on her thumb? And what's that powder around her fingernails?)

"Right, of course!" Myles says, stepping back. "Well, I don't want to keep you guys."

Thornswood's grip on me tightens in a squeeze, whether to send a message to me or because she's nervous, I'm not sure, but it successfully wakes me up.

"She's right. Our teacher expressed that it's an especially important day since she'll be going over partners for our final exams."

"Ah, yeah, I see. Then good luck. It's pretty early for talk of finals though, isn't it? Guess some teachers are just like that."

I nod, done feigning interest in this conversation, and begin walking to the door, Thornswood following closely.

"Hey, wait!" Myles yells after us. "I know you never check your chatroom, so you'll have to give me your number! Otherwise, there's no way you'd be able to contact me, right, Zero?" *Every Kane Academy student has the KA Chatroom (KChat) installed on their phones, a function that allows them to contact any other student as long as they know their name.

So much for hoping he hadn't realized.


Once in the hallway, I turn to the girl at my side. "So, what was that all about?"

Her golden eyes gleam with confusion but, astonishingly, no fear is visible. "You wanted to get out of that situation, right? I mean, you didn't want to do whatever it is that guy was trying to get you to do."

Perceptive. Though she says "that guy" as if she doesn't know who Myles is. I believe he and his friends were good acquaintances with the group Thornswood used to hang out with. Besides, *everyone* knows who Myles is. He's just that type of guy.

"That may be true, but that doesn't explain why you stepped in." I'm not usually one to push this sort of thing, but, well, curiosity is getting the better of me.

"Do I need more of a reason than that?"

"Mmh, no, I guess not."

It's a strange shift in character from last night any way you slice it, so no explanation would likely be satisfactory. I decide to drop it.

When we get to art class, I don't plan on asking her to sit next to me, since my plan should take care of that on its own, but she follows me to my table all the same. With careful movements, she takes a seat while also taking several, what I can assume are meant to be unnoticeable, glances at me. She then proceeds to adjust herself in her chair an unnatural number of times, a pained, barely audible sigh passing between her lips before she settles back into a waiting silence.

"....."

"What is it, Thornswood?"

She startles at the sound of my voice, taking a second to answer. "… I'd prefer if you didn't call me that."

"What should I call you instead?"

"My name—Briar."

Her first name? It seems … too familiar. But I can't deny her request.

"All right. Now, tell me, Briar, what are you thinking about? It seems something's on your mind."

Though definitely not a smile, her lips no longer look to be pressed in the tense line they had been.

"I don't mean to be taking up your time," she begins, "there's just something I wanted to say to you after last night …"

It's like her cheeks grow warmer the longer I look at her, but it's natural to look at someone when they're talking to you, right? Maybe my eyes make her uncomfortable. I look away just in case.

"What is it?"

"It's just—I-I wanted to say thank you."

I can't help it. I look back at her.

"For saving my life," she continues, "and making sure we both got back inside. Thank you."

She's thanking me for *that*?! But wasn't she upset about it?

"I didn't say anything in the moment, but I should have. I was just … I don't know—in shock, I guess. But that's no excuse. You *saved* me, Zero, and I should have acknowledged that."

I don't know if she's just being polite, or if a part of her is actually grateful to have had someone step in and stop what she'd been about to do, but she *sounds* sincere.

"It's nothing. I'm just glad I was informed of your absence, otherwise, I might not have known to go looking for you." I hadn't planned on addressing my reasons for being there last night, but this gave me the perfect opening. It'll raise other questions for her, but any hunches that I might have also been on that bridge to kill myself should be erased.

"Look for me? You were looking for me?"

"Yes. Don't you remember what I first said to you?" *I found you.* (Thank god I'd had the sense to say something I could use later on.)

"Right ... But who asked you to do that?"

"A boy I ran into when walking back to the dorms. He seemed distressed and I heard him muttering something about how you'd been missing all day. I figured I might know a place or two you could have gone, so I went off after finishing up my homework just in case they hadn't found you yet. Guess it paid off. I assume you got stuck out there once the snow started to come down harder. I can understand not wanting to go back in that alone." There, she's been given an out, as well. Unless she *wants* me prying into her true reasons, she shouldn't push back.

"But who was the boy you overheard?"

Huh? She really cares about this, doesn't she? I quickly wrack my brain for the names and faces of the group she used to hang out with, choosing the most appropriate option. "I'm not sure, exactly. I think he was one of those guys you used to hang out with a while back." She flinches, but I continue. "He has curly hair, darker skin—I'm sorry, but that's about all I can remember."

"I see."

She's obviously distressed over this. If I'm truly going to help her, I'll need to get to the bottom of this important part of her past. Aside from the fact that things seemed to take a steep slide downhill after the summer of freshman year, I really don't know much about the subject.

I wonder if she'll question the boy I pointed out to her or not. My guess would be "not," but even if she does, and he inevitably acts like he has no idea what she's talking about, given the bad terms they all seem to be on it's believable that he'd be unwilling to admit the truth to her. At least, that's how it would seem to Thorn—to Briar.

Class starts and Mrs. Michaels reveals the pairings for the final just as she said she would. When it's announced that Briar and I will be working together, my new partner looks surprised but not as surprised as I might have expected.

"It seems we're not destined to part ways just yet, huh?" I say, calling out the weirdness of the situation.

"I—yeah. It's definitely an unexpected coincidence."

(That's one way of putting it.) "I'm not sure if you already had ideas for the project, but if you don't mind, I think I have something that could work."

"Please, go ahead, Zero. Anything you'd like is fine with me—I honestly have no opinions on it."

"I was thinking it would be interesting to go a more untraditional route, creating something bigger than just a painting and more abstract than, say, a film or a performance sketch. Specifically, what if we created a club for our project?" (A crucial step in my plan.)

"A club?"

"I get that it's a bit of a strange choice, but I think it has potential. Mrs. Michaels enjoys out-of-the-box thinking and if need be we can spin it in a way to say that 'the people in the club themselves are the art,' or something artistic," (and pretentious), "like that. The other option would be to have the club produce a product before the end of the semester to showcase."

"I see ... We could even connect the club to the Talent Festival—it'll be going on at the same time as final exams and would be an opportunity to show off whatever we'd been doing all semester."

I raise a brow. She appears to already be on board with the idea. The light in her eyes even tells me she's at least a little excited by it.

"Yes, that's a wonderful idea, Briar."

At that moment, a boy walking by our table to get back to his partner stumbles over his feet and starts to fall.

With scissors in his hand.

Right over Briar's head.

This is sooner than I'd anticipated, but I've been ready all the same. My hand bolts up and grabs the boy by the wrist, stopping the deadly arc the sharp stainless steel had been making straight for the space between Briar's neck and shoulder.

Then the idiot drops the scissors in shock and I'm forced to use even quicker reflexes to release his wrist and catch them instantaneously.

"Uh ..." Briar looks up to where my hand still grips the scissors.

"Ah ... thanks, man," [Uncoordinated Scissor-Boy] says, swallowing hard. "Umm, I don't really need those, honestly. I'll just leave them to you. I—uh—yeah—sorry." His apology is hard to make out as he's already halfway across the classroom by the time he finishes it.

I lay the scissors on my side of the table with a roll of my eyes.

"Amazing."

I blink and look to Briar who is staring at me openly.

"Not really. His face gave away the fact that he was going to drop them ahead of time. I just acted accordingly."

"Still, your reaction time ... That was impressive."

Being openly praised hits me as something even stranger than being thanked.

"I'm glad you didn't get hurt," I cover. "Now, about the club …"

I continue bringing up several possible ideas about what kind of club we could create throughout the rest of the period, incorporating the ideas Briar occasionally contributes. If she really is into this idea of creating a club together, then my plan will be much easier to pull off than I ever could have hoped.

While we go our separate ways for third period, I suggest at the end of art class that we regroup during lunch. A series of conflicting, but readable, emotions flicker in Briar's eyes. Surprise, hopefulness, doubt, and worry, respectively.

"Are you sure? I mean, it's not necessary."

"I wouldn't have suggested it if I wasn't sure."

"It's just—well—" Her eyes travel quickly across the room, settling on the front left corner for half a second before returning to me. "Never mind. My next class is a free period so we can just meet outside the library if that works for you."

I nod in affirmation.

"Ok. I'll see you at lunch, Zero."

She leaves the room in a hurry as I shake off the jolt I get whenever someone says my name in regular conversation. Then I look to where her eyes had briefly landed. A boy with fair blond hair stands there, staring out the door Briar just exited. I recognize him as the leader of the friend group she'd been a part of.

Getting the feeling he's about to pivot his attention, I glance away. Sure enough, a second later, I feel his eyes on me.

Interesting.

I meet Briar outside of the library just as planned. Despite this being her idea, she does a double take when she sees me waiting for her.

"Y-You're here."

"I said I would be."

I continue to get double takes all the way down the hall toward the main cafeteria as people's jaws fall open at the sight of me walking with another student (a girl, no less).

If Briar is bothered, she doesn't show it. I wonder if she gets similar treatment herself and suddenly find myself wishing I'd paid closer attention to her before all of this. Due to personal matters extending beyond my time at this academy, I've always paid at least some attention to her, but I guess that wasn't enough …

"So, did you have a productive free period?" We share four out of our six classes, meaning I only need to learn what her fourth class is to have an idea of her full schedule.

"Productive?" she repeats. "Yeah, I guess it was, in a way."

She doesn't give any more explanation, and I have nothing else to say, so I allow us to continue walking in silence. I predicted doing so would be unbearably awkward and make me wish to dive out the nearest window, but it's surprisingly comfortable. Thank god. Still, I can't help the bubbling curiosity growing inside me. This girl is one big mystery to me. There's a lot I don't know, and while I can usually get a good read on a person from simply observing them in conversation, with Briar, I'm only able to pick up bits and pieces before being led to more questions.

"Briar."

She turns her head, looking up at me.

"I wanted to ask you this earlier, but—"

And God once again proves to me that I am his least favorite. No sooner have I begun to ask my question than I witness another incident about to unfold. Like the scissors, preventing it is mostly a matter of reflexes.

A guy and girl are talking, with the guy's open locker directly behind his head. Coming up on them is a rowdy group of sport boys who are roughhousing each other as they make their way down the hall. [Rambunctious Boy Number 3] gets shoved a bit too hard by one of his buddies and slams directly into the open locker door which swings toward [Oblivious Locker Boy]. Though I have to be slightly quicker than with the scissors, I manage to catch the locker door in the last millisecond before it can slam into the back of the boy's skull. (Jesus. I almost didn't make it this time.)

I make eye contact with [Rambunctious Boy Number 3] who is too stunned even to stutter out an apology. "If you're going to act like a child, might I suggest dropping out of high school and enrolling in the nearest elementary school? Perhaps that environment would better suit your needs." He nods stiffly and I continue past him. "*Dumbass.*"

"How was that even possible?" I hear Briar mutter, presumably to herself.

Many people have caught onto the fact that strange things happen around me, but I should take into account the different effects it will have on someone who is around me for an extended period.

Unsure how to deal with it right now, I deflect. "What do you like to eat?"

"Oh, uh, it depends on the day."

"Then tell me what you'd like to eat today, specifically."

"Mmm," her face twists like she's thinking hard, "I don't know …
But I guess I usually like the pizza stand best, if I had to pick."

"Great. Same here. Lunch is on me."

"No, you really don't have to do that, Zero!"

She grabs onto my arm as if to stop me and I almost laugh at
her concern.

If she thinks buying her a school lunch is going to put me out in
any way … "Trust me, it's not a problem."

"Still, I have the credits to cover my portion and I'd prefer if you
didn't go out of your way—"

"I want to, so please, let me."

This quiets her and she gently lets go of my arm, seeming to have
only just realized she'd been holding onto it. (I again take note of the
small burn on her thumb.)

As we approach the doors to the cafeteria, a particular student
exits. The blond boy from art class who'd been staring at Briar.

I can sense the exact moment she spots him, her entire body
becoming stiffer in response.

This time, I get a better look at the boy's face and see something I
hadn't been able to from the angle I'd been at in class. There's a dark
bruise forming on the left side of his face, starting at his temple. I tend
to be able to tell how someone has gotten an injury, but this one gives
me difficulty—I can't place it as being from any kind of attack I've
experienced or witnessed. A fight? An accident? It could be either.

Just as she's noticed him, he's clearly noticed us. And the closer he
gets, the colder his gaze becomes. Something about those plain, dull
eyes gets on my nerves, so I step slightly in front of Briar as we walk,
discreetly looking down at her as I do so with the intent of analyzing.

I hadn't thought much of it before, but the dark circles under her eyes stick out to me.

With her focus subconsciously directed at me now, it seems she no longer takes notice of [Blond Boy] when he walks by us. I think I have an idea for what I'll need to do regarding him and his connection to Briar, but that's an issue for another time.

For now, I will simply focus on having my first-ever lunch with another student.

The minute we enter through the cafeteria doors, I am hit, not for the first time, by just how disgustingly extravagant this academy is.

The space is cavernous, containing an absurd number of options, from a coffee shop section with its own seating to a bakery, an Italian deli, a sushi bar, and a number of other specialized stations. (I suppose with what tuition costs, it would be unacceptable if it *didn't* go all out like this.)

I tell Briar to pick out a spot for us to sit as I go straight to the pizza counter to order. All but three students end up leaving the minute I join the line, making for one of my quickest experiences yet. Generally I just skip lunch entirely since I find ordering to be a hassle, but my stomach growls at the sight of my pizza slice, reminding me that I haven't eaten anything in two days. That's pushing it, even for me.

I start taking bites before making it back to Briar, unable to help myself. We didn't specify an exact area, but I spot her quickly, sitting in the most deserted corner.

It looks like she's searching around the cafeteria for something—or *someone*—as I approach her. Since she knew exactly where I was going, it can't be me she's trying to find …

"You're really hungry," she observes as I hand her the plate with a side of fruit and the other pizza slice, my own already being mostly devoured.

"It *is* lunchtime." I really should have gotten myself two. No, probably three or four.

Briar's hand twitches toward her bag for a second before she changes her mind and shakes her head. "I-I guess we should talk about our project," she says, switching the subject.

"Sure." (What was that about?)

"Just ... give me one moment." She stands without waiting for my reply and walks away. (Perhaps she needs to use the restroom?)

I start drawing idly in my notebook as I wait.

Hey, since we're both here with nothing to do, humor me with a little game. Can you do that?

Come on, it's not like you have anything to lose. I can't jump out of the page to punish you if you don't win ... right?

Right. It works like this: I'll give you a string of numbers and you figure out the pattern to say which comes next in the sequence. (I'm bored so, really, you have no say in the matter. But I promise I'll go easy on you.)

Give me just a second to think—

Ok, here it is: 3, 12, 6, 24, 12, 48,

What comes next? _____

Yeah, I think that was *too* easy.

How about: 5712, 4610, 358, 246, _____

(Technically there are two forms of logic that you can use to solve this second one, did you figure them both out?)

I'll continue drawing while you think about it.

I've nearly finished a sketch of the main character from Ms.

Kurima's horror manga by the time Briar returns with … another slice of pizza.

She places it down in front of me from behind, peering over my shoulder at my drawing.

"You didn't have to do that," I say. I guess I wasn't masking my hunger as well as I'd thought. But this gesture is still such an unexpected one.

"S-sorry, did I overstep?" she asks, sounding nervous. "I can take it b—"

"No—my apologies, that wasn't what I meant at all." I clear my throat, switching my tone to something gentler. "Thank you, Briar. This was very thoughtful of you."

She doesn't say anything, but I feel an unusual, pleased aura emanating from her. Then she leans forward a bit, once again focused on the drawing. "What style is that?"

"Hmm?" She's extremely close right now, what did she ask me?

"What style of art? I don't recognize it."

"Ah. I'm imitating the style of one of my favorite manga artists."

"Man-ga," she repeats, separating the word into two distinct syllables. I nod at her over my shoulder and she smiles a little, seeming proud of herself for getting the pronunciation. (Cute.) "Is that a character you created?"

"No, not at all. He's actually a character from a different manga than the one whose style I'm practicing in."

"Isn't that confusing?"

She's still directly behind me. "On the contrary, I think it makes the exercise more fun."

"You never show this talent in art class. If you did, you'd probably be the top student."

If I tell her I have no interest in how I fare in that class, it probably won't be very reassuring coming from the boy she's partnered with for her final. "Top student? With people like Alina Carter and Benjamin Hawkins in our class? Not likely." In truth, [Blond Boy] is relatively average in both his artistic and academic achievements—by academy standards, that is. Dropping his name alongside a genuinely talented student like Carter may have been a little too obvious, but I'm curious as to her reaction.

She says nothing for several moments before quietly murmuring, "Downplaying your abilities is a bad habit."

(What?) There was a time when such a statement would have made my blood run cold. (The precise opposite of my father's harshest sentiment.) Now, I'm not sure how to feel. If someone had said this to me yesterday, I couldn't have given less of a shit. But since I'll be staying around a bit longer, it's possible a disruption of my careful attempts to remain inconspicuous could prove problematic.

I have to laugh at myself, at least internally. Barely half a day into my new life of attempting to have a relationship with someone and I've already slipped up.

"I get the feeling there's a side to you that you don't want me to see yet. And that's ok. But you should know, you really don't have to pretend, Zero. Not with me."

These words are even more surprising than her last bombshell. There's no malice or threat behind them, no hint of ulterior motives. She's just ... being honest with me. But for her to have noticed any of this, she must have been watching me for some time. Either that, or she's incredibly, frighteningly, observant.

I wonder briefly if she remembers the day we first met. Then I quickly discard the notion. It really doesn't matter now.

Having said her piece, Briar straightens up and comes to sit in front of me as if she's ready to get back to work on our project. Actually, it looks like she's ready to get her instructions as she waits for me to take the lead.

Biding my time on the question I've been meaning to ask her, I acquiesce to her unspoken request and restart the discussion on potential project ideas while gratefully eating my new slice of pizza. She mostly listens to begin with, but I gradually coax some thoughts out of her, wanting to get a better glimpse into her way of thinking.

I am purposely being open to a myriad of proposals currently, but I'll eventually steer the conversation around to the one I have in mind. It was something I considered carefully on my walk here this morning. The question that brought me to it was a simple one: What is the greatest way to feel fulfilled? Well, it's to make others feel fulfilled. At least, so it seems to be for people who are, deep down, genuinely good at heart. And while I can't say I especially like or know Briar Thornswood on a personal level, I can still say that I believe she is a good person.

Probably.

Close enough, anyway.

And I'd already decided I needed to get her into a controlled environment where she'd be forced to meet as many people as possible, therefore giving her the best chances of making meaningful connections. With these two points in mind, some kind of club that involves helping others is ideal for getting her to a place of self-fulfillment.

Of course, then I ran into my second issue, which is that no such club currently exists.

Well, *technically*, there is a community service club. But that won't do at all. Most community service-type gigs would involve going into town and students aren't allowed off campus without express permission, making the whole thing a giant headache. And it would be unquestionably better to have a club connecting her to people directly from school, anyway.

This left me with two options.

1) Forgo a club of this type altogether while searching for the best alternative. Or:

2) Create my own.

It might be a pain, but I believe the latter is the only viable option since it will allow me to slowly fade away from the front lines into a purely executive position and, finally, out of the picture altogether.

"Zero?"

I snap to attention, focusing on Briar. "Yes?"

"You went quiet for a minute, like your head was ... somewhere else."

"I was just going over the qualifications of creating a new club," I reply, not missing a beat. Besides, this is an obstacle we need to face sooner rather than later.

"That's something I've been thinking about, too. If I remember correctly, you need to fulfill two requirements. The first is that you have at least three members, and the second is that you either have a faculty advisor or you get permission directly from the student council president himself."

So, someone really did do their homework during free period. "That's right. There is a faculty member I could ask," I gulp, thinking of what Ms. Kurima's reaction would be to me willingly coming to her for a favor, "but if I'm being honest, I'm not dead set on going that route." Not that dealing with the president sounds like any more fun.

"You'd rather go to the student council?"

I'd rather break a finger than do either, actually. "I'm not sure yet, but I can assure you that I'll have it sorted out by the end of the day."

She tilts her head to the side and I involuntarily notice the slender curve of her neck as well as the delicate black choker she's wearing. It's an unusual accessory among the academy girls. Where might she have picked that style up?

"Ok," she says, seeming to trust my word, "then we should talk about the other requirement. Do you have anyone in mind to be our third member?"

"Huh? Oh, yeah, I might have someone who could work. Do you?" It's a cruel question seeing as I already know the answer.

"No … Sorry, but I don't think I'll be much help when it comes to that kind of stuff … I don't like that I'm putting both requirements on you to solve, though." Her nose scrunches as she frowns, almost endearingly, and I get the sudden urge to relieve her anxieties.

"If you want, you can come with me to meet our possible third member."

She perks up instantly. "Really? I mean, uh, yes. Of course. Let's do that."

Ah. I already regret inviting her, getting the feeling that my target for a third member is probably less likely to agree with Briar beside me. What a short-sighted idiot I can be.

Briar crosses her arms atop the table and my eyes get drawn to her hands yet again. I glance over them, checking something I'd noticed when she'd touched my shoulder this morning. Though it's only a faint amount, the white powdery substance under and around her nails stands out to me against the black nail polish she's wearing.

First the burn on her left thumb, next the darkened circles under her eyes indicating staying up all night, and now this.

"Tell me, Briar, are you ever going to give me the treats you baked last night, or are they for someone else?"

Briar straightens in her seat. "What?"

"What?" I repeat back to her.

"Treats?"

"Oh, am I mistaken?"

"… No. It's just … y-you knew? This whole time? But I never said anything. How could you know?"

I shrug. "Just a hunch."

She continues to stare at me, waiting for a better explanation. This isn't something I've had to do in a while. Very well, I'll play along.

"The dark circles under your eyes are much worse than last night, pointing to the fact that something kept you up. Insomnia is a possibility—" oh, don't I know it, "—but then I took into account the burn on your left thumb, a common place to accidentally make contact with a hot pan when taking something out of the oven, and the flour residue under your nails. None of which was there before this morning."

"Is that all it took?"

"You also hesitantly reached toward your bag after confirming that I was feeling hungry earlier. That made me curious, so I started thinking about it more. Not to mention, if you had something to give me, it would explain why you looked like you wanted to come up to me after statistics."

"But I already told you why I came up to you then. It was because I could tell Myles was annoying you."

"That occurred after you'd already been looking at me. Unless you can see into the future, that explanation doesn't cut it."

"Oh ... I guess you're right. Zero, you're just—you're really good at figuring things out, aren't you?"

"What can I say, I'm a wealth of inductive knowledge."

I return my attention to my new slice of pizza, but the sensation of Briar's gaze burning into me makes it difficult to digest in peace.

"Go ahead and ask," I say.

"Mmh?"

"Whatever question you have right now, ask it. I can tell you've got one."

"Ok." This response surprises me. (All it takes for her to reveal what's on her mind is a prompting from me?) "Since you're good at figuring things out, then you must have already deduced what *kind* of baked goods I made you, yes?"

"So they actually are for me? Hm, well," I think of the most common sweets given as gifts and name one at random, "are they brownies?"

Briar shakes her head. "That's not really your guess, is it?"

"It's a perfectly reasonable guess. What are you smiling about?"

"If you'd *really* been paying attention, Zero, you wouldn't have guessed brownies."

"Oh?" I'm starting to enjoy this, if only a little. "Do explain."

"One of the clues you used to put this together was the flour around my nails, right? It's true that brownies require flour, too, but if I'm the type to get flour all over myself, wouldn't I have also gotten the cocoa powder all over myself when I mixed the two? That would make the leftover residue chocolate-colored, not white."

Ah ha! She actually figured that out? "Well, well, maybe I'm not as smart as I thought I was."

"I don't think that's a conclusion anyone could come to after speaking with you," she mumbles under her breath. And, for me to hear, "The correct answer is chocolate chip cookies."

"Is it now?"

"But don't worry," she smiles a little, "I'll let you have a chance to redeem yourself."

"I make no promises, but I'll give it my best shot."

She goes quiet for a second, thinking, her expression suddenly growing serious. Then— "Tell me the reason why I made them."

This I must say I actually *don't* have an answer to.

But I'm spared from coming up with one as Briar begins twisting a strand of her long hair, eyes avoiding mine as she bites down on her bottom lip in a way that looks painful.

"Briar, you're going to bite through your own lip. Stop it."

She listens immediately, and I'm left feeling skeptical about her easy obedience.

"I made them ..." she starts, finally looking back at me, "as an apology. For the way I acted last night." She *what?* "I wasn't sure what kind of sweets you like, so I just sort of made a bunch of different kinds, actually, which is why I was up all night. I only brought the cookies, but the cupcakes and peanut butter truffles are back in my room if you'd rather have those. If you don't want any of them, that's fine, too. It's really ok either way."

When I'd asked her if she was going to hand over what she made for me, I'd been half joking. No, more like 85% joking. To find out she made them with such a serious intent, I just—I can't understand where this change came from. It makes no sense.

"You did all that ... to apologize to me?"

She nods and the way her cheeks puff out slightly as the inner corners of her brows draw upward is almost too much to bear.

Before I can tell her that if anyone should be apologizing, it should be me for saving her in such a rough and clumsy manner, Briar keeps going. "Ok, um, I know I've just forced you to talk a lot over this lunch, but I'm hoping you can answer one more question for me, Zero. If you don't mind, that is."

I swallow, regaining composure. "You can make me talk as much as you want. Shoot."

"What were you going to ask me before you had to save that guy from getting smashed with the locker?"

I figured she'd ask about that at some point. But actually, regarding that question, I'm glad I was interrupted because I think it's better if I investigate its answer on my own.

I lean closer to Briar without responding, inspecting her face. Rather than jerk away, as most anyone else would have done, she goes completely still. I push my luck and reach out to grab her chin, tilting her face to show me her left side.

Her fair skin is practically pearl-smooth. Only the most indiscernible amount of red remains behind from what I saw last night. And even that is difficult to say for certain since her cheeks quickly gain color in a deepening flush the longer I hold her in place (a standard response to someone getting in your personal space like I just did).

Releasing her, I finally answer, "I wanted to know how you got that mark on your face last night."

Briar takes a deep breath, giving me a dark glare that elicits a small smirk from me in return; this is the first time today she's expressed annoyance toward me. "I don't have a mark on my face."

(Not anymore.) "Yes, my bad. I must have been mistaken." (At least, not one the normal human eye would pick up on.)

Indeed, I am starting to put together a bit more of the pieces that make up the puzzle of the girl sitting in front of me. Things seem too good, too easy, to be true right now. But with this new information, it's likely all of that is about to change. There's not much I can do until the other, albeit mysterious, shoe drops.

"And what about you?" she asks.

I tilt my head. "I'm not sure I take your meaning."

"You had a mark on your face—a lot of them, actually. And they're gone now."

Naturally, she took notice of that last night before my killer-tree-caused cuts finished healing. "Now I believe you must be the one who's mistaken." I point to my face. "I promise you, my skin is perfectly intact."

"I know; that's what's so strange about it."

Yeah, Briar's powers of observation may prove difficult to deal with. But, in the meantime, regarding the other issue I created for myself … I've kept her talking long enough.

"It's time I go meet with our possible recruit," I say, pushing out of my seat. "Since lunch is almost over, I don't think you can accompany me. I have a free period, but I'm fairly certain our schedules aren't *that* similar—unless you managed to beat the system to get two free periods."

"… What are you saying?"

"I'm saying you should get to class and I'll contact you once I've got this part down."

"You really think this person will agree before we've even decided on what type of club we want?"

"That shouldn't be an issue." Because I *have* already decided. Not that that even matters in this context.

"I still want to come with you."

"Briar, you should really prioritize your classes. You were already absent all of yesterday, so you're ranking could drop and you're going to have to meet with the chairman to discuss that—"

"Exactly, I'm already going to be punished. So what does it matter? Besides, *you* were absent the entire day before that, weren't you?"

She noticed my absence? *It's different for me than it is for you,* I want to say. But going into my "special" treatment probably isn't the best move.

"Zero, I'm sorry, but I won't take no for an answer."

My impromptu plan of preoccupying Briar with conversation until lunch was over ultimately backfires on me.

My other half-hearted attempts at dissuasion also prove to be in vain. I'd underestimated just how stubborn this girl can be. (Sometimes she'll listen to me at the drop of a hat, others, she'll push back till the last possible second.) Well, there's nothing I can do about it now. And I won't deny the fact that not letting her out of my sight makes me rest a bit easier.

At this exact moment, though, I don't feel as if I can rest at all … Actually, I feel incredibly on edge.

I glance around my surroundings as we walk down the halls, scanning for the source of this ill feeling. Could it be that—

"You're going to visit her." This statement comes from none other than the president, who's just turned the corner, coming to a stop in front of us. "That's incredibly kind of you, Zero. Are you sure you're feeling well?"

"I thought I sensed something extremely unpleasant. Glad to see my intuition hasn't dulled completely. And I'm certain I have no idea who you're speaking of. You should know I'm not the visiting type."

His eyes have already moved on from me, fixating on Briar. There's a slight crease between his brows as though this troubles him in some way. I don't like it.

"Ms. Thornswood," he says, tone diplomatic but authoritative, "shouldn't you be headed to class?" It's not really a question. "The bell is about to ring."

"... Yes, you're right. I guess I got caught up in our conversation." She glances at me, though we both know we hadn't been in the middle of any conversation.

"Inform me of its location and I'll escort you there."

"Well—"

"If you ever once minded your own damn business," I begin, "I think I'd die of a shock-induced heart attack."

The president angles his head toward me. "I'll keep that in mind."

It's not as harsh or snappy as his usual comebacks, but I suspect he's toning it down thanks to Briar's presence.

"You were saying, Ms. Thornswood?"

"Um, unfortunately, my class is on the other side of the building—I really wasn't paying attention to where I was going. So, please, don't worry about walking me there. I'd hate to make you late to your own class."

I'm impressed with how calm and honest Briar sounds. Sadly, that won't be nearly enough to trick the president.

"That's of no concern for me. The teachers understand I have other matters to deal with that occasionally take me away from their lessons. The same cannot be said for you, Ms. Thornswood, but if you enter with me, your tardiness will be forgiven."

Cold and to the point. She won't have anything to say back.

"….."

"It's fine, Briar, I'll be sure to meet up with you later," I say with a small, dismissive wave as I continue walking. I'm not a fan of fighting the inevitable.

"Come, let's go," I hear him tell her.

"Yeah … ok."

I roll my eyes as I turn the corner. *So she can be convinced by him, but not me.*

My pace slows to a halt the minute I'm out of their sight, something striking me as fishy. The president had been coming from the same direction we were going in. And if my memory of his schedule stands correct, he'd have no business in this wing of the building, unless …

I spend a minute thinking it over.

By the time the three guys loitering around the door to the nurse's office have surrounded me, I've got a theory. But I suppose I should deal with this predicament first.

***

# Myles Adrian

- **Year/age/student ranking**: Junior, 17, 110 of 150
- **Hair**: light golden-brown, grown out slightly longer than his brother's

- **Eyes**: brown
- **Height/Weight**: 5'9, 159 lbs.
- **Noticeable features**: exceptionally charming smile
- **Favorite item**: a baseball hat he's had since childhood
- **Likes**: Sports of any kind, violin, magic tricks, hanging out with friends
- **Dislikes**: Being compared to his brother
- **Personal comment**: "Woah, we get to have our own personal comment?"
- **Fact**: Myles is a part of three clubs, including both the soccer team (of which he is the captain) and the basketball team. He also takes private music lessons.

*Briar's picture (since Zero didn't give you one)*

**Kane Academy Fact:** Only students placing within the top 50 of their year for at least two consecutive ranking periods are eligible for a room and board scholarship (outstanding circumstances notwithstanding). Only those in the top 10 are guaranteed a full scholarship to the university of their choice upon graduation.

*Answers to Zero's number sequence game:*
1. 24
2. 134

***

# Chapter 6:

## I Meet Three Idiots and Am Forced to Expend Physical Energy (Again)

This is the first time I've been targeted at Kane Academy. How exciting.

In a short two days, things really have turned upside down on me. In a way, it's like I'm back at my old school. And in many other ways, it's not like that at all.

"Hey," sneers [The Ugly One Who's Probably The Leader Of This Sad Gang In Desperate Need Of More/Better-Looking Members]. "*Zero.*"

"Is the number that comes before one," I finish for him. "Yes, that's correct. If that's all you came to confirm, you can go now."

"Let me guess, you're here for Marina?"

"No, I thought I'd come down to the nurse's office and just *not* go in." So this is about Marina?

"Stop playing around, Hale. We know why you're here—you just want to make sure she stays quiet," [Lackey #1] says.

"Why would I need to do that? Because I tried to drown her in the Black River?" Clearly, those rumors have gotten out of hand.

"Stop playing dumb. It's not gonna work."

"In that case, if I wanted her dead, do you really think she'd be sitting comfortably in the nurse's office right now?"

"Goddamn, you know, you walk around like you're the toughest shit—like you're *untouchable* or something—and it's really starting to piss me off. But not one person here has ever seen you in 'action.' Actually, besides some of those random freak accidents, I don't think anybody's ever seen you do *anything*."

The ugly leader's not wrong, in a way. Compared to my past, I've lied carefully under the radar as much as I am capable of doing so. (Though the phrase "some random freak accidents" doesn't even begin to cover it.)

"So then, you're here to teach me a lesson. Or, more accurately, you're here to boost your own social status by being the ones to take me down while 'protecting' your popular-yet-vulnerable classmate."

Judging from the twitch in [The Quiet Lackey #2]'s eye, I've hit the nail on the head. Or maybe he's just confused.

"It's true that you'd become quite the sensation if you managed to take me out. And Marina would be incredibly impressed, wouldn't she? To find out all you big, strong men stood up for her—I'm sure she'd be grateful. One of the most popular girls in the junior class in *your* debt, just think about it."

The three of them shuffle on their feet, a bit restless, a bit agitated.

"But that plan requires you being *able* to take me out. Are you sure you can do that?"

"Huh?"

"Or, allow me to phrase that question differently: **are you sure you want to make me your enemy?**"

All three lose what color was left in their pale faces. But none of them back down. (Their motives must have a secure hold over them. Or is there something else to this?)

I sigh. "Well, I've got business to attend to. If you're going to try something, do it now."

And so it begins.

Gathering all of his courage, [Lackey #1] moves in on me, looking both frightened and angrily determined, but the ugly leader stops him.

Correction, *tries* to stop him. His calls for him to "wait!" go unheard as the other boy gets swept up in the moment. (I can and will continue to say whatever I want about the president, but at least he has control over those working under him.)

I'm actually embarrassed at how easy it is to sidestep the punch. If he's gonna move that sluggishly and that sloppily, I'd be doing this kid a favor by putting a swift end to his fighting career. Sure enough, having expected his momentum to be stopped by contact with my body, he goes stumbling past me.

I straighten and look over the other two standing in front of me. Are any of them worth breaking my impressive no-fighting streak? No, it would be better for everyone if this ends peacefully.

"Well," I clap, "it was a good attempt while it lasted. Full marks for effort. Now, get back to class. Just because there aren't any athletic scholarships in your futures doesn't mean you shouldn't try to keep up with your studies instead. Gotta be useful in at least one category of life, after all."

"I-it's three against one," stutters [Honorable Mention Of Punch-Throwers], trying to give himself a comeback. "You can't win like this. You can't …"

Hm, what do you think? Should I shut them down or stay out of trouble by finding a peaceful resolution? I'll go with whatever you deci—

The sound of footsteps running up behind me has all four of us looking to see who has stumbled across our little party.

Hang on, is that, "Briar?"

What the hell is she doing back here?

Her cheeks are flushed and her breathing is heavy, like she's just sprinted all the way here.

She says nothing, not even glancing at me as she walks directly up to the leader boy, positioning herself between us.

"The hell are you here for?" he spits at her. It almost sounds personal. "This has nothing to do with you. Leave—while I'm still feeling nice."

Briar stays silent, not budging an inch.

"What, can you not understand me? We're in the middle of something. If you're so eager to get in on the action, don't worry, I'll give you some aft—"

That's as far as he gets before Briar's foot slams into his head.

He goes down instantly, body thudding to the ground as my jaw drops open. But I'm not paying him any mind; I'm staring at the girl who just all but KO-ed him with a single kick.

Is she … protecting *me*? Have I been transported into a fight scene from a classic delinquent manga? Who kicks like that? One second she was standing straight, unmoving, the next, her leg was in the air making contact with his head. (Remember what I said about the other shoe dropping? Yeah, it's just come crashing down.)

"Goddammit," the ugly one gasps weakly from the floor, "for Christ's sake, don't just stand there."

[Lackey #2] comes at her next, looking like he's not sure what to do. Before I can react myself, Briar kicks him straight in the face with no hesitation, causing him to swear and stagger backward, cupping his now-smashed nose.

"You bitch," he seethes, pain making his words come out strangled as blood drips down his face. "I'm gonna—"

She takes two steps to spin around and kicks him in the stomach from behind. He folds over immediately, struggling for breath.

Interestingly, it appears she has a variety of moves in her arsenal.

The first kick she utilized was a roundhouse, making contact with the side of the boy's head. Her next was a straight-on frontal attack, and her last was one incorporating a spin while extending her leg from behind and making use of her momentum (ie. a spinning back kick). They're impressively precise, not to mention effective, as she's made clear.

I'm prepared to think it's over when [Lackey #1] barrels forward from behind me, grabbing hold of Briar and pinning her arms back. (Naturally, it couldn't be that easy.) I could step in now, but before I do, I want to see exactly what kind of guys I'm dealing with here. How far are they willing to go? My actions will depend on the answer.

Briar struggles fiercely, finally displaying distress, but the boy's got a strong grip on her. Naturally, though she admittedly has skill, this delicately built, five-five girl can't muscle her way past a heavy-set, six-foot-tall, nearly grown young man.

"Get out of here, Zero! Go, now!" she yells at me, (the first thing she's said since showing back up).

Curious … despite the trouble she's in, she isn't asking for my help.

[Lackey #2] is still nursing what may very well be a broken nose, but the leader picks himself up off the ground, grunting slightly as he walks toward her slowly.

Once in range, he winds his arm back, hand splayed open, glaring pure, humiliation-induced hatred. "You're gonna learn to stay out of what doesn't fucking concern you, you little—"

He starts to swing at her, but, of course, his smack doesn't reach its target.

"H-hey—?!"

"You were actually going to hit her," I say, my tone revealing nothing as I hold onto his wrist from where I caught it.

"What're you—"

"With your filthy hand that might be even dirtier than your filthy mouth." I emphasize my point by swiftly hooking the fingers of my free right hand on the inside of his open mouth, using them to yank him toward me, leaving an uncomfortably small amount of space between us. The experience is a painful one for him (the insides of people's mouths are particularly soft and delicate), but I've moved too fast for him to react and the position I am in makes it impossible for his teeth to clamp down on me.

Having him where I want him, I withdraw my fingers and wipe them on his uniform shirt. He coughs, sputtering as his head bends down as far as my hold on him will allow.

"You're crazy!! What the hell?!"

"I thought your entire reason for being here was to protect a girl," I say, ignoring his hysterics.

"Not *this* girl. Didn't you see anything?! She attacked *us* first!"

I twist his wrist and he cries out involuntarily. He tries to push me away, to rip my hand off of him, but it's of no use.

I lean in another inch, speaking just loud enough that the other two can hear. "I don't give a shit if she stabbed you first. You idiots deserved everything you got, and everything you're about to get. That's been the predetermined outcome since you decided to go through with this little charade. So when we're done, just remember, if you try anything on Briar *or* Marina ever again, I won't hold back against you."

Tears of pain spring from [Ugly Leader]'s eyes as he desperately swats at my hand and arm. "S-stop—stop!"

Any harder, and I might break his bones. I abruptly let go and deliver a solid punch to the left side of his face. Before he can recover, I strike him with my left fist, followed directly by another right hook.

One last hit and he's out cold at my feet.

"W-what? H-h-how?!" [Lackey #1] gapes, his grip on Briar going slack. She could easily slip out of his grasp right now, but she's frozen, staring wide-eyed at the scene unfolding.

The nurse obviously isn't around, just as before, and there aren't many teachers available to be walking the halls, monitoring things, but this affair hasn't exactly been quiet. Sooner or later, someone will come upon us, so I need to make quick work of wrapping this up.

I walk toward the one holding Briar. The second I move, he lets her go, seeming torn between running and coming at me for the sake of his leader (or his pride). Unfortunately for him, he chooses the latter. With a panicked mind and such predictable movements, getting him to fall next is simple. I let him throw his cross, leaning back at the last second to dodge it and immediately moving in to catch the left punch that follows. Pressing on his arm, I use his own momentum to bring him down a bit lower before throwing him back in the opposite direction, lifting my hand up to his face and slamming him backward.

He twists slightly in the air and, before his head can smash into the floor, I catch him by the back of his neck. (I'm looking to teach him a lesson, not kill him.)

"You really are a special kind of stupid," I say, dragging him a few steps to drop him on top of his unconscious friend. "Before you challenge someone to a fight, you should at least learn how to get a single hit in. I mean, if nothing else," I turn my attention to the last of them, [Lackey #2], "you could have at least tried to make this interesting."

He trembles, stumbling a few steps, his hands out in front of him protectively. I decide to take inspiration from Briar and use a kick, shoving him hard enough that he falls onto his backside, letting out a noise somewhere between a grunt and a yelp. (Pathetic.)

The leader is starting to come-to behind me, groaning and rolling onto his side as he shoves his underling off of him. "Th-this is *bullshit* … It w-wasn't … supposed to be like this."

He's about to try getting up, so I kindly help him out seeing as he doesn't seem to understand his situation just yet.

"Where do you think you're going so fast?" I ask, placing my foot on his chest and pressing him down until he's lying flat on his back. *"Stay down on the ground where you belong."*

He goes completely still aside from the slight tremors I can feel coming off of him as he stares up at me.

I direct my next bit to all three of them. "You can wait here for a teacher to find you. Then you'll take responsibility for yourselves, saying you had a disagreement that got out of hand. If you so much as think about telling anyone we were involved in this, I'll hunt you down myself. Understood?"

The one under my foot swallows hard but slowly dips his head. Since he's at the center of their little group, that'll do. For later analysis, I snap a photo of all three.

"Come with me, Briar," I say to her, taking the dazed girl by the arm and leading her to the door of the nurse's office. It'd all be pointless if we didn't now complete our original objective.

I open the door, holding it for her behind me. She takes one last glance over her shoulder at the three boys laid out across the floor and then follows me inside.

<h1 style="text-align:center">6 ½</h1>

I'm not sure what I expected to find upon entering the office, but it definitely wasn't to see Marina, in my uniform jacket, dancing around with her eyes closed and earphones in. Didn't she learn anything from last time? And what kind of dancing even is this? It's sure as hell not any style that comes from technical training, that's for damn sure.

At the end of some kind of little spin, Marina's eyes open and land on us. Her face turns white as she freezes mid-weird-hand gesture. Then:

"I told you to knock!" she explodes. "You were supposed to *knock!* How else am I supposed to know you're here?!"

"Huh?!" Is she kidding? "Marina, you—"

"You just walk in like you own the place every time, giving me no warning—"

"Are you crazy? You'd have to be deaf not to hear everything happening right outside your door," I throw back. "And have you ever thought you shouldn't be doing so many weird things you don't want people seeing to begin with?"

"What are you talking about? What happened right outside my door?"

"There was ... a bit of a fight," Briar answers.

Marina sizes her up, seemingly just having noticed her for the first time. "Hey ... why did Zero bring *you?* And what fight are you talking about?"

"Oh, you know, the one caused by the rumors that I tried to *drown* you. Not that it'll concern you, but you had three guys blocking me from entering your room thinking I was coming to intimidate you into silence or finish what I 'started.'"

"Well, you are acting pretty intimidating, so maybe they had a point ... And wait, it's hardly *my* fault if that's what people are thinking! I've been in here for two days, and I haven't said a word about it, I swear!"

"Ugh." I lift a hand to my forehead. "Stop shouting. I'm right in front of you. And I know you didn't, so just be quiet already."

"Tch." She folds her arms over her chest. "Did you really just come here to insult me and boss me around? You should have started with that."

"I came here because you wanted me to. Surely your memory can't be so bad as to forget the request you made just a single day ago. Or did you hit your head before falling into that ice?"

Really, I came out of an interest in recruiting her. Despite her popularity, Marina is only in a single, fairly low-commitment club and has more than enough time on her hands for another. And her connections could prove useful for a multitude of reasons. However, I'm going to hold off on breaching that subject for now.

Marina eyes me suspiciously, slowly backing up to her bed and sitting down. "There's something different about you today. Like you're even meaner."

I wave my hand. "It's probably because of my good night's sleep." (Plus, I've been on such good behavior all day.)

"You sound serious about that, but that's supposed to have the opposite effect ..."

I ignore Marina and turn my attention to Briar, who is currently looking just as surprised as when she was watching me deal with the three idiots outside.

I guess witnessing me having a passionate interaction with

another student would be a little shocking.

But there's no way her surprise could possibly compare to what I felt seeing her make that first kick. I may have finished them off, but no doubt her attacks will leave a mark on the two she hit. [Ugly Leader Kid] is going to have a bruise on the side of his face for the next week thanks to her.

I'd like to analyze her movements a bit more, however, now that the moment's passed, there's one thing that keeps popping into my brain, making me never want to revisit the whole ordeal ever again. Which is, *did she have to be wearing a skirt?!* I hadn't focused on it in the moment, but now the image is seared into my mind. (Curse the academy dress code—it's absolutely absurd for the female students.)

"Zero, is something wrong?" Briar asks, sounding worried as she cocks her head to the side. "Your face … it's—"

"I'm fine. Are you all right? You're the one who got grabbed."

"Oh, so you can be calm and nice to her, but not me?" Marina questions, suddenly getting up and walking right up to me (she's not even pretending to be hurt anymore). "Every time I think it's not possible, your rudeness gets worse."

"If you had given me five more seconds, I would've introduced you," I say between gritted teeth. "It's hard when you won't ever *shut up.*" (Maybe I should abandon this part of the plan.)

"I don't need an introduction." She looks at Briar, as if evaluating her again. "You're Briar Thornswood." Then to me, "We all have class together, duh."

"I remember you, too," Briar responds, her voice quieter as she moves a bit further behind me. The confidence she displayed just a few minutes ago is gone.

I refrain from sighing in exasperation. *Aren't you the one who wanted to come here so bad?* I want to ask her. Though I'm beginning to see there's something more to her reasoning for this.

Marina's eyes narrow, darting between me and Briar, like she's thinking something through (wouldn't that be amazing?). She decides to get a closer look at Briar, but rather than walking around me like a normal person, she clutches onto the front of my uniform and peers at her from around my chest.

"Marina! What are you—"

Briar moves first, her hand coming forward to reach for Marina's. I'm not sure what she's about to do, but my intuition has me grabbing hold of her before she can do it. My hold is gentle but firmer than I'd anticipated as necessary.

When I turn my head to look at her, her golden eyes have a strange look in them, almost like she's not totally in control or aware of what she's doing. Before I can decipher it, she blinks and looks at me, expression innocently confused. (That's the face *I* should be making.)

"What was that about?" Marina asks, gripping onto me with even more force as she leans away from Briar.

I release Briar and proceed to pry Marina off of me. "Both of you, sit down on the bed. We need to talk."

Marina pouts a little, but they each listen.

I start with Briar, hoping the pouty, invasively troublesome one will find it in herself to be quiet for a few moments.

"So, want to tell me how you knew those guys would be waiting for me?"

Briar shifts a bit under my gaze, doing her best to maintain eye contact. "It's not exactly like I *knew* they'd be there when they were."

"Oh?" There's no way it was a coincidence that she ran back to me when she did.

"It was just something I heard those guys say this morning while I was walking to the main building. 'Someone needs to put him in his place,' or something like that. They didn't say your name, but I just sort of felt … like I knew. And then I overheard them talking about it again during lunch like they were making some kind of plan." So *that's* who she was looking for in the cafeteria. Wait, then was her getting me another slice of pizza just a pretext for her to go and eavesdrop on them? "So I knew I couldn't let you out of my sight all day, even if it bothered you."

"You could have just told me, you know."

"I know …" She looks like a scolded child.

"Just remember that for next time if anything like this happens again." (Because it most certainly will.)

"Huh? Next time? You mean, you'll still be my partner for the final—you won't ask to switch?"

"Why would I do that? That has nothing to do with any of this."

"But I … failed. I thought I could help you, but it didn't even work. I couldn't do anything." Is she … tearing up? Oh god.

"All right," I pat her head in an attempt to soothe her, "I get it. That's enough. You did well. Really well. So just leave it." (It's not like any other person, let alone girl, would have done what she did.)

I half expect Marina to cut in with something like "Zero, did you come to my room to see me or to just talk to Briar all day?" Instead, she appears to be listening rather intently.

"You said when you came in here something about there being three guys. If that's true, how are you, like, totally not messed up?" she asks.

Fair question. I take my hand off of Briar's head. "Briar had already just about taken care of the situation herself; I just helped her finish them off. They weren't experienced fighters, so we didn't take much damage."

Briar raises a brow but doesn't oppose my recounting of what happened.

"Wow, they were willing to fight a girl? Jeez, they must be lowlife cowards. I can't stand guys like that."

Seeing as we were attacked by "cowards" who were acting on behalf of Marina, it would be possible to use that to force her into agreeing to be the third member of our club. But I have other ideas, bringing me to another piece of the puzzle that makes me far more wary than anything I've yet experienced today.

"Marina, you seemed pretty happy about something when we came in." (That's putting it mildly. She was dancing around like a little maniac.) "Did you have any visitors before we showed up?"

Marina's face brightens. "Yeah, I did! In fact, he visited me yesterday too, right after you left, Zero."

"And this person, that would be the president, correct?"

"Yep!" She smiles but then quickly straightens out her face, looking a little suspicious. "Oh, but it's not anything like you're thinking. I just admire him for everything he's done for our school, that's all. Plus, it's not as if he'd ever be interested in *me* like that."

"I don't doubt it. Now, when he was talking to you, did the president make a point of asking you something? Like, say, to join the student council?"

"Uh-huh! Wait, how did you know—did he tell you about it?" She clasps her hands in her lap happily, not seeming to care about an answer. "President Jordan is just the best, isn't he? He says he's got just the position for me and he thinks I'll make a great fit."

It appears my theory is correct. While I can't say *why*, or *why now*, it's clear he's somehow trying to force my hand, aligning his chess pieces to get me involved. Of course, Briar would have thrown a wrench in that, which is probably why he didn't seem to like the fact that we were together earlier. She's a variable he couldn't have predicted no matter how much thought he'd put into this.

I won't go into it now, but something about the three guys showing up to take me down also rubs me the wrong way. Their motive, and something one of them said ... But such brash, impulsive action—it doesn't feel like the president's style at all, which means ...

"And Briar, I'm guessing when he walked you to your class, you spoke to the president about the possibility of getting his permission for a new student club."

"Uh ... I didn't say it was for us, necessarily, I just asked hypothetically speaking."

It's not surprising she took the initiative with him, she'd been wanting to be useful all day. Still, I do wish she hadn't done that.

Question is, what's the president going to do now? Without knowing it, she's given him all the information he needs to re-route his original plan. I rub my temples, closing my eyes for a brief second. Then I sit in the same chair as before.

"Marina," Briar begins, looking at the girl sitting to her left, "is that your uniform jacket? It's ... very big."

"No, Zero wanted me to have it. So I decided to be nice and accept it from him."

"Oh, for the love of—"

"Is that true, Zero?"

"Only in that it technically is mine. And I'd have no problem taking it back."

Marina wrinkles her nose. "Taking back gifts is such a lame thing to do. Even *you* should find that beneath you, Zero. Oh wait, you already did it yesterday, didn't you?"

"Nothing can be beneath you when you've already made hell your home."

"What does that even mean? Seriously, you can be so annoying."

*You're sure one to talk*, I think but don't say.

I thought maybe Marina would play the innocently sweet and bubbly girl she usually does since Briar is in her company now. But she seems entirely unconcerned with her, acting almost as obnoxious as she did when she was alone with me.

"So, Briar, are you and Zero, like, friends or something?"

I hold back a wince at the word friend being flung around so carelessly. I guess it's an understandable question, but at the same time, people with lots of popularity shouldn't pry into the social situations of those without such privileges. It may be of no concern for me, however, Briar is another matter …

"We're partners for a final project," I answer for her. Ideally, Briar will see me as someone she trusts and will listen to, but full-on friendship would likely thwart the entire plan if I'm not careful.

"I don't remember seeing you guys talk at all before this. You seem to have gotten awfully close in such a short, short time."

"Are you saying you actually pay attention to things going on outside of your own personal social sphere? I'm impressed." Marina's correct—it's odd for me to go out of my way to talk to anyone and Briar herself is odd for being so open to it. But like I'd ever admit that to her.

Marina glares haughtily, crossing her arms. "Rude much?"

I sigh, flicking her forehead to get her to lean back out of my personal space that she seems to be steadily making her home. "I mean, yes, you have been rude. But you don't have to atone for it by verbally calling yourself out. A simple apology would suffice."

"Huh? How do you even think of things to say like that?! Uaghh, whatever—just wait, Zero Hale. When I'm on the student council, I'm going to keep *such* a close eye on you. And you'll *have* to respect me then. There's nothing you can do about it. Your stupid, sharp tongue won't save you. And don't think your scary personality or looks will do anything for you, either. I swear, you'll be totally at my mercy."

A terrifying prospect. Also one that won't come to pass; at least, not anymore.

"If you don't mind me asking," Briar says, hands folded in her lap, an unreadable expression on her face, "I'm actually curious as to when you two started talking." She looks at Marina. "You think it's strange Zero and I know each other, but I'd argue you're the stranger pair."

"What, you don't know about what happened yesterday?" This seems to shock Marina more than anything else that's been said.

Sadly, it only makes sense that Briar would be out of the loop. This is just a testament to how isolated she's become over the past year and a half.

With a captive audience member, Marina launches into a detailed, dramatized retelling of the events of yesterday. She does a wonderful job of somehow painting me in both a heroic and villainous light, begrudgingly complimenting how I was able to hold her up while giving focus to how "cruel" I was when I was "ordering her around." Something about my face being wasted on my "horrible, trash personality" is also thrown in there at some point.

She's barely finished the story of when I came to visit her the first time, followed by an account of all her other friends who visited her, when I notice we only have a few minutes until fifth period.

I catch Briar's eye and nod, standing up. "I hate to cut off this fascinating, semi-based-in-fact story, Marina, but we all have US History now, so we'd better get to class."

"But you just got here," Marina protests, grabbing me by the arm. "You said you came to visit me, so visit me." (Since when does almost forty minutes count as "just getting here?")

"You're coming, too," I tell her.

"Huh, don't you see I'm on bedrest?"

I yank Marina off her bottom, placing her on her feet.

"Hey!"

"We both know you haven't needed 'bedrest' since yesterday morning. Let's go."

She complains willfully, but eventually I get Marina to follow us out of the nurse's office. (Once she realizes that I really will leave her behind, she sobers up to the idea pretty fast.) She even goes so far as to walk ahead of us, a bounce in her step as practically everyone we pass smiles and greets her excitedly along the way, happy that she's feeling better. What must it be like in the life of someone like her? I can't begin to imagine.

"So, you're really not upset about what happened?"

I look down to my right to see Briar watching the floor as she walks. I know exactly what she's talking about. "Not at all," I say honestly. "It's not your fault, Briar. Those guys were just stupid enough to try what they did. It's as simple as that and it has nothing to do with you. Just … don't ever start a fight on my behalf again, ok?"

"You think I should have just let them gang up on you? I don't think so, Zero. No way."

"Right, because attempting to deal with everything on your own is a much better way to go about things."

Briar turns her head to me, frowning. "I know I should have thought it through more, but I was trying not to inconvenience you. How was I supposed to know you could do what you did? Like I said, hiding your true abilities is a bad habit."

"Ok, the next time I meet a new acquaintance, I'll sit them down and tell them exactly what kind of combat experience I have, how many years I've trained, and how many guys I've taken on at once," I say sarcastically. "Besides, if you really think that, then you should take some of your own advice. It's not exactly normal for a high school girl to be able to KO a guy with a kick to the head."

"He wasn't *knocked out*. And what you did was way stranger than what I did—once you got serious, you took them all down in twenty seconds flat!"

I reach over and slap my hand over her mouth. "Quiet. This school prefers if students deal with their issues amongst themselves, but they can't turn a blind eye if someone comes forward about a fight with legitimate injuries as proof. It'll be better if this story *doesn't* get out." Especially seeing as I went through the trouble of threatening the idiots into silence.

Just before I uncover her mouth, I feel a light nip on one of my fingers.

I yank my hand away on reflex. "You just bit me," I say in astonishment, looking down at the spot she'd nipped. It was nothing more than what could be compared to the harmless love bite of a kitten, but it's an entirely unpredictable, incomprehensible action nonetheless.

"I couldn't let you cover my mouth like that without some form of payback."

"Huh?"

"And I don't care if you don't want the rest of the school to know about all of this, that's fine—I just want you to teach me."

"You want me to *teach* you? What, how to fight?"

She nods.

"You can't be serious."

"I am! I-I've never seen anything like it. It looked so easy for you." She looks up at me, large eyes almost pleading. "Please, I have to know how you did that."

"… I'll consider it."

I see her arm jut out right before I feel a slight jab in my ribs and look down to find her frowning deeply. (Brave move to elbow the person you want fighting tips from.)

Yep, it seems there are three sides to Briar Thornswood: the silent, cold one from last night; the polite, almost nervous one from most of today; and the fierce, downright stubborn one I'm experiencing now.

No matter what the truth is, the events of today have shown me that I've only just scratched the surface of who this girl really is. What more will I uncover before our time together is up?

"I know you could have dodged that," she mutters. "Also … since you kind of brought it up, how many guys *have* you taken on at once?"

"Hey, are you two coming or what?" Marina calls back at us, saving me from answering that question and causing quite the scene as people in the hallway put two and two together that she's talking to me and Briar.

I would've thought a girl like Marina would be too worried about her social standing to be seen conversing with me in public, but she doesn't seem to care at all. She even stalks back up to us and grabs hold of my shirt sleeve, pulling me along after her.

"Come—on."

That's when I notice she's still wearing my uniform jacket. Or should I now call it *her* uniform jacket? I did gift it to her after all. Still, she can't really wear that thing to class.

"Marina, that jacket is way too damn big on you. You're not actually going to keep it on for the rest of the day, are you?"

She halts for a brief second before picking up speed as she pulls me. "Shut up, of course not. I just didn't want you to feel bad if I didn't wear it at all. You did give it to me, you know."

Yeah, back when I thought I would be dead and safe from the embarrassment of seeing such a ridiculous girl parade around in my clothing.

How much longer will this day drag on?

***

### Bonus: Q & A

Q: "Are you sure you want to make me your enemy?" That's a direct quote. "Stay down on the ground where you belong." So is this. I bet you thought you sounded pretty cool, Zero.

Z: Is that even a question?

Q: "Should I shut them down or stay out of trouble by finding a peaceful resolution? I'll go with whatever you decide." These are also your words, Zero, are they not?

Z: Are you just going to quote back the entire chapter to me?

Q: Irrelevant—are you ever going to make good on your promise here?

Z: I'll consider it. But can I go now? I'm kind of in the middle of an important plot line.

Q: Yeah, yeah, whatever. See you next time.

Z: Yeah, sure … Wait, next time?

**Kane Academy Fact:** Rankings give students a certain number of "credits" that are sent to their ID cards and can be used as currency for various things, including spending money at stores and food stations. Whatever a student is given in rank credits is theirs and won't be taken away even if they drop in rank later on. Those credits are replenished every quarter in an amount dependent on what placement they're at. Ex: 1st gets $1,000 in credits while 150th gets $0.

*Briar in her favorite nightgown*

***

# CHAPTER 7:
## UNPLEASANT ENCOUNTERS

I keep a close eye on Marina's actions in history, having seen her run directly up to the president upon entering the classroom. What I really want to see is how he will react to her, if he'll attempt to watch me and her together. Moderate offense to my overly lively classmate, but there's no way she's a genuine candidate for a prestigious, highly sought-after, by-invitation-only student council seat. And the president knows that better than anyone. But after a polite, if not perfunctory, greeting to Marina, he doesn't so much as glance at any of us, seeming as completely disinterested and superior as always.

Mr. Rubin also acts differently from how I imagined he would. I was decently rude to him yesterday, walking out mid-class. However, he's not nearly as nervous-looking as he should be. He's pretty much back to normal.

I look over to the president again who must sense my eyes on him because, when no one else is looking, he flips me off. *That bastard.*

Since she's already planted the seed, I might as well let Briar finish what she's started with him. It'll be suspicious if I approach him on my own, and I've decided to let things play out more or less the way he wants, for now.

I just want to speed things up a bit.

All I have to do to get her to take the initiative again is pass her a note asking her when she thinks would be a good time to discuss possible plans with the president. Her response is to give me a thumbs up, which I return. At the end of history, Briar approaches him directly, seeming to ignore the displeased expressions of the other girls in the class with practiced ease. (I've got to hand it to her, anyone who can converse so bravely with the president—especially when being watched by jealous enemies—is someone with impressive nerves.)

Meanwhile, Marina gets ready to bounce off to her next class with a group of equally talkative girls. Pausing at the door, she takes a long look at Briar speaking with the president and then glances over at me. For some reason, when she sees me looking back, she quickly turns away and takes her entourage out of the room.

Briar fills me in on the way to English that we are to meet with the president at the end of the day. Oh joy. (I know what you're thinking—"Stop complaining, Zero; you did this to yourself." To which I have this to say: *shut up.*)

Since today hasn't been full of enough exciting fun, I also get to deal with Ms. Kurima going from giving me strange looks to outright staring at me all throughout class. *What does this woman want from me?*

"Zero, come over here for a minute," she says just as I'm attempting to make my escape at the end of the period.

"Ms. Kurima, can we do this another time?"

"Are you trying to say you have something better to do right now?"

"Unfortunately, I have a prior engagement I must attend to."

"Hey, don't give me that. We both know you don't have any—"

"Zero, are you ready?"

Briar appears at my side, not looking at me, but at Ms. Kurima. That expression, it reminds me of the one she wore when she interrupted my conversation with Myles. (What is she—a bloodhound for my discomfort?)

"So, the little punk finally made a friend. Huh," Ms. Kurima says, sounding awed. Then she throws an arm around my shoulder, grinning. "It's about damn time."

"It's rude to involve yourself in the personal lives of others. Who's to say I don't have friends that you just don't know about?"

She lets go of me, chuckling in amusement. "So testy. Maybe I should just ignore you and talk to Ms. Thornswood here instead." She smiles again, slapping my back for no good reason as she turns to her next target. "I haven't spoken to you in quite some time. How are you doing, Briar? I guess if you're hanging with this one," she nudges me, harder than necessary, "you probably can't be doing too well."

"Hey," I warn. I mean, she's not wrong, but still.

"I'm just fine, ma'am. Though Zero's right, we do have a meeting to get to."

I snort at Briar's use of the word "ma'am," receiving myself another nudge to my side.

"Sounds official. Well, I'm glad to hear it. This'll be good for you kids." Ms. Kurima says this like she has any idea what it is we're going to be doing. "But I do want to ask you something before you go, Zero."

"Fine. Make it quick."

She scowls at that last bit and yanks *much* harder than necessary as she pulls me to the corner of the room. I see Briar stiffen, eyes becoming alert, as if she might come over to us again, but I put up a hand, stopping her. (*Jeez, Kyouka, you could tone it down a little, don't you think?*)

"What is it?"

Leaning in conspiratorially, she says, "There's something I need you to look into for me."

"Again?" This wouldn't be the first time Ms. Kurima has asked me to "investigate" something for her.

"Don't be a brat. This is important." (It always is.) "It's been going on for a few weeks now. Assignments and tests that kids swear they've turned in are going *missing*. Just gone. Not a single one of them has been found."

Oh, yeah. I remember overhearing some people complaining about a situation like that in the halls.

"I'm familiar with the fact that it's been going on, but I'll need more details."

"When I get more, I'll give them to you. Just keep your eyes open. It wouldn't kill you to actually pay attention to the other kids around you."

"Right. Ok, bye, now."

"Hold on, kiddo. Not so fast. There's one more thing, and you're not getting out of here until you give me an answer." (Ominous.) "Yesterday, before you left, you put some kind of letter underneath my flower vase." (She noticed that? Freakishly observant; I'll have to remember that.) "But when I went to look at it, it was gone. I want to know why you took it back and what was in it to begin with."

"Would you believe me if I told you someone else took it?"

"Probably not."

"Well, sorry to disappoint, but that's the truth. And before you ask, I have no idea who this person is." (Only that they sent me quite the unexpected package this morning.) "Who knows? Maybe it's the same one who's been stealing people's assignments, huh. If that's all—"

"You can at least tell me why you wrote it and what was in it!"

"You seem really interested in this 'letter' I wrote to you, Ms. Kurima. Why is that?"

She crosses her arms, not budging. "It's only natural I'd want to know. You did intend to give it to me, at least for a time."

"It's nothing you need to concern yourself with." I turn and start heading back to Briar. "Just a little love confession, sensei, that's all."

"A little—wait, what?! Zero, you'd better explain yourself!"

"I can't. I'm too shy."

"Come back here!"

I lift a hand in farewell as I continue walking, ignoring the rest of her demands for me to return. Sometimes I can't help but tease her back, if only just a little. *You reap what you sow*, and all that. Or, alternatively, *Sooner or later everyone sits down to a banquet of their own consequences.*

"Have you always been that close with Ms. Kurima?" Briar asks as we head toward the student council rooms, possibly trying to gauge whether or not I could just ask her to be our faculty advisor and be done with it.

"I wouldn't call what we are 'close.'"

"What would you call it?"

*A less than mutually beneficial relationship in which I am exploited for both mental and physical labor.* "Complicated."

"Compli—"

"Mr. Hale, a moment of your time?" a familiar, deceptively kind-sounding voice calls to me from behind us.

(I knew this was coming at some point.)

Briar turns her head to look at the woman while I remain facing forward as I bring us to a stop.

This timing is nothing short of terrible. But brushing her off won't work and allowing Briar to stay could also potentially result in catastrophe. Besides, we've had a little shadow tailing us ever since we left English, and I want to know what they'll do when I leave Briar alone. Rather than complaining, I ought to simply treat this situation as the opportunity it is.

"Go on ahead of me," I tell Briar. "Wait outside the council room for a bit if you can, but don't worry if they bring you in early. Just say that I'm on my way and don't begin discussing terms until I get back."

"That's ok, I'll just come with you—"

"Trust me, there's no need. I'll catch up with you soon."

"Are you sure?"

"I'll never give you instructions unless I'm certain."

I wait for her nod of understanding and then turn away, ensuring I don't look in the direction of the "shadow" lingering behind a corner when I pass, heading toward the woman who called for me. Her crimson-painted lips open in a satisfied smile as she sees me coming to her; then she turns on her heel and begins walking down the stairs.

I follow her all the way to the first floor, several paces behind until I stop beside her in front of the ranking display boards. To anyone passing by, we'll look to be having a normal student-teacher conversation about the current rankings. Of course, the truth is …

"What do you want?" I say after a few seconds of annoying silence.

"I haven't seen you in a few days." A trace of her smile is audible in her voice.

"And?"

"And I almost started to worry about you. Is that so hard to believe?"

"You tell me."

"I was just concerned that, well, I might have been a little too *rough* with you last time."

I incline my head toward her slightly, brow lifting skeptically as I catch her smirk from the corner of my eye.

"But then I realized that's not possible." She reaches over and touches the base of my neck, running her fingers over the now-healed mark that had been just barely covered beneath the ends of my hair yesterday. I swat her hand away.

"Don't be stupid."

"*Aww,* so mean, Zero. And after all I've done for you."

"I think you have our roles reversed."

She lets out a snort. "You always cut right through the social niceties, with no regard for authority or hierarchy. How cheeky."

"That's never been an issue for you before."

"Yes, I've actually always quite liked that about you. Among other things …"

"Ms. Sharp. I do have somewhere I must be. Did you pull me down here just to say hello, or is there something of importance you wish to tell me about?"

She sighs as though I'm being unfairly difficult to her. "Somewhere to be, huh? With that girl, I suppose. What's her name? Thornswood or something? Have you finally gotten yourself a girlfriend, Zero?"

I don't appreciate the mocking tone she takes on that last part.

When I say nothing, she sighs again, though this time in resignation. "Fine, don't tell me anything, as usual. But yes, your senses are as sharp as ever—there is a reason I brought you down here. You might not give a thought to social hierarchy, but there is one form of hierarchy that you should pay at least a *little* attention to."

"This is about the rankings, then," I say, looking back up at the display boards.

"Right on the money. Notice anything … strange?"

I look over the boards. Of course, it's the same as when I looked at them when I broke into the school this morning.

If you've been paying attention up until now, you'll remember there are two parts to each display: an unofficial ranking, and an official one, both attached to each student's name.

The official is what actually impacts you as a student, giving you credits to spend and determining everything about your life here from what dorm and roommate you'll get to what special amenities (like the movie theater and pools) are open to you and how many clubs you're allowed to join. Certain classes are also off limits to those of a low enough ranking, as are some big, school-wide events, like the annual Fall Sports Tournament. Naturally, your social standing can also be affected.

But official ranks are only given twice a semester, while *un*official ranks are displayed anew every week to give us an idea of where we stand and what we have to do before midterms and finals to maintain our position or fight to claw our way up. At least, that's the purpose they serve for students who care.

"There's a notable disparity," I say. "Between the official and unofficial ranks."

"But?"

"But only for top-performing students." Well, for a rather small handful of top-performing students, really.

It wouldn't be something I'd bother to pick up on except that, even to me, the numbers are intriguing in the way they don't add up. Sure, there's always a bit of discrepancy between the two, but generally, what you have is around what you'll get. Especially for those at the top of their grade. But there are a lot of names to look through— 600, to be exact—so you probably wouldn't even notice unless you were one of the affected or knew what to look for.

"You never disappoint, Zero. I suppose your rank isn't high enough for you to have to worry, but I knew this was information you might find interesting."

Ms. Sharp is not dumb, by any stretch of the word, but I'm certain she didn't notice this herself. It's possible another student brought it up to her, though it's more likely that there was some kind of a faculty discussion on the matter. Since Ms. Sharp is one of the teacher representatives on the board, it could even be that the chairman has weighed in on the issue, depending on how much notice it's garnered.

"Do you know what the chairman said when it was brought up to him?"

So he is aware? I can hear the answer to her question ring out clearly in my mind in his voice: "Let the students deal with it themselves."

"Precisely." She takes a step closer to me, her heels clacking on the floor as her hand comes around to rest on my back. "Well, it may not concern you at all, but I just wanted to pass it along."

The scent of her perfume is impossible to ignore at this distance—heavy and somewhat overwhelming, unlike the light lilac scent of Ms. Kurima's.

It's true that we're alone in the corridor at the moment, but the first floor does have a secret security camera in place. And while its existence is unknown to most of the faculty and students, it is not unknown to Ms. Sharp.

She's always been a bit reckless, that's part of the reason I scouted her out in the first place. But what I had started up as a fling that would give me access to … information that was of interest to me at the time, is now starting to get out of hand. If she becomes uncontrollable, she'll be of no use to me.

"You're right. Should you get anything else on the matter, I'd like to hear it."

"And on top of everything else, you're bossy, too." She pouts, red fingernails lightly scratching across my back as she moves to run a hand through her glossy black hair before tossing it over her shoulder. "But, ahh, I'll see what I can do."

I should cut her off right here and now, but I won't do so just yet. This arrangement could still be useful for me depending on how things go. So I simply watch as my most playable pawn strides back toward the first-floor faculty lounge.

Now then, let's see how the situation I left upstairs is unfolding.

***

I can hear their argument from the steps leading up to the fourth floor, voices coming out in angry, harsh half-whispers.

"I already told you, there's no way I'd ever agree to that!" It's Briar, and she sounds … upset. "That's never going to change."

"Come on, you can't seriously still be acting this way. This is getting ridiculous." And that voice most definitely belongs to Benjamin Hawkins. "Grow up, Briar."

"So the little shadow decided to make himself known after all," I mutter to myself.

"Ben, just stop, please—I don't want to—"

"Aren't you tired of this? It's been over a *year*. And, Jesus, after what you pulled last night, do you really think you have any right to behave this way toward me now?"

"I—I-I'm sorry for … what I did. But I've already told you." She takes a breath and her shaking voice becomes firm once again. "My answer is **no**."

Having enough of an understanding on the situation now, I step out from my spot around the corner.

"You should think carefully before—" Benjamin cuts off the second he sees me.

I offer a little wave and a smirk.

"You've got to be kidding me," he growls under his breath.

"Oh, sorry. Am I interrupting something?"

Briar's eyes are shining in a way that suggests she might start crying. *Should I have come in earlier?* is my knee-jerk reaction. But no, it will benefit her in the end if I can confirm what's going on. And while she was undoubtedly distressed, now that she's looking at me, I can make out a sense of relief as her troubled expression begins to melt away.

"Apologies for making you wait, Briar," I say as I stop before her. "I promise I won't leave you like that again."

It's kind of an extreme statement to make, and it has the desired effect on dear Ben who glares ominously at me.

*Ooh, so scary.*

Just to make sure it really sticks with him, I bring my thumb up under Briar's chin, tilting her face toward me as I wait for her response.

She goes stock still, losing her voice for a split second before swallowing in recovery. "I-it's ok, I'm fine."

"Good." I smile warmly at her and open my arm in the direction of the student council room. "Shall we, then?"

She doesn't so much as glance back at Benjamin as she walks away with me. I don't have to look back, either, to know that his eyes are glued to us all the way down.

*Goodbye for now, Benjamin.*

# 7 ½

The head office of the Student Council is definitely the nicest, grandest room on the fourth floor, and possibly one of the nicest rooms in the entire academy (which is saying something). With the same floor-to-ceiling windows as some of the classrooms, a huge crystal chandelier, and what almost looks like a throne at the head of a long, mahogany wood table, it's impressive to say the least.

"Wow," Briar utters quietly, taking in her surroundings. Since it's her first time here, that's an understandable reaction.

The nine other council members in the room stop talking the moment we step through the doors, and I get the feeling that while they may have been warned I was coming, some of them weren't prepared for me to actually show up. The girl who assisted with my bath the other morning, Annie, looks particularly startled.

Meanwhile, the president doesn't even look up from the document he's going over. "You finally showed."

"Yeah, I'm sure you just didn't know what to do with yourselves in our absence."

"Sorry to keep you waiting," Briar says, giving me a look that says *Stop it already, we want him on our side, don't we? What's your problem, anyway? Don't make me bite you again.*

Her eyes are really quite expressive.

Upon hearing Briar speak, the president's aura seems to change. He places down the papers he'd been holding and stands. "It's no matter. We were just in the middle of a council meeting, so there wasn't any waste of time."

"Should we wait for you to finish?"

"There's no need. The answer to the problem we were discussing should present itself shortly." (What a strange thing to say.) "Please, take a seat, Ms. Thornswood," then, tacked on distastefully at the end, "Zero."

He gestures to the seats near his own. Briar starts to move toward one, but I place a hand on her shoulder, stopping her.

"There's no reason for that. Get to the point, or we're leaving," I say.

The president narrows his eyes, taking his time to walk directly up to me. "Is that so? And here I thought *you* were the ones who wanted this meeting to begin with."

"He's right, Zero," Briar cuts in, sounding a little anxious. "I asked him for this."

"That doesn't mean we all need to sit around the campfire, holding hands and drinking hot chocolate together. Besides," I lock eyes with him, "if that's all there is to it, then I guess you won't be upset if we walk out now before finalizing anything."

It's a small ploy, nudging him toward revealing that he has his own stakes in this matter, even if they are hidden ones. But the president doesn't even flinch.

"You're right. I was doing this as a courtesy to Miss Thornswood. But if you've changed your minds, I have no issue with that."

(So, continue with my rules or see yourselves out, huh?)

To my surprise, Briar doesn't jump in with any dissent. When I glance over at her from the corner of my eye, I can see that she's watching me carefully, like she's waiting for me to make my next move.

"Excuse me, President," squeaks a short girl with dark, curly hair, successfully slicing right through the tension created any time the president stares into your eyes for too long. "Should we stay to listen in, or continue working on the issue?"

"I'd like for you all to continue the discussion amongst yourselves. If you wish, feel free to use my office. As I said before, it would be best if the rest of the student body didn't get ahold of this information yet. If you have any questions, I'll drop by in just a minute."

"Yes, President." She dips her head in a nod and scurries off, gathering the other council members and taking them next door to what must be the president's personal office.

"Even me?" a beautiful girl with dark skin and glossy black hair asks. I recognize her as the Vice President of the student council, Avni something-or-other.

"Yes, Avni, you have another task to do; I trust you didn't forget it so soon."

Avni's eyes light with understanding and she excuses herself, exiting the room so that it is only the three of us left.

"It appears you're feeling better today, Zero," the president muses as the door shuts behind us. "Though I must say, I think I prefer you when you're barely able to move or speak."

"What, so like when I'm basically dead?"

I all but feel the sting of a giant sticker labeled "IGNORED" getting slapped to my forehead as he turns to Briar, saying, "About the question you asked me regarding the creation of a new club, while it's true I can give my seal of approval to allow it, there is another requirement that needs to be dealt with first."

Briar nods, hand under her chin. "The three people requirement. We'll have that figured out by the end of the day." (I guess she trusts in what I told her.) "But is that really it? I mean, once we get that done, will you approve us?"

"Obviously, I'll need to hear the specifics of what kind of club you want to create." That should have been his first question. The fact that it wasn't … is suspicious.

"Well, we—"

"We'll give you the specifics when you tell us what your condition is," I say.

"You think he has a condition, Zero?"

"Ask him and see."

The president's mouth quirks at the side, his eyes remaining cold. "I wouldn't call it a condition—"

"But?"

"*But* someone should have taught you to keep your mouth shut when someone else is talking, *Zero*."

"If I'm quiet, will you finally get to the point?"

He sighs, glaring. "You have the patience and attention span of a child. It would almost be pitying if it weren't so annoying. As I was going to inform you before interruption, there's a little problem I want you to deal with for me." (Problem?) "Consider it a favor." (Favor?)

"A favor for what?" I scoff aloud.

But the president is already moving ahead. "I won't expect you to figure it out right away, since I've had council members working on it for the past two weeks now with little progress. But I trust you'll give it your best shot."

This sounds incredibly sketchy. It must have to do with whatever issue [Little, Dark, and Curly] was talking about before she left.

"In the meantime, I will draft your club contract. If you finish with the problem you've been given, you can come back to me and I'll give you my signature."

"We haven't agreed yet, President. Don't go getting ahead of yourself, it makes you look desperate."

"Are you worried this task will be too challenging since you don't know what it is yet? How cute."

"Cute, huh?" I take a step forward. "Keep complimenting me like that and maybe I'll give in."

"You say that like you still think you have a choice. But if you want to start a club, this is the only way I'll agree to it."

A problem for the president = just more work for me. Great. (*Is this the direction my last few months at this academy will take?*)

"And let me guess," I sigh, "when you mentioned a favor, you meant that solving this problem can be my way of repaying you for dealing with my absences. And Briar's as well." If you'll remember, my chemistry and history teachers seemed to have conveniently forgotten I walked out of their classes. (I don't think he's actually dealt with Briar's yet, though, so I added that in there to make it a reality.)

"You catch on fast." He smiles a half-smile, and my entire body feels twitchy under his gaze. "That might be the one thing I don't despise about you."

Whenever I'm in a room with him, I ought to wear a sign that says *Yeah, the feeling's mutual* just to save myself the time. "Perhaps you can clear up how exactly you managed to do that? I really don't like the idea of you being so involved in my student life." Him taking care of everything on my behalf explains why I wasn't hassled about my early departures of yesterday, but it doesn't explain how or why he did it.

"I'm your student council president; it's my job to be involved in your student life, you idiot. It was fairly simple to do, anyway. I just had to say you were called in for an unexpected council meeting that required your immediate attention."

If the teachers had bothered to check the times of any student council meetings along with the times of both my chemistry and history courses, they'd have realized his excuse for me doesn't add up at all. Of course, they didn't. It's scary, but at Kane Academy, Jordan Adrian's word is absolute. Even when it comes to some teachers. (Not that he'd have issues talking his way out of any questions someone might level at him if it came to that, the bastard.)

"Telling lies to members of the faculty? That's not very responsible of you, Prez. Do you feel no guilt?"

"I'd be happy to take you to the chairman if you'd like to face punishment, instead. You can take Thornswood with you."

(Interesting how he calls him "chairman" and not father.) Neither of us wants this outcome. So what happens when two bluffs coincide? The most stubborn wins out—

"Excuse me, but shouldn't we get back to talking about the club? I'd really rather not take a trip down to the chairman if I can help it."

We both look over to Briar, almost having forgotten she's here. Under the weight of both our stares, she shifts uncomfortably on her feet.

"Umm, whatever the problem is, I'm sure Zero and I can deal with it."

Is that so?

Before I can answer, I hear noisy footsteps approaching from down the hall. How many people is that? Ten? That seems a large number to be going around in a group after classes are finished. And clubs should already be in session.

"So, is that to say you accept the condition?" the president asks while I'm distracted.

"Yes," Briar says, accepting for both of us.

"Oh, so now it *is* a condition?"

"Good," he continues, looking at Briar, "then you're just in time to meet with the 'problem.'"

As soon as he says this, the doors burst open and a group of eleven students comes inside. Each of them looks just as upset as the last. Well, each aside from two, a boy lingering toward the back of the group and a girl with a somewhat vacant expression being led by the wrist by a particularly angry boy at the front.

"It's about damn time you guys actually take action on this," growls [Boy 29 Days Away From Getting His 30-Day Chip From Anger Management]. "If you don't do something soon, I'll do it *myself*."

I notice Avni on the left side of the group along with at least one more member from the student council.

"Have fun," the president says over his shoulder at us, making his way toward the doors. "And remember, this is a trial. If you fail, then there will be no reason for me to sign off on anything."

He nods to Avni and they walk out of the room together. Bringing this little group in to ambush us must have been the "other task" the president had reminded her of. I get the feeling that even if we had declined his offer, there was never any possible future where we walked out of this office without doing as he wanted …

Well, I already have an idea of what the "problem" might be.

Do you?

***

- **Year/age/student ranking**: N/A, 32, N/A
- **Hair**: black
- **Eyes**: brown
- **Height/Weight**: 5'6, N/A
- **Noticeable features**: high cheekbones

- **Favorite item**: a book gifted to her by her father
- **Likes**: teasing her students, teasing Zero especially, traveling, manga, leather jackets
- **Dislikes**: students who inhibit the learning of others, having her advice ignored, not getting a reaction from Zero
- **Personal comment**: "With that terrible attitude and the amount of shit he pulls, it's a miracle and a crime that Zero's rank isn't dead last."
- **Fact**: Kyouka graduated from Kane Academy, rejected offers from six Ivy League schools to travel across the country for a year, and ultimately went to MIT for graduate school before returning to the academy as a full-time faculty member.
- *Note from Zero*: "What else does Kyouka like? Well … she really enjoys baking, but, *dear god*, don't **ever** let her feed you anything she's made. Whatever it is, I guarantee you it's downright inedible. Hey, wait … You're not going to tell her I said this, are you?"

## Bonus: Q & A II

Q: Zero, what is your life motto?

Z: What? Why would you want to know that? You already have our "personal comments," isn't that enough?

Q: Look, we warned you we'd come back, so just answer, please.

Z: Fine. I guess it'd have to be … "I do what I want—it's not my fault what I want to do is nothing." Or something like that.

Q: Wow. That's …

Z: …

Q: …

Z: …

Q: … terrible.

*Zero Hale: chibi-style*

***

# Chapter 8:

## The Case Begins

"So the president couldn't even bother to stick around this time?" [Angry Boy] hisses. "Do you guys not take this seriously? Any of you? I guess it'd be different for people on the 'special,' protected student council, but for the rest of us, having your student rank drop is the same as losing a limb."

Well, that's incredibly dramatic. But I see what he's getting at.

"James," says [Pretty-But-Apathetic-Looking Girl Connected to Angry Boy], "could you try to rein it in, please? I'm tired, and your voice is too loud."

James scoffs. "Are you serious? Not you, too. Analisa, you've had six taken yourself—that's more than almost anyone else!"

Analisa frowns but doesn't pull her wrist from James' grasp.

"Actually, I think it's Daniel who's suffered the most," a frightened-looking blonde girl quietly interjects.

Several of the students shift their eyes to a dark-haired, good-looking boy toward the center of the group. Daniel offers a small, amiable smile, seeming to be meant to reassure the rest, though a worried edge remains in his light eyes.

"Yeah, well, at least *Daniel* isn't graduating in the next few months, though."

"Hey, don't talk like that to him," a spunky girl I recognize as a junior cuts back at James. "You think you're the only ones with real problems just 'cus you're seniors? Gimme a break."

"Please, there's no need to argue like this," Daniel cuts in, trying to diffuse the situation. "I'm sure we'll all find a way to work through—"

"No one's saying you aren't being affected, Nina, but you can't understand the stress we're under in our final semester!"

Well, it looks like this is the situation I anticipated. (I just hope it's not too much of a headache in the end.)

"You're here concerning the missing assignments," I say, interrupting the bickering and getting confirmation from the surprised glint in several of the group members' eyes. "Have you all been targeted or are some of you just here for moral support?"

"By 'missing' I guess you mean *stolen*," James seethes. "And no one's done a goddamn thing about—wait." He looks me over as if seeing me for the first time. "Why are you here? What do you have to do with any of this?"

"We're here to help solve the problem," Briar answers, entirely serious. "If your assignments really were stolen, then I promise we will figure out a way to stop it from ever happening to you again."

"What the hell? Is the student council taking on freelancers now?" James mutters, sounding halfway between suspicious and confused.

"If we're going to do this, can we get on with it?" voices the boy lingering on the outside of the group. It's Alek Slate. "I'm starting to get bored. And there's nothing I hate more than that." He's as jarringly captivating to look at as usual, his half-black, half-dyed-green hair making his bright green eyes pop noticeably. Then there's the Band-Aid over the bridge of his nose, two on his left cheek, and the bright blue and pink sticker on his right cheek just above his jaw … What a weirdo.

James turns his annoyance toward Alek. "No one's forcing you to stay, Slate."

"And yet here I am anyway—aren't you lucky?"

"Mr. Slate is right," the other student council member I recognized, a girl, finally steps forward, "we should focus on the problem at hand. And Mr. Blackwell is right in that arguing will get us nowhere."

I survey the rest of the group. Roughly half look determined to be here, while the other half are carefully avoiding my gaze and looking like they're about to make a bolt for the door.

"Are you facilitating this?" I ask the council girl as she steps to the forefront between us and the complainants. The answer is a clear yes.

"That's correct. I'm Charlotte Atwell, the student council's parliamentarian."

"In that case, I want all the information the student council has compiled on the issue so far."

[Council Girl—I Mean, Charlotte] stares at me, slightly flustered. "Information compiled?"

"You were all in an emergency meeting about it yesterday, weren't you? Surely the entire council isn't so useless that you've discovered *nothing*." I'm going out on a limb here, but the president was obviously already familiar with the issue, and both he and Alek had been missing from at least some of their classes yesterday.

"Well, yes ... we were discussing it yesterday, and I do have some information we can give you, I suppose."

"Wonderful." The only reason I can think of for her to be hesitant about handing over what they already have on the case is that the president instructed her to avoid giving it to me if possible. A test through and through, huh?

"Hang on a minute," Alek says, pointing a finger at me. "How do we know you're trustworthy? You have no stakes in any of this. So what are you doing here?"

"I asked the same damn thing earlier and you brushed it off and said we should get a move on!"

"Please, James, if you could stay focused on the issue at hand that would be great. Zero, I asked you a question, do you have an answer?"

As if it isn't clear I'm here on behalf of the student council ... "Actually, you're wrong, Alek. You see, I do have stakes. Or, more accurately," I pull Briar to me, to the shock of her and everyone else in the room, "*we* have stakes. Though she's been worrying how to come forward about it until now, Briar's had two assignments of hers stolen over the past two weeks. As her partner for a very important final project, I can't just let her be targeted by this thief, now can I? So we're joining the cause of getting to the bottom of this thing."

At this moment, I am glad for Briar's high aptitude for academics. Her rank may not be as impressive as the rest in this room, but it's still a believable lie. And while I can feel her confused stare, she smartly looks away after a second, going along with me.

Alek glances at Briar and then shrugs, losing interest in the matter. "Fine. Then let's continue."

"Oh, I'm sorry, are *you* the one facilitating this now?" James asks, crossing his arms.

"I could be."

"Why, you little—"

"That's enough, James, Alek." Analisa makes an unexpected, assertive stance between the two. "This case isn't going to make any progress unless you allow Charlotte to do her job."

*Case.* Is that what we're calling this?

"Indeed," Charlotte agrees. "While I get everything sorted, why don't you all go around the room and introduce yourselves to Mr. Hale and Ms. Thornswood? They will be assisting us with the issue and so you may answer any questions they have."

Briar nods her head, still taking this all very seriously.

"Right …" James clearly remains suspicious, but I suspect he's too relieved to finally be having real meetings facilitated by the student council to raise much more of a fuss.

I survey the group more closely, paying extra attention to one person in particular that I made eye contact with a little earlier in the discussion. As it stands, here are how the introductions go (points of interest only):

1. Daniel Blackwell (Steps up after Analisa physically holds James back by his collar): "These have been a difficult past few weeks, for all of us, but I am confident we'll get to the bottom of whatever is going on. I promise those in my grade will cooperate to the full extent of our abilities."

2. Nina Taylor: "You guys better fix this frickin' mess. I'm missing soccer practice for this, you know?"

3. Maggie Arrowood: "I-I don't know how much help I'll be on this investigation, but I'll do my best, like Daniel said."

4. Alek Slate: "I showed up today out of curiosity. But I'll leave if it turns out to be less interesting than I thought."

5. James Hudson: "Jeez, don't any of you have any respect for your upperclassmen? How come the juniors started first? I'm missing club practices too, goddamnit."

6. Analisa Weston: "James, shut up. Zero, you mentioned a thief, earlier. Is that to say that you agree the assignments and tests have gone missing due to ill intent? … I see."

7. Thomas Kang: "Regardless of what the rest of my classmates do, I won't back out of this investigation until I get results. The lack of proactiveness this 'elite' academy has taken so far has been nothing

short of appalling."

8. March Haskins: "My mother is going to end my life if my grades and rank don't improve again soon."

9. Sam Dixon: "I-I'd like to go home, please ..."

10. Briar: "Right! Let's all do our best."

In other words:

1. [Nice And Seemingly Respected Pretty Boy]

2. [Feisty Sports Girl]

3. [Blondie Who's Good At Eliciting Sympathy]

4. [Half N' Half]

5. [Ill-Tempered Senior Boy With A Passion For Upper-classmen Respect]

6. [Cleverly Blank-Expressioned Girl With Decent Conflict Resolution Skills]

7. [Tall, Serious Senior Who Cannot Converse With Others Sans Scowling]

8. [Soon-To-Be Murdered By Her Mother Girl]

9. [Fairly Forgettable Sophomore Boy Who Is A Member Of The Go-Home-After-School Club]

10. And [Troublesome Girl Whose Blatant Lack Of Concern For Her Own Safety Is Probably Going To Make The Remainder Of My Life Much, Much Harder]

So, this is what I'll be working with, huh?

## 8 ½

After returning with a rather thick file, Charlotte makes the suggestion that we all take a seat at the conference table to make things easier. As it stands, students from the same grade level seem to stick together, choosing seats beside each other, with the exception of Alek, who chooses to sit directly beside James—much to the latter's annoyance.

"Hey, you following me around or what? Go sit where you're supposed to."

"I had no idea there were seating assignments. And is there really something wrong with me wanting to be close to the upperclassman I so admire?"

"You son of a—*ouch!* Was that really necessary, Ana?"

When making our way to the seats, I have Briar go in front of me while stopping at the chair directly to the right of the head of the table, successfully getting Briar to sit front and center while Charlotte takes her place at Briar's left. I receive a strange look from my art class partner, but I pretend not to notice and she accepts the seating arrangement regardless.

It's true I may have to do a fair bit of the talking during this trial put upon us, but since it essentially marks the start of our club, it would be best if people didn't see me in an authoritative position. Instead, I can slowly nudge Briar toward fulfilling that role until she's able to comfortably take it on by herself. (Either that or find someone else she wants in the role—either is fine with me.)

"I assume since you asked for it now that you're ok with sharing the contents of this file with everyone in this room? It's true some of this was discussed yesterday, but the exact details contained here have not been shared as of yet." Charlotte looks at me, but when I defer the question to Briar by looking to her myself, she shifts focus.

"Uhh ..." Briar trails off, noticing everyone's waiting stares. Of course, they all wish to see the total of what's been gathered, as well.

I give her a nearly imperceptible nod and she swallows, a bit of relief easing the tension visible in her features.

"Yes, that is all right with us."

"Very well, then." Charlotte opens up the file and spreads out several pages of documents. As she goes about explaining their contents, I look each of them over individually, allowing Briar to focus on listening like the rest of our complainants.

The information the council put together is roughly what I expected it to be: Lists of all the students affected, their grade and ranks (both official and unofficial), the classes that have been targeted, the assignments and tests that have disappeared, statements taken from various complainants and teachers alike, and notes about any suspicious activity in recent weeks. Meanwhile, Charlotte's retelling gives a vague but accurate account of everything I'm looking at. There are still some other pieces of info that I want filled in, but, considering the president's actions of the past few days, a way of getting that info should arrive any minute now.

Unfortunately for me, even with only what I currently have in front of me, I am beginning to get a foreboding inkling that this might not be the best challenge to force Briar to the head of.

*If I'm right about what I'm seeing, this is not good for anyone.* **Very** *not good …*

(Why must all my plans go awry?)

"Now that you all have an understanding of exactly what's going on here, I will go over the timeline of these events. We are in our third week since the start of the semester, and in week one, the class History of Europe was hit first that very Monday, followed by English 300 on Tuesday, English 100 and Logistics & Enterprise on Wednesday, Advanced Algebra and Physics on Thursday, and, lastly, Visual

Studies and Mastering the Written Word on Friday. Week two saw Chemistry and Economics taken on Monday, then Humanities that Tuesday, Popular Literature and English 400 on Wednesday, Astronomy and Literary Analysis on Thursday, and Comparative Government, US History, and Psychology that Friday. As of this week, ah, well, Media & Technology was targeted Monday and Tuesday saw Economics hit."

I continue to pay attention to Charlotte as I check back over the charts for the affected students. It's an overwhelming sum of classes and students when said aloud in one go, but it aligns roughly with what I expected after seeing the ranking board this morning. (However, this pattern I'm putting together …)

"And you should know, while the vast majority of these instances have occurred, obviously, since the beginning of this semester, the first known case actually occurred at the end of last semester. Ms. Arrowood can give you more details on that fact seeing as the information was not volunteered to us until yesterday," she finishes.

Out of the corner of my eye, I watch Maggie shift uncomfortably at being called out like that, pulling at the hem of her slightly too-big uniform shirt. But Daniel places a hand on her shoulder and she quickly settles down. He then provides clarification on her behalf. "The courses she was targeted in last semester were English 300 and Organic Chemistry."

"Charlotte," I say, and look up from the documents at her.

"Y-yes?"

"Did the president offer any particular advice to you and the council when you presented these pieces of data?"

"Well, no … He mostly listened and instructed us on what data to collect, not yet what to do with that data. I assume that's why he brought you and Ms. Thornswood on. He's a busy man and doesn't have time for every issue that comes up."

"But this isn't just *some* issue," James speaks up loudly. "If Hale is right, then it's just like I told you when we first came to you about this whole thing—your school's best students are being attacked! On purpose! These 'details' you have here prove that."

"So from what you've all gathered, these … attacks have been random aside from the fact that they generally are aimed at students of high rank?" Briar asks in clarification.

"Yes, that is correct."

James shakes his head, seeming ready to jump in again, but Analisa quiets him with a cutting look.

"And what significant event occurred this Monday?" I ask, pointing my question to the entire group.

Student council meetings that occur during the school day are rare, with mid-day meetings that involve non-council members being even rarer. If they all got together during class time yesterday, it would have to be for a surprising and important revelation regarding the previous night. Whatever it is, it's likely the 'information' the president mentioned he didn't want spreading around to the rest of the student body.

"The MO changed," Analisa answers before Charlotte can. "Rather drastically. Instead of a single assignment or just a few, a total of twenty tests were stolen."

I raise a brow. That's quite a number—an entire class, to be accurate.

"Which class was that again?" Briar asks.

"Media & Technology."

"Nobody outside of this room and the student council knows this yet as we've made an agreement with Mr. Henderson, the teacher, to avoid submitting grades for the test until we've gotten closer to figuring this out," Charlotte adds, not needing to expressly state that we are expected to follow their lead on this.

"Thank god for Mr. H," the girl called Nina sighs, shaking her head, "he's a real one."

"Yes, his cooperation has been appreciated. However, the incidents didn't stop there; the very next day, things went back to normal."

Normal, eh? This specific incident from Monday wasn't written about in the documents from the file—they must really be trying to keep it under wraps. Or, they were simply discussing something completely different yesterday. I wonder if any of them, aside from the president, understand just what this means for the case and the type of person we're dealing with.

"You know," Alek drawls lazily from his kicked-back position, "I think I have a way to solve all our issues."

"If you're going to say security cameras then shut your trap because you know damn well we've already tried getting that approved—"

"No, I'm not talking about cameras, Jamesy. I'm talking about updating the entire academy's system of turning in tests and assignments in the first place. It's simple, really; if we didn't allow certain teachers to have their own archaic ways, we could just have things submitted online. Then, once your work's in, it's in. No one can come and steal it out from under you."

Nina frowns and rolls her eyes from across the table. "Well, duh. If we could fix it that easily then none of us would be here in the first place. But there's no way we could ever get every single teacher here on board with that in time to make any damn difference for us. Plus, it's not like all these things could be turned in online, anyway. A lot of the missing work has been quizzes and tests, in case you didn't notice, which are always taken *in* class."

Alek shrugs, unconcerned with his argument being shut down.

"Umm, but about the security cameras, maybe if we all banded together they wouldn't be able to say no?" Maggie suggests, pulling again at her large sleeves.

"Unfortunately," Daniel begins, another small, wry smile on his face, "that's not the way this academy operates. They'd consider security cameras as both an unnecessary action on their part and an easy way out for us. As their top students, if we can't get ourselves out of a mess they see as being of our own making, then we aren't truly deserving of our spots, anyway."

It seems he has a better understanding of the underlying truth and values of this school than most of its students. But what else can you expect from the number three of the entire junior grade? (Though I guess if things continue to pan out the way they are, he'll end up around number one hundred and three of the grade.)

"That's such bullshit!" Nina groans. "Do they want us to suffer?"

"I suppose the way I phrased that sounded rather negative. Another way to look at it is that they have faith in us. The academy trusts us to get through this on our own."

"... Still stupid ..."

"It's truly a strange situation we find ourselves in," Analisa muses, a hand under her chin. "Whoever this is, what they're doing, they wouldn't be able to get away with it at a normal school."

"Huh? What're you getting at?" James asks, not yet following.

"Always a step behind, Jamesy," Alek adds unproductively.

"Oh, like you get it? Yeah right."

Alek just smirks, not bothering to prove whether or not he does in fact "get it."

Daniel, on the other hand, nods in agreement with Analisa. "Yes, that's true. Aside from what we've already pointed out regarding the academy's stance on these matters, since nearly all teachers are afforded their own classroom unshared with any other staff member, they're able to leave most work behind overnight, rather than always taking it all back to their living accommodations. In a way, that kind of arrangement opens up the perfect opportunity for the situation we're seeing now."

"Of course," Analisa cuts back in, "it doesn't explain *how* they're doing it. Just because, in the least strict sense of the word, it's *possible*, that has no bearing on the fact that someone pulling this off is wholly improbable."

She's right. The entirety of this "problem" is, in her own use of the word, improbable.

James looks disgruntled. "All right, so what exactly does that mean? Like, does any of this tell us anything?"

No one has an answer.

"As of this semester, who was the first to have their work go missing?" I ask, looking to move the conversation forward. I already know the answer, thanks to the thorough documents, but I want Briar to hear as well.

"That would be me." Analisa raises her hand. "The class was History of Europe, in case you're wondering."

"And the most recent?"

"Me," Thomas says frankly. "Economics, obviously. Because the teacher refused to see reason and would not agree to our request that previously targeted classes take all their work home."

My attention catches on Briar, noticing that she appears to be lost in thought throughout all of this. "Hmm, actually ..." she begins but cuts herself off, taking another second to think something over.

"What?" Nina presses. "What are you gonna say? Just spit it out."

I lock eyes with the impatient girl. She swallows and her gaze skirts sideways, a defiant little pout on her mouth. (Cutting remarks from classmates can't be good for Briar's self-esteem and social standing, so, at least at the moment, I cannot allow them to slide.)

"Nina." Daniel says her name like a light warning and my opinion of the boy rises a notch. "Remember what we've talked about."

"I just mean if you have something to say, we'd all like to hear it, or whatever," she corrects, sullenly feigning a newfound interest in picking at a rip in her uniform jacket.

Briar nods, her brows still slightly pinched together. "Well, I know we already went through this, in a way, but I was just thinking it might help to go through each class in order along with what was taken and from whom and put it all into a single document or a chart that we can all look at together. Maybe we'll notice something we hadn't before. A pattern, even."

"I see, that's not a bad idea," Analisa agrees. "As of right now, everything we have is here but separated. There might be missing information that we haven't even considered yet."

Finally finished analyzing its contents for the meantime, I slide the entire file over to Briar to look at. A pattern. Yes, I just need a second to see if I'm rushing ahead of myself and seeing things or if it's all as it seems. (If only I had Lila's mind, I'd have already sorted through it all with a clear mental image of the entire case and all its individual elements connected perfectly.)

"What do you think, Zero?"

"I think that's exactly what we should be doing, Briar," I answer her. "We need each piece of the puzzle in one place if we're ever going to get an idea of the full picture. Analisa, would you be willing to write it out for us as Briar reads off the data?"

"Of course."

"Actually, that's a lot for one person to read. Briar, pass around some of the documents to the others and you can take turns." I've already mostly memorized the contents, so if someone attempts to slip something by, it won't go unnoticed. "I'll start creating a chart as well and then we can compare the one I make to the one Analisa makes to see if there are any mistakes or notable differences in how the facts are organized."

"Is that really necessary?" questions Analisa.

"Indulge me."

No one steps up in dissent and we begin. In the few seconds it takes for each of them to get their hands on the documents, I shut my eyes and clear my mind of everything else as I run through the data again in my head.

Yep.

It's the same as I calculated before. My ill suspicion appears to be correct; this case does not offer the right opportunity to push Briar toward taking control. No, something … *else* is going on here.

This calls for a change in tactics.


In the end, the chart Analisa puts together is a good one, matching up well with the one I created in my head. So rather than giving you the raw data to look over yourself, I'll simply show you it (at least, the important parts):

# The Charts

**Time Frame**: Beginning of the semester — present (January 20 - Feb 4), not including the original incident of last semester (final two weeks before winter break)

**Affected Classes** (in order of incident) + affected students (rank and year included, representatives starred):

<u>Week one</u>:

| Monday - Jan 20 | Tuesday - Jan 21 | Wednesday - Jan 22 | Thursday - Jan 23 | Friday - Jan 24 |
|---|---|---|---|---|
| 1. History of Europe Students: Analisa Weston* (2/150, senior)<br><br>Assignments: Paper | 1. English 300 Students: Daniel Blackwell* (3/150, junior) Fredrich Sanderson (27/150, junior)<br><br>Assignments: Paper, Quiz | 1. English 100 Students: Seth Parker (134/150, freshman)<br><br>Assignments: Worksheet<br><br>2. Logistics & Enterprise Students: Analisa Weston* Daniel Blackwell* Nina Taylor* (9/150, junior)<br><br>Assignments: Test | 1. Advanced Algebra Students: Emma-Carla Tosto (56/150, freshman)<br><br>Assignments: Quiz<br><br>2. Physics Students: James Hudson* (8/150, senior)<br><br>Assignments: Worksheet | 1. Visual Studies: Art History Students: Eli Young (94/150, junior)<br><br>Assignments: Art Piece<br><br>2. Mastering the Written Word Students: Daniel Blackwell* Nina Taylor* Alek Slate* (30/150, junior) Kirstina Collins (71/150, junior)<br><br>Assignments: Paper, Reflection |

<u>Week two</u>:

| Monday - Jan 27 | Tuesday - Jan 28 | Wednesday- Jan 29 | Thursday - Jan 30 | Friday - Jan 31 |
|---|---|---|---|---|
| 1. Chemistry<br>Students:<br>Yasmin Iravani<br>(84/150, sophomore)<br><br>Assignments:<br>Worksheet<br><br>2. Economics<br>Students:<br>Analisa Weston*<br>James Hudson*<br>Thomas Kang*<br>(6/150, senior)<br>Alek Slate*<br><br>Assignments:<br>Project, Worksheet | 1. Humanities:<br>Religion & Culture<br>Students:<br>Analisa Weston*<br>James Hudson*<br>Maggie Arrowood*<br>(18/150, junior)<br><br>Assignments:<br>Project, Reflection | 1. English 400<br>Students:<br>Analisa Weston*<br>Parker Lee<br>(24/150, senior)<br><br>Assignments:<br>Test, Report<br><br>2. Popular Literature<br>Students:<br>Ollie Adams<br>(122/150, junior)<br><br>Assignments:<br>Worksheet | 1. Astronomy<br>Students:<br>Uliana Lopatkina<br>(14/150, sophomore)<br><br>Assignments: Quiz<br><br>2. Literary Analysis<br>Students:<br>Maggie Arrowood*<br>Nina Taylor*<br>Daniel Blackwell*<br>Camila Santiago<br>(134/150, junior)<br>March Haskins*<br>(7/150, sophomore)<br>Sam Dixon*<br>(19/150, sophomore)<br><br>Assignments:<br>Worksheet, Paper | 1. Comparative<br>Government<br>Students:<br>Ivy Wicker<br>(66/150, senior)<br><br>Assignments: Paper<br><br>2. Psychology of Man<br>Students:<br>March Haskins*<br>Sam Dixon*<br><br>Assignments: Quiz,<br>Worksheet, Project<br><br>3. US History<br>Students:<br>Nikolai Anderson<br>(11/150, junior)<br><br>Assignments: Paper |

<u>Week three</u>:

| Monday - Feb 3 | Tuesday - Feb 4 | Wednesday - Feb 5 | Thursday - Feb 6 | Friday - Feb 7 |
|---|---|---|---|---|
| 1. Media &<br>Technology<br>Students:<br>Everyone in class<br>(range: 97/150 -<br>3/150)<br>Repeat targets:<br>Daniel Blackwell*<br>Nina Taylor*<br><br>Assignments: Test | 1. Economics<br>Students:<br>Thomas Kang*<br><br>Assignments:<br>Quiz | N/A | N/A | N/A |

**Note** 1: Though assignments and tests were taken on the days indicated, they were not technically discovered missing until the following morning or afternoon.

**Note 2:** Many representatives had multiple assignments and/or tests stolen in a single incident.

**Core representatives (nine total) ordered by number missing:**

- **Seniors:**
1. <u>Analisa Weston</u> (rank 2, unofficial rank 89, six missing)
2. <u>James Hudson</u> (rank 8, unofficial rank 75, four missing)
3. <u>Thomas Kang</u> (rank 6, unofficial rank 54, three missing)

- **Juniors:**
1. <u>Daniel Blackwell</u> (rank 3, unofficial rank 103, eight missing)
2. <u>Nina Taylor</u> (rank 9, unofficial rank 78, five missing)
3. <u>Maggie Arrowood</u> (rank 18, unofficial rank 51, four missing)
4. <u>Alek Slate</u> (rank 30, unofficial rank 69, three missing)

- **Sophomores:**
1. <u>March Haskins</u> (rank 7, unofficial rank 63, three missing)
2. <u>Sam Dixon</u> (rank 19, unofficial rank 50, two missing)

**Note 3:** ranks of representatives range from as high as 2/150 to as low as 30/150 (which is not technically low but is still notable).

**Note 4:** representatives comprise the nine students who formed the group to speak with the student council. They make up the students with the most work stolen, as well as the majority of those targeted more than once, and have been chosen by fellow students to represent their concerns for the issue.

At the bottom, I see Analisa included profiles of all the affected students (~~complainants~~ representatives and otherwise). It features their year, rankings, class schedules, and club affiliations. Every single student is a part of some club or sports team, with, once again, the exception of Alek (no surprise there). These extracurriculars include soccer, volleyball, basketball, swimming, fencing, ballet, orchestra, private instrument lessons, art club, literature club, home economics club, film club, photography club, history club, mathematics club, and chess club. Again, it's a wide variety, to be sure.

Of course, there's a notable exception missing from this list …

There's also a section dedicated to unaffected students whose ranks are actually going to benefit from the plummeting ones of their targeted counterparts. But the data here is limited by comparison. It would seem the president didn't instruct them to focus on this area. All in all, not particularly interesting.

An area he did include info on is the students (affected and unaffected) who requested for the representatives to, well, represent them. And that *is* something I find interesting.

•••

So then, what do **you** make of all this?

You might not yet know, but I'll still be asking you again in the near future, so prepare yourself.

"All right," Analisa begins, looking at me expectantly once we've finished going through her chart, "where's yours? I'd like to make the comparisons as you suggested, Zero."

Casually, I push the paper I've been working on to the center of the table. As I do, a weighted hush falls over the room. Then—

"What the hell is that?" Nina asks.

Slowly, Analisa picks it up and looks at it, a small crack

running through her calm exterior in the form of a slight crease on her forehead.

"You think the one responsible," she says, maintaining her composed, steady cadence, "is among us, in this room."

"Huh?!" A noise of confused protest slips from Nina's consistently vocal mouth.

Daniel shakes his head, eyes widened with what looks like real horror. "It can't be. I—I don't …"

"Lemme see that, Ana." James snatches the paper from Analisa's hands. "The hell—this ain't a chart. What're you sayin' with this?"

Apparently, James is ruffled enough to nearly completely drop the careful masking of his southern accent.

"I think it's fairly obvious what I'm saying. But if you need someone to spell it out for you, Analisa should be up to the task."

He slams the paper back down on the table and the rest of the representatives who haven't already looked at it up close gather in. While it may not be my *best* work, it's certainly not the worst I've ever done.

In great detail, I drew the likeness of the council room and included in it ten sheep sitting around the table with one, large, grinning wolf hiding amongst them. *To the sheep who have all gathered in the killing pen, now the real fun begins.*

Briar is the last to take a close examination of it. She leans down, looking at the drawing from all angles.

"Wow," she says, mostly to herself, "this is very good."

"This is very good?" Nina scoffs. "Do you hear yourself right now?"

"We're representatives in the middle of an investigation, not students hanging out in art class after hours. *Drawing* isn't what you should be focused on." This exasperated snap comes from dear

Thomas whose tan skin is starting to turn pale.

"Look, sure, objectively speaking I guess it's an ok drawing, but couldn't you have just told us straight up? I mean, I don't get it."

"Wow, that's a first, Nina."

"Tch, shut the hell up, Slate! You've done nothing helpful this entire time."

"Nina, it's all right. Let's just refocus, ok?"

"Come on, Daniel! How am I supposed to just sit here and let him say this crap to me?"

"Please, can I go home yet?"

"No, you can't," Analisa responds to the increasingly anxious-looking sophomore, Sam, before James can jump in on the back-and-forth between Nina and Alek. "None of us are going anywhere." She turns to me. "Zero, explain yourself."

All eyes—at least, the ones not already looking in my direction—pivot to me.

I place my chin in my hand, crafting a languid smirk on my face. "Someone here is a liar. And they're willing to betray all of you in order to get what they want. Those are just the facts of the case."

"Facts ..." Analisa repeats at the same time Briar murmurs, "A liar."

"A 'traitor,' so to speak." I hold a long pause as everyone waits for me to speak again, for me to give them answers. But I have no intention of giving them anything of the sort, yet. "All right. That's enough for today. You're all dismissed."

Immediately, the room erupts into a symphony of indignation.

James: *slams fists on table* "This is bullshit!"

Nina: "You can't dismiss us just like that! Who do you think you are?!"

Charlotte: "A-are you sure, Zero? I think we can make a bit more progress—"

Analisa: "I'm not following your line of thinking. This hardly counts as an explanation of anything."

Thomas: "Of course you'd end up being even *less* helpful than the council. This is what happens when the president allows his work to shift off to the untrained and unqualified."

Maggie: "Does this mean we can go now?"

Daniel: *sigh* "If that's what you think is best for now."

March: "Please, you have to help us! If my scholarship is taken away, this is it for me! Please!"

Alek: "Hahaha!"

Briar: "....."

Sam: "Oh, thank god. We can go home."

The doors suddenly crash open and Marina marches through, right into the brewing eye of the hurricane. Later than I expected, but here she is. And she doesn't look happy (so she fits right in).

"Marina," I say, as if we're just two acquaintances coming together for a class project, "so kind of you to join us."

She folds her arms, already having moved on from the strange situation she's walked in on. "President Jordan sent me here."

"Yes, he did," I affirm. I knew he'd send her in eventually. I'm surprised it took as long as it did.

"He said you'd be expecting me."

I nod.

"Well? What's going on? Is anyone gonna tell me or are you all just gonna stare at me?!"

"Actually, we just wrapped up here." I clasp my hands together on the table. "But I'm sure we'll have something useful for you to do soon.

We'll meet here, in this room, this time tomorrow." I do have something I want from her, but it can wait.

"But, Zero …" Charlotte's mouth is open as if she's going to continue her sentence, but nothing else comes out.

Analisa, who's been watching quietly, steps in once again. "If nothing is done now, they will attack again by tomorrow. More students will be hurt, including students in this room. I know you think one of us is … well, the 'traitor,' as you've titled them, but that doesn't mean we can just give up."

"No one's said anything about giving up."

"Oh? Then what do you propose we should do?"

"As of now, I say … we ignore them."

"What?!"

I can see Marina shifting on her feet from the corner of my eye, impatient at being left out of the loop. Without looking at her, I make a gesture toward one of the open seats. "You can sit down, Marina."

She scoffs but does as I say (though not before noisily dragging the chair into the space between me and Briar).

Analisa is still waiting for a better answer, as is everyone else. Posture relaxed, I lean forward. "Whoever this is, all they are is a childish little attention-obsessed whore." Breaths of surprise suck in around me. "Why continue to expend energy on them? At the rate they're going, it's a short matter of time before the traitor all but unmasks themselves."

"You think we can just ignore them? Are you for real?" Nina asks. "But isn't that, like, just taking the easy way out? I mean, how can that solve anything?"

"They believe themselves to be very clever, but they're just the same as all the other desperate, acknowledgment-seeking students that crawl all over this school like maggots. There's nothing special about them. They may have stepped out of their comfort zone on Monday with that little stunt with the tests, but they don't have it in them to do something like that again."

At this point, all eyes are on me ... except for one pair. Briar, I notice, is glancing at every other person in the room, examining their expressions. Smart girl. Nothing works for getting people to show glimpses of their true selves quite like pissing them off.

I re-examine one last, possibly significant detail and dismiss them all again, this time with a promise that ensures they'll leave.

Me: "If you all continue to do as I say, we'll have the traitor caught by the end of Friday."

Analisa: "You mean the end of next Friday?"

Me: "I mean the Friday that's coming in two days."

Thomas: *incredulous snort* "We'll just see about that."

James: "You better be tellin' the truth or I swear I'll make you sorry, Hale. I don't give a damn about the kind of reputation you got."

Briar: "What do you mean 'make him sorry?' Are you planning to try and hurt Zero?"

Analisa: "Two days? That sounds impossible but ... Fine. I'll put my trust in you until you give me a reason not to."

Charlotte: "Um, I suppose we will all meet here tomorrow at four p.m. For now, everyone can go back to their rooms."

Sam: *relieved sigh* "Back to our rooms."

March: "I don't know if I can make it back to my room, I'm shaking too much."

Nina: "This is stupid—I'm outta here." *looks down at her partially ripped sleeve* "Damn. Looks like the tear is getting bigger. Daniel, you can fix it, right?"

Maggie: "Wait, Nina! I'll come with you! Let's go back to our room."

Daniel: "Ok, see you tomorrow. March, I can walk you back, all right? Let's go. And yes, Nina, I'll fix your sleeve."

Marina: "Ugh, seriously, why was I sent here if we didn't even do anything?"

Alek: "Heh. I have a feeling things are about to get interesting."

***

### Daniel Blackwell

- **Year/age/student ranking**: Junior, 17, 3 of 150
- **Hair**: brown
- **Eyes**: blue
- **Height/Weight**: 6'0, 176 lbs.
- **Noticeable features**: classically pleasing features, bright blue eyes
- **Favorite item**: a "lucky" tie gifted to him by fellow student Alina Carter
- **Likes**: helping others, figuring out peaceful solutions, spending time with friends, ensuring his classmates are doing well
- **Dislikes**: conflict
- **Personal comment**:

"Oh, you'd like me to give a comment—" *girls calling Daniel's name in the distance* "Sorry, could we have a rain check on this?"

- **Fact**: Daniel is in love with a good friend of his. So, despite being one of the most sought-after boys at the academy, he has never pursued a romantic relationship with any of his admirers. Also, he has trained in Taekwondo since the age of 10, though he stopped upon coming to the academy.

## Nina Taylor

- **Year/age/student ranking**: Junior, 16, 9 of 150
- **Hair**: dark brown
- **Eyes**: brown
- **Height/Weight**: 5'7, 133 lbs.
- **Noticeable features**: athletic frame
- **Favorite item**: the blue pen Daniel gave to her last semester for her studies/the set of matching PJs she shares with her co-captain, Alina

- **Likes**: soccer, winning, beating other people at things, competition
- **Dislikes**: losing, homework, people who pick on others
- **Personal comment**: "When I find out who the traitor is, *first* I'm gonna punch their lights out, *then* I'mma knock their teeth out and—hey, wait, you're not actually gonna use this as my comment, are you?"
- **Fact:** Nina is roommates with Maggie. She is also co-captain of the girls' soccer team with Alina Carter and known for her powerful athletic ability. She's lagged behind in academics the past few years, but, thanks to the help of Daniel, she has worked hard to improve her scores. This is the first semester she's been in the top 10. Now, if only she could apply that dedication to keeping her uniforms intact …

**Kane Academy Fact:** The Kane Academy words are *"Sui Super Omnia."* Translating to "Self Above All."

**Zero Fact:** Zero used to have a popular, anonymous MyTube channel in which he—ah! Hey, Zero, you can't do this! Let us speak the tru—

**A Note to You, the Reader:** If you are having difficulty reading the charts, please make your way to zerohale.com and select **The Charts**. And if you wish to see all profile pictures in color, please select **Characters**.

***

# Chapter 9:
## Traitor

Everyone clears out of the room aside from two other people. Marina (still annoyed) and Briar (confused) sit side by side, bursting at their seams with questions.

"Marina, why are you still here?"

"Whuahh?!?" Was that a human noise? "You told me to sit!"

"My apologies. You can go, too."

"I'm not going anywhere!" She crosses her arms and digs herself further into her seat. "I have every right to be here. President Jordan is the one who told me to come, and you don't have more authority than him. Just more attitude." (Debatable.)

*Your Opinion: Who has more attitude? (Zero will not be shown your answer.)*

1. *Zero* __

2. *Jordan* __

Briar raises her hand.

I hold back my desire to facepalm and nod at her. "Yes, go ahead, Briar. Also, there's no need for you to raise your hand."

"Do you know which of them is the traitor, Zero?"

I shrug. "I'm not even sure there actually *is* a traitor among them. It's just a fair possibility."

"What?!" squawks Marina, ten decibels too loud. "You don't even know? Then why did you say all that?"

"Because it would be much more convenient for me if it is true."

"*Huh???*"

"Think about it. If you want to get technical, anyone in the school could be a suspect. But that's not very likely, is it? This is a very direct and calculated attack focused on a very specific set of students of a very specific quality." I lounge back. "Even *if* the whole school *could* technically be a suspect, that would be wayyyy too much work. And it makes much more sense that whoever is responsible has personal stakes in the matter, making it more likely that they're closely tied to the case, in one way or another. Concentrating our focus here is the best move we can make." *And then there's that pattern I saw* ... A pattern that changes the entire identity of the case. That, paired with a few other details I picked up on in the room, gives me a ~~bad~~ good feeling that I'm right.

"So you just made a random conclusion 'cus it would be too much work for you if you solved things the right way," Marina summarizes unhelpfully.

"Did you hear anything else I just said?"

She shakes her head, still disregarding my words. "And after you made such a big thing out of saying you'd catch them. What's everyone gonna think when you totally fail?"

"It's fine. What I said about the case's timeline still stands."

"That you'll uncover them by Friday? Yeah, good luck. President Jordan's been working on it for weeks and they *still* don't know who it is."

"If my theory is correct, we should get a response from the traitor by tomorrow. Depending on how they go about it, we'll be able to get more information from it."

Briar goes to raise her hand again but then lowers it when she sees my expression. "By a response, you mean ..."

"Yes, I mean that they'll be making their next move. More than likely, they're stealing assignments during club activity hours, or possibly in the middle of the night, rather than during the day when everyone is around."

"But didn't you say that the traitor won't be willing to step outside of their comfort zone again? Does more of the same really count as 'making a move?'"

"Consider everything I said during the meeting to be more of a provocation than actual fact."

"So, basically, you're full of crap," Marina sighs dramatically. "This is just great."

"In the meantime, how about you try to narrow down the pool of suspects?" I say to Briar, casually brushing Marina off when she attempts to fiddle with the cuffs of my shirt. "For the sake of the exercise, let's just agree that the traitor *does* exist. Now, how do you root them out?"

"Um …"

"First, we can start by covering what we already know. For example, if we're running with the hypothetical theory that said-traitor's plan requires they be involved in the case, then we know that they're someone meticulous—someone who's gone through the trouble of taking from their own assignments, at least occasionally, just as they've gone through the trouble of taking assignments from both classes they're in and a lot of classes they're not in. As for their goal, well, it seems pretty clear: sink the reputations and rankings of high-level students, many of whom are in the top ten of their year. But, naturally, that's only part of it; *goal* doesn't equal *motive*, after all." And 'motive' is undoubtedly the thing that's bothering me the most about all of this.

"If they've thought so far ahead, how can we ever narrow it down?" Briar asks.

"Yeah," Marina drawls with a yawn. "I've changed my mind—this whole thing is too hard. Can't we do something else for President Jordan?"

"Again, no one here asked for your assistance. You can leave at any time, Marina."

"Why're you being so rude? I can be useful too, you know."

"What I know is that showing up late and complaining is a very loose definition of the word 'useful.'"

A full-lipped pout appears on her face. "Zero Hale, if you keep being mean to me, I'm gonna—well, don't you know what I know that you don't want anyone else to know?!"

"I don't have any idea what you're talking about." In times like this, it's best not to indulge her at all.

"Really, huh? Then I guess it won't matter if I tell Briar right now. Briar, are you aware of the super popular MyTube channel Ze—"

I slap a hand over her mouth (a move I've now pulled twice in one day) and level her with a stern glare. "Marina, you have two options: stay quiet and listen, or *leave*." Then I look to Briar. "Let's start by figuring out which year the traitor is most likely in, as that is one way to help simplify the problem. Of the group that came to us, four are juniors, three are seniors, and two are sophomores. What does that tell us?"

I feel something soft and wet press forcefully against my palm.

"*Eughh.*" I make a sound of disgust and drop my hand away from Marina's mouth. (Was that ... her tongue?) I scowl murderously at her, but she glowers back just as fiercely. (Seems she's going to stay.)

Briar places her hand under her chin, brows furrowed in concentration, oblivious to what's happening right beside her. "I'm assuming what you're getting at is that we should proceed as if we know the traitor is a junior, since they're probably most interested in affecting the rankings of their own grade level and that's the year the majority of the most affected students are from. But it's by such a small amount, only one person, can that really be considered evidence?"

"You're right. That hardly provides a lead on its own. But let's think about what classes could possibly include this mix of grade levels. Because of the way our school operates, it's not uncommon for students of a particular grade level to be in some courses with students of the grade levels directly above or below them. However, very few courses could allow for, say, a senior and sophomore to intermix. Just as it would be unlikely for juniors and freshman to share together. On the other hand, juniors *will* commonly have classes with both sophomores *and* seniors, accounting for the exact variety in grade level we're dealing with. Especially if the traitor is a smart, high-level student who has many classes with seniors, which goes along with the profile we're currently operating under. And targeting students you share classes with, regardless of their year, would hold relevance due to the fact that individual class placements impact your overall ranking pretty heavily." A clever way for the school to allow some additional competition between the grade levels.

"But you said yourself that the traitor has been careful enough to steal assignments from classes other than their own. Shouldn't they have also stolen from classes including freshman?"

Pleased with her questions, I nod. "If you look at all the classes that have reported missing assignments the past few weeks, they have. There are actually two missing from classes with freshman students. English 100 and Algebra are both introductory courses, are they not? However, we've established the ones that have been hit the hardest are most definitely those of the upper three grade levels. That is where the focus of the traitor has been."

"What if they're just a very careful sophomore or senior who's covering for themselves by taking more from a year they don't intermix with often?"

"If they're someone who had thought *that* far ahead, then they would have protected themselves even more by stealing just as much from the freshman classes, too. Besides, like I mentioned before, we can't forget that this traitor has their own motive in mind, not just tricking us. There's something else they're after by manipulating these rankings. And spending too much time fooling around with red herrings would be a waste to them."

Marina shifts in her seat, already unable to remain silent. "Red 'hairings' ... What are you even talking about?"

"Our representatives all happen to be of a specific, high-level rank whereas the majority of those attacked from outside their group appear to be of random selection," (some high, some low, some in-between) "as if the traitor either didn't care about who they targeted from those classes or didn't have enough information on them to know which students to take from. Though since student rankings are publicly displayed, my guess is the former. Either way, the point is, they are not the traitor's true focus. Thus, you can consider them akin to red herrings."

Though she's the one who asked, it's clear Marina has stopped listening entirely as she goes back to attempting to mess around with the buttons on my cuffs, followed by the ring on my right-index finger. Rather than shaking her off, I stand and begin pacing the room.

There's still a lot that isn't adding up here ...

And Briar, unsurprisingly, has more questions.

"So then, given everything you've said, should we re-examine the charts and see which representative has the most crossovers with the others? Maybe that will tell us who the most-likely traitor is."

"I don't think so."

"Why?"

"One: the data doesn't narrow it down as much as you'd think." Feel free to write it out for yourself and see—they made sure to target students that happen to have a lot of courses together, in various combinations. "Two: the traitor's entire goal may not center around tricking us, but they still wouldn't be that obvious. Whoever this is has been clever enough not to get caught until now, and there's a reason for that. And three: my intuition tells me that's not all there is to this."

"Hmmm," Briar's nose scrunches slightly, "this is difficult."

"It's all right. You're doing well."

Her eyes skirt to the side. "L-let's go back to discussing the method of stealing the assignments." *deep breath* "Zero, you said it's possible they're acting in the middle of the night, but the school locks itself after club activities finish. Wouldn't it be easier to take assignments in the middle of the classes themselves? That would eliminate the need to return."

"Remember, the traitor is intent on also targeting numerous classes they are *not* enrolled in themselves."

"Yes, but would they not even do it in their own classes? Just to make it easier on themselves?"

"Always have something to push back against, huh? But no, I don't believe it was any in-the-moment sleight of hand. Let's, for a second, imagine ourselves as the traitor:"

**You have your target picked out, one of the smartest kids in class, and you know the assignment you want. The teacher comes by and collects them, all of them getting shuffled into a pile at**

the front. On your way out, you discreetly pass by the pile, reach in, and grab an assignment.

It's not your target's, of course. Unless you have an ability that rivals the best card counters in gambling, you have roughly a 1/25 chance of getting the right one—or around 4%. What do you do now? Attempt to shove the assignment back in the pile and get the right one? No, you don't have time. People are watching and staying around any longer would be suspicious—even the move you've just pulled is a risky one. Say you try this method once, you'll likely never try it again.

"Oh," Briar says, tilting her head. "You have a point. I wonder though, if they're able to get in without anyone else around, why not just take all the assignments like this Monday? Wait, then I suppose the teachers would have to act if their entire class's work kept going missing … and it might cause excessive damage for the traitor if they always had to hurt themselves each time they made a move like that."

"Yes, that's true. Well," I pause briefly, "actually, I'm not so sure …"

"What do you mean?"

"I mean that I'm not sure if 'hurting themselves' is something the traitor is trying to avoid. Whoever they are, they've already significantly damaged their rank. They knew what it would take to get themselves in the middle of this investigation, and they did it anyway."

"But why?"

I shake my head. "That question brings us back around to the most important factor we're missing: motive. If I'm being honest, I truly have no idea what's fueling them." Revenge/personal grudge? A desire to crash and burn with everyone around them? A need to stay relevant? To garner sympathy? The buildup of pressure to continuously excel that's caused them to—no. That's not quite right.

*None of this is right.*

"Is it possible this 'traitor' is doing this for … fun?" Briar offers. "I mean, what if they really are just trying to stir up trouble among those of us in the top percentage of our years?"

"No," I say, finally stopping my pacing to face her. "Consider who was here today and all the other students our group is representing." This was something I noted as soon as I saw the affected student profiles. "When looking at the club affiliations, it's clear this traitor has carefully avoided one thing: **targeting anyone in the student council along with anyone that a council member is close to**, regardless of how highly ranked they are. They've been resolutely avoiding getting the council," or more accurately, *Jordan Adrian*, "involved for as long as possible, not wanting their concrete goal to be obstructed—whatever it may be. If they were simply in it for fun, or for blood, rather, then they'd most definitely include prominent members from the council among their victims. Nothing stirs up trouble and panic quite like going straight for those considered most 'untouchable.' And whoever it is we're up against, it's clear that hitting a member of the council is not something outside of their abilities."

Briar doesn't even look down at the profiles to confirm what I'd said to be the truth. She simply stares at me with large, honey-colored eyes. "Oh."

I'll have to make Marina double-check that part about not targeting anyone within the social circles of council members, but I'm fairly certain I'm correct. At the very least, seeing how difficult the representatives found it to get in contact with the council, it's safe to say none of *them* have any ties to it.

Besides, the repetition and meticulous attention to detail—none of that strikes me as someone who simply desires chaos and chaos alone.

But then there's that damned pattern again … It's like I'm piecing together the psyche of someone with major internal contradictions. Do they want to be cautious? Or do they want to be involved? Do they want to send a message? Or do they seriously think they *need* to do this for their own personal well-being?

(Wait.)

Mmm …

I see.

An idea comes to mind that suddenly appears so obvious that it *must* be the truth. "Or at least part of the truth. It doesn't answer everything, not by a long shot, but it *does* make sense …" *Zero is unknowingly muttering to himself.

(All of this hypothetical theorizing is feeling less hypothetical by the minute.) But that's enough for now. There's only so much detective roleplay I can handle.

Deciding it's time for the next step, I go to the doors and beckon Marina over while Briar remains seated, lost in thought.

"First you clap your hand over my mouth like a muzzle, and now you're calling me over like I'm your dog or something. You really do have a lotta nerve." She shifts all her weight into one hip as if striking a pose. "Let me guess, you're about to ask me for a favor?"

"A favor?" I repeat. "No, I wouldn't call it that. I just have a request for you. And if you fulfill it, I'll consider allowing you to remain in on our investigation. After all, you want to prove you're suitable for an official position on the council, right?"

"Yep. Definitely treating me like a dog."

"What's with all this hesitation? Worried you won't be able to do what I need?"

"No! Just tell me what it is already … I can do it."

"Great. Here's what I want from you …"

After receiving her instructions, Marina looks at me sideways. "Really, I have to do *that*? I don't see how that's gonna help anything."

"It should be an easy task considering your social position."

"Is the picture part really necessary? I mean, I don't even know her that well."

"Marina, I'm counting on you."

As soon as I say this, her mouth closes on her next complaint and she makes an audacious huffing noise before resentfully taking off, leaving only two of us. Since Briar's not looking, I take the time to loosen the laces on my left boot enough so that one end trails dangerously, just above the floor. Finished, I focus my attention on her.

"You're trying to think of how the traitor could be getting into the school after hours."

Briar blinks, eyes flitting over to where I stand, arms folded, leaning back against the door. "Yes," she admits, "but none of my theories seem … right."

From my back pocket, I take out the unused security card I swiped off of the security guard's desk last night. "I have an idea about that."

Her expression grows puzzled as she focuses on the card, but before she can respond, the sound of a knock interrupts. Now, who could this—oh. Great. (Didn't I tell him I'd get back to him later *tonight?*)

Telling him to leave me alone won't work, so I stand out of the way of the entrance and say, "Come in, Myles."

The door pushes open and, sure enough, Myles Adrian walks in. Shockingly, he's alone. And not at soccer practice.

"Ah, did I just come in on the middle of something?" he asks, looking at Briar with his hands clasped in front of his chest. "Sorry—

I was told I could find you here, Zero, so I came, and—"

"Would it really make a difference to you if you were interrupting something?" I ask. "But no, we were just about to leave ourselves. What do you want?"

He smiles, a smaller, more sheepish smile than his usual, wide grin. "Well, I was hoping I could talk to you about that favor I need from you."

Yeah, that's what I figured. Favors seem to be spreading around this school like a contagious disease. "You'll have to wait, Myles. To be frank, I probably won't have the time to help you until after this case we're working is solved."

"Case?"

"But we'll be done with it by this Friday," Briar adds.

"Oh, uh, that's totally fine by me … yeah, cool, ok. This is good." He begins to back up toward the door and reopens it, that smile still on his face. "I should get over to practice now. Best of luck with your case, though! Let me know if you need anything and I'll try to lend a hand in any way I can."

"Wait." I stop him before he can shut the door. "I don't know what you want my help for, but whatever it is, I'll agree to it," his face brightens, "*as long as* you agree to accept a condition of my choosing later on. Do we have a deal?" (This is me making use of Jordan Adrian's tactics.)

Myles cocks his head, light brown strands of hair falling in his face. "That … doesn't seem right—agreeing to a deal when you don't know exactly what you're saying 'yes' to?"

"Currently, we both have unknown requests."

"And I guess it won't do me any good to ask you to tell me what yours is now?"

"Ever heard the phrase 'that's for me to know and you to find out?'"

He's suddenly back to flashing that famous, cheeky grin—a *real* one now. "You're an interesting guy, Zero. I think I might kick myself for this down the line, but ok, I accept your condition, 'whatever it is.'"

"Then as a show of good faith, I'll take you up on your offer to lend a hand."

"Oh? I didn't expect that, but sure, hit me! What can I do?"

"I want you to look into these students." I hold up a list of the people responsible for volunteering the representatives. "Please ask them this specific question: **Why did you choose your representative?**" I proceed to elaborate on the question, as well as the exact information I want Myles to get out of these students. Just like Marina's newly delegated task, this is something best done by an extremely well-liked and, in this case, well-trusted peer.

"All right," he gives me one last (slightly confused) smile along with a mini salute, "I don't get what any of this means, but you can count on me."

Then, he's gone, almost more abruptly than when he arrived.

It was annoying at first, but I'm actually glad Myles came when he did since this is information I'd have to gather one way or another. And, besides all that, I'm beginning to think it's a good thing I was interrupted before I could explain to Briar what the security card was. (I probably shouldn't have her with me when I'm testing it out.)

"Come on," I say, motioning with my head for her to join me. "We're gonna head back for now."

Briar stands and—

*CRASH!*

The sound of glass shattering from several rooms over causes both of us to freeze.

"…?"

Briar instantly looks to me as if I can determine the cause of the sound just from hearing it. In truth, I have no idea what the hell just happened, and I'd rather not spend the energy it will take to find out.

"We can probably ignore that," I say, just moments before I hear Ms. Kurima's voice echo down the hallway.

"What the—! Hey, you, go find Zero Hale for me! Tell that brat his skills are needed, and don't let him slip out of your sight once you get him!"

*sigh* "If only we'd left five minutes earlier."

The first thing I notice in the classroom is the shattered glass from Ms. Kurima's flower vase littered across the floor. The second thing I notice is Ms. Kurima herself staring at me expectantly with her hands on her hips. And the third thing I notice is the message written in dry-erase marker on the whiteboard behind her:

**ZPV SFBMMZ GFMM GPS UIJT?**

I press my fingers to my temple. "You really fell for this?"

"Excuse me?" Ms. Kurima asks, her expression simultaneously asking, "Did you seriously just ask me that?"

"That's what it says," I clarify. "The message. It's a simple shifted alphabet code. The kind grade schoolers put together to send each other secret notes in class."

"I don't know what kind of grade schooler you were, but I definitely never did that ..."

"Shifted alphabet code?" Briar tilts her head, brows furrowed.

"Yes. Essentially, you create a message you want to encrypt and then shift each letter down the alphabet by a set number. In this case, you only shift it down by one. A becomes B, C becomes D, and so on."

"So, ZPV SFB—uh, and the rest of the message, becomes ... It becomes … What was it again?"

"You really fell for this." I turn to Ms. Kurima. "I'd stay to try and explain things to you further, but I have a feeling this was all just a trick to get us to rush over here."

"You mean my favorite flower vase was broken so some idiot could play a 'grade school' level prank on you?"

"Precisely." I'm already walking out of the room, scanning the hallway for someone I know won't be here. "If it's any consolation, I promise I'll get you a new vase, Ms. Kurima." *There's no way the traitor would still be hanging around.*

"Yeah, you'd better!" she shouts after me. "And make it a nice one!"

I head straight for the student council room to see if my suspicions are correct, but something momentarily stops me when we pass back by the president's personal office. I've noticed it before in the past and never thought much of it, yet, for some reason, today it sticks out to me.

"What are you looking at Zero? Is there something on President Jordan's door?"

More like something above his door—engraved over the frame is an unusual symbol: an arrow pointing in four directions encased in a ring of three circles.

Huh. I have no idea why this detail would suddenly catch my eye, but since I'm pointing it out to you, let's just say that it will have some significance later on. For now, we can focus on the student council room and … how not a single thing appears out of place.

Seriously, everything is exactly as it was when we left it, from the furniture to the case files to the pens on the table.

Nothing is different.

So why doesn't this fact alleviate my suspicions?

9 ½

As we walk down the empty halls after returning the case documents to Charlotte, I'm reminded of the other task I have at hand—something I'd nearly forgotten about after the strangeness of that amateur code.

The plan I've put in place for this particular task will be difficult seeing as Briar doesn't go on her phone much (an understatement), but I'll improvise. I just need one other person to pull it off. (Technically I could have used Charlotte, but it didn't feel right, so … time to stall.)

Discreetly, I fully unlace my left boot mid-stride by stepping on the loosened end I'd created earlier, pretending my clumsy footing is due to my laces being untied.

Of course, Briar pauses beside me as I lean down to tie them, *slowly*, back up. Rather than standing when I'm done, however, I take out a notebook from my bag and start to look through it.

"Apologies, Briar, I know this is sudden, but I need to check for something. Feel free to go on ahead if you need to."

"No, no, I don't mind."

I intend to wait here as long as it takes for someone else to come walking down this hallway. Taking out the notebook had just been for show, a reason for my delay, but then I notice something strange sticking out of it. No, make that *two* strange things sticking out of it. The first is a message from [~~Woman I Apparently Owe A New Flower Vase To~~] Ms. Kurima that makes me roll my eyes: ***Zero, meet me this Saturday for lunch, ok? There's something we need to discuss, so don't make any plans. - KK.***

The second is something entirely different.

It's a detailed drawing ... of two wolves facing off, snarling wickedly at each other.

*So this is the reasoning behind that little distraction just now.*

"Heh, guess I was right after all," I say under my breath. (All those hypothetical deductions Briar and I made are officially *un*-hypothetical.)

One wolf is black, and the other is white; both impressively ferocious. Though there's an especially demonic gleam to the red eyes of the wolf with midnight fur, and I wonder, only partially offended, if that one is supposed to represent me. The white wolf, on the other hand, has a confrontational wickedness that draws the eye, something undeniably cunning in its expression. (Yeah, it's pretty clear who's who.)

On the front, beneath the animals, is a quick sketch of a sun. When I flip to the back, I see a moon done in the same fashion.

*But why risk returning for something this nonsensical? Could they really not help themselves? Or ...*

I'm so intrigued by what I'm looking at that I almost don't notice the sound of approaching footsteps. (*Ah*, here we go.)

A boy rounds the corner, coming toward us from the other end of the corridor. When he's about twenty feet away, I ask, "Briar, do you have the time on you?"

"Sure," she says, surprised at my sudden question but taking out her phone nonetheless. "It's four—"

Then things happen very quickly.

I slip the pen I've been carrying on me all day (inspiration from Myles's close call with it) out of my pocket and throw it around Briar's back so that it lands under [Unsuspecting-But-Useful Bystander Boy]'s foot at the *exact* right moment.

He steps on it and begins to slip just as I abruptly stand, my elbow "clumsily" jutting out and knocking into Briar's side—not particularly hard, but enough to push her a step to her left and therefore directly into [Toppling Boy]'s path.

She starts to fall, letting out a small noise of surprise and catching herself before she can go all the way down but not before her phone drops right out of her hands. It lands with a satisfying clamor as it skids across the floor.

"O-o-oh! I'm sorry! I-I didn't mean to—I-I swear, r-really," the boy stammers. "I'm so sorry. So so sorry!"

I go over and pick Briar's phone up, handing it back to her. "Are you all right?"

"Yes, I'm fine. Really, it's not a big deal."

Indeed, she looks more confused than anything else. Meanwhile, [Unnecessarily Frightened Pen-Slipper] has already scampered off down the corridor and around the corner.

"It was just poor timing—I should've paid attention to my surroundings before standing up. It's fully my fault. But as long as you're not hurt …"

"I'm not," she says quickly. "Please, there's no need to apologize, Zero."

"That's a relief. Then let's head back to the dorms."

You may not see why, now, but there will come a time very shortly when I benefit from all this (i.e. in the next scene).

***

"So, I guess we'll work on this more tomorrow?" Briar asks as she pauses outside of her dorm room.

"Yes. Just try to get some rest now, all right?"

Her mouth wobbles a bit as she continues to hang onto the door frame, not yet stepping inside. Very clearly, she wants to ask me more questions—no doubt about the security card I'd flashed at her earlier, the shifted alphabet code, or the mysterious condition I have for Myles Adrian in exchange for my help. But I don't intend to give her a chance to ask about any of it.

"Briar, although you almost fell directly on your face, you didn't seem particularly shaken afterward."

This isn't what she expected me to say. "Oh …" Her cheeks flush pink, the warm color contrasting with the ivory-paleness of her complexion. "… Well, I guess I just have a hard time feeling scared about anything when you're right there."

"I see." (This is not good.)

"Did I just … say something weird?"

"Not at all. I'm simply surprised given how you felt the need to step in and protect me from our fellow students only a few hours ago."

"That was *before* I saw everything you could do. Besides, when it's you who's in trouble it feels different."

"Different?" (Definitely not good.)

Briar's cheeks pool with color again. "Ah, um, I mean …"

"Sorry, I shouldn't be prying like that. Forget I asked; I'll see you tomorrow—wait, actually, before I go, we should exchange contact information. It'll make things easier."

"Uhh, really? Yeah, ok!"

"Here, give me your phone and I'll put my number in. I never really use the academy chatroom, so this is just more convenient."

I watch as she enters her passcode and hands it over to me. I take it and input my number. Before giving it back, I pretend to inspect it closely. As it turns out, the screen is perfectly intact without a scratch. The fall didn't succeed in breaking it. To amend this, I press my thumb hard into the lower right corner of the phone screen. (This is, once again, not something a "normal" teenage boy is capable of. So before you start asking me "Zero, how are you able to do that?!!" I'm gonna stop you right here and tell you to leave me alone.)

"Is something wrong?"

"Briar, did your phone take any damage when you dropped it earlier?"

"No, I don't think so."

"Are you sure?" I hold up the phone for her to see. "Your screen is cracked. You didn't notice?"

"If you already knew the answer, then why did you ask?"

A small snort escapes me at her sudden feistiness. "You're right. Regardless, you're going to need to get it fixed. It's not too noticeable right now, but if you drop it even one more time, the damage will probably be pretty severe."

"I guess I'll have to go to tech support tomorrow morning ..."

"No need."

"Hm?"

"I'll take care of it. I've been meaning to get myself some new earphones for a while, anyway."

"But I can't possibly let you do that!! I should use my own credits for that, not yours."

"Do you think I don't have the credits to spare?"

"Um ..." She struggles as she decides whether or not to make reference to the lack of credits my low rank would give me. "No, that's not it. It's just that you already paid for lunch."

Clever cover. "I told you, I did that because I wanted to. And I'm already going to the tech store later so it's not a problem. Believe it or not, I have enough credits saved up that the fee should be covered without extra cost. Besides, it's at least partially my fault you dropped it to begin with."

She looks at me skeptically, still unsure if she should allow me to do this. (She just needs a little *something* to nudge her over the edge.)

"What's the matter, Briar?" I say, leaning down until our gazes are level. "Do you trust me to do this for you, or not?"

"I …" She looks up at me, determination suddenly gleaming in those wide eyes. "I do."

The honesty and certainty in her voice take me aback for a moment. We're just talking about a cell phone, are we not? How does one respond to this? In what is hopefully not a diffidently clumsy manner, I reach a hand up to brush aside a strand of hair that's fallen in her face. "Right. Good."

As I leave, I just barely make out the words Briar whispers under her breath in response. "*Goodbye, Zero.*"

***

I unlock her phone as I walk to the tech store. Lucky for me, her finger motions were easy to read when she'd put in her password before exchanging our numbers.

Once inside, I type out and send off the text I'd planned.

I haven't ever had cause to break someone's phone before. It was a lot more difficult than I expected it would be; I guess grip strength exercises have more of a use than I'd once thought. Maybe I'll start them up again—

"Are you freaking kidding me? Someone came and printed them here but you don't have any recollection of any of that? Don't play with me."

An argument up at the counter catches my attention—there's a student fiercely leaning over [Profusely Sweating Store Clerk Who Wishes To Melt Into Nothing Alongside The Lingering Snowfall Outside]. "I'm not sure what else you want me to say, miss," he just-about whimpers. "That's the honest truth—"

"Bullshit! I know about you. I know that you're willing to take bribes from students when it comes down to it. How much did they pay you? Did they threaten you?"

Accusing the store clerk of bribery? I have heard whispers of this being a place where "shady deals" go down, but I didn't take them as anything other than meaningless gossip. Ah, well, it's none of my business, anyway.

"I-I have no idea what you're talking about, miss. I'm very sorry."

I expect the girl to blow up at him again, but, instead, something interesting happens.

"No, I'm sorry—I shouldn't have raised my voice. I think this whole thing's just made it, like, really difficult for me to keep a cool head; it's embarrassing, *haha*." Her tone has done a one-eighty, all signs of fierceness replaced with a sweet shyness. "Maybe I should come back another time, you know, when I have someone else who can help me say what I need to say. I've been told I can get too emotional sometimes. Just, please, don't be mad at me, ok?" She tops off this little performance with another soft, tinkling laugh.

"O-oh, no! Don't worry about it! I'm here to help." [Now-Smitten Store Clerk] gives his own nervous chuckle and leans toward the girl who, in turn, leans ever-so-slightly in toward him, causing her long, golden hair to spill over her slender shoulders.

"Really? That makes me feel *so* much better, sir."

I'm starting to see what's going on here. Everything she's done and said since the shift in tone … has been calculated. Even that bit about coming back later with another person, it was to nudge him into giving her what she wants *now* when she's alone and unguarded.

"But I guess there isn't much you can do about this, is there?" she asks, voice dancing skillfully on the line between cute and seductive. When she rises up and down slightly on her toes, her skirt brushes up against the counter, revealing a sliver more of her thigh—the skin there looking as fair and soft as the rest of her. (Again, I can't wrap my head around the academy's dress code for girls.)

"Well …"

"Mmm … yes?"

"There might be *something* I can do."

"Oh," she perks up, deliberately turning up her excitement with a little hop, "that would be amazing! Any help I can get, I'd be so thankful for."

*unappealing grunting noise* "Of course, of course." He brings a wide hand up to wipe the sweat beading on his slick forehead. "But … maybe there's something you can do for me, too?"

(*Sigh.*)

"What would that be, sir?"

He shyly slides a notepad across the counter, a pen sitting atop it. "If you write your number down here, I'm sure we'll be able to work it out."

Judging from the way he's eyeing her—not focused solely on her *face*, that is—I can guess what "working it out" means for him. Surely, she must know, too.

"You see," she starts, voice still lilting, "I sort of need the answers to this as soon as possible. You understand, right?"

"I-I'm not sure I do. Like I said, there's not much I can do for you right *now*, but if you contact me later, say when I get off work and have more time, I'll be able to assist you."

"… You won't help me … unless I give you my phone number, is that it?" Her delicate hands clench into fists, knuckles turning white. "Are you serious? Are you *actually* serious?"

I'm surprised I'm not able to see curls of steam coming off of her; *she's about to blow up again.* But since neither of them have noticed my presence, I can easily choose to remain a spectator in the corner. (Let's hope they finish this little spat soon. I'll be taking bets now, who do you think will come out on top? The primadonna student or the desperate tech store worker?)

"I am serious. Do you have a problem with that?" And now, [R/Nice Guys Clerk] is getting an attitude as well.

"Why don't you look me in the eyes and tell me if I have a problem or not? Did you really think I'd give you my number just like that? What's wrong with you?!"

"You were the one flirting with me!"

"*Me*, flirting with *you*? Tch. Guys are the worst, always thinking I owe you something. I came here for some basic information, and you can't even give me that—"

His hand slams violently down on the counter, making the girl flinch. "For the last time, *you're* the one flirting with me!!"

"I—"

"You girls are all the same." His voice has lost any of the shy-waver it used to have as his meaty hand grabs hold of her wrist, wrapping fully around it and pulling her to him, hard.

"*Ahh!*"

"That's right. Just because you're pretty you think you—" He cuts off, startled, and looks down at where my hand is gripping his arm.

"I've been waiting for some time," I say flatly. "What exactly does it take to get some customer service here? Because I'm not sure I'm willing to go quite this far." Pointedly, I look down at the notepad and pen.

[R/Nice Guys Clerk Who Is Regretting His Decisions] releases her wrist immediately, backing up until he bumps into the shelves behind him. Seeing him like this, with nowhere to go, his small, skittish eyes darting around, I can't help but be reminded of cornered prey.

I slide Briar's phone onto the counter. "I want this screen fixed. You can charge me for the credits after it's done."

Wordlessly, he takes the phone and backs away into the staff room behind him. Then, finally, I look at the girl, knowing exactly who I'll see staring back.

Tumbling waves of golden hair frame a perfect face with rosebud lips, a delicate nose, and large, jewel-blue eyes that are looking me head-on. Really, she has ... the strangest eyes. I've never known what to make of them. Sharp and intense in a way that should make them appear harsh, they have a contradicting innocence that softens them, pulling you in and taking hold of your attention for as long as she pleases.

*Alina Carter.*

Her name's come up several times so far, so you may remember. She's a talented art student and singer as well as co-captain of the girls' soccer team. She was also a one-off victim of the traitor—hers being one of the twenty tests stolen in Media & Technology. Not to mention, she's literally known as "The Princess of Kane Academy," outshining even Marina's reach when it comes to connections and admirers. (So what's she doing here alone?)

It's no exaggeration to say she's probably the most beautiful girl I've ever seen; a fact I find as disgusting as I do annoying. But her beauty isn't the reason I'm still staring, her *expression* is. After what had just happened, I knew she'd be shaken, and probably somewhat frightened. At least, that's what I *thought* I knew.

Instead, I'm faced with a look of pure FURY.

"What are you doing here?" she asks, each word sharp and dripping venom.

"Sorry, have we spoken before?" I'm certain the answer to this is "no." In other words, she has no reason to be this hostile.

"Acting like you don't know who I am—your arrogance makes me sick."

"That's clearly not what I meant."

"I almost had the situation figured out, and then *you* stepped in. Thanks for ruining all my hard work."

"Almost had it figured out? Yeah, those red finger marks on your wrist certainly back you up there."

She jerks her arm behind her back, chin remaining level. "I had it under control."

"Did you now? And which part, exactly, was going according to plan? The part where you lost your temper and blew up at him, or the part where he grabbed you and you screamed?"

"I did not *scream*—you don't know what you're talking about!"

"I watched the whole thing."

"And you only just stepped in at the very end, huh? What's that about? I mean, what kind of guy does that make you?"

"So you're saying there *was* a time I should have stepped in earlier?"

Her lips come together in the most impressive pout I've yet to see (sorry, Marina) as she glares at me and crosses her arms over her chest—a chest which is, to put it kindly, not exactly *ample* (just what was the store clerk looking at?).

I say nothing else, now curious which of us will win this stare-off. But we both lose when the door to the store opens and Daniel Blackwell walks in.

"Sorry I'm late; mending Nina's uniform took longer than expected. But, Alina, you should've waited for—oh, Zero? Hello, I didn't expect to see you here. What a nice surprise." Words that would usually sound cruel or contrived sound genuine and friendly when coming from him. (What a gift charisma and kindness must be.)

"I needed my phone screen fixed."

"Oh, I hope the break wasn't too bad."

"It wasn't."

"That's good to hear." Daniel smiles and I hold back a grimace. Some people just have an intimate smile, one that gets under your skin and warms you up whether you like it or not. Daniel has one of those smiles. "Do you and Alina know each other?"

"Ha! Yeah right, Danny," the Carter girl cuts in, coming over to him and leaning against his arm. All of her previous animosity is gone as she slips back into the role at hand: being Daniel's charming, cheerful classmate. "Now, can we get out of here? The store clerk was totally giving me the creeps."

"Alina, that's not polite. Besides, I thought you wanted help with—"

She waves him off, simultaneously dragging him toward the exit. "It's fine, he couldn't help us, anyway. Honestly, I can't believe I wasted my time coming here. Plus, like, I really need to make it over to Mr. Henderson before practice—our meeting's gonna make me late and I just *know* Jackie's gonna be a bitch about it."

*tired exhale* "All right … Then I'll see you tomorrow, Zero. Take care."

I lift a hand in farewell. But, naturally, Alina Carter wants the last word.

"Ok, bye now, Seven!"

"Alina!"

"Oops! Sorry, sorry, my bad. What's his name again—Three? Six? Well, anyway, we're gonna take off now. See ya."

Daniel gives me an apologetic look, mouthing, *"I'm sorry,"* over his shoulder. Carter looks back, too. This time, outside of Daniel's range of view, her angelic features are composed into something lethally serious. It's as if she's giving me a message. One that says, "*I'm watching you.*"

What the hell is her problem?

The store clerk comes out shortly after they leave, still mumbling nonsense about stuck-up girls not giving him a chance. But he shuts up pretty fast when he sees me watching him.

He doesn't speak again until he scans my ID to pay for the repair (and the earphones I threw in—I really did need some). "Hey, what is …"

"Something the matter?"

Dumbfounded, he looks from his computer screen, to my ID, to me. "I-I've never seen this many … H-how—how do you have so many credits?!"

That's right. Those at the cafeteria stations have grown used to seeing the unusual number of credits I have. But I haven't had cause to come to the tech store in a long time.

I take my purchases without bothering to answer. However, there is something *I* want to know. "One more thing before I go. That girl, what did she want from you?"

On my way out of the tech store, I take out a very different kind of picture from the ones the Carter girl had apparently been so upset over. It's the drawing I found stuck inside my notebook.

And its existence confirms what I'd already put forward as a theory: **there really *is* a traitor among us.**

"Now, isn't that fun?" I muse to myself.

Just then, Briar's phone buzzes. I check the message and smile.

(The bear has fallen for the bait of honey I've laid out for him.) *So … I flip the phone once in my hand. It's time I get myself a bear skin.*

I already have a pretty good picture of what happened to Briar yesterday before I found her up on the bridge. In fact, after *that* interaction I saw unfold earlier today, I'm all but certain of the general idea.

But I'll confirm the specifics when I meet the person I texted.

***

### Alek Slate

- **Year/age/student ranking**: Junior, 16, 30 of 150
- **Hair**: half black, half dyed-green
- **Eyes**: emerald
- **Height/Weight**: 5'9, 148 lbs.
- **Noticeable features**: everything about him is weird …

- **Favorite item**: assortment of colorful Band-Aids and stickers
- **Likes**: a good time, any and all sweets, night-core hyper-pop songs, pain (*jk*)
- **Dislikes**: being bored
- **Personal** ~~comment~~ **motto**: "Better to arrive late than to arrive ugly—this doesn't apply to me, but I really wish others would take it to heart."
- **Fact**: Alek's stepfather was murdered in front of him when Alek was 12. His mother is currently institutionalized at Blackthorn Asylum.

*Zero * 238*

- **Year/age/student ranking**: Junior, 17, 18 of 150
- **Hair**: blonde
- **Eyes**: pale green
- **Height/Weight**:  5'4, 120 lbs.
- **Noticeable features**: round cheeks, large eyes
- **Favorite item**: stuffed bear Daniel gifted her last year
- **Likes**: romance movies and books, baking, chocolate
- **Dislikes**:  violence, disappointing her parents, having to wear her glasses, her ex-boyfriend, girls who obsess over Daniel
- **Personal comment**: "I just … want things to go back to the way they were."
- **Fact**: Her boyfriend broke up with her last semester in a nasty way. Having her work be the first to go missing on top of that—knocking her out of her previous place in the top 10 for the first time in three semesters—was a near-fatal blow, and the one to get her through that hard time was Daniel. She looks up to him more than anyone else. She is also roommates with Nina.

## Bonus: Q & A III

Q: I have a really bad feeling about this. You're up to something aren't you, Zero?

Z: Don't worry about it.

Q: You're always getting into trouble—for once, couldn't you get into the *fun* kind of trouble?

Z: I wasn't aware there was a fun VS not-fun kind of trouble.

Q: I'm just saying, would it kill you to let loose and get yourself a girl—

Z: Contact me again when you have something worthwhile to ask. I'm busy.

*Additional comments*: Zero really went about getting Briar's phone in the most convoluted, unnecessarily thought-out way possible, didn't he?

*The two wolves*

***

# Chapter 10:

## Brutality

I arrive behind the old movie theater several minutes ahead of time. To keep myself entertained, I put in my new earphones and shuffle one of the fifty-two MyTube playlists I've so carefully put together over the past few years. I'd give you an earphone to listen, but, well …

Ah, I know. As I wait, how about you and I play a little game? Yeah. A game.

Rock, Paper, Scissors.

That's as simple as it gets. Obviously, you already know how to play, so, how about it?

I can hear you wondering, *"Zero, how the hell are we supposed to play an interactive game?"* But it's really easy, I promise. All you have to do is make your decision about which move you're going to throw before flipping to the next page, and I'll do the same.

It's an unusual thing for a book character and reader to do, but that's fine. You adjust to this sort of thing really fast, anyway.

So, are you ready?

You better be, because I'm not waiting.

**Rock.**

**Paper.**

**Scissors.**

**Shoot—**

*Zero's Choice: **Scissors.**

So, which of us won?

Hm. I guess it's not easy for you to just tell me, is it? What a shame. This'll just have to be one of those one-sided things where you know the truth and I'm left guessing.

If I had to choose, I have this feeling that you came out on top this time … but I'll have you know that if you pulled a gun, that does *not* count and I will not accept your victory.

Still, let's play again sometime. I'd offer another round right here and now but …

I need to focus.

Because here comes my target.

I watch, seated against a tree in the shadows, as he looks around nervously and smoothes back his hair. (What an embarrassing little fool.)

Another text pops up on the phone.

*Ben: Where are you? I don't see you anywhere*

*Me: I'm right here.*

*Ben: This isn't funny Briar. Come out before I leave. You're the one who wanted this right?*

I stand and walk over from my partially hidden position. Benjamin Hawkins stiffens, straining to see just who is coming toward him in the dark.

"What are you doing here?" he asks, taking a defensive stance once I step out of the shadows.

"You know, you're the second person to ask me that this evening. The first time was annoying, but this time, dear Benjamin, I'm mostly feeling disappointment."

"What're you going on about—"

I hold up Briar's phone, shaking it with a little smirk.

"This some kind of joke?"

"Not one you're going to find funny, unfortunately for you."

"You stole her phone?!"

"'Stole' is a rather strong word. What would you say if I told you she *gave* me her phone? After I asked, of course. I wonder if that makes it better or worse."

"....."

"You're starting to get the picture, right? See, Briar *used* to belong to you and to your group. Now, she belongs to me."

"W-what?"

"To put it in terms even you can understand, Briar is," I smile, leaning over him, "*completely under my control*. She does anything I say. Including handing over her own cell phone, password and all."

Benjamin seethes, a deep hatred burning in his plain, brown eyes that's visible even in this dim lighting. "Why did you call me here, Hale? Just to tell me this, to rub it in?"

"Isn't it obvious? I called you here to tell you to back off. I saw you looking at her today. And then you had the nerve to stop her in the hallway when I wasn't there. You think I didn't know what you guys were talking about?"

He blanches.

(This possessive villain act is tiring, but I've got to see it through, so bear with me.)

"You're the reason Briar wasn't at school yesterday," I continue. The fact that she'd still been wearing her uniform when I found her up on the bridge told me that she'd been *planning* to come to classes that day.

My best guess was that Benjamin asked to meet her in the morning beforehand and things took a turn for the worst when he'd brought up whatever deal he'd proposed—the one they were arguing about again this afternoon that Briar made clear she'd never agree to. Looking at their text history only confirmed this. Of course, just as she'd turned him down today, she'd turned him down that morning, too.

Except they were alone that time, and Benjamin didn't react so well … This is where the other two strange observations I'd made earlier come in: The red coloration I noticed on the left side of Briar's face last night, and the dark bruise still prevalent on Benjamin's left side right now. *See pages 97, 122, & 133.*

"She rejected you yet again, and you slapped her for it." His reaction, eyes enlarging with fear, tells me all I need to know. "You must've slapped her pretty good, too," I go on, "since the mark remained hours later. Getting out some pent-up frustration, were you? But Briar's not one to take abuse lying down … so she kicked you in the head."

After all, the placement of his bruise is the exact same as where [Ugly Gang Leader] is going to have his thanks to his run-in with Briar outside of the nurse's office.

I take a step nearer to Benjamin and trail a finger over the purpling skin starting at his temple. "And that's an injury you're going to be feeling for a while, eh, Ben-boy?"

He smacks my hand away. "You don't know anything about me and Briar."

"Oh, so you haven't been in love with her since freshman year? And I suppose that isn't the reason for your falling out over the summer. To think, you've been trying to get her back all this time—has no one told you women find desperation unattractive? Hm, well, that would explain a few things."

"You bastard!"

Benjamin swings his fist at me, but I don't bother to slip; I catch it. *Slipping: a common boxing term for dodging.* It's clear he's had no martial arts training, much less actual fighting experience. He's no different than the three idiots, with his feet too close together, his posture abysmal, and his muscles slow. He grunts with back-breaking effort, trying to pull his fist away, but I keep it firmly in place.

"Is this how you treated Briar?" I ask. "Because it's no wonder she rejected your advances. You're ..." I lean down and whisper into his ear, "*pathetic.*"

His knee comes up, aiming for my stomach. But I catch that, too.

"What now?" I say, clenching his thigh where I'm holding it with one hand and using my other to spread his palm out until my fingers interlace with his. "Should we stay like this for a while?"

In a last, frenzied attempt at escape, he uses his left arm to aim another punch at me. I let go of him, knocking his oncoming fist aside, and smash my head into his nose. He crumples to his knees instantly, the only thing stopping him from sprawling out on the ground being the fistful of his hair I grab, tilting his face up to look me in the eyes as I kneel down.

"*Shit,*" he gasps, voice hoarse. "Someone! Someone, help!"

"Face it, you've agreed to meet after hours in a place with no security cameras. No one is here, and no one is coming. You're not leaving until I want you to."

"Why?! What do you want—is this seriously all about Briar?!"

"Hey," I grin, releasing his hair to clap my hands, "look at that. You're starting to catch on, you worthless piece of shit ♥"

"This, this doesn't make any sense," he groans, cupping his nose. "Why do you care?"

"Sorry, but you haven't earned the right to ask questions yet. So, here's what's going to happen. You're going to leave Briar to me and never bother us again. From now on, you'll acknowledge that she's *mine*."

Blood drips down his face and he looks down at his hands as if he's never seen himself bleed.

"Benjamin."

"Fine! Ok, whatever, just, *ah*, just leave me alone!"

"I want to hear you say it."

"*Argggh*, all right! All right, Jesus, just, ugh … You … You can have Briar. Is that what you wanna hear? I don't give a damn anymore—she's been nothing but trouble anyway—do whatever the fuck you want!"

My entertained expression disappears, the curtain finally falling on my performance. "I always knew you were a sorry bastard, but this must be a new low for you."

"Wait, what?"

"You'd give her up just like that. Despicable."

"But you …?!"

"Benjamin Hawkins. I know all about guys like you." His pupils dilate twice in size, his body frozen in place. "Perfectly average in every way, never able to stand out due to your own merit, and so you hide your insecurities and overcompensate in every way you can, relying on others to uphold your image. Because that image is all that matters. If it crumbles, you crumble." Sweat drips down the side of his face. "It's a fragile existence. That's why you don't surround yourself with just *anyone*, you protect yourself with a leadership position you've made in an easily controllable group of followers—all the while being afraid of being found out for the weakling you really are. And the second you're rejected by someone in that tight, carefully crafted circle, you freak out. Especially if that someone is a *girl you like*. Am I wrong, Benjamin?"

"I don't … I don't …?"

"Tell me I'm wrong, *Benjamin.*"

"I-I …"

"That's the secret to what happened between you and Briar. She rejected you at the end of freshman year, and you made her life a living hell because of it. You turned everyone in your group against her—even to this day, those she considered friends barely look at her in the halls. What exactly did you tell them?"

"You don't know what you're—"

"You've gotten so used to seeing her alone and miserable, always figuring that one day, she'd come back to you and accept your ultimatum: 'Be with me, and I'll let you back into the group.' But she never took you up on it. Heh, it must have really screwed with your psyche when you saw that I was getting closer to her. That's why you began tailing us, and why you jumped out at Briar the *second* I walked out of sight."

"You knew …"

"Obviously, you don't have Briar anymore. You haven't for a long time, thanks to your own selfishness. But if you ever bother her again, you won't have any of your other friends, either." I take out my cell phone, showing him the blinking red line that means this entire conversation has been recorded. "That image you've created, it'll all come crashing down, dragging your true self into the light: a sniveling, pitiful, entitled scumbag."

"You recorded—but that recording has you on it, too! Everyone would hear you beating the shit out of me! You can't—"

"Do you really," I lift his chin with my thumb, "think I care?"

"I-I never said you were right about everything. I never admitted to any of it."

"I think I have more than enough evidence. But if you'd like to add to your statement, sure, I'll allow it. I mean, you haven't received your full punishment yet, anyway."

"Punishment?"

I delicately pick up his right hand, the one he'd first tried to punch me with. "Because you really did hit Briar."

"I—*AHHHH!!!*"

He screams as the bones in his ring finger snap.

"Oh, god! My finger! My fucking *finger*—!!"

"I'm going to go easy on you this time because I don't think you're going to be stupid enough to try any of this again, will you, Benjamin? Briar doesn't belong to you, me, or anyone else. But you'll stay away from her from now on. Or else I will see it as a personal attack. And then this recording getting out will be, to put it generically, the least of your worries."

"Holy-fucking-shit! You're insane!!"

"Maybe. But you're the one with a broken finger. You should really go get that checked out. Just know, if you ever hit a girl again, next time, **I'll crush your entire hand.**"

I stand and he begins shuffling away on the ground, clutching his hand to his chest, anguished noises of pain and desperation escaping him.

"Before I let you go," I place my boot on his good hand, preventing him from going further, "there's something I want from you. From this day on, you know that your life is in my hands—you're going to do exactly as I say, when I say it. Understand?"

Benjamin nods vigorously, whimpering.

"Prove it."

"W-what?" he sniffles out between sobs.

"Prove you're willing to listen. Go on, *PROSTRATE YOURSELF*. Bend your head and lick my boot."

His dull eyes are as wide as saucers. "A-are you serious?"

"Do I look like I'm fucking joking?"

"....."

Still cowering, and somewhat in shock, he lowers his shaking head, his tongue brushing against the top of my boot. Rather than picking himself up after, he drops his head all the way to the ground, still weeping (now, quietly).

"Good boy. If you're obedient like this, everything will be just fine. I take care of my pets. Now … as my new dog, here's your first command."

I wait as he slowly looks up, eyes glazed over with disbelief, just barely meeting my gaze. Then, I hold up my phone screen, indicating a picture there.

"If I'm correct, you know these three idiots. They targeted me earlier today. Find out why."

***

"Disgusting," I mutter, wiping the specks of blood off of my hand as I walk back to the dorms.

Well, that was unpleasant. But I had to break him thoroughly, completely, to really build him back up as something useful. (It's good for me that he didn't have a particularly strong will to begin with. I've crushed people's hands before, but only breaking a finger or two is much easier.)

The meeting was originally, in part, to see if I could get Briar's old friend group to take her back. But I don't see any way to make that happen that doesn't also involve Briar having to come into contact with the piece of human trash by the name of Benjamin Hawkins. So the other reason for the meeting will simply have to do: Briar will no longer be bothered by that trash or his friends ever again. It's the existence of people like them that make living so unbearable. No doubt, that entire situation of her being shunned while secretly getting pressured by Hawkins is one of the main reasons for Briar ending up on that bridge. Well, I say this but …

… Briar Thornswood …

Things about her just don't add up. I'd been looking for signs of a girl ready to end her own life all day and coming up short. (Is it possible I read the situation on the bridge wrong? Is there actually any need for me to "help" her?)

Perhaps she doesn't need me at all.

She's proven herself to be pretty tough, and clever, too. Though I'll acknowledge that me dying will take away her protection against both Hawkins and the Three Idiots. That could prove to be an issue. I may need to find a way to deal with them permanently.

Hmm?

What's that? Oh, did you think I'd forgotten about my desire for suicide? Before your thoughts start running wild, I'll tell you right now that nothing's changed.

I will ensure the safety of Briar Thornswood. And then I will kill myself.

But that's beside the point right now. Right now, what I have to know is, "Do I have the wrong idea about you, Briar?"

As if in answer to my question, I spot her about fifty feet away, sitting up on the grassy hill beyond the dorms. (What the hell is she doing out here? It's past curfew by over an hour. And the temperature's cold enough for more snow.)

She's out of her uniform, wearing only a soft-looking silk nightgown complete with lace around the shoulders and neckline, and doesn't see me as she sits, one knee extended, the other propped up with her forearm resting on it. She doesn't notice me when I approach, either—her expression unchanging while the gentle wind blows her hair around her face.

Since the clouds have all but disappeared, the moonlight shines without hindrance, pouring down on the hill and Briar in a way that leaves every part of her visible.

She looks … so …

Sad.

For a moment, I pause and watch.

You know, there are different types of sadness.

Despair, heartbreak, betrayal—those tend to fall under a feeling of cathartic sadness, something grand in scope, as if fireworks could go off in the background, lighting up the sky as all your emotions consume you.

Loneliness, well, that's an example of the quiet kind of sadness.

I wonder if I'm not explaining properly ...

In the media, there are certain films that make tears seep from your eyes as your heart swells with both pain and awe, forcing you into a cathartic release of all those feelings; perhaps you can think of one such piece of media that has affected you personally in this way. But, on the other hand, while not as bold and spectacular, there are also pieces of media that hold all the weight of those extreme, epic stories while being much *quieter* in their sadness. They elicit no such cathartic emotions and leave you staring blankly at your screen, or page, unable to move. A subtle, emptying feeling.

And then there are things that don't quite fall into either category. Instead of anguish or emptiness, you're left with the kind of sadness that has you sitting down in the grass by yourself, looking out at the view as the breeze gently moves your hair ...

I can't explain it, but her being here like this, something about it just ... it just ... (God, what is this feeling?)

The second I'm within roughly fifteen feet, Briar turns to face me. She doesn't say a word, but, like a spell being lifted, the sadness in her expression melts away before my eyes. It's as if the very space around her brightens. (She's spectacular at putting on a front when it counts.)

"You'll catch a cold. Come inside with me," I tell her, now standing over her.

"Z-Zero, what are you doing here?"

"Retrieving you, obviously." This marks the third instance I've answered this question in a single night. And yet, this time, I feel no annoyance whatsoever.

"Do you …" she starts and trails off.

"Do I what?"

"Do you mind if I stay out here a little longer? I just, I … I want to stay like this a little longer."

"How do you plan to get back in on your own?"

*uncomfortable twitch* "Mmm …"

So she *didn't* plan to get back in tonight. My, what work this girl is. "Fine. I'll join you."

She looks startled by my decision to stay but listens when I tell her to put on the black sweatshirt she'd discarded in the grass beside her. In fact, it's not until I take off my coat and drape it over her slim, lightly shivering shoulders that she protests.

"But now *you'll* catch a cold! At least wear your coat, Zero—"

I place a hand on her arm as I sit down, preventing her from taking it off. "I don't get cold, and I don't get sick." *Note: This is true only when Zero is functioning at normal capacity. Chapter One Zero was … a different story.*

Briar looks at me questioningly and, very slowly, reaches a hand up to my cheek. Her touch is so soft, her fingertips brushing against my skin as if adding any pressure might shatter me.

So I take her hand and press it flat to my face. "Can you feel it now?" I ask.

"Yes," she breathes, surprised. "You're *warm*."

We sit beside each other in silence for several minutes. When I glance at her, she has her eyes closed and I see the hint of a smile on her lips. But there's no denying what I saw as I was coming up here. So what is she hiding from me?

"Hey," I start, keeping my voice gentle, "in case you've forgotten, you never gave me those cookies you baked for me."

"Oh." Her eyes blink open. "You're right."

I can practically feel the weight of her heavy lids as she fights off the desire to close them again. And the dark circles under her eyes are worse than before. She's exhausted. (Well, she did stay up all night ...)

"Never mind that now," I say, bringing two fingers up to press at the center of her forehead. "Rest."

She allows her eyes to shut and, after wobbling back and forth for a few seconds, becomes limp. (What?! The hell?!) I catch her head smoothly before she drops over and discover that, miraculously, she's asleep. *Asleep.*

Just like that.

"Where did that come from?" I murmur.

Curious, I set her head on my shoulder (where she continues to sleep peacefully) and stare down at my hands, at the two fingers I'd tapped her with. It's not something I've ever done before. But I didn't even think about it—I just *did* it. Surely, that can't be the reason she ... No, that's nonsensical. Briar was simply already on the verge of passing out due to exhaustion.

"And now what do I do?"

I was going to suggest that I climb in through my window and open the doors from the inside while creating a distraction for the guard, but I'm not about to leave her alone like this. So I send a chat message to the last person I ever thought I'd send one to.

"What a pain." I scoop her up into my arms, coat and all, making sure not to disturb her. "You must be one heavy sleeper."

By the time we reach the dorm entrance, it's already open, and *he's* standing inside. I'm glad he responded promptly, and that he informed the guard we were outside with his permission as head of the dorm, but did the president really need to greet us here himself?

"This your doing?" he asks, sharp eyes narrowing as Briar's head nuzzles deeper into the space between my neck and shoulder.

(Well, maybe.) "No. I found her like this; she fell asleep while relaxing on the grass."

"That doesn't explain why *you're* out after curfew. You remember what I said last time, don't you?"

I shudder, remembering his promise to give me a roommate should I continue testing him.

"I'll take your eloquent silence as a 'yes.'"

"Look, you can threaten me all you want later, Prez, but there's a sleeping girl in my arms who needs to be taken back to her room."

"I'll see to that," he says, coming toward me as if he's going to carry Briar himself. I'm aware he's strong enough, but—

"No. Shifting her around too much will wake her." (Honestly, will it?) "I'm already carrying her, I ought to finish the job myself."

I don't wait for permission and begin to head up the stairs. I'm aware of the president's eyes on my back until I'm out of sight, at which point I continue to the third floor. Reaching Briar's room number, I mentally apologize before slipping my hand into the only place her ID could be (sweatshirt pocket). Hmm, with my fingertips skimming over her side and only the thin silk fabric between me and her skin, I can tell there's … almost no fat on this girl!

Do I need to start making her eat more?

Shaking my head, I quickly let myself into the room and deposit

Briar onto her bed, moving as quietly as possible so as not to wake her snoring roommate in the other bed. I decide to leave my coat with her, pulling it up so it covers her from the shoulders down. On my way out, I spot something sitting on Briar's desk and grab it to take with me, putting her repaired phone in its place.

***

"What a long day. Interacting with other people is so tiring—how do they all do it all the time?" I wonder aloud, walking over to my window to open it for some fresh air.

As soon as I turn my back, I hear something jumping through it, landing with a light thud beside me.

"It's been a while, Marius. But I'm too worn out to entertain you tonight. Want a cookie?" I hold out an offering, part of one of the chocolate chip cookies Briar baked me, which I swiped off her desk. *Zero has eaten three already.*

He meows haughtily in response and proceeds to rub himself up and down on a particular part of the bed frame before jumping onto the covers and curling up beside me. Meanwhile, I munch on another cookie and check my phone to see what information Marina's sent to me.

*Marius*

Nothing unexpected. The picture is exactly what I asked of her. As for the rest of her messages, I use what she's gathered to privately contact the other top students outside of the representatives who have been affected, planning to corroborate their accounts with the data compiled by Charlotte and the student council. Though there's always the possibility something has slipped past me, I am confident that none of these less-than-NPC-lvl characters—aside from the data they provide—are of importance regarding this investigation. The heart of what is going on will be found within the group that has come to me and Briar.

Those nine students.

This fact is only reinforced once a second chime from my phone alerts me to the answers Myles retrieved on behalf of my earlier request.

(Things are shaping up nicely.)

I take another look at the wolf drawing, comparing it to the anonymous note I'd gotten when my things were returned to me this morning. Since one's a picture and the other is writing, it's impossible to say if they were done by the same person.

But I'd be willing to make a bet.

As for the security card, I didn't get a chance to try it out. *i.e. Zero is occasionally prone to laziness.* And that's ok, because I have plans to spontaneously visit a certain woman's office tomorrow who can answer all my questions regarding it.

"That ought to fill in the rest of the blanks, don't you think, Marius?"

Before passing out on my bed, there's one last thing I have to do: I sweep my hand under the bed frame and take out the small listening device stuck to it, crushing it between my fingers. I check the rest of my furniture and the bathroom as well but find nothing there. At the time, I didn't care that the president had sent Annie up to bathe me for reasons other than benevolence, but now things are different. I don't need a spy meddling in my affairs. But, knowing him, I half believe the prez *assumed* I would end up finding the bug he'd had Annie plant. Such work is beneath doing himself, I suppose.

I flip the lights off and lie back on my comforter, hands behind my head.

Lately, you know, it feels like there's been a lot of eyes on me …

***

- **Year/age/student ranking**: Junior, 17, 98 of 150
- **Hair**: blond
- **Eyes**: brown
- **Height/Weight**: shorter than Zero, who cares
- **Noticeable features**: N/A
- **Favorite item**: N/A
- **Likes**: being secure and in control of those around him
- **Dislikes**: having his true self laid bare
- **Personal comment**: He does not get one.
- **Fact**: Benjamin has been trying to force Briar into dating him since the summer of their freshman year.

## Bonus: A Look At What The Senior Representatives Are Up To Tonight

Analisa: James, it would appear we have our own bonus installment. How do you think we ought to make use of it—

James: Hey! How come that boring junior asshole up there got a profile and I didn't?

Analisa: I don't think it's something you should take personally—

James: Fine. I'll just make one myself. Name's James Hudson, I'm a *senior*, I've got reddish-brown hair, blue eyes, I'm 6'0—

Analisa: Try 5'9.

James: Goddamnit, Ana—who asked you, huh?! It ain't like you know how tall I am or anythin'.

Analisa: I know you're one inch taller than me. I'm 5'8.

James: Ana! Quiet down, jeez.

Analisa: Shouldn't we be more focused on the case at hand, hm? You are aware that if our spots in the top 10 are taken out from under us, we're no longer guaranteed scholarships to the universities of our choice, yes?

James: … yes.

**Bonus Part II: What Song Was Zero Listening to on MyTube?**

*Insert your response here:* _______________________________

**Kane Academy Fact:** KA uniforms are custom-made per each student. There are two options for shirt colors—black or white. Most students have several of each. Examples provided below:

*Typical female & male uniforms*

***

# CHAPTER 11:
## WHY DO PEOPLE WANT ME TO SING SO DAMN BAD?

*BANG. BANG. BANG!*

"Lila?" I groan, sitting up in bed as the loud knocking continues. "What do you—" (*Wait, of course, Lila isn't here.*) "Then who the hell …?"

God, I hate being woken up. I'd lie back down and go back to sleep, but that damned banging is going to rattle what's left of my brain and shatter all of my remaining sanity along with it.

I walk to the door, debating whether or not to open it. "Whoever you are, you'd better have a good reason for being here," I warn, voice still rough with sleep.

"*Zeeerroooooo*, open up," comes the whining response. "Hey, why does your voice sound so deep? I mean, like, extra deep, even for you."

Dammit. How did she figure out which room is mine?

I'd ask her what she wants through the door, but I know she won't be satisfied enough to leave until I let her in.

Resigned, I swing the door open and Marina bursts through it.

"Finally, I—" She stops, gawking in horror before whipping her head to the side, squeezing her eyes shut. "Zero!! You're naked!"

"I'm *not* naked—don't say such weird things. I'm clearly wearing sweatpants. And hey, don't you know it's rude to just show up at people's doors uninvited?"

"But where's your shirt?!" she squeals, clutching her arms around herself as if her shirt is about to disappear, too. "What if someone saw us in here alone? Did you think of that, walking around shirtless? Just imagine all the rumors that would spread! Is that what you want?!

How do you have a *tattoo*, anyway—you're a minor!"

"Quiet down. It's too early for you to be this annoying." I walk over to the dresser and take out my uniform. "You're the one who came to me. This is *my* room, and you showed up without notice, so you can't be upset."

"Ugh, you're unsufferable, Zero! I don't know why I bothered to come here."

"*Insufferable*. And me neither, because you still haven't told me. But insulting me with made-up words can't possibly be it."

"I came because today is an important day! It's the last one you have to catch the traitor thanks to the time limit you made up. And I didn't trust you to get yourself to class on your own, so I figured I'd make sure you didn't skip today."

"How thoughtful."

"Well, how well you do on this affects *me*, too. In case you forgot—"

"I haven't."

Marina has now opted to cover her eyes, but her hands might as well be translucent considering the way she's peering through her fingers so obviously.

"Marina," I fold my arms over my chest, "my eyes are up here."

"What, I wasn't looking at you!"

"Whatever. You haven't seen me naked yet, but you will if you don't wait outside so I can change."

Her cheeks burn a bright crimson as she drops her hands from her face, taking one last look at me before dashing out the door, slamming it behind her. (She sure has a thing for slamming doors, doesn't she?)

But hey, you, yeah, I see you. You can wait out there with her, too. *Pervert.*

***

**A look inside Marina's mind while she stands in the hallway:**

*Oh my god, oh my god, oh my god!!!!!!!!! Zero!!!!!! Since when???? How?!!!?!?! I knew I felt muscle when he was holding me in the river, but I never imagined ….!!!!!*

***

"Wait, you're wearing a sweatshirt now?" she asks once I invite her back into my room. "Is that allowed in the dress code—where's your coat?" She sighs with exasperation. "Never mind, we're gonna be late, Zero."

*I'd be perfectly fine if you'd just gone without me*, I think, but am too tired to bother saying.

"Hey, can I ask you a question?"

"No."

"How did you get that tattoo? It's really big—does it mean something?"

"That's two questions. The answer to both being 'none of your business.'"

"Then can I ask you another question?"

"Again, no."

"Who is Lila? At first, you thought I was her … I heard you saying her name through the door."

"……"

"Zero?"

"Come on. I thought we were going to be late."

We make a stop by Briar's room once I explain to Marina that she wasn't feeling well last night so I need to check on her. Except when we arrive ... Briar isn't there. It's not exactly *weird* given that she likes to be punctual, but I make it to class in record time nonetheless, with Marina huffing and puffing behind me.

"You're," *labored breathing* "the worst," *huff* "Zero. You were trying to ditch me like—"

"Marina, over here!"

"Hey, Marina!"

Marina looks over her shoulder and suddenly forgets all about me and the ways I've spurned her. "Oh my god, hey guys!"

Well, would you look at that? It's Girls 1, 2, and 3 from Chapter 3 (otherwise known as Lacey, Kate, and Sophia, in case you care). Oh, and there's one more girl with them—Marina's useless friend from the river disaster (Rosie? Rosalie? Rosaline? Something like that). I'd say it's been too long, but I'm trying to cut back on lying when possible.

"We're so glad you're feeling better, Rina, but, uh, what are you doing with him ...?"

I leave them to their gossip and enter the classroom for statistics. (Oh, thank god.) Briar's sitting exactly where she should be, staring down at her phone in worry.

"Hey, good morning," I greet her, sliding into my seat.

She turns, startled. "Zero, I'm so sorry! I didn't see your text until now. I should pay more attention to my phone; I would've been happy to walk with you."

"Don't worry about it. We can walk together tomorrow."

She smiles warmly, eyes darting down to her lap. "Yeah, that sounds good. Oh—but your coat! It's still in my room! I-I promise I'll give it back tomorrow."

"Keep it as long as you like."

I'm about to ask her if she's had any other ideas about the case when I notice something up on the whiteboard that's … well, I'm not sure *what* to make of it. More so than being something sinister, it's just something *weird.*

I'm puzzled to find the same thing taped to the whiteboard of my second class, art. I'm staring at it in confusion, trying to figure out what the hell is going on, when Ben Hawkins slinks into the room right as the bell rings, his right hand wrapped in bandages.

For a brief moment, his eyes lock with mine, but he quickly averts them and goes directly to his seat, head down. (*Good. He won't be a problem anymore, Briar.*) Really, the gaze I need to be concerned about is the one I'm getting from Alina Carter. She stares at me, unabashedly, throughout the entire period. Yet at the end, she gets up and walks out without a word, instantly swarmed by a large group of adoring ~~fans~~ friends. This doesn't stop her from glaring at me over her shoulder. I once heard someone refer to her as the "Ice" Princess, and I'm starting to understand why. (A problem for another time.)

Keeping with the pattern, my third class also displays the same weird thing stuck onto the side of its whiteboard. I look carefully around the room to see if anyone else is in on this, but everyone appears to be going about their usual business. (God, won't you let me have just one semi-normal day?)

At lunch, both Briar and Marina find me at the back of the cafeteria, scratching my head over my discoveries.

"Zero, what are you looking at?" the annoying one asks, bouncing around to sit beside me. "Is this a puzzle?"

Spread out before me on the table are three sticky notes, each containing different Japanese characters spelling out what appears to be nonsense at first glance.

To give it to you in Romaji, it would sound like this:

1.  Ni 5-kai renshu-shitsu

2.  1 de atte kudasai

3.  Zero-san, hiruyasumi

Rearrange it, and you get, *Zero-san, hiruyasumi ni 5-kai renshū-shitsu 1 de atte kudasai.* Which roughly translates to, *Zero, please meet me in practice room one on the fifth floor during lunch.* Either the notes were put up out of order to be a hassle, or whoever did this simply does not know my class schedule very well.

"I ... don't know what to make of this," Briar says after I explain the situation.

I nudge the plate of tacos I got toward her. "Eat your food. I'm going to check this out. I'll be back soon."

"You can't go alone! What if it's a trap or something?"

"A trap?" I ask, deadpan.

Briar folds her arms. "Yes, a trap. It could be. You can't deny this isn't strange, Zero."

"I'll say," Marina comments, mouth stuffed with the taco she's stolen. "It's creepy."

I lightly swat her on the head.

"Ow!"

"Don't chew with your mouth open. And stop taking Briar's food."

"Hey—"

"Just stay here, you two, will you?"

"... Fine."

*They do not, in fact, "stay there."

"This is so, so creepy." Marina squeezes tighter onto my arm as we exit the elevators on the fifth floor. "So, so, so cre—" I pinch her cheeks together to get her to shut up.

She has a point, though. It's dark up here aside from the light glowing from beneath the cracks of Practice Room 1. (So someone really is here.)

Impressively, Marina continues to talk even with her mouth squished into fish lips. "Ooo, I don wiike ii, Zewoo. Do wiiikee iii a aaal. Le go baaa. Le go baaac riii now!"

I release her jaw. "If you're scared, then just stay here, dummy. You don't have to come in. Better yet, just go back to the cafeteria by yourself."

"I'm part of the case you're working, too! Don't treat me like a child."

"This isn't related to the case."

"Whaaa??"

While I'm distracted dealing with Marina, Briar sneaks ahead of us. Before I can stop her, she opens the practice room door. I practically pick Marina up as I rush forward, unsure of what or who will be waiting behind that door.

"Umm ..."

"Y-you, you actually came!"

But whatever I was expecting, it wasn't this. Sitting on the bench is a girl with large, dark eyes and her hair twisted up into two buns. It's ... the girl I saved from falling down the stairs the other day! The one who thanked me. *See page <u>59</u>. She's—

"Juri?" Marina steps out from behind me. "Juri! It's you!"

"Oh, Marina!"

The two girls rush toward each other, embracing.

"I thought you were a psycho leading us to a torture chamber!" Marina wails. "You seriously creeped me out!"

"Sorry, sorry! I didn't mean to scare any of you, I just wanted to get Zero's attention. I'm so sorry. Please, forgive me."

[Sweet Girl With Cute Hair And A Strange Way Of Getting A Guy's Attention] Juri turns toward me, looking particularly vulnerable. She takes a step but is blocked when Briar comes to stand between us.

"I don't understand. Who are you? What do you want with Zero?"

Juri wavers on her feet, hands twisting in front of her. (She's so small, even shorter than Marina.) "I see how this might seem unusual ..."

"Briar, it's all right," I assure her, stepping around her. "Juri, is it? Well, Juri, tell me what you need and I'll see if I can help." Because right now, I don't see how any of this can possibly come to make sense.

"Umm, well ... you see, I needed to find a partner ..."

"A partner?"

"Like a boyfriend?" Marina asks, hands on her hips as her face scrunches up. "No way, you don't *like* Zero, do you, Juri? No way, no way! That's not possible, you're way too good for him!"

"Oh, no, that's not what I meant at all!"

"No one said anything about a 'boyfriend' so stop saying things without thinking," I grumble. "Juri, what do you mean by partner?"

"Someone to perform with me for the end-of-year Talent Festival. I wasn't sure who to turn to, so I went to someone for help ..."

***

*Juri's search for help—a re-telling:*

Juri: Ms. Kurima, I want to perform a song for the Talent Festival.

Kyouka: That's a great idea, Juri! :)

Juri: But … it's a duet and … it's in Japanese. You see, I don't feel fully comfortable singing in English … *Juri is a Japanese exchange student.

Kyouka: Japanese, did you say? And you need help finding someone who can sing in Japanese with you?

Juri: *nod, nod*

Kyouka: Preferably a boy, I assume?

Juri: *nod, nod*

Kyouka: *devious chuckling* Oh, I have the perfect person for you, heh heh heh ♥ Here's what you need to do, follow my instructions *exactly* …

***

"Juri, let me ask you something," I begin after she's finished, "why did you follow Ms. Kurima's directions knowing they were this absurd?" I should have known there was only one person at this academy who could be responsible for such a ridiculous scheme involving no-context, broken-up messages in Japanese writing all directed at me.

"Because … I had nowhere else to go and I needed help. She said this was the best way to get your attention."

"Next time, just ask, ok?"

"Does this mean you'll do it? You'll sing with me for the Talent Festival?"

"I didn't say that … You haven't heard me sing."

"But you can, can't you?" Juri fiddles with her hands again and looks up at me, making the purest, most sinless expression I have ever seen. "Please, Zero?"

(!!!!)

*11* ⅓

"Well, this is a welcome surprise—you using your free period to come see me." In the corner of her private office, Ms. Sharp makes herself comfortable on a plush, red loveseat. Thick raven hair tumbles over her shoulders, falling in waves past her breasts (which are shown off to their *very* full extent with the tight, low-cut dress shirt she's wearing). As always, her smokey, half-lidded eyes make it appear as if she's either just gotten done in the bedroom, or she's just about to drag you into it.

If Alina Carter is the most beautiful female at this academy, then Natalia Sharp is, without doubt, the most sensual. It's no wonder why so many of the male students are head over heels in love with her.

"After how impersonal you were last I saw you, I must say I didn't expect this. Tell me, Zero, did you miss me that much?"

(But, as it turns out, she's only interested in one of them.)

I stand over her, opting not to take the seat she's made for me beside her. "We both know I don't feel emotions as kind and sentimental as that."

She sticks out a plump, glossed bottom lip. "Maybe so, but did you ever think about the effect your coldness has on *my* emotions?"

"Only every night I have trouble falling asleep."

"Zero! You're so cruel; how could you say such a thing to me? As an esteemed faculty member, I should really have you kicked out for talk like that."

"What's wrong?" I kneel down to lean in close to her, ignoring the overpowering smell of jasmine perfume poisoning my lungs. "I thought you'd be happy to hear how often I think about you, Natalia, late at night, when I'm alone ..."

Her cool, slender hand lifts my chin, tilting my face up. "You naughty, naughty boy. Don't you know school is still in session?"

"It's a bit late to be acting the role of the pedagogue now."

"Is that so ...?" Her eyes gloss over as I turn my head just enough to bite the tip of her finger. Legs parting and un-parting, she leans in. "Zero ... won't you ... come closer."

I release her finger and reach behind her neck, pushing her head down until her ear is level with my mouth. "I meant what I said last time."

"That you won't be doing this sort of thing as often?" This is not what she wanted to hear. "It's a rare enough occasion as it is, don't you think?"

I pull back and stand up, choosing not to provide an answer.

Ms. Sharp huffs in disappointment, running a hand through her hair. "Always so distant. But you know I don't have to go through you to find out what you're up to. In fact, I heard you're working a 'case' with the student council now—how cute. I guess you found what I was saying to be of interest after all."

"....."

"You're here for more information, aren't you? Sorry to disappoint, but nothing else has come up that I'm aware of."

"Actually, there's something specific I want to know about."

She raises a perfectly arched brow. "And what would that be?"

I hold up the security ID I've been keeping on me. "How long would it take for one of these to be deactivated after being taken?"

"Where'd you get that?"

"Natalia." I say her name in warning.

She leans back into the loveseat, folding her arms and recrossing her legs. "It depends on when it's discovered missing. But from that point on, it would likely be reported and dealt with within the hour."

Essentially, if you were to get your hands on one, you'd have a limited, one-time use of it. "And how many of them have gone missing lately?"

"Oh, you think the one responsible for this whole rank mess-up is getting into the school using these ID cards. Not a bad theory."

"This would go much faster if you'd just answer my questions. If you don't know, then just say so—"

"*Six* have gone missing. Though it seems you're responsible for one of them."

(Six, huh?) "When was the first taken and when was the last taken?"

"Mm, this is getting boring, Zero. I'd have to look it up, and that sounds like so much *work*."

"Indulge me a bit more, and I'll make it worth your while."

"My, the things I do for you ..." Ms. Sharp spends a minute clicking through her phone. Then— "The first account of a security ID going missing this year was January 20th, and the last was February 4th."

The 4th would be from the night I took this one. "How about the second to last?"

"January 25th."

(So, about two weeks ago.) "Wait, are you sure the first to go missing was the 20th? And that includes the entire academic year?"

"Yes, and *yes*, I'm sure."

(January 20th—but that means ...)

"Are we done here?" she asks, tone whining.

"Not quite." From my bag, I pull out something I printed at the tech store: an old map of Kane Academy grounds. "I already know of an unused entrance into the main building here," I point to the area with the door I broke into the school through yesterday, "but I need to know of all other possible ways in."

"After the IDs stopped being stolen, you think their MO changed and now they're coming in through some secret entrance? How do you know they aren't just using the one you pointed out?"

I shake my head. "The amount of rust on the hinges showed that no one had opened that door in years before I did. So, can you be of assistance here, or not?"

Ms. Sharp just smirks. "I'm sure you're more than capable of finding out the answers to that on your own."

"So am I. But to use your words, that sounds like so much *work*."

"Hah! All right, I'll tell you something. But I'll expect something in return, later."

"I already said I'd make it worth your while. Just come out with it."

She leans in a final time, whispering the answer in my ear.

Oh?

Now this changes things.

***

At the end of the day, the representatives—along with Briar, Marina, and I—meet at the scheduled time in the student council's main office.

The energy in the room is …

TENSE.

Gravely, Charlotte sets down a new file, which I immediately pass off to Briar. (There's a piece of paper poking out of someone's bag that already gives me an idea about how this is all about to go down.)

"So?" James asks, ever the first to speak. "What is it—give us the update. Was Hale right, or what?"

Briar opens the file and tilts her head to the side.

"*So?*" James pushes again.

"Mmmm ..."

Nina looks her over, making a face. "Is she ... confused?"

Charlotte takes a deep breath and steps in. "Mr. Hale was right that the traitor didn't make the bold decision of targeting another class by taking all their assignments." She closes her eyes, steadying herself. "They targeted *four* classes and took all the assignments of the top student from each. Four completely *new* classes."

"My god," Thomas mutters as James's fist re-familiarizes itself with the table.

"This has to be a joke!"

Analisa places her hand on his, quietly stopping him. "And what would these classes be?"

"Rhetoric, Entrepreneurial Skills, Oral History of Storytelling, and Zoology," answers Briar.

This gets my attention. "Say that again?"

"Rhe—"

"No, no, I got it. Ah ha, that's really kind of funny, actually."

"*Funny?*" James asks. "Just what about this is entertaining? Care to share with the class?"

"Heh. Heh heh heh." I fold my hands under my chin, still chuckling. "So, the traitor has a sense of humor."

"Now what?" Nina demands, pushing her chair back as she stands. "Since your whole 'ignore them, they won't break pattern again' thing turned out to be *dead wrong*. We're back at square-frickin-one."

"On the contrary," I stand as well, "things are progressing quite nicely." This just confirms what the drawing placed in my notebook was saying. (Now, it's time to bring attention to another secret note.) "Nina, tell me, what's that sticking out of your bag?"

All heads in the room swivel to Nina's bookbag, but Alek is the one to snatch the folded piece of paper out of it.

"This is a list," he says, the corner of his lips tugging up at a wickedly sharp angle. "Of the top students in Rhetoric, Entrepreneurial Skills, Oral History of Storytelling, and Zoology. Well, well, isn't that something?"

"The hell you talking about—" Nina grabs the list from Alek's hands but cuts off the second she sees what's on it. "But … no, I didn't … I don't know where this came from."

"It was you?" James looks like he's about to blow up in a way that will make even the Carter girl's explosion at the tech store look tame.

"Hold on, James, this could have been planted on her. We don't know enough for this to tell us anything." Analisa is as level-headed as always.

(If only the rest of them could follow her example.)

Nina is anything *but* level-headed and wastes no time in whipping out her phone and firing off multiple lightning-fast texts—as if she's updating someone on the situation in real-time. *But who could she be messaging?* I want to know.

James, apparently, wants to know, too. "You sending off some secret code?" he demands.

"None of your business, Hudson!"

"If you don't hand over your phone, I'mma make it my business. You're acting super shady, Taylor."

The ensuing scuffle results in Nina literally escaping underneath the table (still sending off texts) and popping up on the other side as Analisa incapacitates James via a shin kick to prevent him from giving chase.

"Maggie, are you crying right now?" Nina asks, finally looking away from her phone and to her roommate now seated across from her. "Shouldn't *I* be the one … Hang on …" Perplexion gives way to hurt. "You don't actually think …"

Maggie's doe-like eyes are filled with genuine tears as she refuses to face her friend.

"Oh my god. You do."

"Nina …"

"You're actually buying into this crap, aren't you?"

"Nina, i-it's just …" She trails off again, unable to finish her thoughts. "I-I mean …"

"*What?* What do you mean? Tell me to my face."

"Everyone, just calm down," Daniel interjects, his tone uncharacteristically firm as he takes hold of the list. "Zero, how did you notice this?"

"It was sticking out rather obviously. I'm surprised no one else noticed."

"Meaning it was likely planted on her, as Analisa suggested," says Thomas, eyes narrowed with unchecked suspicion.

"What if that's just what she wants you to think?!" cries March, her cracks of fear deepening. "She's probably going to try and pin it on someone else. Oh, god, maybe she's going to come after me next!"

"No, they can't do that—they can't take you away from me!" The other sophomore, Sam, clutches onto her arm. "Please, don't leave me here *alone*."

"They're gonna expel me, and my mom's gonna *killlll meeeee!*"

"No, no, no, you can't leave, March! Please don't get framed—please! If you go home, you have to take me with you!"

The two begin rocking back and forth together, one crying, the other hyperventilating. (Are they really representatives of Kane Academy's best and brightest?)

Maggie turns inward toward Daniel, laying her head on his chest. "I just want this to be over."

"You think *you* want this to be over? I'm the one with the freakin' fake evidence put in my bag!"

"Nina, lower your voice."

"You're on their side, Daniel? You think I did this?"

"There are no sides here except for us against the traitor. I don't believe you're responsible, Nina. But getting worked up over it won't help anything."

"All of you, shut up. Briar and I already have our next lead, so there's no need for us to stay any longer. You're dismissed."


"Ughhh, I didn't understand any of that," Marina whines as we make our way down the hall. "Why'd you even make me go in the first place?"

"No one asked you to come, Marina. You just showed up."

"What are they all getting so upset over anyway? My rank is a hundred nineteen and I'm doing just fine."

"For some people, being below average is seen as a negative."

"Zero! Was that an insult?!"

"Hey," Briar rushes in, "I'm sure he didn't mean it that way, Marina."

"I did mean it that way."

"Please, Zero—"

*from behind* "Zero, wait!"

We're about halfway down the hall when his voice stops me. I do as he says and pause until Daniel is beside me. "What do you need?"

"Nothing; it's just an invitation." He smiles, the same warmth to it as yesterday in the tech store. "If the lead you mentioned can spare the time, I would really like for you, Briar, and Marina to join us for karaoke."

"Us?" I repeat, wondering who else he's including. *Karaoke?!*

Behind him, I see Maggie and Nina standing toward the opposite end of the hall, each of them awkwardly avoiding eye contact while they wait for their mediator to return.

"As diverting as that would be, I think I have some shirts that need ironing," I say, using the first excuse I can think of. "And Briar has … some buttons to sew. You can take Marina, though."

Daniel laughs a little. "Sorry, I'm not trying to torture you. I just think it would be a great opportunity for us to all wind-down after, well, you know …"

Torture. That's exactly the word I'd use to describe the prospect of group karaoke. But—

"Nina! I got your texts and came as fast as I could," a new girl's voice yells as its owner races toward us. "I already talked to Mr. Henderson, because this is seriously getting out of hand, but what the hell does any of this—"

Alina Carter cuts off as our eyes meet and the temperature in the hall drops by several degrees.

Every nerve in my body goes on alert. (*Her? Now? Why?!*)

"You," she says, with even more animosity than I thought possible. "You're the one who 'found' the list in Nina's bag."

"Are you making an obtuse observation or a baseless accusation?"

I ask as she comes to a stop beside the other girls. "I can hear the verbal quotation marks your putting around the word 'found.'"

So **this** is who Nina was firing off texts to.

The aforementioned girl faces Carter, putting on what I can assume is meant to be a brave face. "Thanks for coming, Alina." *with unintentional puppy-dog eyes* "It means a lot."

"Wait," Maggie says, sounding as confused as I am (for, albeit, different reasons), "d-did you say you talked to Mr. Henderson?"

"Yeah," a fourth, athletically built girl chimes in as she rounds the corner. "She was late to practice yesterday 'cus of it, and today she ran out on us midway through just to come sprinting over here." Judging from her cutting words and sports uniform, she's also a player on the soccer team.

"And I'm glad that I did," Carter says, pointedly looking at this girl in a way that almost demands for her to try making another snide remark. *That's right,* I think, finally taking in Carter's jersey and high ponytail, *she and Nina Taylor are co-captains of the girls' soccer team—a truly fearsome duo.* "Mr. Henderson needed to be updated on the situation," she goes on. "I mean, his is the class that had the most stolen from it. It only makes sense."

"Yes," a deep voice echoes from down the hall. "Alina is right. Something had to be done."

Just like that, we're joined by [Ridiculously Attractive Media & Technology Teacher] as he attempts to step through the crowd of students clogging up the pathway in front of him and my unhappy-looking statistics teacher, Mr. Davis, who stands by his side.

"Mr. H!" Nina cries, halfway between a sob and an exalted exclamation. (So much for her brave face.) "Did you hear about what happened?"

"Of course. Alina provided me with most of the information yesterday and called to fill me in on the rest just a few minutes ago."

"Then she told you how they're gonna kick me out?!"

"No one's kicking you out, Nina," Mr. Henderson says with an exasperated smile. "Please, try not to worry so much."

"Yeah," Carter steps up to her co-captain, taking her by the hand, "no one's gonna do *anything* to you. I swear to God, they won't."

The fierceness in her tone has me believing she's telling the truth.

"See?" Mr. Henderson says, attempting to step through the crowd once more. "You're in good hands—"

Nina jumps back in front of him (a fearless action to take considering the sheer size of the man she's cutting off.) "So now that you know all about it, what's gonna happen? Are you gonna let us make up the missing test?"

He stares down at her, still partially amused (a trait no longer shared by Mr. Davis) as he runs a massive hand through his dark locks. "An important half of the test was to include the robot you created— so even if you recall the answers you'd made for the questionnaire portion, you're still missing too much to get a passing grade."

"Ahhhh, come on, Mr. H!" she wails, jumping in front of him a second time, suddenly switching concerns from getting framed to getting credit. "But I handed in my new robot already!"

"You handed in a paper airplane, Nina."

"So what? I was limited on time! The thing still moves on its own, doesn't it? The last one took me and Daniel two weeks to make, how am I supposed to do that in one day?"

"You're not. I never asked you to attempt to recreate anything. I asked you to wait patiently until we figured out a solution."

"Patience seems to be something your students could stand to have a lesson in," Mr. Davis snaps, checking his watch as he taps his foot. (Are they late to something?)

"In the meantime," Mr. Henderson continues as though my statistics teacher hadn't spoken, "even if I understand the issue, it's not like I can suddenly give you all full credit. The best I can do is to hold off on submitting grades until the actual 'traitor' is caught. And believe me when I say I *really* want that to happen as soon as possible. Mr. Davis feels the same way. We're headed to a meeting to discuss this very topic, after all."

"Really?" Nina, Carter, and Maggie ask at the same time.

"If we could ever *get* to the meeting," Mr. Davis cuts in again. (Ah, so they are late to something.)

"Really?" Nina asks again as Maggie wonders, "Who are you meeting with?" while Carter questions, "Is it the chairman, like we talked about?" and [Soccer Girl] gives a sharp one-word inquiry of, "Why?"

"That is not information that you students are entitled to," Mr. Davis says crossly.

But Mr. Henderson only smiles wearily at his overly enthusiastic students. "Yes, it's a meeting with the chairman."

"But how?" Daniel asks, stepping in as Maggie, Nina, and Carter simultaneously grab onto him with varying degrees of excitement.

The Media & Technology teacher shrugs, the muscles under his button-down shirt swelling with that small movement alone. "Alina made a strong case for you all. I wouldn't be too good a teacher if I just brushed your concerns aside, would I?"

"No, but you're the *best* teacher, so you would never do that!" Nina shouts as she throws her arms around him.

The act startles him, but he plays along good-naturedly and pats her back as Mr. Davis scowls with disgust. "Students should not be invading the personal space of their teachers."

"Sorry ..." Nina says sheepishly as Daniel pulls her away whilst making apologies on her behalf.

So, I think to myself, *Mr. Henderson has the power to get the chairman to act? And on such short notice? Impressive.*

(That's all thanks to the Ice Princess, is it?)

Not that it's going to change anything. The most that could happen is for all rankings to get officially frozen until the situation is resolved. And even that would be a miracle. But there's no way he'd ever allow any faculty member to interfere beyond that in what he considers to be "student affairs." Ms. Sharp confirmed as much yesterday.

(Still ...)

"I know I made a strong case, but how did you manage to pull it off so *fast?*" Carter asks, sounding genuinely perplexed as she mirrors my thoughts exactly.

"I called for an emergency meeting after we spoke yesterday," Mr. Henderson answers. "The chairman trusted us teachers enough to believe it was worth responding to immediately; and it just so happens that the full-faculty conference he scheduled is happening now. But," his tone shifts to something polite yet firm, "Mr. Davis and I are going to be late to it if you don't let us get on our way."

Carter makes eye contact with him and nods in an unspoken "thank you" as she smiles and takes her co-captain by the arm, ready to stand aside.

But Nina has more to say. "Wait, so, can we come to this meeting, too, or—"

"For the love of god, will you get out of the way!" Mr. Davis hisses, hand reaching out to physically move the girl aside.

He doesn't get far.

To everyone's surprise, Mr. Henderson takes him by the shoulder before he can stretch his arm halfway. What's incredible is that it doesn't look like he's putting any force whatsoever into his hold, and yet it's clear that Mr. Davis can't move a single inch from where he stands.

What I'm more interested in, however, is how Daniel Blackwell was moving in on him at the same time. (If Mr. Henderson hadn't been so quick to act, I genuinely believe he would have stopped Mr. Davis himself.) *Fascinating.*

"Jackson?" my statistics teacher says, his voice almost faltering as he faces the colleague he suddenly has a newfound image of.

Mr. Henderson, meanwhile, looks just as calm as he did before. "Mr. Davis, you correctly commented that it's inappropriate for students to invade the personal space of teachers; but the same sentiment applies the other way around." His tone is as mild as his expression, but there's no way to interpret such an action other than as a threat.

"I simply meant," Mr. Davis starts slowly, "that I refuse to let a couple of little girls be the reason I become in bad standing with the chairman. You know how little tolerance he has for being kept waiting."

"Yes. No tolerance at all." He flashes a charmingly crooked smile at the group. "Then we'd better be off."

This time, both Daniel and Carter take Nina clear out of the pathway as the teachers proceed down the hall.

"I promise to do my best for you," Mr. Henderson says over his shoulder. "But I can't make any promises on the chairman's behalf. Remember that."

"Yes, sir," Daniel answers. "We're just grateful to have your support."

(I wonder, now, how will news of this development affect the traitor?)

"You can get anyone to do anything for you, can't you?" [Sour Soccer Girl] asks Carter as the two teachers are finally out of sight, making her the second person to perfectly mirror my unspoken thoughts. "I doubt you even needed to be late to practice to get him to listen. You could've just sent an email and he'd have done it."

Carter's smile drops the second she turns on her teammate. "I told you that everyone was free to continue practice on their own, Jackie. You easily could've done that. Or do you need Nina and me to hold your hand through every drill?"

"I'm just saying," [~~Soccer Girl~~] Jackie starts, her face turning red, "it's not like it's any of your business, anyway. You're not one of the 'representatives' or whatever they're calling themselves."

"I'm in Media & Technology, too, duh. Besides, there's no way I'd *ever* let Nina suffer on her own like this. Someone had to do something."

"And that someone just had to be you, of course."

"Jackie, Alina—this isn't a productive conversation," Daniel says, forcing his way between them. "Since you're both already out of practice, why don't you come with us to karaoke?"

But neither girl pays him any mind.

"Please, can we not get upset with each other?" Maggie entreats. "We already have enough to deal with, and …"

She falters when Carter and Jackie turn their attention on her, their hot gazes melting her fragile defenses as she instinctively turns to Daniel (the way she so often does).

"Who else is going?" Carter eventually says, flipping her ponytail over her shoulder as she rests her arm on Nina's shoulder.

"Well," Daniel looks around the hallway, "originally it was going to be me, Nina, Maggie, and Jake." *Jake Parker, the other most popular student at Kane Academy—no, you haven't met him yet, calm down.* "But the more the merrier."

**The more the merrier.** A sentence that could only ever be uttered by a true, self-assured extrovert.

"In fact," Daniel continues, "Zero's group might be coming now, too."

*I guess shirt ironing and button sewing may have to wait,* I think as, suddenly, all eyes in the hallway shift to us.

It's only then that I realize Briar has been hanging onto my arm this entire time. (I'm guessing the excitable interaction with Mr. Henderson and Mr. Davis sparked her nerves a bit.)

"Oh, you invited them, did you?" Carter asks, her tone making a neck-breaking shift into one of deadly cheerfulness. "Don't you usually prefer karaoke when it's just a few of us, Danny?"

"We don't have to come," I intercede. "Really. It's fine." At least, that's what I think until I notice the slight deflation in Briar's shoulders as I say this. Is she disappointed?

"Actually," Daniel counters, "I was really hoping you would come. You see, I'd like for you all to get to know each other better."

"Why would you want that?" Carter wonders in a still-overly-cheerful voice. (Though I don't enjoy admitting it, she's still keeping up with my own internal dialogue quite accurately.)

He gives her a knowing look. "Because I want my friends to get along. Besides, karaoke is more fun when you have a bigger group. So, Jackie, how about it?"

Did he say *friends?* Does Daniel Blackwell consider me his friend? No, I won't let myself be distracted by such a ludicrous sentiment.

Daniel may be friendly, but even he can't really mean that. (This is reminding me of Myles trying to get me to lunch with him before revealing he needed my help on something.)

I don't even listen to the ensuing conversation that results in [Sour Soccer Girl] stalking off alone.

(So … Daniel Blackwell wants something from me. And it has to do with the "princess" standing in front of me, staring me down as she likewise ignores everything else going on …)

Carter doesn't look away when I meet her gaze, apparently eager to continue the staring match we'd been in during our last unfortunate encounter.

"That sounds like fun to me," Briar says, oblivious to the dangerous undercurrent of this interaction.

Marina grabs onto my other arm, adding, "I mean, I'm not completely against it. And after what Juri said, I want to hear Zero's voice."

*uttered flatly* "Thirteen can sing?"

"Alina, what did we talk about last night?"

*back to joyful* "Sorry, Danny!" Carter matches Marina, grabbing onto his arm. "Some people are just hard for me to remember, you know that."

"Anyway, are you sure now's the time for karaoke?" I ask him, looking at Nina who's been uncharacteristically quiet since Mr. Henderson left. She's still heated from the new accusations. Or, more specifically, from one person's *reactions* to the new accusations … (Her eyes have been compulsively flitting back to Maggie this entire time.)

Daniel catches my meaning and turns to her. But Nina is already stepping forward, hands on her hips.

"Look, I don't give a damn what anybody says, I'm not gonna go back and wallow in my room 'cus some bastard thinks he can pin this shit on me. I won't stand for it."

Carter squeezes her shoulder. "And you shouldn't have to, Nina. So don't worry." Her eyes fix on mine again, though she isn't talking to me. "Six here is on the case, right? From my understanding, he promised he'd solve the thing by tomorrow. Only a complete loser would say something like that just to let you all down."

Daniel's face falls into his hand. "Alina, please …"

"Besides, even if he fails, Mr. Henderson is still looking out for us. This traitor will be caught, one way or another."

She says this last bit while walking toward us, taking one slow step after another until she's only a few feet away. *What does Briar see when she looks at her?* I wonder, noticing the way that the girl clutching onto my arm is currently looking at Carter in awe.

*Inside Briar's mind: "Wow! I've never been this close to Alina Carter before. She has to be the prettiest girl I've ever seen."*

Well, if it *were* somehow possible to get Carter to accept Briar, Briar's chances at making friends would go up exponentially thanks to Carter's extensive connections. Karaoke, as much as it pains my rotted soul to say, might be a good opportunity for them to "get to know each other," as Daniel said.

I sigh. "If it's what you all want, I'll accompany you."

"Really, Zero?" The shine in Briar's eyes assures me I've made the right choice despite this unpleasant feeling in my stomach.

"Wonderful." Daniel sounds relieved, and I have to wonder if he's been pushed to his limit trying to keep all the representatives from exploding at one another. "Then shall we go?"

"I'm not sure if *Maggie* will still want to come, though." Nina doesn't bother hiding the contempt in her voice as she finally says what she's been wanting to say all along. "Seeing as she actually thinks it's me who did this to us."

"Nina, no! That's not what I—" Maggie breaks off, bottom lip trembling. "I didn't mean it. I'm sorry. I'm just … scared."

"Yeah," Nina says, more quietly, "me too."

The two girls look at each other, each unsure of what else there is to be said.

"We're all a little scared." Daniel puts his hands out in a welcoming gesture. "So, for an hour or two, let's put that aside and go enjoy ourselves."

"I'm not scared," Carter scoffs. "The one who ought to be scared is whoever's doing this to Nina. They mess with my friend, they mess with *me*."

"Oh, well, now that you've said *that*, we're probably all in the clear," I say with a clap of my hands. "No doubt you've singlehandedly frightened the traitor into submission, Carter. Bravo."

"*What* did you just call me, Seven?"

Whatever relief Daniel had felt is gone.

"Zero's not great at remembering names, either," Marina jumps in jovially. "Kinda like you, Alina, so don't feel too bad. He only remembers people he finds super important—like me! Right, Zero?"

"If you say so."

"Well, isn't that sweet?" Carter smiles, all angelic innocence. "Then at least you'll have someone here who can recall who you are—"

Daniel takes Carter by the arm and starts walking forward. "Ok! Follow me, everyone. I've already reserved one of the rooms, so we can go straight there."

(*Mental note:* Alina Carter and Marina are not on friendly terms, despite both being among the popular crowd. Reason: Because their names rhyme?) *Though by that logic, she shouldn't get along with Nina, either—which is clearly not the case,* I think as Nina joins Daniel and Carter at the front and Maggie runs after them.

A few words are exchanged and soon Maggie is walking arm-in-arm with her roommate (Nina, in case you forgot) as if nothing had ever happened.

I don't miss the look over her shoulder Carter shoots me before proceeding to laugh and banter with "Danny" all the way to the cafe, also like nothing had ever happened.

I shake my head. "Girls are confusing."

"Sorry, what was that?" Briar asks.

"Nothing," I reach up to pat her head, "let's not fall behind."

"O-ok."

Marina bumps into my other side. "Hey. Don't forget about me."

"Would that I could."

"What's that mean?"

"It means you need to keep up, shortcake."

"Did you just call me … HUAAH?!"

‖ ⅔

The Karaoke Cafe is located near the new movie theater and other recreational hang-out spots on Shopping Row.

Compared to much of Kane Academy's grand, Victorian-meets-Medieval-Gothic architectural styles, the Karaoke Cafe is notably modern. A large, shiny red booth circles around a low table with drinks and snacks, a flat-screen monitor mounted at the front of the room and multiple microphone stands set up. It's fairly big for a private room, and yet, not big enough for the crowd Daniel's gathered here this evening.

Everyone is talking excitedly, the volume in the room continuing to climb as dialogue overlaps and seemingly multiplies.

I, on the other hand, sit as far into the corner as I possibly can, regretting all my life choices as I watch the scene before me unfold:

Carter and Marina argue at the front for who will sing the first song (unwilling to perform a duet); Daniel tries to break them up; Jake Parker and Myles (because somehow he was already here by the time we arrived) go back and forth on whether singing and dancing, Jake's specialty, is as physically taxing as sports, Myles's specialty; and Nina pulls Maggie into a duet while everyone else is distracted, singing horribly off-key to a song better left in the 2010s as Maggie attempts to sing along without tearing up out of social anxiety.

Oh, what's Briar doing, you ask? Well, she's glued to my side as she looks on with wide eyes at everything going on, overwhelmed.

I lean down to speak into her ear. "You ok? We can leave whenever you want."

"I'm fine! Just … it's a lot."

"Do you want to sing a song?" I'll confiscate all the microphones if need be.

"No, I don't think so. Will you?"

"Not a chance."

She looks a little disappointed, but there's no way I'd ever willingly subject myself to such an experience.

"Come *ooonnnn*, Zero." Suddenly Marina is in front of me, back to her habit of invading my personal space. "Just one song." She puts a finger up in front of her nose, pouting. "Just *oneeeee*."

"I'll give you just one word, instead: No. And weren't you just arguing with Carter for the first song? Did you really let her win?"

*sulky huff* "Don't remind me. She's impossible to reason with. Some people, you just can't get through to them no matter what you say, you know?"

"Oh, I know."

It's now that the conversation between Myles and Jake Parker catches my attention.

"Look, I'm just saying," Jake starts, one hand on his hip, the other waving around, "I don't get why this assignment thief didn't target me, too. What, am I not good enough? Why didn't they want one of *my* tests?"

"Man, I don't think this is something you want to be a part of," Myles says, laughing a little. "Hey, I didn't get one taken, either."

"Exactly. So now I've been lumped in with the likes of you. Meanwhile," Jake's eyes flit to me, a bright hazel-green in color even in the dim karaoke room lighting, "someone like Hale *does* get to be involved in it. He's second-to-damn-last—tell me how that makes sense!"

"If you'd like to take over the case on my behalf," I reply, "by all means, be my guest. Though I should warn you that you're on a bit of a time crunch; you'll have to solve it in less than twenty-four hours. I don't believe it's something you can sing and flirt your way out of, but you're welcome to try."

"This is what I'm talking about. What do you have aside from attitude?"

"The attention of everyone else involved in the case that you will likely never be a part of."

"Excuse me? You've got some real nerve—"

"Jake, are you really upset over this?" Carter interrupts, coming to sit beside him and Myles. "I don't see why it matters, but I'm sure if you ask nicely, the culprit will consider you for their next target. Will that make you happy?"

"Don't patronize me, Alina," he grumbles.

Seeing the two of them side by side is interesting, from a purely visual standpoint. Jake's golden-brown skin and voluminously styled chocolate-brown hair contrast well with Carter's fair complexion and long locks of pure, silken gold. Even her deep, jewel-toned eyes pair well with his softer green ones. It's easy to picture them on a poster together, and easier still to see why the academy arts department insists on partnering them for every singing competition that comes around.

"Stop whining and come do a song with me," Carter says, nudging him off the booth.

Jake sighs heavily but gives her a sweetly exasperated smile and stands. "All right. What do you wanna sing?" (It appears Carter has this boy wrapped around her finger, too—she can go from teasing him to getting him to do exactly as she wants in the span of a few seconds.)

"Have you ever heard her sing?"

I turn to look at Daniel as he sits on my left, his gaze still fixed on Carter. "No, I haven't," I answer.

"Just wait."

The song they pick is a ridiculous choice. Even I, who avoids having to use my voice as much as possible, am aware that it's difficult to sing. I'm not even sure why they include it as an option in the queue. And yet ...

From the first note, everyone's attention is on her.

A foreign chill slips down my spine and I sit forward, listening.

Then Jake's part begins and the song really kicks off. He's good. They're both good.

But Alina Carter … Her voice is almost as beautiful as her nauseatingly perfect facial features. She might be a talented art student and an even better soccer captain, but it's clear this is where her passion lies. *This* is where her true talent lies. If I hadn't already met her, hearing her now might have convinced me she really was the lovely, charming princess everyone else seems to see her as.

Beside me, Daniel's hand unconsciously touches his tie; there's a soft smile on his face, different from the usual, warm cheerfulness he spreads around him at all times. It's much quieter, a smile only for him and the one he's looking at.

But his expression isn't what catches my eye. It's the muscles in his forearm as his fingers lightly press against his tie—with his jacket off and sleeves rolled up, they're easy to see now. Though I have nothing other than his almost-interaction with Mr. Davis to back this up, I wonder, is Daniel secretly trained in any martial arts?

Marina gets the next song, as promised, yet it turns out she's less sure of herself than she first appeared.

"Zero, please, come on, don't make me do this alone!"

"We all must lie in the beds we make for ourselves."

"Don't just throw a random quote at me, help me!"

"Hey, hey, I'll sing with you, Marina—don't worry, I got your back!"

"Um, thanks, Nina, but that's what worries me."

"What're you trynna say?"

"All right, all right, calm down, girls. I'll do it."

"Thanks, Jake! You're the best ♥."

As that ^ conflict resolves itself, I notice Carter slip out into the hallway. Daniel notices as well, but he doesn't go after her as I expect him to. He just sits with his hand still at his tie, a deep crease forming in his brow. (Hmm …)

"I'll be right back, Briar," I say and follow right behind Carter.

I find her directly outside our private room staring down at her phone, an emotion etched into her face that she would never show in public: fear. It dissolves almost immediately as she senses my presence and looks up.

"And what do *you* want?" (It's amazing to think that the beautiful voice I'd just heard could now be filled with such vitriol.)

"Who's to say I want anything?"

"So you just happened to come out into the hallway at the exact time I did. Yeah right."

"What were you looking at? On your phone, I mean." I already have a pretty good idea given what the store clerk told me yesterday, but I want to see if there's any chance in hell she'll tell me the truth herself.

"That's none of your business, Seven."

(Of course.)

But if I'm to have any hope of salvaging whatever this strange, antagonistic relationship we seem to be building is, now's my chance.

I step forward. "I think we got off on the wrong foot. Let's start over."

Carter doesn't even look at my outstretched hand; her ice-cold eyes remain locked on mine, burning with the heat of blue fire. I'm not sure how much time passes as we stare at each other, both unwilling to stand down. *Those eyes of hers …*

"When you look at me," I murmur, the words coming out on their own, "it's like you're seeing something no one else does."

"Because I am." Her response also comes without thought.

"Tell me, then. What do you see?"

"What do I see?" She takes a step closer. "I see *you*, Zero Hale." Closer. "And I really, really wish I didn't."

I blink. (That was the first time she's ever said my name.) "I don't think I understand what you mean."

She moves back, some of the intensity from a few moments ago gone. "No, and you never will."

"Have you always disliked me, or was it something specific I did?"

*laugh/scoff* "Why should I answer your questions, Thirteen? And if you're not going to sing, then why even bother coming to a karaoke cafe?"

"Unless you suffer from extreme short-term memory loss, then you'll recall that Daniel is the one who requested we be here."

Her glare deepens. "And why is that? Why did Daniel want you here? You're not working on the case, clearly, so what's the point of you?"

That's ... actually a good question. (Not that I'll tell her that.) "I guess we'll have to be patient and wait for him to reveal the answer to us."

"Oh, you're both out here, too," a soft voice interjects before Carter can respond.

We turn at once to find Maggie Arrowood gazing down at her shoes, hands behind her back.

"It was getting loud in there, so I thought I'd take a little break."

"Maggie!" Carter says cheerfully, all hints of anger long gone. "I'm glad you came out. You saved me from having to be stuck here with Seventeen all by myself."

"What—you mean Zero?"

"You say that like I was keeping you prisoner, Carter."

"Ugh, will you stop it with that? Why do you insist on using my last name—do you think it makes you cool?"

"What I *think* is that you're not in a position to talk." From our very first interaction, she's seemed insistent on calling me every number in existence *aside* from the number that is my name.

"See what I'm dealing with, Maggie?"

"Uh—"

"Alina, hey! I knew I heard your voice."

(And who the hell is it *now?*)

[Boy With Either Impeccably Bad Or Impeccably Good Timing] sticks his head out of the private room across the way, grinning.

Carter grins back with ease. "Lee, what a surprise."

"You here singing?"

"Of course."

"Nice, so are we." He nods toward the room behind him. "Why don't you join us for a while?" His eyes land on Maggie for the first time. "Oh, hey, Maggie. You can come, too." Then his gaze falls to me and he quickly looks away, back at Carter.

(Should I be offended at my lack of an invitation?)

"Thanks, Lee, but Maggie and I are actually here with a group already. Maybe next time."

"What, you guys in a group with Hale? Really?"

"Like I said, maybe next time, ok?"

"Aww, come on." Lee steps fully out of the room, approaching Carter. "You can spare a few minutes for *one* little song, can't you?"

"Lee, I already said—"

"But the guys heard me say I'd bring you in with us. Don't make me let 'em down, Alina. *Pleaseeee?*"

"Hah." Carter crosses her arms, holding her ground. "That sounds like your problem."

*exaggerated wince* "So cold. I guess you really are the Ice Princess, huh? Still," he moves closer, hand outstretched, "I think you're being difficult on purpose, aren't you?"

Usually, I'd have left the second [Boy Who Can't Take No For An Answer] showed up, but I wanted to see what would happen when *he* arrived. Just on time, right before Lee's hand can grab Carter's shoulder, another hand shoots out and stops him.

"What the—*ack!*"

With an expertly efficient pull, turn, and twist, Daniel has Lee's arm pinned behind his back. (My hunch was correct; Daniel Blackwell is no stranger to martial arts or self-defense.)

"What the hell, man?!" Lee grunts. "What's the big idea—let go!"

Heh. He just became a lot more interesting in my eyes. (And it seems Mr. Davis was actually rather lucky that Mr. Henderson reached him first.)

"Daniel, what are you doing?" Maggie cries at the same time Carter says, "Danny, I'm all right. Lee didn't do anything."

"Oh." Daniel sounds almost startled as he releases Lee and stands back. "I'm sorry. I'm not sure what came over me—I didn't realize it was you, Lee."

"Daniel?!" This revelation seems to shock Lee more than the act of having his arm twisted.

"I shouldn't have done that. I apologize. But," he straightens, "you also shouldn't go around grabbing girls by the shoulder, even if you're familiar with them, Lee."

"Always ready with a moral lesson, aren't ya?"

Daniel shakes his head but turns to Maggie. "Sorry, did I frighten you? I didn't mean to."

"No, of course not! You could never frighten me, Daniel ..."

"Hey, and what about me?" Carter asks. "Did you not think that *I* could be frightened?"

"I know it takes more than that to scare you, Alina."

Carter smiles, a blinding, mischievous quirk of her lips, and bounds up to Daniel, taking hold of his arm for what feels like the fifth time. "But I can grab *your* shoulder, can't I, Danny?"

After a few more words of apology and promises to hang out in the future are exchanged between Daniel and Lee, we all re-enter our room.

"Daniel! Perfect, you're back—now help me out," Nina pleads up by the monitor. "Jake keeps trying to take the mic away from me, but I only got to sing one song! It's not fair—"

As Daniel deals with the newest conflict, I see Briar, Marina, and Myles caught up in a lively conversation. The instant I walk in, Briar's attention cuts to me. I wave and she almost breaks away toward me, but I put up a hand and motion for her to stay where she is, trying to convey that she doesn't need to stop talking with them on my account. Reluctantly, she listens.

*She's building relationships.* Good.

Even better, Myles calls Carter over to join in on their discussion.

I smile in satisfaction to myself. It appears Myles is doing his job perfectly—telling him we'd be here was the right decision. Yes, I'm the one who contacted Myles, figuring I could get him to show up if I mentioned this gathering. Naturally, he's probably hoping that I mean to speak to him more about that favor of his, but I'll be out of here before that happens. I've got a lead to follow, after all.

**Your Opinion Part II:*

*a) Zero actually has a lead* __

*b) Zero is just making things up and lying to us* __

*c) Somewhere between both these options* __

Disappointing Myles aside, this is all going fairly well. Briar and Carter are talking, and Myles is there to buffer—I know he won't let anything bad be done to Briar. What I also know is that my presence would ruin any chance of creating a bond between Carter and, well, anyone, apparently, which is why I opt to sit beside someone else entirely.

She doesn't notice me at first, her attention directed wistfully, almost painfully, elsewhere.

I look to where Maggie is looking. At the other end of the room, Daniel talks to Nina in a low voice—a conversation meant only for the two of them. He'd been calming her down, and now he's making her smile as she nods to something he says.

Maggie continues to watch, quiet.

"You really value Daniel as a friend, don't you?" I say.

She startles. "Z-Zero!"

"Apologies, that was personal."

"No, no … you're right …" Her hands twist in her lap. "I do."

I wait for her to continue.

"Things have been … difficult this year, but he's been there for me, all this time."

"Since your boyfriend left you, you mean. Or are you talking about how you were the first target last semester?"

This startles her again. "Um, well, yes, I guess both of those are right."

I nod toward Daniel and Nina. "Have those two always been this close? Or is that just how Daniel acts with everyone?"

I don't miss the way Maggie's fingers tighten around the fistfuls of her skirt she's gathered. "Daniel's nice to everyone. That's just who he is. But I'm sure you already knew that."

I nod in agreement, waiting for her to go on.

"I guess ... his relationship with Nina is a little different, though," she starts hesitantly.

"Yeah, he always seems to be looking out for her, doesn't he?"

"Well, uh, I mean," she shifts around in her seat, "they got closer this past year as he helped her break into the top ten."

"You think it's his doing that Nina made it to where she is."

"Of course it is. That's just a fact. I love Nina, but there's no way she could've done that on her own. Daniel ... he's a great tutor."

"Did he tutor you as well?"

For a second, Maggie's hands tighten around her skirt again. Then, all at once, they relax and she lets out a soft sigh. "No. He was already helping me with ... other things."

"Other things?"

"Yes. You see, Zero," she faces me, pale green eyes lighting up with a rueful smile, "I wouldn't be here without him, either."

Ah.

"Do you know what that's like? To have someone else be the entire reason your life is what it is?"

I look over Maggie's shoulder at Briar. She's tucking her hair behind her ear and laughing, albeit tentatively, as Myles shows the little group around them a magic trick. "Yeah, I think I take your meaning."

Right, then. It's almost time I take my leave, too. The last thing I need to do here is send off a quick text to a certain student in this room.

Marina gets the notification and looks down to read my message. She frowns at its contents before finding my eyes across the room and attempting to mouth something in my direction that I pretend not to understand. Since she won't stop mouthing things, I send off another text.

*Me: You still wish to be useful, yes?*

At this, she finally walks over to my side of the room. But instead of coming up to me, she waltzes up behind Maggie and practically jumps her, grabbing hold of her shoulders as she exclaims, "Maggie! Come on, you need to sing with the rest of us!"

I watch as Maggie winces sharply and attempts to lean away from Marina's face which is now so closely pressed to hers. "Umm ..."

"*Please?* It's making me sad just watching you sit all alone over here."

"I'm not alone, I'm with Zero—"

"Same thing! Now, come on already!"

Maggie shudders again as Marina squeezes her tighter. Poor girl *really* does not want to sing. But it will do her more good to be a part of the group than to sit on the sidelines with an outlier like me.

"All right," Maggie relents with a small, nervous smile. "I'll come with—"

*BAM.*

The door to our room swings violently inward, revealing Alek standing in the doorframe, his leg outstretched from where he'd kicked it in. No, correction: revealing Alek along with *all the other representatives* behind him.

"Jesus, Alek!" Nina yells. "There're door handles for a reason, you know!"

"What have I missed?" he asks, sauntering in, nursing a lollipop.

"Who is this?" Jake asks, automatically wary.

"I'm the one who's going to challenge you to a dance battle," Alek declares confidently, popping the lollipop out of his mouth to stick it in Jake's face. "And win."

"What are you talking about? This is a karaoke cafe, you freak!"

"Oh, is that what this is?"

"Conspiring about the case without us, are you?" James asks, pushing his way inside.

"It wasn't exactly a secret that they were coming here," Analisa supplies, following.

"Still, a gathering like this without getting the consent of the whole group is unacceptable," Thomas says.

"Actually," Daniel steps in, "I'd already invited you all at the meeting. I'm afraid you were just distracted by the other conversations you'd been in at the—"

"Oh, you mean the panic we all got into after Hale told us to shut up?!"

"Well, James, that's not exactly what I—"

"Because *that* part I remember well. Where is he, anyway?"

Yes, definitely time to slip out.

In the commotion, I manage to do just that. Analisa catches me going by, but she doesn't say anything, only giving me a barely visible nod. *I'm in the clear.*

As I make my way back toward the main building, I shoot a text off to Briar.

*Me: Sorry, something came up. I had to go.*

*Me: Don't worry about the lead or the case tonight. Leave it to me. I'll see you tomorrow. Sleep well.*

Ok. Now it's just us. Are you ready to do this thing, or what?

**Insert your response here:** ________________________________________


***

*Karaoke Café: Private Room*
*(KA's most modern facility)*

## Q & A With <u>You</u>

Q: Zero didn't sing a single song, which disappointed everyone greatly. How should we punish him? *Place a checkmark next to your choice.*

A) Force him to give you a private concert __

B) Force him to go shopping and get a damn makeover already __

C) Force him on a date __

D) Free Answer: _________________________________

Thank you for your time. Your response will be recorded.

## Bonus: Meanwhile, Back at Karaoke ...

Myles: Anyone seen Zero?

Alek: *playing with Myles's hair and sticking stickers on his face* Eh, who cares?

Myles: Alek, I appreciate this mini-makeover you're giving me but, uh ... why are you doing it?

Alek: You and Jordan have such nice hair; but Jordan would never let me close enough to touch his, so you'll have to do.

Myles: You're kind of weird, you know that?

Alek: *humming a breakcore hyper-pop song no one's ever heard of* Hold still. I'm gonna add one more sticker, ok?

Myles: *obediently holding still* Seriously, though. Where's Zero?

Alina: Did Thirteen take off? Hm, I didn't notice his absence.

Jake: *looking at Briar* Well, someone did ...

Briar: *staring at the door* ...

*Briar Thornswood: chibi-style*

***

# CHAPTER 12:

## I TAKE BRIAR TO HELL

I spend an hour poking around the academy grounds (in the dark) to find what I'm looking for.

*"I've been told that under the school, there's a secret network of tunnels. They say … it connects the entire campus,"* is what Ms. Sharp whispered to me.

Secret tunnels. It's hardly the first time I've suspected there being such a system underneath Kane Academy. But the question is—

"Where the hell are they?" I seethe, taking a seat on the railing of the small, stone bridge by the Northernmost wing of the main building.

The entrance has to be somewhere a student would be able to access without a stolen security ID, given how they moved off of using that tactic, but it also has to be somewhere that *no one* aside from people who already know it's there can find it. Unfortunately, the information Ms. Sharp gave me was limited to the fact that there *are* tunnels under the school, while any maps of the system or even how to get in count as info "outside of her pay grade."

"If it turns out she was full of shit, I'm going to—oh, Marius?" The black cat jumps onto the railing opposite of me, his yellow eyes flickering in the twilight. "This is pretty far for you. You've been venturing out more and more, it seems."

His tail swishes and he leaps back down, walking off.

"Leaving so soon?"

He pauses at the other end of the bridge and turns his head as if he's waiting for me. Wordlessly, I follow him.

I follow him all the way to the North Garden where he curls up at the foot of the water fountain and closes his eyes.

"Well, I'm not sure what I …" Hang on. "Is that … ?"

Directly under Marius, the words "Abandon Hope All Ye Who Enter Here" are engraved in the ground along with a symbol. That's the message said to be inscribed at the entrance of Hell in *Dante's Inferno* (an odd thing to etch into a garden). The symbol, however, is unique. Four arrows encircled by three rings.

"Now where have I seen that symbol before?"

Above the president's doorframe, to be sure. It stuck out to me last I saw it. But there's another place I'm thinking of … A place you have yet to see.


The moon shines high in the sky by the time I reach the graveyard. Sitting at its center is the answer I'm looking for: The Kane Family Crypt, which has the exact symbol from the garden engraved beside its name. The atmosphere is as foreboding as I remember it from the last time I came here to draw; curls of lazy mist stretch into the distance, weaving in and out of headstones, reaching to the outskirts of the surrounding forest where towering trees encase the entire cemetery in a coffin of its own.

"This isn't morbid at all."

I'm about to try opening the door when a voice from behind startles me.

"What are you doing?"

"Jesus Christ, Briar," I spin around, "what are *you* doing? You scared me."

"Really? I didn't mean to—I just, I followed you."

She followed me? And I didn't notice? "I thought you were staying with everyone at karaoke."

She shrugs. "It wasn't fun without you. Besides, I think everyone's gone back to the dorms by now."

"You really shouldn't be walking around late at night by yourself."

"But that's exactly what *you're* doing."

"……"

"You're looking for a secret way into the school, aren't you? That's the lead you were talking about. I was doing the same thing this morning—that's why I wasn't in my room." She looks up at the crypt. "That symbol, it's in the garden, too. Or one like it, at least. And the dorms. Have you noticed?"

"The dorms, did you say?"

"Over the fireplace in the library."

I guess I've spent more time in this graveyard than in the dorms … (I hereby award Briar Thornswood 10 observation points. When she reaches 100, I'll give you a surprise.)

"Do you think the symbol means something?" she asks.

"I do. I'd ask you to take me to the library, but I think it will still be too crowded right now, and we don't have time to waste. So this will have to do."

"For what?"

Naturally, the door doesn't budge. I could force it open, but I'm looking for something that another person would be able to regularly come in and out of, not an entrance only a freak is capable of opening.

I come around to the back of the crypt, searching for another symbol. There, right in the middle, I find it.

"I wonder how I never noticed this before."

A large, rectangular slab of stone about the width of a door is the only part of the crypt free of the vines of ivy growing wildly over the rest. And at chest height, illuminated by the nearby lamppost, is an arrow pointing down with the three circles around it. I press my palm to it. When that fails to do anything, I look at the four smaller, circular symbols surrounding it. They each contain a letter: R, M, O, S. I passed over them completely at first, so it takes me a second to puzzle out. Then I press them in the order of M, O, R, S, followed by the arrow.

Mors, the Latin word for death and destruction. (The things you see when you finally open your eyes.)

"What is—"

The slab of stone gives inward before sliding to the side, revealing—rather than the interior of the crypt itself—a set of stairs leading, well, I think you know.

"The entrance into Hell … and apparently death and destruction. Huh, she wasn't screwing with me. I really am going to have to 'make it worth her while.'"

I step inside the totally-not-suspicious-secret-crypt-passage and begin to descend the stairs when I notice Briar is still following me.

I turn and place both my hands on either side of the entrance, blocking her way. "Where do you think you're going?"

"With you, of course."

"No."

"You can't just—"

"No. Stay."

I start to descend again but don't make it far before I hear footsteps coming in after me. Since she's incapable of listening, I pick her up and physically carry her back outside. After repeating this process three times, Briar lets out a frustrated grunt and plops down on the ground.

"If you won't let me come, I'll just sit here until you get back, no matter how long it takes or how cold it gets."

I stare down at her pouting lips and narrowed eyes. *I thought there was no time to waste so why are you making us sit here like this?* they appear to say. Very expressive eyes.

Letting out a final sigh, I shake my head.

"Just stay close."

*excited smile* "Here. I thought these might come in handy." She hands me a flashlight from her bag and takes another out for herself. (That's right—normal people need flashlights in these situations.)

"If you want to turn back at any time, Briar, just say the word. I promise I won't hold it against you."

At the base of the stairs is a hole just wide enough for one person. It appears to drop straight down but is in fact only about six feet deep. However, whatever ladder had been there is no longer bolted in place.

"Wait up here for a second," I say, jumping through the opening and— *"Son of a bitch."*

Blood trickles from the fresh wound on my shoulder as I land; a piece of what used to be the ladder had fallen outward, horizontally, sticking out at an angle perfect for slicing an unsuspecting hole-jumper such as myself.

"Zero! Are you ok? Zero?!!"

"I'm fine. Now, Briar, I want you to sit at the edge of the hole, ok? But don't jump. Scoot over to the right side—I'm going to lower you down."

She does as I say and I gently grip her by the waist, lowering her with care to avoid any other sharp things that may be sticking out on the way. She's incredibly light, making the task remarkably easy. (Though the stinging in my shoulder won't be going away any time soon. That pine tree seriously has nothing on this metallic incarnation of a Geneva Convention violation.)

"You're hurt, aren't you? Show me."

"I'm not hurt. Now, let's get going."

"You're lying. There was something sharp that cut you when you jumped, wasn't there?" She shines her flashlight around the small, musky stone room to look for the culprit.

"Wait," I say, grabbing her arm and moving it until the light is back on the ladder scrap that tried to KO me. There's something … hanging off it. I walk over and snatch the torn piece of black fabric, looking over my shoulder to see if my uniform really got ripped this badly, or if …

Ah.

"Briar," I hold up the fabric, "here's a piece of solid, physical evidence. It's part of someone's uniform that tore off when they jumped." I put it in her hand and close her fingers around it. "Keep hold of it, all right?"

"All right … but are you ok?"

"Stop asking questions I've already answered. You don't have to worry about me."

Once we exit the room under the hole, the tunnels open up into an expansive space that seems to be as deep as it is dark. Not a sliver of light is present aside from the beams produced by our flashlights.

"Let's keep moving."

Judging from where we started, we're about a half mile away from the main building. I can create the outline of a primitive map when I try to picture it—at least enough to tell us when to make a turn and when to continue straight.

There are a surprising number of off-shoots—narrow, twisting and turning passageways leading in all directions. Curiously, most of these passageways have their own symbols or writings above them, many of which are in Latin. Aside from unknown messages being scrawled on the walls and over entrances, there is also a delightful number of cobwebs that I have to knock aside every time we come through a passage with a lower ceiling.

I cringe at the thought of Briar coming down here by herself. As you may have gathered, I really, *really* didn't want to bring her with me. These tunnels have been closed off and erased from history for a reason. Who knows what's down here … or where they all lead. (She really does have fantastic timing.)

"What if they show up here?" Briar asks me now. Her quiet voice echoes eerily, as do the sounds of our footsteps on the rough, stone floor. "The traitor."

"I don't think they will. After this latest move, they're likely collecting themselves for the finale."

"About that …"

"Hm?"

"About the traitor's latest move, I mean … Zero, you knew they'd do something like this, didn't you? You noticed what it meant when I read off the classes. Rhetoric, Entrepreneurial Skills, Oral History of Storytelling, Zoology—if you take the first letters and rearrange them, it spells out your name. It spells out ZERO."

"Yes. And," I smile at her approvingly, "I'm proud of you for getting that so fast. Just a hunch, but I think Alek and Analisa got it as well."

Briar goes quiet, but I see the pleased upturn of her lips as she glances away.

"So," I pivot her focus, "what do you make of the new faculty involvement with the case?"

She thinks over my question for a moment. "Hm, I guess I'm surprised that they're willing to do anything at all, considering their hands-off approach to student conflicts." I cringe again as she stumbles over a crevice in the derelict pathway. (That was close.) "But it's definitely good news," she continues as if nothing happened. "Because now things might finally calm down for a bit. Like, the traitor will probably want to lie low, right?"

"Not quite."

She looks at me, confused, and nearly missteps again.

This time, I manage to hold back my cringe and continue, "Everyone's assumption is that this is when we can finally take a breath and relax. Whatever mistakes we make, the faculty will surely come to our rescue eventually, correct? Well, anyone who thinks that sentiment through for more than five seconds will come to the conclusion that it's not correct at all. Not at this academy. In truth, we'll be lucky if Mr. Henderson can convince the chairman to allow for rankings to momentarily freeze."

"So you don't think anything will change?"

"Oh, things will change all right. But in quite the opposite way." I steer us through a fork in the path. "Between my fast approaching 'deadline' for solving the case and the unexpected attention garnered by teachers, the traitor has their back against the wall. And that wall is closing in. In their eyes ... the final act is about to go down. For better or worse."

"Final act," Briar murmurs to herself.

"Hey, be careful where you walk," I say, unable to hold it in this time as I see the *fourth* bump in the path that she's *almost* tripped over.

"I am being—" Her boot catches on something and she plummets forward. Her hands shoot out to stop her fall, dropping her flashlight in the process, but the ground is made of unpolished stone that will cut the flesh of her palms to pieces.

I reach out and grab the back of her shirt collar, pulling her back to a standing position. "You were saying?" I don't know if I should blame this accident on my curse or on Briar's clumsiness.

"Thanks … You know, you really are amazing, Zero."

"Quiet."

"Did I say something—"

I grab Briar and duck into a nook diverting to the right, my hand over her mouth and her back pressed flat against my chest.

The echoing of distant footsteps sounds from ahead. *Dammit.* The flashlight! The one that fell out of Briar's hands is still lying directly in the middle of the tunnel. And the footsteps aren't going away, they're coming toward us. I uncover Briar's mouth, making a "quiet" gesture over her lips with my finger before bending down and picking up a pebble. Luckily, the flashlight's switch is facing up, so I can do this—I throw the pebble with precision, making sure it hits its mark and flips the light off. That made some noise, but whatever sound it caused will be less conspicuous than a bright stream of light.

The footsteps are heavy enough that I have an idea of the height and weight of our unexpected tunnel-exploring companion. An adult male or a sizable male student, ie: likely not the traitor. (All the boys in the representative group, aside from Daniel, are either average or lighter than average.)

The footsteps keep coming forward until they stop directly beside our hiding place.

He has a flashlight as well, whoever he is, and he must be looking at the one we left in the middle there. With one hand atop her head, I re-cover Briar's mouth on the off chance she makes an accidental sound that gives us away.

I can hear the man pick up the light, turning it over in his hands as he likely scans the path for signs of company. He doesn't say a word as he begins walking away, still holding onto it. Thirty seconds later, his footsteps become more distant and the sound of a door creaking open and shut is the last thing we hear before the tunnel becomes dead silent again.

I wait another ten seconds to be safe, then I drop my hands away from Briar and nudge her out of the nook. "We need to move."

"Zero, who was that?"

"I'm not sure. But now isn't the time to find out."

She nods and starts to step forward, but I grab her hand, my fingers sliding up to her delicate wrist.

"I thought so."

"Thought w-what?"

"Your pulse," I say, voice quiet, "it's racing."

"It is?"

"I was under the impression you didn't get scared when you're with me."

"I don't. I guess I'm just," she smiles up at me, "excited."

"Weirdo."

"Says the one who keeps grabbing me and picking me up."

"Yeah, well, I'm about to do that again."

"Grab me, or pick me up?"

"Both. We're not alone down here—at the speed we're going, it's not safe. Besides, I'd rather we get back to the dorms before curfew if possible."

"Ok, that makes sense. So what are you proposing?"

I walk around in front of her and kneel down, facing away. "Get on my back. It'll free up my movement."

"How could that free up your movement?"

"You trip too easily and I'm constantly paranoid you're going to wander into another passageway and get lost."

"I-I wouldn't do that," she protests, but climbs onto me, anyway. "You're certain I'm not too heavy?"

"I'm certain."

After a few minutes of walking, I feel Briar's cheek press into the nape of my neck. Her breathing has become soft and rhythmic. (You're kidding.) She's asleep. I didn't even do the weird, two-finger-to-forehead thing this time. Does my presence just make her pass out? No, she woke up early this morning again, that idiot, trying to help *me*. And although I'm certain from the slow steadiness of her pulse that she's sleeping, I could swear I occasionally feel her deeply inhaling, as if she's sniffing the back of my neck.

"Yep," I whisper. "Weirdo."

We should be right around the beginning of the main building now. I make a left turn as if I'm "entering" the school and abruptly halt. There's a large wooden door in the side of this passageway—the only door I've seen since reaching the underground equivalent of the main building.

"Signasti Fatum Tuum," I say, reading the ominous message scrawled atop it, translating from Latin to *You Have Sealed Your Fate*." Carved into the doorknob is the symbol from the garden and the crypt, something I now believe to be a sign of either an entrance or an exit. Hey, what do you think we should call this symbol? I think I'm going to go with **Infernum**. After all, the message of Hell is what brought us here …

The door opens easily when I try it (no rust) and, after deciding no one's there, I step inside.

"What's this?" I take in my surroundings, shining the flashlight over every surface, almost not believing what I'm seeing. "Impossible …"

At the center of the chamber is a long, flat-surfaced rock. It could almost be a table, but its similarities lie closer to a sacrificial altar. On top—covering the full length of it and stacked into neat, orderly piles—is every single missing piece of work.

Every test, paper, worksheet, and assignment.

They're all … here.

(Wait, so these assignments aren't simply being destroyed immediately after being stolen?) Not only that, but they're all being kept in pristine condition. "*Why?*"

Briar stirs, her head lifting. "Mmh, where are we, Zero?" Then she sees what I'm looking at. "Are those what I think they are …?"

I set her on her feet and flip the switch on the old, bronze-encased lantern sitting among the papers, flooding the room with red-orange lighting. "Yes."

"*Auhh!*" Briar gasps, staring wide-eyed at the writing on the wall behind the altar.

I don't need to look to see what's caught her attention—written in the same handwriting as the note I'd gotten, it was the first thing I saw when I stepped foot into this chamber:

There, scrawled in messy red paint, covering half the wall behind the altar, **is my name.**

***

# Natalia Sharp

- **Year/age/student ranking**: N/A
- **Hair**: black
- **Eyes**: gray
- **Height/Weight**: N/A ("never ask a woman her weight")

- **Noticeable features**: curvaceous figure, thick raven hair, sultry appeal
- **Favorite item**: a secret
- **Likes**: mind games, flirting, smoking, a challenge
- **Dislikes**: being sidelined
- **Personal comment**: "Despite what he may think, I have Zero wrapped around my little finger."
- **Fact**: Natalia had a fascination with Zero before he ever transferred to Kane Academy as she was appointed in charge of his transition by the chairman. They didn't have any contact until the beginning of his sophomore year when he was in an ethics class of hers. Zero started up their affair shortly after in order to have eyes on the inside of the academy. Recently, she feels he's been pulling away from her.

James Hudson

Analisa Weston

*The North Garden*

*Kane Cemetery*

***

Zero * 321

# CHAPTER 13:

## THE TRUE TARGET

I pick up the papers on the altar and flip through them, puzzled. Meanwhile, Briar picks up the flashlight and wanders around the chamber "looking for clues."

"Try not to touch anything," I say offhandedly, my focus on the small pile of work I notice set aside from the rest. It's the missing work belonging to the student I've suspected since the beginning. I quickly riffle through it. "Not a single mistake, huh?" Every question is answered perfectly. *Too* perfectly.

But, just as interestingly, there's one student whose pile is nowhere to be found: Nina Taylor, the representative who had a list of the top students from the recently attacked classes on her. Her assignments are the only ones entirely missing from this altar of stolen work. Vaguely, I hear the sound of stone shifting as I continue rifling through the papers. "Say it is her, it still doesn't make sense. Why keep them all? *Every single* missing assignment is here except …" (*Oh.*) "Hah. Really? I didn't even *think* of that. How stupid of me—"

*SLAM!*

I whip around at the sound of stone slamming shut to find that Briar is gone. "Briar, you touched something, didn't you?"

"Zero!" Her voice comes muffled from behind a wall of rock. "I pressed something on the wall and it opened up, but then it just shut behind me the second I walked in!"

"What did you press?"

"O-oh …"

"Briar?"

"… Th-there are a lot of spiders in here …"

"Spiders?" (*Spiders?*)

"Oh, god, they keep coming out of the cracks and the ceiling, everywhere—"

"Briar, you're ok. You're not scared, right? I'm right here. Now, what did you touch?"

"A circle with a, uh, a face on it. A grinning face."

Of course she'd have to go around touching the creepiest things in the room, and the creepiest of all would be the half-sneering, half-smiling face of a joker painted onto a round slab in the wall. I press it, but nothing happens.

"Briar, you're going to have to open this thing from the inside. What do you see in there?"

"I don't know; it's really small. I can barely turn around."

*And you decided to go inside it?* I think with a groan. "Are there any other painted faces or symbols on the walls?"

"T-the walls, the walls are covered in spiders! There's more every time I look—they won't stop!"

"I didn't take you to be one with a fear of spiders."

"I'm not, but … but, Zero, they keep biting me."

(Biting her?) So that quiver in her voice isn't due to fear—she's shaking in *pain*. My fist pounds into the rock. "Briar, I know it's hard, but if there are too many crawling on you, stop trying to get them off. Spiders tend only to bite when they're trapped or need to defend themselves." She doesn't answer, so I assume she's trying to stay still. "Good. Now, tell me, what is it you see in there? If there's a way in, there's a way out."

"I-I see a painting, but nothing that can be pressed on. Oh, except below it, there are three circles! Just like the grinning face—"

"Don't touch them!" I yell. Breathing in, I take a split second to calm myself. "Do the three circles all look exactly like the joker face out here?"

"N-no … It's hard to make out since spiders keep crawling over them."

"Just try for me."

"There's a fox, I think, some kind of bird, and the outline of, o-of a, a person."

"Ok, you're doing well." (The hell does any of this mean?) "And you said there was a painting—what's that of?"

"F-four half-suns—I mean rising suns, two full suns, and three moons, I think?"

A fox, a bird, a person, and four rising suns, two full suns, and three moons … *What the fuck?* I rest my head against the wall, squeezing my eyes shut to think. If I have her press the wrong circle, I have a feeling something very bad might happen. Spiders will no longer be our main concern. But what is this getting at? What kind of trap room …

My eyes open.

"Briar, press the circle with the outline of a person. Do it now!"

The grinding sound of stone sliding to the side lets me know she's done it. But then it stops part way, leaving only a three-inch-wide gap. *What, but why?!* We answered the riddle correctly. Of that, I'm sure.

"Zero, it won't move any further!"

"Damned trap room doesn't even work properly," I mutter, sticking my fingers in the gap and gripping on. Instantly, spiders come crawling out onto my arm. "If they're gonna make it a death trap and an arachnid den, the least they could do is get the mechanics of it right."

The stone grinds against itself as I force the wall open using my right hand while supporting myself on the opposite wall with my left.

It's heavy, easily over a thousand pounds. And I'm moving it, but not fast enough.

I need to get her out *now*.

Come on.

Pull harder.

*Harder.*

By the time I've got the thing wide enough for Briar to step out, I can feel a drop of sweat rolling down my forehead and another sliding down my chest.

I yank her toward me and hit the joker's face again, slamming the wall shut on all the spiders about to swarm out. But that doesn't take care of those already crawling up and down the shaking girl in front of me. I swiftly brush them off her, counting at least thirty.

"All right, there's no more—"

"I can still feel them," Briar whispers, "in my clothes."

"Jesus, just how many were there?"

Briar reaches down the front of her uniform, looking like she's in shock. "I can feel them moving, but I don't know where they are ..."

Part of me wants to turn around and tell her to deal with it, but another part of me knows it's better to finish this quickly before any more spider bites are acquired. (Shit.) "Ok, I'm going to get them all off of you, but I'll have to take some of your clothes off to do it."

She nods, still shaking as she lifts her arms to the side, waiting for me.

Precise, controlled, and collected, I slip Briar's jacket off, followed by her uniform blouse and skirt, leaving on her stockings, underwear, and bra.

A number of eight-legged bastards are uncovered in the process and I knock each of them off clinically—shoulders, arms, chest, stomach, back, thighs, calves, ankles—until I'm sure there are no more. Briar stays still the entire time, obediently turning this-way-and-that when I ask her to.

"That's the last one," I say, resting my arm on my knee as I bend my head down in relief. "You're clear. Oh—the bites!" My gaze snaps up and I'm prepared to assess the bites she's received when the vulnerability of her countenance suddenly hits me.

*Huh …*

It … reminds me …

It reminds me of *that* time …

Nine years ago.

I blink.

(What ... just happened?) This look she's giving me, I was suddenly transported back ... **Back to that day** ... For a second, it was like I was there.

Briar mistakes my hallucinogenic episode for irritation. "I'm, I-I'm sorry. I shouldn't have been touching things."

I stand and place her jacket around her shoulders, handing her the rest of her uniform. "It's not your fault. You couldn't have known it would have a secret death room."

Though the damage has been done, I turn around as she gets re-dressed. (That wasn't only a hallucination just now. That was a memory flash. The memory of when we ... )

"I think there was something hanging from the ceiling in that room," Briar says tentatively. "I couldn't really tell what it was, so I'm not sure if this is true, but I think ... I think it would have dropped on my head if I pressed the wrong symbol."

"Given what else we know, that's a high possibility."

"How did you know which one I should choose?"

"It was like a game, a riddle, actually. The question was asked in the painting and the answer choices were each of the symbols. The riddle was the famous one given to Oedipus by the Sphinx: What goes on four legs in the morning, two in the afternoon, and three in the evening? The answer is man, who crawls as a baby, walks on two legs as an adult, and uses a walking stick in his final years. The rising suns, full suns, and moons were used to represent this."

She touches my arm, gently prodding me to turn back around, so I comply. "That's unbelievable. How could you figure that out so quickly?"

"Like I said, it's a fairly famous riddle, so not nearly as impressive as it may seem."

"And you … you moved the wall! With your bare hands, you pushed the stone aside."

"It's not as heavy as it looks." (Lie. My back is going to be aching later tonight, I can feel it.)

Briar walks over, puts both hands in the slim crevice of the door, and starts to pull at it. She grunts with the effort, feet almost slipping out from under her.

"Hey, hey!" I place a hand on her shoulder. "You have nothing to grip onto, of course you won't be able to move it. And before you get yourself trapped in another death room, let me check out your bites."

Thankfully, no spiders of the venomous variety bit her. There are no signs of swelling or notable inflammation and she claims not to have any muscle pains or cramping. But, as I brush her hair aside to assess her neck, she *does* appear to have an unusually high heart rate. Her breathing is faster and a light coat of sweat shines on her forehead. When I press my fingers to her pulse there, it seems her heart picks up in speed again.

(Is she ok? In shock? What's wrong?) She claimed last time that her racing heart was due to excitement, but I *know* that can't be the case right now.

"Let's get you back and put a cold washcloth on these. It'll help soothe the pain. Here, get on my back again."

"But what about the evidence?"

"We've got what we need from down here."

"And what was it we needed?"

"The thing we've been after since the very beginning."

I stand with Briar hanging onto me tightly, taking one last glance at my name on the back wall before switching off the lantern.

"**Motive.**"

***

After dropping Briar off at her room, I head down to the library and check the fireplace for the Infernum. As it turns out, there are three different symbols etched into the bricks. When they're pressed in the correct order, another stupid riddle, the entire fireplace moves aside just enough for a person to slip inside.

Back in the "Sealed Fate" chamber, under a different Infernum in the ceiling, is a trap door leading into a classroom of the main building.

Further down the tunnels and up several secret staircases is another exit leading directly to the president's office, as I expected given the sign over its entryway. *See page <u>223</u>.

"Fascinating."

Is it possible this system of tunnels and chambers really could get you *anywhere* in the entire academy? It makes for a wonderful method of carrying out nefarious deeds without being caught, I'll say that much. As long as you don't get lost or trapped in a secret room of death, that is …

Hey, I want you to make a decision now. Yeah, it's time.

Who is the traitor?

Come on, tell me. Put an X next to your guess:

| Analisa __ | James __ | Thomas __ | Daniel__ | Nina__ |
|---|---|---|---|---|
| Maggie__ | Alek__ | March__ | Sam__ | Other__ |

Other? Yeah, I guess that is a vague option. But for all you know, *I* could be the traitor. *Just joking.* Don't take it so seriously.

This'll all be worked out soon enough. You'll see.

"Zero Hale, is that you?"

The sound of Analisa Weston's voice gets me to look up from where I am on the library floor, attempting to reach behind my back with a washcloth to clean the cut I'd received from jumping through that damned hole.

"If you're having to ask," I say, crossing my legs and leaning back on my hands, "then your powers of observation aren't as strong as I'd believed they were."

She gives me a small, tired smile. "Pardon me if seeing *anyone* sprawled out, shirtless, in the middle of the library at two a.m. with a bloodied towel is something I find to be a strange sight."

"I suppose you have a point. What are you still doing up? I'd have thought the karaoke debacle would've tired you out."

"It did. And yet, I couldn't sleep. I often come here when that's the case." Analisa looks around admiringly at the rows and rows of books. "Even when I have nothing else, at least I have reading."

"Nothing else? I think that statement would hurt James's feelings, don't you?" Standing there in her matching blue pajamas, silvery-colored hair falling to her slim waist, Analisa makes it very easy to see how she could have such a hold over someone like James Hudson. But does she feel the same?

"It looks as if you could use some help," she says, ignoring my comment and bending down beside me to take the dirtied cloth out of my hand. "Here, let me."

After getting a new towel from her room and soaking it in soap and water, Analisa begins dabbing at my wound. Her touch is gentle but firm, and I get the feeling this isn't her first time taking care of a person's injuries.

"I won't ask where you got this, because I already know you won't tell me. And I won't tell you to have it treated properly by the infirmary, because I know you won't listen. But ... how are you not wincing at all? Doesn't it sting?"

"Only a little." Telling her that I'm actually enjoying the feel of her soothing touch would probably creep her out.

"You must have a high pain tolerance. This is a nasty cut."

"It'll be fine in the morning."

"I think you mean in a few days, or maybe even a few weeks. Just how fast do you think gashes like this heal? It could very well get infected."

"Analisa, you come in here when you can't sleep, isn't that right?"

"... Yes, that's what I said."

"How often would you say that is?"

"Probably every other night, or so."

(That may explain why the traitor has been using the crypt entrance at times rather than only the convenience of this one.) "Have you ever seen anyone else down here? Late at night, I mean."

"Hmm, well, yes. I have. I'm not the only one with sleep issues and a love for books."

"Did they appear startled to see you—nervous, even?"

"That's one way to put it. Though that only makes sense, doesn't it? Not many are awake at this hour, much less out of bed and wandering about." She takes a breath, pausing for a second. "Zero ... maybe I'm just a bit slow, but I don't see how this line of questioning is relevant to anything."

"I wouldn't call the number two of the senior class 'slow.'"

"I—" Analisa cuts off, towel falling away from my back as if something's startled her. "That's ...?"

"Analisa, are you all right?"

"Your wound, it's … If I didn't know better, I'd say it almost looks healed already."

"You probably just washed away all the blood, which was making it look more serious than it was."

"That's not all. I don't know how I didn't notice at first, the cut must have distracted me, but … this tattoo you have, something about it is familiar."

I sit up straighter. "Unless there's something you're not telling me, then you've never seen me without a shirt on and therefore have never seen this tattoo until now."

"No … not all of it. Just," her fingers trace over the lines of dark ink spreading across my back, "this portion of it. It's so unique, yet I swear, I've seen it before."

*That's. Not. Possible.*

"Thank you for the help." I stand, leaving a still-confused Analisa on the floor. "We should both go back to our rooms now. Tomorrow's a big day, after all."

"Very well …"

"There are just two things I need from you before that. First, have you heard any updates from the faculty meeting yet?"

"There was one significant development. Though it's nothing you wouldn't have already foreseen."

"So, rankings are frozen, then. For now." (Yeah, that sounds about right.)

Analisa nods, still staring up at me from the ground. "This is the end of the line. Whatever final move the traitor plans to make, I'm guessing it will be done tomorrow."

She's certainly right about that.

"And the last thing? You said there were two that you needed from me, Zero."

"Yes. The last thing I need is for you to confirm the name of the one you've run into here before …"

*The East Dorm's Library*

*13 ½*

I sit with my eyes closed and feet up while the mayhem in the room continues to escalate.

"I didn't do it! I didn't fucking do it!" Nina yells, the crunching of paper sounding in my ears as she balls up the assignment in her hand and throws it.

"Then who the hell did?!" James yells back with just as much enthusiasm. "The goddamn tooth fairy? But instead of money, she's brought you the miraculous discovery of *all* your 'missing' assignments?!"

"Well, when you put it like that of course it sounds awful!"

"James, calm down."

"I am calm, Ana!"

"Nina, please, stop trying to hit—"

"Daniel, you gotta tell them—you know I didn't do this!"

"Ahhhh!! I knew it was you! Sam, get behind me, this girl is probably going to try and frame one of *us* now that she's been caught. There's no hope left. If I go down, just remember me the way I was, ok?"

"M-march, y-you're scaring me."

"Hey, Hudson, you and Kang both had assignments found, too! So how come you're acting like that ain't also suspicious?!"

"We each had one assignment found, Taylor! One! And it was the most useless assignment outta all of them! Not to mention, it's awfully convenient how the only people who had work found were two guys who ain't in your grade that just 'happen' to not have any classes with you, don't ya think?"

(So Thomas and James also had assignments returned.) Looks like someone went back to the Sealed Fate chamber for a few more things after Briar and I left. Well, that makes perfect sense given the way this finale is meant to play out.

"Oh, yeah? Well, if I was actually the traitor, I wouldn't return any of your stuff! I'd burn all of it—so there!"

"Come over here and say that to my face!"

Small hands suddenly wrap around my arm, gripping me tightly. "Zero," Briar whispers. "Zero, *do something*. They're going to kill each other."

I let out a breath and lower my feet as I push my hands down on the table, standing.

When I open my eyes, Nina is being held back by Daniel with her foot in the air poised for a kick, James is on the ground with Analisa standing next to him—holding him by the shirt, March is sobbing in the arms of Sam, and Alek is in the corner of the room cackling at the entire situation with laughter that would put a hyena to shame.

(Indeed, any semblance of peace of mind Mr. Henderson was able to offer us yesterday has been completely undone by today's 'unexpected' turn of events.)

"Everyone," I say, and wait as they all slowly turn to look at me, "let's change venues. Come."

A bickering procession of disgruntled representatives follows me from the student council room to the cafeteria. They remain arguing as I go up to the smoothie counter and order two strawberry smoothies, one of which I hand off to Briar. It's been proven that people are more likely to listen to you when you ask them to come to a different location. (Plus, I felt like having a smoothie.)

Taking a long sip from my straw, I survey the group of students before me. Then the cafeteria doors fling open and Marina comes running in, startling everyone and putting an end to any lingering squabbles.

"I knew it! I knew you were about to start without me," she huffs. "But I made it, so there!"

"Perfect timing, Marina. You've sliced through the tension excellently. Now," I smile and sit down atop one of the lunch tables, "shall we begin?"

"Dude, are you really drinking a smoothie and smiling right now?" James asks. "Slate, you too? Man, why am I not surprised?" *Alek decided to follow in Zero's footsteps and is currently ordering a pina colada.

"I'd say bringing this investigation to a close is reason enough to smile. So, let's start by looking at what's caused everyone here today to get their panties in such a twist." I turn to Nina. "All of your work was mysteriously discovered in a random, unused locker this morning, wasn't it?"

"I mean, yeah, but I swear to god I didn't put it there—I have no idea where it came from!"

I hold up a hand. "Let's examine the facts: Nina, you were found to have a list of the recently targeted students in your bag yesterday, and today all of your work, and your work alone, has been found, allowing your unofficial student rank to skyrocket back to its former position due to the deal the student council made with teachers to allow targeted students to have their work counted should it be discovered. On top of this, there was a rip in your uniform two days ago. You even asked Daniel to mend it for you, which he did that night." (Recall Daniel's excuse for being late at the tech store with Alina Carter.)

"What does that have to—"

"For the rest of this to make sense, you should all know that

Briar and I discovered the way the traitor has been getting in and out of the academy after hours. At first, they were stealing security IDs and using them until they were deactivated. But this was a risky method and had limited uses per stolen card, so they changed tactics ... You see," I lean forward, and everyone in the room seems to instinctively do the same, "I'd appreciate it if this information wasn't shared outside of this group, but ... there is a secret system of tunnels running under this school."

"Secret tunnels?" Nina and James say at the same time. "Are you for real?"

"I'm afraid I am, in fact, 'for real.' And at one of the entrances, a torn piece of fabric was found." At this, Briar takes out the scrap of clothing I'd asked her to keep safe and hands it to me. I lift it up for them to see. "This is from a Kane Academy uniform. And," I get up and walk to Nina, placing the fabric on the stitches of her now-mended jacket, "it fits exactly with where you had Daniel fix up the back of your sleeve."

As it turns out, this tear in her sleeve is the "possibly significant" detail I'd taken note of the first afternoon we'd all met. *See page <u>205</u>.*

"W-wait, but, I ..."

"James, given all of this disconnected information, who do you suspect the traitor to be?"

"Huh?" He frowns, affronted at being put on the spot. "Well, I'd have to say it's Nina, of course."

"Yes, you're right." I pat him on the shoulder as I pass by, beginning to pace. "At least, that's the conclusion one would come to if they were an idiot."

"The hell did you just say to me? You callin' me stupid?"

"All suspicion has been firmly placed on Nina. As of right now, she is the only one to have benefited from this mess. Except … has she really benefited? She's now the number one suspect, and therefore the number one candidate for being blamed for everything and expelled as a result."

"Well, obviously she didn't intend for it to go down this way! She was probably planning to steal as many assignments as she could for as long as she could, and then, at the end, return all of her own along with a couple more of the unimportant ones for everyone else to throw off suspicion—but that was all screwed up when her hiding spot was uncovered too early. See? It makes total sense."

"So you think if that hypothetical plan you just created were to actually play out, she would benefit from it?"

"What're you even askin'? I mean, sure, it's a risky play, and she'd probably still be the number one suspect all right, but even with this mistake, there's already a good chance she won't actually get charged with nothin'. And if that's the case, of course she's benefited! Once the rankings unfreeze, hers'll go right back to what it was while all of ours drop," James goes on.

"Yes, her rank will stay the *same*. Maybe it'll rise by a slot or two, but nothing that will make a distinctive difference. Why is that, you ask? Because consider the rank Nina was already at. Nina, tell us, what official rank are you?"

"Umm, well, it took a while to get there but, with Daniel's help, it's gotten to ninth place," she states proudly.

"Ninth place. In other words, already a part of the top ten. The benefits belonging to those at the top of Kane Academy were benefits Nina already had. Of course, this ends up being a problem for most of you, as most of you already had secured top ten spots. Really, this was an issue that bothered me for a long time. For a multitude of reasons, I couldn't seem to pinpoint the motivation behind the traitor's thinking. That is … until the discovery Briar and I made down in the tunnels."

I do my best to paint the picture of the contents inside the Sealed Fate chamber.

Analisa's eyes grow wider with every word. "You mean to tell us that you've found all the missing assignments?"

I nod. "It wasn't just Nina's. And it wasn't just the 'unimportant ones' for everyone else. It was *all of them*. Now, it was then, and only then, that I finally began to understand the true intent behind this whole case. There's just one reason why someone would keep all the evidence of their crimes hidden safely away in perfect condition: the traitor's plan, from the beginning, was to return all of the assignments. All of the assignments, starting with those belonging to junior representative Nina Taylor."

"Just what are you saying …?"

"This left me with a question—one not accounted for in the case file, or asked about by any of the representatives or council members: What happens to everyone and their ranks if this entire business of missing assignments and tests gets **overturned**? At first, it appears that overturning the whole thing won't do anything for anyone—things would just go back to how they were. But that's only true if no one is *caught*. If the blame were to be pinned on just one of you, a serious violation and misconduct inevitably resulting in one person's expulsion … who stands to gain?"

"….."

"It wasn't until I started suspecting the end goal being the outcome of framing someone rather than the outcome of the crimes themselves that things started to fall into place. Suddenly, the reasoning for focusing on a select group of students, the nine of you, began to make sense. At least, when combined with the other important clues here it does. It's akin to gathering all the players together on the board of a mystery game, creating a core cast and therefore a core set of suspects. This way of thinking, as if it's all a theatrical production, makes sense when paired with the patterns I noticed."

"Patterns?"

"Yes. Allow me to show you."

I take everyone with me to Ms. Kurima's classroom where I find her grading papers at her desk. This ought to make for a good final stage.

"Zero, what are you doing here?"

"Mind if we use your whiteboard?" I ask as we all file in. "If you say yes, you can stay and watch what happens next."

"... Ok."

I walk up to the board and grab a dry-erase marker. "Here's where things get tricky ... So try to keep up." I begin making a rough replication of the original charts Analisa created. "Each day for the past three weeks, without fail, at least one student of high rank was targeted. This is where the repeat attacks on those of you who became representatives come into play. However, at the same time, seemingly random students of seemingly random ranks would also have work stolen. Briar, what did I tell you we could consider these attacks as?"

Briar sits up in the seat she's taken, suddenly very awake. "You said they were like red herrings."

"Exactly. All the attacks in this chart can be split into two groups, those that focused on members of the high-ranking representatives, and those that took from random, singular students. If we ignore the red herrings," I begin crossing them out, "and look only at the classes of the representatives, we are left with History of Europe, English 300, Logistics & Enterprise, Physics, Mastering the Written Word,

Economics, Humanities, English 400, Literary Analysis, Psychology of Man, Media & Technology, and a repeat of Economics. Without all the excess information and attacks, do you see what this means?"

Analisa gasps quietly. "I hadn't been looking for a pattern—not one like *this*. I never thought there'd be a message hidden in …"

James groans, leaning back in his chair. "Well, I ain't seeing it, so can someone explain?"

"I'm not seeing it, either," Thomas says, frowning so deeply I believe he may give himself permanent wrinkles.

"Allow me to make the visualization clearer."

| Monday - Jan 20 | Tuesday - Jan 21 | Wednesday - Jan 22 | Thursday - Jan 23 | Friday - Jan 24 |
|---|---|---|---|---|
| History of Europe | English 300 | ~~English 100~~<br><br>Logistics & Enterprise | ~~Algebra~~<br><br>Physics | ~~Visual Studies~~<br><br>Mastering the Written Word |

| Monday - Jan 27 | Tuesday - Jan 28 | Wednesday - Jan 29 | Thursday - Jan 30 | Friday - Jan 31 |
|---|---|---|---|---|
| ~~Chemistry~~<br><br>Economics | Humanities: Religion & Culture | English 400<br><br>~~Popular Literature~~ | ~~Astronomy~~<br><br>Literary Analysis | ~~Comparative Government~~<br><br>Psychology of man<br><br>~~US History~~ |

| Monday –<br>Feb 3 | Tuesday –<br>Feb 4 | Wednesday | Thursday | Friday |
| --- | --- | --- | --- | --- |
| Media &<br>Technology | Economics | Rhetoric,<br>Entrepreneurial<br>Skills, Oral<br>History of<br>Storytelling, &<br>Zoology<br>(ignore for now) | N/A | N/A |

Analisa walks up to the whiteboard, staring hard at the chart. "This message … is incredibly unnerving."

For those still not understanding, I continue writing it out.

History, English, Logistics, Physics, Mastering, Economics, Humanities, English, Literary, Psychology, Media, Economics.

Or …

History, English, Logistics, Physics, Mastering, Economics, Humanities, English, Literary, Psychology, Media, Economics.

Put it all together …

HELPMEHELPME

HELP ME HELP ME

"Help me, help me," Briar murmurs, also coming up to the board. "You figured this out on the first day, didn't you?"

Alek leans forward, brows furrowed as he examines the chart. Meanwhile, James and Thomas gape, jaws open.

"Care to finish off the message for us, Briar?" I say and step out of the way.

She takes the marker from me and carefully writes out what's left—the part of the message we'd discussed down in the tunnels.

"Rhetoric, Entrepreneurial Skills, Oral History of Storytelling, and Zoology," she says the names aloud as she writes. "You have to re-arrange them, but if you take the first letters again and put them together ... they spell Z-E-R-O."

Rhetoric, Entrepreneurial Skills, Oral History of Storytelling, Zoology →

Zoology, Entrepreneurial Skills, Rhetoric, Oral History of Storytelling →

Z, E, R, O → ZERO.

"Very good."

"Now *that* part," Alek cuts in, "I did get. But the first half ... Heh, I'm almost a little disappointed in myself."

"So, the full message isn't just Help Me, Help Me." Analisa's fingers lightly touch my name on the board. "It's Help Me, Help Me, Zero. Incredible. But ..."

I know exactly what she's going to bring up. "But you wish to know how the traitor could have foreseen that this exact group of students would make up the representatives on the case, therefore making it possible to spell out this message."

She nods.

"I," (Myles), "did some digging on the students who volunteered you all." *See pages <u>221</u> & <u>257</u>. "Most of you volunteered yourselves, this was practically a guarantee for those of you who had an excessive amount of work stolen, but some of you only joined the cause because your classmates asked it of you. In those cases, each student who volunteered you reports the same experience: they were messaged by an anonymous account over the chatroom app and offered an exchange of credits for submitting your name to the council."

"So they were truly determined for this outcome, hm."

"Wait a goddamn second." James, finally out of his stupor, joins us up front. "You mean this whole case, all three weeks of it, all the theft and—and *bribery* and everything else, has just been *this?*" He slaps my name on the board. "This traitor trying to send a message to Hale?"

"Not exactly. It's more like … there's a conflicting set of ideologies at play."

"In English, thank you very much," Marina mutters from her chair, not bothering to get up like the rest of them.

I shoot her a look and continue. "What was clear to me from the beginning is that there are **two** very different minds at work here. One, a cautious, obedient pawn with something to lose. The other, a cruel mastermind with a sick sense of humor and no regard for anything other than their own enjoyment. But where did I get these conclusions from? It's all there in the data. Actually, this is something I touched on with Briar and Marina a while ago."

"Oh!" Briar exclaims. "Wait, do you mean about them not targeting the council and how that conflicts with the idea of someone who wants to enjoy causing trouble?"

"Yes, actually." I'm surprised she got there so quickly. "All the students attacked are a part of a wide variety of clubs. But something I noticed immediately was that none of the students attacked, *not a single one*, was a part of the student council. I had Marina gather some extra information and was quite surprised to find that not only are none of the affected students in the council, despite some of them having a relatively esteemed ranking, but none of them are even in a social circle *containing* members of the council. This was a very deliberate, thought-out choice that directly opposes the impulsivity of, say, stealing an entire class's worth of tests in a single night. Why be so careful only to turn right around and be so reckless?

"Then there's the matter of spelling out secret messages. Why make elaborate moves that have no impact on a plan to get the benefits of sabotaging your classmates while simultaneously stealing the assignments of high-ranking students so consistently, so *methodically?*" The same could be asked about them taking the risk of returning to the council room just so I could receive that little drawing of the two wolves—a declaration of sorts to let me know my challenge had been accepted. (But I won't bring that up right now.)

"The message is still bothering me," Analisa says, looking it over again. "There's something about it that doesn't feel right."

"That's because there is something not quite right about it. Before it was fully spelled out, I believed the message of help was directed at the president. But then I realized that made no sense. If you wanted to aim for the president, you'd begin with members of the council, or his family—after all, Myles Adrian was never targeted the entire time. Instead, the traitor brought me into the mix—a student of incredibly low rank and altogether inconsequential social standing. An outlier amongst the elite representatives."

"They must have *really* wanted trouble if they decided to bring you into it," Ms. Kurima says from behind her desk. I'd almost forgotten she was there.

"Other actions taken by the traitor that had no impact on their final goal of raising their position by expelling a classmate include a note I received before taking on the case, a code written on Ms. Kurima's whiteboard, a mysterious drawing I found placed in my bag, and my name written in the chamber with the assignments."

*See pages 107, 222, 225, & 318.

"What can we divine from this? A conclusion none of us expected to make: There are, in all likelihood, *two* traitors. For one of them, Nina has been the true target all along. And for the other

… the true target has been me."

A quiet "woah" leaves Sam's lips.

"We may know the identity of the first. But, unfortunately, I'll admit I still have no idea who the second might be. They will be much harder to catch. They're clever, the mastermind behind the entire plan, and they did it all without getting their own hands dirty since it seems they successfully used the original traitor to steal all the work. If I had to guess, I'd say they're someone who has stayed far away from this entire investigation."

"Um," March speaks up for the first time, "you're saying this like we know who the first traitor is already."

"What, didn't I say?"

"Uhh … no."

"Oh." I lean back against the board. "It's Maggie."

"*MAGGIE?!*" everyone shouts at once.

"Given that Nina is the one being targeted for expulsion, the traitor had to be in the junior class to get any benefit from that. You can already discount Nina for obvious reasons, then you can eliminate anyone who's already in the top ten since taking down someone below you won't help you—say goodbye to Daniel as a possibility—and a person whose rank is too low for it to matter is also not going to gain anything, so you can cross off Alek, too. This only leaves Maggie. To double-check, I ran a calculation based on the scores she would've gotten on her assignments which I found in the tunnels, and if Nina were to disappear, she would have a clear shot at rising back to the top ten so long as she maintained that quality of result.

"It's hard to say for sure since a lot goes into calculating a ranking, but each assignment of hers was perfect." *See page 322. "Not a single question wrong. Curious, I double-checked with an outside source,"

(Ms. Sharp), "and found that all of her work has been perfect the whole semester. That's rather suspicious, too, if you think about it … It's very likely that was part of the deal she cut with the mastermind. If she followed his instructions, he'd get her back into the top ten no matter what. Be it through expelling another student, or helping her cheat. So he pulled her strings and she danced to his tune."

"'He?'" Analisa and Briar both ask.

"Statistical probability."

Ms. Kurima shakes her head. "All this brain power and you're still second to last in your whole damned grade."

"Also, it shouldn't be controversial to say that Maggie's mental health is relatively unstable at the moment, so if it weren't for someone like the mastermind to help her out, she'd probably have continued on the decline that dropped her out of the top ten last semester, making her lower in status than even what her current unofficial rank is."

"*You're* the unstable one if you think *Maggie* could have pulled this off," Nina says, hands on her hips. "She's not capable of something like this! She's not a liar."

"She's not capable of it *on her own*," I counter. "But if you want more evidence, let's go back—"

"Wait," Daniel interrupts, suddenly looking very troubled. "Where is Maggie?"

(What does he mean where is she? She's gotta be … wait.) I scan the room. Then I scan it again. "It appears … Maggie is not with us."

***

**Bonus:** Are you kidding? We don't have time for a bonus! Get to the next chapter!

***

# Chapter 14:
## Something I've Missed

"It's fine even if she isn't here," Alek remarks, unconcerned as ever as the rest of the representatives begin to panic. "It's not like she can go anywhere. No matter what, it's over for her. That is … if she's actually the traitor. What were the other pieces of evidence you were about to give, Zero?"

"Alek is right," Analisa says. "If it's Maggie, then it doesn't matter where she is. There's nowhere to run. Her time at this academy will be finished."

"I don't know …" Briar looks at me, golden eyes especially turbulent. "It's like Analisa said about the message—don't you feel it, Zero? Something isn't right. Why isn't she here right now?"

"I just can't believe he started his whole big reveal when the one he knows is responsible isn't even in the room," is Ms. Kurima's helpful addition to the conversation.

"As I was saying," I pick my momentum back up, "regardless of where she is right now, evidence points to her." My hand flicks toward Nina. "Take your uniform here to begin with."

"My uniform that's being used to frame me?"

"Yes."

"What about it?"

"It fits you perfectly."

Nina's fierce expression suddenly dissolves as her dark skin tinges red. "Uh, w-what? Is that a compliment?"

"Oh my god, Zero!" Marina finally acts interested, bolting upright in her chair. "Did you really just give her a compliment?!"

"Both of you calm down. I'm making a point. Her uniform fits perfectly because of course it does. All academy uniforms are custom-made for each student." Hey, if you've been paying attention to the bonus content, you know this. "But, Nina, let me guess, this isn't your first uniform to have a mysterious rip or hole, is it?" (Traversing the tunnels would likely leave a few scrapes and tears—as I learned firsthand.)

"I mean, yeah, they've been getting a little roughed up, I guess. I kinda just have a tendency to do that, though … Daniel's always tellin' me I'm real hard on my clothes."

"So you haven't noticed an increase in damage?"

"Well, I didn't say that … But I swear I'm tellin' the truth that I really got no idea why they keep ending up like that."

"It's simple. The reason is because someone else has been wearing them. And that someone is Maggie Arrowood, your roommate, who has easy access to your personal items at all times."

"And this has to do with uniforms being custom made … how?"

"Nina, you're about 5'7, and I'd put your weight at around 135 lbs—" *See Nina's profile on pg. 207 (Zero is only slightly off.) "And Maggie is … roughly 5'4, 120 lbs." *See Maggie's profile on pg. 239 (Zero is actually dead on.)

"How the hell could you—"

"That is to say, a uniform that fits you would be slightly too big on her. And, on the first day we all gathered in the council room, Maggie continuously pulled at her sleeves as if their large size was bothering her. How would this be possible if her uniform was custom-made? I have no doubt she received instructions to use your uniform when entering the tunnels due to the danger of leaving evidence behind. That is certainly not outside the realm of the mastermind's calculations … Actually, let's call him 'X' for now."

"Can anyone back this up?" Alek asks, looking around.

Hesitantly, Daniel nods. "Yes, though I always assumed tugging at her sleeves was just a habit of hers."

"I don't require any 'backing up;'" I motion to Marina, "the evidence of this claim has already been retrieved."

Marina sighs as though I've greatly put her out but stands and shows an image on her phone to everyone. "Zero rudely ordered me to take this picture for him after he told everybody to get out of the room a couple of days ago." *See page <u>219</u>. "I had no idea what he was getting at, and it was super weird, but I did it."

It's a selfie of her and Maggie, both grinning and holding up peace signs, as instructed (the kind of task only a popular, friendly girl could naturally pull off). Directly beside Marina's form-fitted uniform, the extra room in Maggie's is clear as night and day.

"Huh, yeah, I guess it does look a little funny on her," March says timidly.

"Furthermore, I enlisted Marina's help once again to double-check this finding. Do you recall what I told you to do in the karaoke room?"

"Seriously, again, how could I forget something so weird?" She sighs and then walks around behind me before forcefully jumping onto my back and hugging me tightly. "It was like this."

Ms. Kurima's eyes look like they're about to pop out of their sockets and Briar's face has gone whiter than the stacks of papers we found in the chamber.

"You told me specifically to make sure I made contact with her whole left arm, so of course I thought *this* was the best way to do that—"

"Thank you, Marina," I say shortly while unhooking her arms.

"Though I think we all could have done without the reenactment."

"You were trying to gauge whether or not Maggie was wounded there," Analisa explains for me. "The left sleeve is where Nina's uniform was ripped."

She has a good memory.

"I don't have it on video, but I can assure you all that Maggie immediately recoiled at the contact. It was clear she was in pain."

"Maybe she was just recoiling out of distaste for Almandez," Thomas grumbles. "I'd probably have a similar reaction."

"Hey! What the hell is that supposed to—"

"Next," I begin, taking back the dry-erase marker, "we come to the issue of the timeline. As Briar and I discovered, we know the traitor began by stealing security IDs, the first of which was reported stolen on January 20th." *See page 272. "Why is this a problem with our case?"

Before James and Nina can utter a "How the hell should we know?" Analisa's mind makes the connection. "Because January 20th isn't when this is all supposed to have started."

"Exactly." I circle the date on the chart. "This is when the traitor's methods began, but supposedly not when the *case* actually began. According to Maggie, the first time she was targeted was at the end of last semester, all the way back in December. But if that's true, why were no security IDs taken? You could argue the traitor opted to change MO, but since they hadn't begun using the tunnels, that would mean a change from taking assignments in the middle of the night to during the school day. That's a big change. Even more suspicious than this is how these 'first' attacks fit in with the message carefully crafted these past three weeks. Or, more accurately, how they *don't* fit. Anyone recall what classes Maggie's work was said to be taken from?"

"English 300 and Organic Chemistry," answers Daniel.

"Which makes no sense when added onto the beginning of the message," Analisa mutters. "Zero," she locks eyes with me, "I'm guessing you're about to bring up the fact that Maggie is the one I saw at the library in the middle of the night. Is there an entrance into the tunnels there?"

She just seems to get sharper and sharper. "Yes. There is an entrance there. She was likely looking to use it that night but was prevented from doing so when she saw you. She left shortly after to find another entrance." (The crypt.) "There are multiple of them around campus. Even I don't know where they all are."

"Hang on," James tilts his head, "why would she lie about English 300 and Organic Chemistry?"

"The answer to that is also the answer to why X chose Maggie as the one he'd use."

"So 'X' is really what we're going with?" Ms. Kurima questions.

"Ms. Kurima, if you could keep your comments until the end, that would be best."

"Why you little—"

"It's actually true that she had missing work from both those classes. It's the *reason* behind that missing work that she is lying. When I went through Maggie's pile in the chamber, no work from either of those classes was found, because it never existed to begin with."

Analisa places a hand under her chin. "Are you saying that she simply never completed the work back then and used this case as a reason to cover for that and get credit regardless?"

"I am." (Granted, that's a small part of a much larger picture.) "My guess is that X has been holding these pieces of work, in particular, over her head this entire time with a promise to help her forge them anew before planting all the missing assignments to be found together. They were the original losses that kicked off her downfall, after all, and represent two large 'zeroes' she'd have no chance of making up for by herself.

"So, taking all of that into consideration," I stop pacing and look out at my audience, "put yourself in the mind of X for a moment. For exact reasons we still don't know, you want to create enough trouble to challenge me directly while also protecting your identity so that *the game* may continue as long as you want. Who would you recruit to pull off this scheme? Someone smart, of course, as someone less intelligent than those in the upper ranks—the ones you're targeting—would have a high chance of screwing up and you wouldn't want your game spoiled before you ever get to play. But, even more important than choosing someone smart, you'd need to choose someone *vulnerable*. Someone who is weak and desperate enough to listen to your every command. A puppet whose strings you could pull at will. Essentially, someone who has hit rock bottom and needs to believe you'll save them in order to cope. Those are the easiest people to control and therefore the best pawns."

"So," Briar starts slowly, "Maggie was at this rock bottom, you think?"

"Consider her situation before all of this began. Daniel, you're the one who had to help her through it, weren't you?"

He blinked. "Well, of course she was in a rough spot. Her boyfriend broke her heart and then she dropped in rank all the way to eighteenth place because her work went missing. She needed support."

"I see; Maggie was someone who used to be in the top ten." Analisa looks to Nina. "But while in a state of emotional distress, her attention to her work slipped. And while Daniel was providing her with emotional support, he was also providing you, Nina, with academic support. You've stated multiple times that the only reason you got to where you did is because Daniel helped you with your studies."

"Yeah ... he did help me ..."

"Precisely," I say. "Maggie told me much the same last night when I pressed her about it. And that's not the only thing that became clear to me. Upon hearing what she has to say about you," I look at Daniel, "and watching the way she watched *you* the whole night, it was painfully obvious that Maggie Arrowood has feelings for you. In fact, I don't think it's a stretch to say that she's in love with you."

A collective intake of breath ripples through the room.

"But I'd be willing to guess that you already knew that, didn't you, Daniel?"

His expression is grave, as if being put in this position is the last thing he ever wanted. But he responds, "I had my suspicions."

"Similarly, I'd also wager that Maggie believes you," I continue speaking to Daniel, "fancy Nina. And that Nina feels the same way."

"Say what now?!! She thinks Daniel and I are a thing?"

"Well, he does go out of his way to help you on a near constant basis." Granted, that is more out of necessity than anything else, but ... I let my point stand. "So, I'll ask again, as X, who would you single out?"

*Zero's mental image of "X"*

"A timid girl who'd just been broken up with and lost her place in the top ten to her own roommate, who was now getting the attention of the boy she loved and viewed as her savior, all in the span of a couple of weeks, would be a good choice. I know that's the kind of person I'd pick."

"So *you* could be X?" James all but shouts.

I stare dumbfounded at him. "What is it like to be so blissfully ignorant to everything going on around you?" (Though me and this X, we may have more in common than not …) "I am simply pointing out that Maggie has the disposition of the perfect pawn. But there's one last piece of evidence I have to give—the piece that made me have suspicions about Maggie from the start."

"Let's hear it then," Thomas says grimly.

"Oh, yes," Alek grins, "let's hear it."

"First, I-I have a question, if you don't mind."

"What is it, March?"

"Umm, how was X able to communicate his instructions to Maggie? I mean, if he wanted to stay far away from the case and protect his identity … how could he do both?"

All heads snap from March to me. (Huh, isn't this part obvious?) We already went over it with the bribery reveal. But I don't have to say anything, because Briar steps up beside me and displays her phone screen with the answer.

"Through the Kane Academy Chatroom, of course," Analisa clarifies. "It's a function installed on all academy-issued phones allowing any student to send messages, anonymous or not, to other students so long as they know their name. It's like it was *made* for something like this."

"Yeah, yeah, that all makes sense." Alek dismisses this bit of the conversation and turns back to me. "What was the reason you first began to suspect Maggie?"

"It was a small slip-up she made—a look she gave me on the first day of this investigation." Alek and Analisa appear intrigued while Thomas and James give me looks of skepticism. Ms. Kurima, meanwhile, only looks amused. "A look she gave me … when I told the lie that Briar had had two assignments stolen." *See page <u>185</u>. "At the time, the information about which students got what stolen from them was still being kept under wraps by the student council, meaning no one in the room had any reason to doubt me. Except for one person, the person who would know *precisely* what was taken and from whom."

"The traitor," Briar says, soft voice carrying across the now dead-silent room.

"Oh, yeah, I remember you saying that!" Nina exclaims, pointing at me. "But it was a lie? Hm, I guess Briar's name never did show up on that chart thing you guys made. Not that I really looked that close at it, anyway."

"It was just for a split second, but her eyes flitted to mine involuntarily—a knee-jerk reaction. It wasn't enough for me to accuse her on the spot or anything, but it had me watching her closely from the start. And that," I sit down atop Ms. Kurima's desk, folding my arms, "brings this case to its end. Given her fragile personality, if we present her with this evidence and thoroughly accuse her, Maggie will crack and confess to everything."

The sound of clapping from the doorway gets all of our attention. With a half-pleased, half-relieved look on her face, Student Council Parliamentarian Charlotte Atwell walks in. "It sounds as though you've solved it. For that, the council is grateful. If this wasn't wrapped up soon, it could've spelled disaster for us."

I cock my head at her. "Yes, we've solved your little 'problem,' so tell the president I expect him to make good on his deal by the end of the day."

"Of course, though, while you've found her out," Charlotte looks around, "I don't see the culprit here."

"She's hiding." James cracks his knuckles, eyes alight with anger. "She knows what's comin' for her."

"Well then, we'll consider your end of the deal met once you've brought Ms. Arrowood to the council, Mr. Hale. After that, I assure you President Jordan will be more than willing to follow through with your request." Charlotte gives me a slight nod and walks out of the room.

(That son of a bitch.)

"Is the council capable of nothing on their own?" I sigh deeply, running a hand through my hair. "Nina, when was the last time you saw Maggie?"

"This morning, I guess? Wait, actually, I think she was already gone when I woke up. I don't think I've seen her all day, then. Not since karaoke last night. Where do you think she could be?"

"If I knew that—"

"Zero." Briar cuts me off, focus trained on the message written on the board. "I don't know why ... but I feel there's something we've missed."

"Something you've missed?" Alek bounces over to us, craning his neck to try and see what Briar could be talking about. "With this message you mean?"

"It—it still feels wrong."

"The message feels wrong because it *is* wrong," I say. "It's nothing short of cruel. X used Maggie to create a stir, knowing she would be caught and have her life ruined, all while forcing her to spell out a message equivalent to her crying out to be saved from her own wrongdoings. If that's not twisted—"

"No!"

Her sudden rise in volume takes me by surprise. "Briar ..."

"I'm sorry, I didn't mean to raise my voice. But there's something *else*. I-I can't figure it out. But you can, Zero. Whatever it is, if I can sense it, you must be able to sense it, too."

"I can't say why," Analisa begins, "but I have a feeling Briar is onto something."

Suddenly, everyone is looking at me again.

"They might be right, Zero," Ms. Kurima says from behind me. "Is there something ... you've missed?"

"I'm not ..."

Briar's hand abruptly reaches out and grabs hold of my arm. "What if we've been taking the message the wrong way?"

I look down at her, curiosity and skepticism fighting a war inside me. "What do you mean?"

"What if it's not just X making fun of Maggie? What if ... what he's forced her to spell out ... is a real cry for help? **What if Maggie's in danger?**"

"In danger?" I repeat.

"Yes, she could be in trouble! Maybe X has done something to her now that she's been found out."

"Maggie might actually be in danger?" Nina asks, looking slightly worried for her roommate despite all that she's done. "Like, really in danger?"

"If that's true," Daniel stands, "then we have to find her."

"Yeah, she might have been trying to get me expelled, maybe, but ... she's still my friend. I won't let her get hurt."

"Woah, everyone settle down," I say. "This situation of danger is all hypothetical—"

"Why should we help her?" Thomas questions, still looking at Daniel and Nina. "She's the reason behind all of this. Have you all suddenly forgotten that?"

"When there's a girl in trouble, you help her," James says seriously, surprising everyone aside from Analisa, who looks on at him with approval. "It doesn't matter what the circumstances are, if that's what's going on, we have to save her. Then she can face justice the right way."

"But she could quite literally be anywhere. This campus is huge," Analisa reasons.

"Then we start looking." James walks toward the door. "I might be mad at her, sure, but it sounds like this 'X' bastard is the real one to blame. I won't have him getting the last laugh if he intends to do something to her."

"Zero, please," Briar says quietly. "Just try to see if it's possible."

The back-and-forth arguments become background noise to me—something I'm only distantly aware of as I stare at the charts on the board. In my mind, I conjure up images of the original charts from the case file.

"Something I missed," I murmur to myself. "Something I missed …" But what could I have overlooked? What—

(No way.)

"Briar!" I say, and the background chatter ceases. "Where's the marker?"

"Um, it's in your hand, Zero."

Right. Something I missed, something I glanced over. "Of course. I was being careless." And X was not. "It all means something."

I rapidly scrawl out the "red herring" classes.

| English 100 | Algebra | Visual Studies | Chemistry |
| --- | --- | --- | --- |
| Popular Literature | Astronomy | Comparative Government | US History |

I twist all of the letters around, upside down, and come up with nothing. No, but I'm certain—wait, *what if it's not about the classes this time?* With more urgency, I add to the chart the names of the students attacked from each.

| English 100 | Algebra | Visual Studies | Chemistry |
|---|---|---|---|
| Seth Parker | Emma Tosto | Eli Young | Yasmin Iravani |
| Popular Literature<br><br>Ollie Adams | Astronomy<br><br>Uliana Lopatkina | Comparative Government<br><br>Ivy Wicker | US History<br><br>Nikolai Anderson |

Follow the pattern, but this time, take the first letter of the first name and …

Seth, Emma, Eli, Yasmin, Ollie, Uliana, Ivy, Nikolai → SEEYOUIN

→ SEE YOU IN

*But it's not complete.*

"Someone, quick," I say, not looking away from the board, "tell me the names of the last four students attacked in the most recent classes." This is information I never bothered to gather.

Daniel steps in, because of course he'd care enough to memorize the names of all his affected classmates. "Rhetoric was Lucian Di Carlo, Entrepreneurial Skills was Edward Sin-Claire, Oral History was Logan Reed … and Zoology was Hunter Foster."

Somewhere behind me, I hear a creaking sound coming from above as I continue to work.

Lucian, Edward, Logan, Hunter →

The creaking sound intensifies, followed by a slight rattling.

The order that spells my name: Hunter, Edward, Lucian, Logan →

Something in the ceiling is coming loose, but I'm still focused on my discovery.

…

HELL

I write the final message across the top of the board:

SEE YOU IN HELL

"The tunnels." I turn around, my eyes immediately finding Briar's just as the cast iron chandelier drops from the ceiling, right above James's head.

Shouts of alarm ring out, but I reach James before the chandelier does, knocking it aside with a push hard enough to send it slamming into the wall across the room, creating a distinct crack in the stone.

If I thought they'd been silent before, that was nothing compared to the stricken hush that descends upon us now. (It's been a while since I've had to prevent one of these, hasn't it?)

I straighten, my hand still outstretched. "She's in the tunnels."

***

Umm ... something has to go here! Hey, author, don't get lazy—

***

# CHAPTER 15:
## I FINALLY DIE (SORT OF)

I practically kick in the door to the president's private office (the room with the closest entrance into the tunnels). If Briar and Analisa are correct, saying we're running on borrowed time is a dangerous understatement.

Reaching the rug under the desk, I toss it aside and open the trap door, slipping through it into the secret stairwell that reaches the tunnels if you follow it down to the first floor. *The president's office is on the fourth floor.*

I was lucky to have Ms. Kurima with us as she was able to keep everyone calm and in the room as I left. Well ... everyone aside from two people, since she refused to let me go alone.

"Zero, catch." I turn around in time to catch the flashlight Daniel throws at me before he lowers himself through the trap door. "Briar," he puts his arms up as she sticks a leg through, "I'll help you down."

"I don't have time to wait for you two," I say, beginning the descent. "I'll have to go on ahead. We'll meet up once one of us finds Maggie."

"I know," Daniel agrees. "Go ahead. We'll catch up with you."

"Wait, Zero, you shouldn't go on alone!"

"Just be careful and listen to my instructions exactly: these tunnels are no joke. Don't wander inside *any* chamber unless you've found me first. And make sure not to try any of the false entrances along the way. The only entrance you can use will be a red-painted hatch at the very bottom of the stairs."

"I understand."

"Wait, Zero—!"

"And, Daniel," I tilt my head around just enough to make eye contact with him, "your only reason for being here is to watch out for Briar. Make sure you do your job."

"No—"

"I will," he assures me. "Now go."

I face forward, bracing myself. Then, I run.

The second I'm out of Daniel and Briar's line of sight, somewhere around the third floor, I jump down the middle of the spiral staircase, plummeting straight to the bottom.

I land on my toes and fold into a crouching position. Then I enter the red hatch, skipping the ladder by jumping again.

Now, I'm right at the heart of the underground system.

I inhale the faint scent of smoke and look at the flickering, still-lit torches lining the tunnel wall pointing forward.

"This is new."

Seems I don't have to worry about which direction to head in— my path has already been marked for me.

That adrenaline-inducing sensation I get before an accident occurs starts to bubble within my gut the further I race down the passageways. (Is it possible Maggie is in *real* danger? *Life-threatening* danger? But that's such a step up from taking students' assignments.)

I continue running for a quarter mile. The place she's being kept is deep into the tunnels. There must be a particular chamber X wanted to use for her, otherwise, it doesn't make sense to take her so far away. Thinking of this, I recall the hidden room of spiders and riddles Briar got stuck in last night. (What kind of horror is Maggie Arrowood being subjected to right now?)

Whatever it is, I must retrieve her, or else all my plans for Briar will go up in flames alongside my deal with the president.

(Hey, is that the sound of running water? Or is the rushing blood of adrenaline getting to my head?)

The last of the torches are lit side by side over the largest iron doors I have yet to see down here. Arching over them are the Latin words "Respice Finem."

"Consider the End," I murmur the translation as I fling the entrance open. I immediately wonder if X chose this chamber only for its fitting name, but once I enter inside, I see that I am wrong.

The entire chamber is lit up by magnificent crystal chandeliers and everything, from the floor to the impossibly high ceiling, is made of gleaming white marble—a shocking difference from the previous chamber we'd been in. At its center, sunken into the floor and made of the same marble material, is a slowly filling pool with four large spouts, each pouring a constant stream of water.

And there, sitting at the bottom of the pool, blindfolded, the water already up to her neck, is Maggie.

"P-please." She trembles and I realize that both her arms and legs are chained down to the bottom of the pool. *"Please, let me go."*

Since she's blindfolded, she likely thinks I'm the one who put her here. That fear in her voice, I've heard it before. It's the kind of fear a person can't fake, the kind that one only experiences when they truly believe they are about to die.

"Please, I'll do any—"

"Maggie, I'm not here to hurt you. I'm going to get you out of this." I slip off my jacket and boots and hop over the side of the pool, creating a loud splash as I join her. "I promise. You're not alone now."

"Z-Zero? Is that, is that really you? H-how d-did you find me?" She stutters over her words, shivering. (Drenched in water in these piercingly cold tunnels, she must be freezing.)

"It's me." I take her blindfold off and examine the chains. Snot, tears, and drool mix together on her face as she continues crying. "Everyone is worried about you." I keep my tone as soothing as possible. "They sent me to look for you."

"W-worried about me? They don't kn-know what I've done!"

"They do, Maggie. And it's going to be all right. But I need you to help me out here. Before you were blindfolded, did you see how the water spouts were turned on?" The handles on top did nothing when I attempted to turn them.

"N-no."

"Did you see a key to these chains get placed anywhere? Or did the one who did this to you take them with him?"

"I … I-I don't know! He grabbed me from behind right when I came into the tunnels—I just w-woke up chained down here! Oh god. Oh, god, I'm sorry." She bends her head down, her expression one of pure agony. "I'm so sorry. I was trying to put a stop to all of it, I swear, but I-I—"

"Shh, it's ok. Keep taking deep breaths. You're ok."

"Just, please—help me, Zero. *Please!*"

This is bad. The chains are secure, fully wrapping around her thighs in an intricate way and stretching her arms out to either side so that she is entirely unable to move. At the rate the water is going, we have only a minute or two before her nose and mouth are covered. I need to see if there's any other way to unlock her bindings or turn off the water.

I pull myself out of the pool and begin circling around it, searching for something, *anything.*

"No! Where are you going?! Don't leave me, Zero!! Don't—"

"I'm not going anywhere. I'm just looking for another way to get you out of this."

"I-I'm … I'm going to die, aren't I?" Her broken voice is quieter than before, the panic and fear finally putting her into shock.

The water's reached her chin.

"No, Maggie, you're not." Think. *Think.* What can I do?

"Oh, god," she trembles, "Nina … It's all my fault."

What can I possibly do?

*"It's all my fault."*

There's nothing to press or solve to get the spouts to shut off—the only notable detail is that the front handles have carvings of suns and clouds etched into them and the two in the back have stars and moons, but that's just design. *Design that reminds me of something else, but my brain's too scattered to remember what.* Then there are the chains which are made of steel and bolted into the pool's walls. (Was this chamber designed to trap and kill someone as well?) The amount of strength it would take to pull all four of them free … in such a short amount of time … that's just not possible—even for me.

"Fuck!" I slam my foot into a marble pillar, causing the whole chamber to shake. (Is there no way I can save her?!)

My breathing becomes rapid as the sound of Maggie's cries overwhelms me. My body feels painfully hot, like I'm burning from the inside.

(… No. There is *one* way.)

It's like each of my muscles is on fire—

(It's something I promised myself I would never do again.)

I clench my fists, the searing heat inside me growing to an unbearable temperature. *God, it hurts!*

(And it could result in an even worse outcome than this girl's death.)

But there's no other choice.

"Zero!" Briar's voice is barely audible to me as she shouts my name. "Zero, we found you!"

I'm already halfway there, anyway.

"Briar, Daniel." I don't turn around to face them. "Leave this chamber and get as far away as you can. If you want Maggie to live, do it now."

"But—"

"Ok. Do what you have to do, Zero. Just ... save her."

"The next time you see me, if I don't speak back to you ..." I step up to the foot of the pool. "**Run.**"

The instant the chamber doors close, I jump back in.

Maggie can no longer speak, too preoccupied with crying and tilting her face up to evade the water about to drown her.

"Maggie. Listen to me closely." There's no more gentleness in my tone; it's as ice-cold as the droplets clinging to the ends of my hair. "Right before your head goes under, you need to take in as deep a breath as you can and hold it. No matter how much it hurts, don't breathe in the water. And when I get you out, stay as still and quiet as possible. This is the most important part."

There's no time to see if she understood me so I dive beneath the water behind her and lie down at the bottom of the pool, closing my eyes. Then I do exactly as I told her not to do: I breathe in. I can't wait until my lungs naturally suck in water out of desperation—I must speed up the process of drowning myself.

But it's hard. Breathing underwater goes against every instinct the human body has—no matter how painful the feeling of running out of oxygen is, a person won't inhale until they are on the verge of unconsciousness or have given up.

Pushing past all of this, I do it again. The new burning in my chest simply melts into the burning across the entirety of my body. One could throw me into lava and I would feel no difference. I …

This is the right thing to do … isn't it?

There's … no other way … and I …

*"It's because we're friends, Zero. Now, and forever. Whether you like it or not, ok?"*

Zero * 372

---

I promise it will be different this time.
Please. Just …
Forgive me.

*When Zero is no longer conscious, control of the story will pass to someone else.*

# 15 ½

*Daniel*

"Daniel?"

Someone … Someone is saying my name.

"Daniel? Daniel?!"

"Mmm …" My head pounds, my vision slowly coming into focus.

"Are you all right? You just fainted out of nowhere!"

All at once, my mind clears and I find myself leaning against Briar as she holds us both up against the tunnel wall. *We haven't made it very far.* Immediately, I get off her, scanning her for any possible injuries I may have caused.

"Pardon me," I say, straightening my classmate up. "I'm not sure what happened, but I'm ok now. Please, tell me, did I hurt you when I collapsed?"

"Hurt me?" Briar looks surprised that I've even asked. "I'm fine—but, Daniel, I … I can't leave Zero. I have to go back for him."

The reality of our situation hits me. *Maggie, Zero—we must get help for them.*

"We left him," Briar continues, her soft voice filled with a mix of panic and determination. "We left him alone in there!"

She wants to go back for him? Of course she wants to go back for him.

"That's what I've been trying to tell you. I can't just leave him—"

I gently take hold of her forearms. "Briar, do you remember what Zero said? He told us to leave as fast as we could if we wanted him to save Maggie. We need to go get help now. There was nothing else we could do for them." The responsibility lies with us to get the school officials who can deal with this properly.

"No!" She tries desperately to maneuver out of my grip, twisting and turning with a ferocity I had no idea she was capable of. "Let me go, Daniel!

"Briar—"

"Let me go! Now! If you don't …! Something is happening to him—I have to go to him!"

*Something is happening to him?* Yes, I think she's right about that. Which is exactly why I can't let her go. Whatever is going on back in that chamber, every instinct in my body is telling me to listen to Zero's warning: *"Leave this chamber and get as far away as you can."*

"I'm sorry," Briar says suddenly.

What's that? "Sorry?"

Her knee rams into my stomach before I understand what she means. Shocked, I release her and clutch at my middle, nearly upturning the contents of my breakfast. The second she's free, Briar sprints back the way we came. *Years of martial arts training, and I'm bested by a frightened girl's knee.* I'd almost laugh if the situation wasn't so horrifying.

Now what?

Do I try to get help on my own?

No, we've wasted enough time as it is; either Zero is successful in saving Maggie, or it's all over. And I can't let Briar go back there alone. Not when I have this feeling …

I suck up the pain and use the wall as support to reach the chamber. But the closer I get, the more foreboding the feeling becomes. It's enough to make me ill all over again, my legs beginning to shake as I open the doors.

*Is Maggie all right? Did he get her?* is what I want to ask, but nothing comes out of my throat. Whether a physical or mental block, I'm not sure. All I know is that when I step inside, the hairs on the back of my neck stand on end.

The first thing I see is Briar standing perfectly still, her eyes fixated on something in front of her. But Zero is nowhere to be—that's when I notice the girl still chained to the bottom of the pool, the water above her head. She's ... she's drowning.

*She's drowning!*

"Maggie!" I hear myself call out as if someone else is controlling my voice.

Movement finally finds my legs and I take a step to run toward her but, this time, Briar is the one who grabs me. She doesn't even turn to face me; she just remains staring forward, holding me in place.

"Briar," I look down at her hand's iron clasp on my wrist, "there's no time for this! Please! She's going to *die!*" And I know this is the truth. If nothing happens, Maggie will drown in a matter of se—

I see him slice through the water just as the sound of something being ripped loose from the walls of the pool cuts through the air, silencing me.

*Zero.*

The instant one set of chains is tugged free, he's already at the next. A single, smooth motion and it's pulled out. Then the next, and the next. I can't speak, I can't breathe, I can't blink. I can only watch as he takes hold of Maggie from underneath and, together, they rise from the water.

There is no possible way to describe this sight.

It's like ... It's like I'm not looking at a man, but at a ... a ... Heaven help me, I don't know.

*What **is** he?*

Zero steps from the pool in silence. The only sounds are those of the water droplets falling from his hair and soaked clothing. In his arms, Maggie is shaking and sputtering, but … I can tell she's trying not to. She's trying to stay still? To stay quiet?

"Zero," I begin and immediately cut off. He shows no reaction to his name.

What were his exact words? *"The next time you see me, if I don't speak back to you … Run."*

But I can't run. I can't move a single inch!

Beside me, Briar's frozen as well. She must be able to feel it, too. The primal sensation of being before a beast this much stronger than yourself—

*—it's overwhelming.*

Zero, just what have you done …?

**"Stand aside."** A booming voice and the sound of multiple sets of boots enter the chamber. "We'll handle the situation from here."

It's security. Ms. Kurima must have told them we were down here.

"I said stand aside," comes the head officer again. He roughly pushes Briar and me out of the way, knocking Briar hard enough that she goes sprawling forward. I'm not prepared when it happens, and at the trajectory she's falling, her head will smack right into the marble floor. I need to reach her in time, but … my legs won't move?!

My limbs feel locked into place. *Is his very presence enough to do this to me right now?* But if I don't move, she'll—

"*Ah—!*"

In the last instant before she makes contact with the marble, I manage to throw myself underneath her. I don't notice if it hurts the spot my stomach was kneed, too relieved to have reached her and regained control over my body.

Meanwhile, the security officer doesn't so much as glance at us as he stalks toward Zero and Maggie. "You there," he directs at Zero, his large, muscular arms already outstretched, "hand that girl to me."

"No, wait!" I shout.

But it's too late.

In less than a second, Zero's leg is in the air. It lifts high—higher than should be possible, all the way up to his head—and slams down on the security officer's shoulder. *An axe kick?!*

The officer must be half a foot taller than Zero and weigh twice as much, yet he crumples under the blow like he's a paper mâché doll.

*He knows Kyokushin?*

The next two guards rush him at the same time. Without letting Maggie go, Zero shoves one guard back with a snap kick until he's parallel with the other. Then he takes two steps forward—

*Is he about to do what I think he is?*

He pushes off from his second step, his right knee contracting in for the briefest of moments before both his legs explode outward: a scissor kick. *And now Taekwondo?* (I remember seeing my instructor demonstrate this move when I was a child. But never did I reach a level close to being able to attempt it myself.) The guards are simultaneously slammed in the chest by his feet, knocking one of them to the floor. The other staggers backward as Zero continues toward him, his expression never changing from its cold, inhuman intensity.

"Hey, kid, just wait a second …" The guard puts his hands out uselessly. "Just—"

At a speed almost impossible to follow, Zero spins into a back kick. There's much more power behind this attack than his last, and the guard goes flying, a horrible cracking sound reverberating across the chamber as he crashes into one of the marble pillars. *A flawlessly executed back kick.* There's no uncertainty in my mind when I vividly imagine all the bones that have just snapped in that man's body.

"My god," I murmur, stunned. "He's going to kill them."

There's a sharp tug at the back of my jacket as the last remaining security guard yanks Briar and me into a standing position, attempting to pull us away. "It doesn't make any sense. This ain't possible …" He tugs harder at Briar when she doesn't move. "Hey, *come on,*" he urges. "You brats wanna die? We gotta get outta here before—" Words fail him as Zero's attention slowly turns on us.

Those eyes … It's like he's not really seeing us. In this moment, under his gaze, all we are is prey.

The back of my jacket is released as the guard stumbles his way to the chamber doors. But without him, that means …

"Wait!" I call. "Sir, please, help them—something is wrong with him! Isn't it your job to protect the students of this academy?! They need you!"

"That's not a student." The guard trips over his own feet in his haste to abandon us, sweat dripping down the side of his fear-drenched face. "That's a fucking *monster.*"

"What's going on? Did you find them?" Ms. Kurima's voice carries from down the tunnels. She, and whoever she's brought, will be here any second.

In all this time, Briar still hasn't turned away from Zero. When my gaze returns to him, I find I can't look away, either. His focus has gone to the officer now crawling his way to safety across the floor. He doesn't make it very far. Zero's foot comes crashing down on his back.

"*Aackkk!*" The officer chokes on his own scream, his chest being crushed into marble.

If Zero wasn't barefoot, I can't even think of the damage. *Perhaps for him, it wouldn't make a difference either way.*

Horror-struck, I watch as Zero reaches the one he'd sent slamming into the pillar. The guard can see he's coming for him, too, but there's nothing he can do. The moment he staggers to his feet, Zero's leg is there, his knee pinning him against the pillar before jerking forward. This time, it's hard to tell what is bone cracking and what is marble cracking as the pillar splits in two and collapses with the guard.

The entire chamber shakes.

*Such power isn't possible, is it?*

Possible or not, anyone who enters here—no, anyone who catches his attention—will be taken out. That is if he doesn't bring the place down on our heads first.

From the corner of my eye, I see Briar take a small step forward and stop. What is she doing? No ... she can't really ...

Yet I recognize the look on her face as she stares at Zero, the one that says "I have to help him no matter what."

"Briar." I say her name, but she doesn't hear me. Like Zero, her mind is miles away. All she sees is him. And nothing will stop her from reaching the object of her fixation.

The two of them face each other, Zero remaining preternaturally still as Briar makes her way to him. She halts, as close to him as she can get with Maggie's body between them. *Too close!!* The intensity of their energy seems to feed off of one another, making these next seconds that go by the longest stretch of time I have ever endured.

"Briar," I say again, helplessly.

Slowly, she brings a hand up to his face.

"Briar, stop."

Her fingers are about to graze his skin—I have to do something!

"Briar! Stop!"

I knock her aside with just a hair's breadth of space left between them. Though I tried not to use full force, she still goes skidding across the floor. *Oh, god, I'm sorry.* But there was nothing else I could do; I couldn't just let her step into harm's way like that! Too many have gotten hurt already.

And I'm about to be next.

Zero's eyes are on me. I don't have time to make a stance because his foot has already shoved into my chest. I don't even have time to feel the pain because the force of his kick rockets me across the chamber, my head smacking against the far wall.

I … I-I'm … barely conscious. I think I taste blood in my mouth, but even that I'm unsure of. *Did I bite my tongue?*

One thing is certain: there's no possible way for me to get back up. Whatever happens to me now is out of my control.

Dark spots flicker in and out of my waning vision as I look up at him. He walks toward me without a hint of emotion or recognition—Maggie still shaking in his arms, her eyes squeezed tightly shut—and I've never seen something so magnificent yet so intrinsically terrifying. This kind of fear is something I've never experienced. I'd say it's that of life or death, but the truth of it goes beyond that.

This feeling, in this moment, transcends anything the human mind or body can comprehend.

I only hope ... *that Briar ...*

Wait, Briar?

My death is about to greet me, one long, lean-muscled leg prepared to slice into the crown of my head and shatter my skull. But the blow never comes. It never comes because *she's* stepped between us, her hand shooting up, cradling the side of his face and—

And something extraordinary happens.

He stops.

It all stops.

Zero wavers on his feet, as if he's about to pass out. The expression on his face goes from unreadable and otherworldly to pained and confused—to human.

The last pathetically useful thing I'm able to do is crawl over in time to have Maggie's body dropped onto mine as Zero releases her and collapses to the floor. There, he leans over on all fours, making an ear-splitting retching sound as water spits from his mouth. It just keeps coming up—the sheer amount implying his lungs must have been entirely full of it.

But no one could do what he did without the ability to breathe. *No one could do what he did no matter their physical circumstances*, rings in the back of my mind. Yet here we are.

When the last of the water has purged itself from his body, Zero slumps over.

Finally, **he is out.**

Only then does Briar allow the full extent of her emotions to take over. She collapses on top of him with a sob, clutching onto his chest as if letting go of him means death.

"You did well," a deep male voice says from above me. I look up to see Mr. Henderson, my Media & Technology teacher, stride over to Briar and Zero. "I've got him now."

With care, he picks Zero up in his arms, the action looking effortless. Never have I seen Mr. Henderson this way, with his rolled-up sleeves showing the hardened muscles of his tattooed forearms, his whole appearance suddenly contradicting the role of a well-respected academy faculty member. *He must be extremely strong.*

"Jordan," he continues, "please take Maggie for me. Kyouka, we'll have to send more down to retrieve the security who got here before us. I don't think any of them will be moving on their own any time soon."

The student council president steps forward and bends down, scooping Maggie off of me just as Ms. Kurima rushes to my side.

"Daniel! I'm so sorry. I went to get security immediately, but we were late finding you."

"You'll all be all right now," Mr. Henderson says, a soft, reassuring smile on his lips. "It's over."

*It's over.* But what *was* it?

Now that the adrenaline is subsiding, the sharp aches firing across my every nerve ending prevent me from saying anything in return.

"Zero," Briar sobs, being helped off the floor by Ms. Kurima, "is he going to be ok? Please, is he going to be ok?"

Zero looks almost delicate in Mr. Henderson's arms—his long neck arched back, eyes closed, and lips slightly parted.

If I didn't know better, I'd say he was a prince straight out of a storybook, fast asleep until someone breaks the spell and wakes him. But his peacefulness does nothing to calm Briar's fears.

"I have to know he's ok!" she cries, tears falling and mixing into the puddles of water on the marble floor. *"He has to be ok."*

This must be the most emotion I've seen Briar express in all our time at this academy. Just when did these two get so close? Though I've always watched them both, ever since Zero came here two years ago, did I ... miss something?

Mr. Henderson appraises her for a moment before continuing to carry Zero out of the chamber. "He'll be just fine, I promise you. We'll make sure of that."

Briar's tears continue to flow and my vision blackens even more, my head filling up with muffling liquid as I finally sink into darkness.

***

- **Year/age/student ranking**: N/A, 35, N/A
- **Hair**: dark brown
- **Eyes**: dark brown
- **Height/Weight**: 6'4, 240 lbs.
- **Noticeable features**: extremely tall/muscular build, defined chest, tattooed forearms, scar running from his left brow to his left cheekbone.
- **Favorite item**: N/A
- **Likes**: playing sports, maintaining a healthy diet, working with his hands/working with technology, MMA fighting
- **Dislikes**: N/A
- **Personal comment**: "No, I will never date a student. No, that will not change no matter how many times one of you asks me—"
- **Fact**: Jackson has 20 years of training in mixed martial arts and frequently won national championships when in his prime. He decided to quit pro MMA three years ago after his then-fiancé gave him an ultimatum and went into teaching instead. Though he's no longer engaged, it's certainly not for lack of options …

## Martial Arts Terms
### (What was Zero doing?)

*Axe kick*: A kick used in a variety of martial arts in which you bring your leg straight up to crack down on your opponent. Daniel attributed this to Kyokushin Karate.

*Scissor kick*: A Taekwondo kick used to hit two opponents at once by making a split in the air.

*Back kick* (or spinning back kick): Taekwondo's most iconic attack in which you spin into a kick aiming straight back.

***

# Chapter 16:
# Everyone I've Ever Had the Misfortune of Meeting Comes to See Me Even Though I Didn't Ask Them to

Maggie Arrowood is safe.

It … worked. I think. My mind is hazy with half-memories and emotions—what really happened, and how much did I miss when in that state?

If it isn't already clear, that state is the reason killing myself has never been as easy a task as it seems. If I don't end everything swiftly, instantaneously, then *that* has a possibility of happening.

But I really … don't want to talk about that anymore.

So, long time no see. Did you miss me? I didn't have time to warn you beforehand, but you're still here, so I assume my absence was bearable. Hey, what's that?

**Insert your response here:** ________________________________

Tch. You really shouldn't say such things to me, you have no idea how much it screws with my head. Anyway, who did you pass on to while I was out?

Daniel, was it? Really? Seems like a random choice, but very well. Did you at least find out any helpful information when you were with him?

Right … I guess that's too much to ask. You're not capable of telling me that sort of thing.

"What are you mumbling to yourself about? If you're awake then you should sit up and greet your guests, not lie there like an overdramatic coma patient. After all, you're fine."

There's no mistaking that cold, offensively impersonal voice.

I crack open my eyes, the action taking a surprising amount of strength. (God, my body feels like it went to war with a two-ton truck and lost.)

"Prez, did it really have to be you that I woke up to? Don't you know the first face a person sees after experiencing great trauma is very important?" Looks like I've been taken to the infirmary—a building about a quarter mile off of the main building. If they didn't just take me to the nurse's office, that must mean they didn't want me to be seen.

"Complaining already, I see."

"Why are you here, anyway? Have you been worried about me and awaiting my recovery?"

"Careful, or you'll wake her."

Wake her?

That's when I feel the weight on my (very sore) lower half. Sitting up a bit higher against the bed frame, I look at Briar sleeping with her head and arms draped over my legs.

"She's refused to leave your side the entire time you've been here. Which is approximately three hours, before you ask. Ms. Kurima and the nurses attempted to insist you go to the hospital, but the chairman saw to it that you didn't."

"Well, at least that's something to be thankful for," I murmur, keeping my volume lower now that I know Sleeping Beauty is in the room. (This marks the third time she's been asleep in my presence.)

"Let's not waste any time here." The president pulls out a piece of paper from the leather satchel beside his seat. "Sign this contract and your club will be official."

I pick it up and read over it. *Sneaky goddamned bastard*, I think upon finishing. "This contract states that we will technically be a branch under the student council. I don't remember discussing this."

"Yes. You're free to decide the specifics about what you do within your club, but as per the contract, should the student council encounter another issue such as this one, we are at liberty to enlist your services."

"Oh, so we're the 'Problem-Solving Club' then, huh?"

"You're also free to decide the name." He leans forward, elbows on his knees. "Though perhaps that's a fitting one."

I stare down at Briar's peacefully sleeping face. *Do I take this deal, or not?* As I've mentioned before, the ideal club would be one where I can take an executive position so as to watch her while also staying away from the groundwork of the club that would involve her being exposed to a lot of new relationships, therefore optimizing the possibility of meeting someone she clicks with. Having the student council controlling us from the shadows, however, is not ideal in any way shape or form.

I don't suppose you'd have advice on what decision to make.

"I don't like to be kept waiting, Zero."

"Shh. If you wake her, I definitely won't be signing anything."

The president rolls his eyes and takes a pen out of his shirt pocket, tossing it to me. "We both know you're going to accept the contract, so just sign it already. I have someplace to be."

"What about us needing a third member?" I question, recalling one of the arbitrary rules for establishing a club.

"As a gesture of goodwill for your new club, I'll provide you with some temporary aid. Tell Marina her status as a council member has been approved and that she's been assigned to your branch. What position you choose for her is of no matter to me. Do what you'd like with her."

"Don't evoke her name, she might be summoned here," I say, scribbling out my signature.

(So, he really was taking advantage of my connection with Marina, knowing he could make use of her.) Fine. If he wants to get closer to me, I'll let him. Because all the while, he'll be letting me get closer to him, too. That's just how the game is played.

And since Briar brought him the issue of us needing his help to create a club on a silver platter, there's a high probability that he thinks this is what I've been planning for all along as well. I wish I could say something like "arrogant opponents make foolish mistakes," but Jordan Adrian doesn't conform to normal human standards. Getting the student council off our backs will be no easy task.

Ah, well, if I have to tough it out here for a while longer, it's only fitting I should have to suffer like this. It'll be just like the old days, huh.

*Isn't that right, Jordan?*

"You're awake!" shouts Marina, flinging her way into the infirmary room, closely followed by Myles. She immediately falls silent upon seeing that the president is here, however, her eyes fluttering to the ground nervously. (I wish this was the effect *my* presence had on her.)

The president gives me a smirk that lets me know he is the one who contacted my excitable new club member, but any trace of amusement vanishes the second he lays eyes on his brother.

Myles, if possible, looks even more startled.

"Jordan?" he says, clearing his throat. "I didn't know you were here. You came to see Zero, too?"

"I was just taking my leave." The president dons his heavy gray coat, his mask of control back in place, and pauses before stepping through the doors. "Zero, we can debrief the incident in the tunnels another time. I've got a particularly important meeting to attend." No doubt a meeting that is also about the "incident in the tunnels."

But right now, I don't have time to worry about that because Marina's loud entrance also woke Briar (even though I'd attempted to cover her ears).

"Zero?" She looks at me, honey-brown eyes brimming with too many emotions for me to place. "Zero! You're ok! You're really ok!"

Her arms wrap around my neck as she buries her face in my chest. It hurts, but I don't tell her to stop.

"I thought you were going to die—or get put into a coma!"

"I'm all right," I say, rubbing the back of her head. "I'm all right."

Never one to be left out, Marina throws herself onto the bed, too. "If you ever almost die again, I'm going to kill you, Zero Hale! You understand? How dare you worry everyone like that? Couldn't you have just saved Maggie in, like, an easier way or something without all the extra complications? Why do you always make everything so difficult?"

"I'll keep that in mind for the next time I—wait, extra complications? Just what do you think went on down there?"

I briefly glance at Briar, who's finally released me enough to look at my face, but she shakes her head in an "I didn't say anything to anyone" motion.

"We really don't know *what* you guys went through," Myles says, taking hold of Marina from under her arms and lifting her off of me. "Nobody will tell us anything. But all club activities were canceled and everyone was sent back to the dorms, including teachers. My father even stopped by. I think the only ones to stay behind were him, Ms. Kurima, Mr. Henderson, and a few other board members and security guards. Hey, Marina, come on, you're going to crush him."

"I don't care if I crush him," Marina huffs, finally allowing Myles to pull her away. "It's what he deserves for causing everyone so much trouble."

I'd like to know the truth about what I did to save Maggie, but I can't ask Briar about it while they're here. The less people know, the better.

"Where is Daniel?" I ask, remembering he was with us. I'd told him to keep an eye on Briar, actually.

"That's right ..." Myles starts, his usually pleasant features looking apologetic. "You wouldn't have heard, but Daniel's in the hospital. So is Maggie, though she's there for shock, not actual injuries, really. And they'll both make full recoveries, so you don't need to worry about them. From what I understand, they almost brought you to the hospital, too, but I guess your condition wasn't serious enough, luckily."

The hospital? *Damn.* He didn't listen to my warnings. How badly did I hurt him?

Indistinct flashbacks come to me of Daniel shouting something at me, Briar cradled in his arms on the floor of the chamber. Then I see a blur of movement that looks like my own foot coming up to kick him—

I wince, not liking where these omniscient flashbacks are headed. *Especially since they don't even seem to be from my own eyes.* It's like ... Like before ... Fragments of memories that aren't mine, but that showcase me in them.

Ever observant of me, Briar sits back. "You ... you should rest now." She turns to Marina and Myles. "We should let him—"

There's a polite knock before the doors open once again and in file all of the representatives (save for the two currently hospitalized). They form a sort of half-circle around my bed with Analisa stepping up front. She places a basket of fruit and chocolates on my bedside and gives me one of the most unfeigned smiles I have ever received, the sight of it momentarily stunning me.

"I'm so glad you're awake. We came here to give you our sincerest gratitude, Zero. Words are not enough to express how thankful we are for what you've done for us, so please accept this gift on behalf of us all." She gestures to the basket.

I don't know what to say, so I say nothing.

I've never been given anything like this before.

Analisa subtly elbows James in the ribs. "*Ow*—uh, I mean, it's nice that you didn't die or anything and it's good you were able to back up all of your talk, 'cus otherwise I would've been real pissed—ow! Again, Ana? I told him I'm glad he's awake and whatever, jeez."

"Thanks, Zero," March says, one hand grasping onto Sam's arm. "I didn't totally get everything you said when you explained the reveal and all, but Analisa talked with the chairman about the stuff you told us and our rankings and grades are gonna be safe now—"

"Forget about that, can you tell us what happened down there?" interrupts Alek, a hungry gleam in his emerald eyes.

"*Slate*," James says with a growl. Then he looks to Analisa. "What, aren't you gonna tell him now's not the time?"

"It's true, now isn't the time," Thomas says. "You ought to get your rest, Hale."

"Aww, but I wanna hear all the detailssss," whines Alek. "Please?

Aren't you all curious? There are secret tunnels, Daniel and Maggie are in the hospital, Zero was carried out like a fairy princess by Mr. Henderson and remained unconscious for three hours, and at least four security guards were fired! How could you *not* want to hear that story?"

Security guards were fired? Why? No, I already know why … This has *him* written all over it. The chairman.

He's become involved.


After Analisa and the representatives leave, Myles, Marina, and Briar stick around. I have a feeling the chairman will come to see me very shortly, but I ought to make the most of my time until then.

"So, Myles, are you here to tell me about your request, or what?" I ask.

He smiles, sitting forward in his chair. (Marina is back on top of my bed and Briar never left it.) "Yeah, I hate to put this on you now after everything you've just gone through, but I'd be lying if I said we're not on a deadline."

"You need Zero's help, too?" Marina asks. "Do you have some secret traitor after you?"

Myles tilts his head back and forth. "I'm not sure."

Is he serious? "Myles, are you telling me that you're being targeted by X as well?"

"X? I don't think I know what you're talking about, but it's definitely not something that has to do with any of you, or your case, if that's what you mean. This is … a problem solely connected to me. I mean, to a specific hobby of mine."

"Which is?"

"I play the violin." (Ah, yes, I do remember this about him.) "Pretty seriously, actually. And I have an upcoming competition in the city. It's in two weeks, to be exact, and I've been practicing for months, but … something happened. About a week ago, Chris, my accompanist, injured his arm and had to quit."

"He injured it himself?"

Myles shakes his head. "That's the weird part. He was mysteriously pushed down the stairs, and no one knows who it was. Then I found a crumpled piece of paper stuffed inside my violin saying I'd be next."

"So you're worried this person will be coming after you since you still intend to compete," I say, trying to sum up his request.

"Sure, that's part of it, but, like, that's not the most *dire* part of it."

"Then what is?"

"I need an accompanist, of course! A really good one. And no one at this academy is up to the task of playing at this level. No one … except you, Zero."

"You need me to be your accompanist?"

I suddenly remember sitting down at the piano earlier this week and playing "The Moon Over the Ruined Castle." There had been someone listening to me at the time …

"It was you," I say, putting the pieces together. "You were the one outside of my practice room on Tuesday." *See page <u>86</u>.

"Uh, well, yeah. I was up there to practice myself when I heard you playing and I just knew I had to work with you. I remembered you were good at piano, but I didn't know you were *this* good. The sound of your playing literally brought tears to my eyes—it felt like God had brought me a piano-playing guardian angel! If we start practicing now, doing the competition together in two weeks will be a piece of cake, I'm sure of it."

"Ok." Why not? I'm already doing a performance of another

variety with Juri Izumi later in the year—might as well brush up on my musical capabilities now.

"R-really? You mean it? You'll play for me?" Myles is so excited and emotional now that I fear I may unintentionally bring another tear to his eye if I'm not careful.

"Yes. But remember I have a condition for you in return."

"Anything! Just tell me what it is, and it's done."

So he's no longer wary of me now that I've given in? "If I do this for you, then, for at least the remainder of the semester, you must become a member of the club Briar and I are putting together."

"… Huh?"

"Will that be an issue?"

"No! Sure, I'll join whatever you want me to. It'll be hard between soccer and violin practices, but you can put my name on it and I'll be there as much as I can."

That's good enough for me. "Then we have a deal. Myles Adrian, welcome to The Problem-Solving Club."

"It's official?" Briar asks, surprised. "President Jordan signed off on it?"

"Is that really its name?" Marina asks, displeased. "Is that seriously the best you could come up with?"

"It's a shame you don't like it, Marina, seeing as you're a part of it, too."

"What?! What did you just say, Zero? Hey, don't kid around about stuff like this."

"I'm not particularly pleased, either. But that's where your beloved President Jordan has placed you as a new council member."

"I-I'm a council member? I'm a council member! Hah! Of course I am—I did it! But, wait, I have to stick around with *you* guys?"

"You follow me around enough as it is, so things probably won't change much from how they are now."

Before Marina can pinpoint a comeback, the doors open for a third time. But this time, the air seems to squeeze out of the room, the temperature around us plummeting as our new guest enters. No one dares to say a word. Marina's openly gaping, Briar's subconsciously gripping my bedsheets, and Myles looks as though he may actually be sick as he jumps to his feet.

Chairman Callan Adrian ... **is here.**

He's not a particularly tall man, but there's something about his presence that is undeniably large, taking up all the space of any room he steps foot in. The kind of presence that ensures, no matter what angle you stand, you'll be forced to look up. It doesn't take an expert to recognize the strength of the body covered beneath his suit, either. For as long as I can remember, and assuredly much longer than that, the chairman's always taken pride in his form. Clearly, that hasn't changed.

Then there's his voice; I haven't heard it in person in over a year, but I remember it vividly, its deep bass reverberating in the depths of my mind. (Yet it turns out recollection does not do justice to the real thing.)

"My son," he says to Myles, the hint of a smile in his cold eyes, "so this is where you are instead of practicing for your competition. You must be very confident in your victory. I look forward to you taking home first place."

Myles flinches, eyes flicking away from the chairman's before he forces himself to look back. "I was just working out the details about that now, sir. Zero will be my accompanist since Chris is still recovering."

"Allowing those you rely on to get hurt is as selfish as it is foolish. Though in this case," his gaze lands on me, "your solution may just prove to be better than the original."

*What is it about the eyes of the Adrian men that is so unnerving?* I wonder as I look right back at him. It must be the color. No, something *behind* the color. A chilling intensity they have (save for Myles).

The chairman acknowledges Briar and Marina, with his attention lingering on Briar for a second too long. (Don't tell me … is he going to take an interest in her now that he's seen *I've* taken an interest in her?)

"Son, escort your classmates back to the dorms. I'm going to have a talk with Mr. Hale."

Myles swallows hard and nods. "Come on, girls, let's go."

Marina's already standing behind him, but Briar hesitates, looking between me and the chairman.

"I'll see you tomorrow, Briar," I say, silently urging her to go with Myles already. It would be much better for her if he doesn't associate the two of us.

The chairman notices her hesitation and laughs, low and deep. "Ms. Thornswood, I promise he's not in any trouble. On the contrary, I think an expression of thanks is in order for Mr. Hale's quick thinking and valiant work today, don't you?"

"O-ok." Briar blinks, reluctantly joining Myles and Marina. "Yes, sir, I'll see Zero tomorrow, then."

Once they're gone, my remaining company takes the seat across from me, taking his time to lean back and situate himself. Chin resting on his fist, he assesses me.

"It's been quite a while, Zero. Tell me, how have you been? Have you heard from your father recently?"

"I think you're more likely to have heard from him than I am, sir."

"You're probably right. It's a shame; even with infinite potential before him, Luc never knew what to do with it."

The mention of my father's name is meant to have an effect on me, but, employing my talents for disappointing others, I show no reaction. Both of us are well aware that Luc Hale wants nothing to do with me.

"I do hope our families can reunite again one day," he continues. "It's been too long since I've seen my old friend. But that's not why I came to you tonight." He tilts his head, looking me over again. "You must know that your stunt in the tunnels had considerable repercussions, yes?"

"If you came here for details, I'm afraid I can't give them. I blacked out for most of it."

"Then I will enlighten you. At approximately five p.m., you entered the academy's underground tunnel system with Mr. Blackwell and Ms. Thornswood to find and rescue Ms. Arrowood, whom you believed to have been abducted by an unknown assailant. You reached the chamber with Ms. Arrowood before your companions only to discover that she was chained to the bottom of a pool and about to drown." (He must have debriefed with Maggie and Daniel.) "Upon their arrival, you instructed Mr. Blackwell and Ms. Thornswood to leave for unknown reasons. Then you miraculously rescued Ms. Arrowood from a watery death by pulling the chains free from the walls of the pool. At five-fifteen, security arrived on the scene, but when they got there, they described encountering a young man possessed with inhuman strength.

The results of the ensuing fight are as follows: one officer hospitalized for a fractured shoulder and cracked ribs, one officer hospitalized for head trauma, one officer hospitalized for a fractured spine and cracked ribs, and one officer declaring his resignation despite receiving no physical wounds. Mr. Blackwell is also in the hospital for a fractured sternum, and Ms. Arrowood is there for trauma-induced shock."

It's so much worse than I thought, but not as bad as it could have been. (Is the proper response here to be relieved or horrified?)

"In conclusion, due to your actions today, Zero, the entire student body may soon learn about the existence of the tunnels—a secret I have been keeping for years from both students and staff for reasoning you'll now understand—*and* I was forced to lose four quality officers who happen to make up four of only *five* faculty members with knowledge about the true nature of the tunnels, all while paying them each a handsome sum to keep quiet about what they experienced. I'm sure I don't need to tell you why this was necessary."

No, he doesn't.

"On top of all this, two dear students were hurt badly enough to require medical attention."

"Then have you come to expel me, sir?"

The small inkling of amusement in his eyes catches fire, spreading into a full, animalistic smile. "Zero, Zero, *Zero*." (The way he's saying my name …) "Didn't I already tell you? I came here to give you my thanks on behalf of the academy. This is a school for the supremely intelligent and extraordinarily talented; this afternoon, you expressed both qualities to an extent I have been waiting to see ever since you enrolled here. I've asked myself again and again, 'When will that boy finally show me what he's capable of?' And now, it seems the time has come."

"Don't get your hopes up. What happened today was a result of adrenaline and luck."

His smile broadens even more. "Yes, solving the case my son and his council have been working on for weeks in a matter of days was luck—and pulling four chains free from marble before taking on three trained officers at once was all due to adrenaline!"

I keep my expression impassive as he laughs. Then he jerks forward and grips my jaw with iron fingers, his face inches from my own.

"Come on, Zero! Tell me the truth! How did you do it?"

*What the—*

"It's driving me mad—why won't you tell me? Must you continue taunting me, pretending like you're *normal?*"

I don't recoil, being careful to maintain steady breathing. "Sir, I really … don't know how to respond when you say such things. None of it makes any sense to me."

There's a long beat of silence between us as the wild look in his eyes dissipates and he leans back, releasing my jaw.

"… I see. You remain as stubborn as ever. Well, you may keep your secrets for now, Zero. But one day, you must know, they will all be dragged into the light. And on that day, trust that I will be there to witness the truth of all that you are, no matter the fallout."

"That's a very ominous thing to say, sir. If I'm not to be expelled, perhaps I should transfer, instead."

"If you had anywhere else to go, that threat might work in your favor. But you and I both know that's not the case."

I look down at my bedsheets, suddenly feeling very tired. "Chairman, if it's not too much to ask, I'd like to get some more rest now."

He waits another beat before nodding and standing. "Of course. You must be *exhausted.* You've had a long day and I was far from the first visitor you've entertained. In fact," he raises a brow, "I heard that Ms. Thornswood stayed with you the entire time until you woke up. I wasn't aware you two had such a relationship."

My stomach sinks.

"She is an interesting girl though, isn't she? Considering how you first met, I'm surprised it's taken you this long to make contact with her. But I wonder, what does she remember of that day? Or is it too far in the past, jumbled with all the other memories from such a traumatic time?"

"In her eyes, are you truly just like any other boy, a classmate and a friend? Or—"

"It doesn't matter to me either way, sir. Whether or not she remembers—the only important thing is that she's happy and safe now."

"Yes, she's come a long way from where she started. But for you," he opens the doors, turning his head just enough to show his profile, "there's still much room left to grow."

Only when he's gone am I finally able to take in a solid breath. I hadn't realized how hard my heart had been pounding or felt the cold sweat beading on my forehead.

I thought since he'd been quiet the past year that he'd forgotten about me and let his curiosity go. But the chairman's fascination hasn't dwindled. If anything, the incident today reignited the flame of his determination in full force. Rather than being upset that I've lost him four of his best men, he's *excited* by this fact. And now, because of me, Briar has been caught in the crossfire.

I bring my knees up under the covers and rest my head on them. (What a mess.)

Did I really deal with things the best I could? Was everything I did worth the consequences? Five people have been hospitalized. *One of those people would be dead, otherwise,* I reason to myself. Her life must serve as a worthy justification, no? Yet even she is traumatized. And her life is as good as over, anyway, since she'll be "tried" for her crimes and expelled.

No one came out of this unscathed. But still ... something about this ending doesn't sit right with me.

When I think of Maggie, alone and blindfolded, every inch of her body in chains, I can't find it in me to blame her for what she did. She was manipulated, her weaknesses exploited and used. At its core, this was just a story of a scared girl desperately looking for someone to save her. X clearly never intended to do this. But shouldn't someone?

Hah. It's a laughable thought—me playing "hero." I won't kid myself; anything I do now is equivalent to me trying to vindicate the violence I've committed.

Even so, taking some more time to think it over, I come to a decision: I'll see to it that Maggie Arrowood is not expelled from Kane Academy. I'm sure, if I ask, the chairman will grant me this one request as a favor for dealing with the council's problem and preventing headlines of a student's death.

A buzzing from my phone has me looking up.

There's a message in my chatroom, an app I *never* use, and I know who it's from before opening it.

*You managed to save my pawn. Nicely done :)*

*Of course, if you'd just figured out the real solution, maybe less damage would have been dealt. After all, I gave you the answer you needed a while ago. Didn't you see it? Oh, well, how can I be disappointed when you gave such a fantastic performance? I look forward to our next match, Zero. Until then, rest up and rest well.*

*— Your only friend*

My only friend, hm? What does he mean by "real solution?" There must have been a way to shut the water off is what it likely means. And the answer for how to do so was something I'd already been given … I close my eyes and picture the marble chamber again. Then I picture the clues leading up to it all. The things he gave me: my book bag, my letter to Ms. Kurima, the drawing of the two wolves, and my name painted on the chamber wall with the assignments—wait.

The drawing.

How could I be so *slow?!*

Of course it wasn't random. He went through the trouble of landing it in my hands for a reason.

And the answer was right there. The drawing he gifted me hadn't just portrayed two wolves; there had also been a sun on the front and a moon on the back. The spouts in the chamber were of a very similar design, with suns on the front handles and moons on the back ones. I'd be willing to bet another visit from the chairman that turning the sun handles forward and the moon handles backward would have shut the water off.

Instead, this was my solution.

Instead, I committed an act of betrayal and did the one thing I promised myself I would never do again.

No, please, don't show me that.

*"It's because we're friends, Zero."*

My head finds its way to my knees again.

*"Now and forever."*

Stop.

*"Whether you like it or not."*

**"I said *stop*!"**

"Woah, but I haven't even done anything yet."

My head shoots up to see Ms. Kurima entering the room. "Kyouka?" I say, mind fuzzy.

"Oh, 'Kyouka' now, is it? What kind of manners are those—calling your teacher by her first name?"

It's strange seeing her out of her teaching attire. Here, in jeans and a sweater, with her hair and makeup a little messier, she looks even younger.

Paying no mind to my stare, she sits at the foot of my bed and hands me a pink box encased in a ribbon.

"Looks like you already have some get-well treats, but I thought you might appreciate some cookies, too. I know they're your favorite."

"… Thank you."

"And I know you've gone through a lot today, but I wanted to tell you in person that I'm proud of you, kid."

I scoff. "Proud of me? You do realize everyone involved other than Briar and me ended up hospitalized, right?" (Shouldn't she be afraid of me right now?)

"It was our fault for not getting to you sooner. The situation shouldn't have been left to you students, and for that, I apologize." She bends her head down slightly. "The emergency faculty meeting was entirely concerned with grades and rankings when what it really should have been about was *safety*."

"You couldn't have known." No one could have.

Still, Ms. Kurima isn't done. "I promise that I made every attempt to get to you as fast as I could, but it wasn't enough. And it was my mistake to allow you down there in the first place. I am truly sorry, Zero."

"How … are you so calm about this? Don't you realize the cause of all of this was … I mean, that I am the one who—"

"I know there are things that I don't yet understand about what happened. And I have a feeling they won't be explained to me anytime soon. But I know you, Zero. I know you wouldn't have hurt Daniel or those men on purpose, or for no reason. So please, don't start worrying about what I think of you, because it hasn't changed. I just hope that you can put your trust in me again, as your teacher and as an adult whose duty it is to look after you."

"Come on, Ms. Kurima, there's no need for you to be like this. If you don't start teasing me and giving me a hard time again, I won't know what to do with myself. Don't make this weirder than it already is."

She picks her head up, smiling, but there's a distinct misting in her dark eyes. "You really are such a brat."

I look away, finding myself at my emotional limit. "That is my natural state of being."

"Since we arrived late," her tone becomes serious once more, "I don't know all that happened in that chamber, Zero. But if you ever want someone to talk to about it, you know I'll probably find you before you find me."

"Oh, I'm aware."

Her hand reaches out and swats me over the head.

"Ouch." I pretend to wince. "I thought you were here to make me feel better? Handing me my favorite dessert as a gift and then physically abusing me, the mixed signals are very confusing."

"Cut that out. I should've known I couldn't have a nice moment with you that lasts longer than thirty seconds."

"Well, I'd hate to be so kind that you unintentionally fall in love with me, Kyouka. That would really complicate things."

"You're a fiend for even joking about stuff like that and you know it!"

For the first time since waking up, I crack a small smile. "You're right. Though I only give out as much as I take."

Ms. Kurima goes quiet. Then, softly, she says, "I sometimes forget you can do that."

"Do what?"

"Smile."

...

"Hey," I say, switching subjects, "I've got a question for you."

"Oh, yeah? Well, ask away."

I focus on the pink box in my lap. "It's about these cookies—I just have to know, did *you* make them?"

"Huh? And why would you need to know that?"

"Because adding food poisoning to the list of my current issues seems like a bad—*ow*." This time it's a forehead flick instead of a head swat.

"I bought them, smartass. Well, aside from *one* of the cookies. But I hid it with the rest from the bakery, so you won't have any idea which is mine and which isn't."

I give her a deadpan look while undoing the ribbon and sticking my hand inside the box, rummaging through it for about three seconds before finding what I'm looking for. "Is this it?"

She looks at the cookie in my hand and startles. "What?! How could you tell?!"

"Because the rest are normal and this one," I hold it up, "is the shape of a decapitated t-rex."

She snatches it from me. "Fine." Then she stuffs it into her mouth, speaking through full cheeks to say, "*Hmph*, forget about it, I'll just eat it myself, then—"

"Hey," I lean forward, ignoring the sharp pain in my back and abdomen as I move, "it's rude to eat a gift you've brought for someone else. Give it back."

What I pull away in the end is a half-eaten, t-rex-adjacent-shaped "cookie." I place it neatly back in the box regardless.

"You're not actually gonna eat that still, are you?" Ms. Kurima asks skeptically. "I mean, I already took a huge bite out of it. Just let me make you some more, and—"

"No." I put up my hand. "Half of one is more than enough. This is just fine, really."

"… Somehow, I'm both flattered and offended."

"There's no reason for you to be either of those things." I pause, remembering something else. "Kind of like how there was no reason for you to stick a secret note in my notebook when you could have just told me in person what you wanted to discuss over lunch." *See page <u>224</u>.

"Oh, I guess I did put that in your notebook, didn't I?"

"Well, you're already here, and we've got some 'food' with us, so let's just get it out of the way now."

"It wasn't anything big. I just wanted to hear what you thought of Juri and what song you're thinking of for the Talent Festival."

(Is she serious right now?) "You say that like you know I agreed to do it."

"Because you did, didn't you?"

(Well …) "What made you so sure I could sing, anyway? Did you really only pick me because I happen to know Japanese, or did you just want to torture me? I mean, if she wanted a singing partner so bad, you could have just gotten her a Vocaloid—there's nothing I can do for her that KAITO can't."

"I picked you because I know it will be good for you."

Wow. I think she really *is* serious about this.

"Plus," she grins mischievously, "Juri's pretty cute, isn't she?"

"Get out of my room so I can sleep."

She throws her hands up and stands, beginning to back up toward the doors. "All right, all right, grumpy pants, I'll go." But she stops, cocking her head to one side, clearly thinking of something else she wants to say.

"Why are you looking me over like that? Aren't you leaving?"

"….."

"Jeez. What is it?"

"… The thing you were yelling about when I got here …"

*sigh* "Don't even bother. It was nothing."

"Say what you will, but …"

"But *what?*"

"I could tell you were experiencing real pain."

"As opposed to fake pain?"

To my surprise, she doesn't react to my sarcastic retort. Instead, she walks back over to my bed and kneels beside me, taking one of my hands in hers. (They're so soft and delicate.) "You went through something difficult tonight, kiddo," she says, voice exceptionally gentle all of a sudden. "And it's ok to let out those emotions."

I can feel my entire body flinch inward. "What emotions?"

*No.*

"Zero."

*No, no, no, don't make me think about it.*

*Not now, not now, not now.*

"You're always holding back. Did you know that? Sometimes I don't even think you're aware of it, but that's the truth."

"Ms. Kurima …"

"I know you'd never do this in front of another human being, but," she brushes aside the hair on my forehead, that little bit of contact making me shiver, "it's ok to cry."

"Why would I cry … over something like this?"

"Until you open up to me, I can't answer that. But it's something I wanted you to hear all the same." Then Ms. Kurima bends down and kisses the spot on my forehead where her hand had been. "Sleep well. I'll see you in the morning."

***

It's the late hours of the night when the world is quiet and it feels like you're the only person on Earth, and I can't sleep.

No matter how many people told me to rest tonight, I can't.

I'm so tired and sore that I can barely move, but no amount of exhaustion calms this quivering pain inside me. It's like a living, breathing thing, mocking me with its constant presence. It's been with me since I woke up. But I ignored it with all the people coming to see me, pushing it down as deeply as possible.

(Now, alone, I must face the consequences as it all comes back up.)

"*Why?* Why did it have to be you?" My fist rubs against my chest—*it hurts*. I want to claw my heart out; whatever it takes to get this pain to stop. "Anyone else, I could take anyone else. Selene, Mom, Father, Lila—but *you* ..."

I haven't let myself think of him since that night over four years ago. I haven't so much as dreamed of him. I've locked him away in the deepest part of myself.

But now, what I've done ... it opened the door, shoving those memories in my face.

"Of course it had to be you," I whisper, fingernails digging into the flesh of my stomach.

The one I saw as I let the life drain from my body.

(My greatest regret ...)

I shake my head, the ache growing.

(... and my greatest treasure.)

"*Zero, it's ok to cry.*"

If only I could.

With one last shiver, I say the words I know I'll never get to say to him: "I miss you, my friend."

***

### Callan Adrian

- **Year/age/student ranking**: N/A
- **Hair**: chestnut brown with streaks of gray
- **Eyes**: steel gray
- **Height/Weight**: N/A
- **Noticeable features**: cold eyes, intimidating presence
- **Favorite item**: N/A
- **Likes**: N/A
- **Dislikes**: N/A
- **Personal comment**: We didn't feel comfortable asking the chairman for this information.
- **Fact**: Callan Adrian was childhood friends with Luc Hale, Zero's father. Like his son, Jordan, he never takes unnecessary actions, and he always has a plan.

Zero & his friend

***

# Author's Note

Hey there.

Thanks for reading the first volume of *Zero*. (Or maybe you just skipped to this note, but let's say that's not the case.)

Ok. You've just finished reading the last normal sentence of this afterward.

Things are about to get really weird, really fast.

So, if you don't want any part of that, just close the book now.

I only take partial responsibility for how strange this is gonna be because, technically, under the rules we'll be using, you *are* a part of this and could stop it at any time. Also, I swear if I could have written a normal author's note, I would have. I tried about 50 damn drafts and all of them were shit. Desperate times.

Here's some context for why things are about to go the way they're about to go: I've realized there's a "problem" with most author notes. This problem is that there's no plot, there's no setting, and there's no character. It's all just random words floating on a page with nothing for you to hang onto which, personally, just doesn't get the job done. So, to amend this issue, I'm going to turn **you** into a character. And I'm going to make *this* into a setting.

Basically, you're about to enter a scene.

Ready?

If you're still here, I'm taking that as consent.

Ok.

At first, I thought of making our setting a bedroom because that's what came to mind for a quiet chat, but then I realized, no, that's way too intimate way too fast (not that anything would happen—calm down). So instead, I'm taking you to a cathedral (yeah, you read that right). More on that in a bit. For now, we need to figure out your character.

You have it easy; you can just picture my profile (you'll find it if you flip forward a bit), but I'm working off of nothing when it comes to imagining you. First, what are you wearing? I'm giving you the all-black KA uniform because it's simple and looks good on just about anyone. For me, well, you can imagine the same thing (or any all-black outfit and that'll be close enough).

Now, would you look at that. We're kind of matching. Cute.

But for the rest of your appearance … I'm going to keep what I'm picturing to myself. Why overload you with more information than necessary, right?

Finally, our setting: the expansive, empty roof of the Kane Academy Cathedral, overlooking the nearby lake. You can hear distant piano playing coming from inside and the sound of birds from the surrounding trees. It smells like petrichor and pine.

All right, now that you're immersed, let's talk.

**Scene Starts Here:**

"You can sit up on the wall railing," I say, "I'll rest my arms on it next to you … Mm, yeah, you're right, it's kind of weird you can't actually talk back to me, but we'll both get over it."

I look at you and do my best to picture your face, but I don't want to make you uncomfortable so I look out at the trees after a few seconds.

"All right, what's something you'd like to know about that's usually given to you in author's notes? The history behind the story?"

You nod, since you don't have a choice, so I continue.

"It all started with a drawing."

You tilt your head skeptically.

"I'm serious; this entire series is based off of a single drawing. It's something I drew as a gift for someone a couple of years back, and it happened to depict a very troubled-looking teenager with dark hair and pale skin, sitting out in the snow, completely alone. He was wearing a black cloak and a white winter hat, and he had this completely apathetic yet ruthless look in his eyes." (Yes, I switched out the black cloak for a black coat.) "I don't know *why* I drew him; all I know is that once he appeared, **he wouldn't go away.** So, obviously, I had to write about him."

You adjust yourself on the railing and I momentarily worry you might fall. Turns out, you're just reaching back to catch the sudden rainfall in your hand. It's only a light misting, so we'll be fine to stay as we are.

"Next," I say, following your lead and catching a raindrop in my palm, "I'll tell you a little secret regarding the making of this volume. But you need to keep it between us, ok?"

Of course, you'll oblige.

"The entire ending to *God Complex* was unplanned." I smile. "Sort of. I'd planned out the charts/messages/clues long in advance, but the conflict in the tunnels was something that came as a surprise. Actually, the only reason this volume wrapped up the way it did is because of a conversation I had with a girl."

You seem to want to know what the conversation was, so I continue.

"Basically, it went like this: she asked how Zero was going to solve the case. I told her, and she said, 'Ok, cool, so what does that mean for Maggie?' I answered, sounding incredibly intelligent, 'Huh?' And she replied, 'Well, X made her beg for help—she must be in real danger. What's gonna happen to her?' And that's when my brain momentarily went blank."

You shift on the railing and look at me skeptically for the second time.

"Yeah, I guess you could say ... my thought process was originally exactly like Zero's: that **Help Me, Help Me** message was just a creepy, cruel way to taunt Maggie by forcing her to unknowingly spell out a cry for help. '*Ok, that's the end of it, everyone can go home now, the case is solved.*' But suddenly I had to think about it differently. Honestly," I consider it for a moment, "'that girl' sounded almost exactly like Briar did, come to think of it, raising the same questions and pushing back against my thought process. So, yeah, I pretty much wrote out that precise exchange."

I start pacing as the rain comes down harder.

"The actual finale of the volume seemed obvious from there. It wrote itself and, once it was finished, felt like the inevitable conclusion to this part of the story. Like it literally couldn't have gone any other way. You know what I mean?"

The rain picks up yet again and I turn to face you.

"Are you bothered by getting wet?" I ask. "Would you like to go back inside?"

You kindly inform me that you're perfectly fine. In fact, you like the rain. (Sometimes.)

"Ok. Then I'll keep going." I take my hands out of my jacket pockets and lean up against the railing beside you. "I guess this is the part of the note where I actually ought to get to the acknowledgments. So, I'd like to thank 'that girl' as well as everyone else on our team who made this thing happen." I begin to list them off on my fingers. "A filmmaker & composer, an actor, an ex-dancer, an officer in training, and a writer all come together for a project. What the hell does that lead to? We're still figuring it out, so don't expect an answer anytime soon. But," I look at you seriously for the first time, "most of all, I want to thank **you,** the one sitting here with me/reading this right now, for giving this story a chance—you have no idea how much that means to me. Just know that, as someone who's here, now, at the very beginning with me, you'll always have a special place in my heart."

I could undercut this line now with a sarcastic quip, but I really do mean it. Thank you.

"Since you've come this far, I hope you'll join me in Volume II. It should be out shortly, if not already, but if there's any kind of delay with future releases that makes you unhappy, please don't hesitate to reach out and give me a piece of your mind."

You smile and let me know that you won't be shy about doing so; nor will you be shy about speaking your mind in any capacity, for that matter.

"Good. Then there's just one last thing I have to tell you. Actually, *show you* is a more appropriate description for what's about to happen ... Do you trust me?"

You answer smartly.

"Yeah," I smile once more as I move to stand directly in front of you, "I thought you might say that. But, well, I was going to do this either way." Then I lift my hand and push you.

Off the railing.

You don't scream. Only a slight exhale of breath releases from your lungs while you fall freely from the roof.

By the time you take your next breath, **he's already caught you.**

Below stands Zero, staring up at the roof with a look of murder in his already blood-red eyes. In his arms, he's got you. He sets you on your feet swiftly.

"The fuck is going on here?" he asks. But before I can answer, he turns to you. "Hey, are you all right?"

You nod, unsure of how else to react.

Zero sighs with relief. Then he fixes his glare back on me.

"Zero?" I ask, cocking my head and pretending as if I didn't count on this outcome. "What are you doing here? Your part of the book ended."

"No," he says harshly, "the *entire* book has ended. So you need to let them go already—you're basically holding them captive at this point." He looks at you again. "I'm sorry about this. Please, just, if you see a weird note like this at the end of the next volume, use that intelligent mind of yours and *don't* read it."

"Oh, come on, now," I chide, grinning down from above, "let us live a little. The push was necessary. It was the only way to ensure you'd make an appearance."

"And why would I need to make an appearance?"

"So you two can properly introduce yourselves, of course." I nod between you and Zero.

"We've already met," he pushes back. "In fact, we know each other quite well. But you should already be aware of that."

I shrug. "It's different 'in person.'"

"Yes. It's much more *dangerous* in person."

I open my mouth to respond, but, just then, the rainfall turns into a downpour. Before I have time to blink, Zero opens the umbrella he'd been holding and puts it over your head.

"You couldn't even provide your own reader with proper cover from the rain you're inflicting on us for unknown reasons?" he asks flatly.

I shrug and make eye contact with you, giving you a knowing look. "The reader doesn't mind. Right?"

You simply shake your head with a roll of your eyes.

"Come on," he tells you, no longer interested in me. "Let's go somewhere and get you dry. As an apology for what the author has put you through, I'll get you something to eat, too. What would you like?" He listens to your response. "Sure. That's all right with me. In fact," the look in his eyes shifts slightly, "I've been wanting a chance to go over some of the 'answers' you gave throughout the book, anyway. Seems this is the perfect opportunity."

"Good luck getting specifics out of them," I drawl as the two of you turn and begin walking away. "By now, we all know that's not how this works." (Yet.) And to you, I call, "Hey, maybe next time, we can go somewhere even more fun than an old cathedral, like Zero's personal suite—or the tunnels. How about it?"

In response, Zero raises a singular/particular finger, not bothering to turn back around as he continues to hold the umbrella over you while you walk.

Yeah, you two will be just fine.

Let's end this experiment here. *See you next time.*

    - J

- **Year/age/student ranking**: N/A, 23, N/A
- **Hair**: dark sometimes, light other times
- **Eyes**: blue
- **Height/Weight**: now, this just seems inappropriate
- **Notable features**: ^ same issue (though for the sake of the author's note, let's just say dark hair "in need of a cut," fair complexion, blue eyes, & average height with the appearance of being taller)
- **Favorite item(s)**: headphones and drawing tablet (J would like to get good enough to draw the pictures used in these books)
- **Likes**: writing, sketching, music, manga, late-night drives, dancing, spending time alone, all-black attire, more music
- **Dislikes**: being told what to do
- **Personal comment**: "Damn. I really don't know how to write an author's note."
- **Fact**: J wrote this novel two years ago and is relieved to finally be publishing it. The series is just beginning and **Volume II** will be out shortly (if not already).
- ***Note***: "I'm not including an image of myself, so here's one last picture of Zero, 'cus I like it."

# Thanks for reading!

If you have thoughts to share, please leave us a review (it would really help us out) and Zero will be indebted to you forever (I mean it). And if you have anything you'd like to ask or share privately, just shoot us an email (teamzero@zerohale.com) or DM (@zero.hale). We'd love to hear from you.

Goodreads

Amazon

**Preview:**

**Up Next in *Zero: Volume II - Fatal Genius of an Arrogant Bastard***

Field trip time! What new case has Zero and the rest of the Problem-Solving Club intertwined with Alina Carter? What is X planning for Zero now? Will Lila ever show up? Who is this "friend" Zero speaks of? Why is there a 17+ chapter? And why is everyone boarding a train with Mr. Henderson as their chaperone?! As long as it all wraps up by the annual soiree for Kane Academy's brightest students, maybe Zero can finally get a moment of peace. But, as you know, he shouldn't get his hopes up …

*Non-canon cover of Vol. II*

***

Don't be shy

***

END